THE UNDE

FOURTE
TO
ONE

Jason Nightingale grew up in London. He has previously taught English in Cyprus, England and Poland. *Fourteen Million to One* is his first novel. He now lives and works in London. You can contact him at jsn_nightingale@yahoo.co.uk

> Cry if I am to cry
> Rage if I am to rage
> Reach if I am to reach
> Die if I am to die
> But breathe if I am to live
>
> Jarek 84

FOURTEEN MILLION
TO
ONE

JASON NIGHTINGALE

Published by the Underground Press Ltd 2006

Copyright © Jason Nightingale 2006

The right of Jason Nightingale to be identified as the author of this work has been asserted by him in accordance with the copyright, Designs and Patents Act, 1998

This book is sold subject to the condition that it shall not, by way of trade or otherwise, be lent, resold, hired out, or otherwise circulated without the publisher's prior consent in any form of binding or cover other than that in which it is published and without a similar condition including this condition being imposed on the subsequent purchaser

The Underground Press Ltd

This book is a work of fiction. Names, characters, places and incidents either are products of the author's imagination or are used fictitiously. Any resemblance to actual events or locales or persons, living or dead, is entirely coincidental.

A CIP catalogue record for this book is available from the British Library

The Underground Press Limited Reg. No. 5872350

ISBN-10 before January 2007 0-9553813-0-4
ISBN-13 after January 2007 978-0-9553813-0-0

Printed and bound in Great Britain by
Intype Libra Ltd, London

for Agata and my niece, Reagan

Acknowledgements

Thanks are due to many friends and family members, but in particular Ahmet Ozgerek, Asim Mehmet, Ragip Mehmet, Robin Yu, and Tim Dalrymple. Of course I can't forget to mention my favourite editor Hanna Drzewiecka – sorry I didn't follow all your suggestions. A special debt is owed to N. Okena A.K.A 'The Naj' for his help and input in all things technological. Love and kisses for my cousin Dil, who lent me the suit I never gave back. Lots of appreciation must be shown to Hasan Ozerman at the Simsak Studio in Green Lanes. I am very grateful to Ercan Yerlikaya for his various suggestions concerning the front cover even though they were never used. As ever I am indebted to Levent Hasan, the finest legal mind I have ever had the fortune of meeting. For their deep insight into the upcoming media campaign I would like to thank Sami Berik and David Chan. I would also like to thank Nicky Harris for her help, however small she thinks it was, and to Matt Stanley, who first aroused my interest in writing. Last, but not least I'd like to thank David Garrett at the Stanton School of English for keeping me in employment all these years.

There have been various people along the way, who in someway have helped me in my life and whom I have been unable to return the gift they have given me. For them I would like to send out my sincerest apologies; first and foremost to my blood, Michael – sorry I let you down. For the man we all called 'The Bruce' – I now see how wrong I was. And last for Miriam, I may have lied but the poem really was mine.

THE UNDERGROUND PRESS LTD

The Underground Press Ltd was established with the intention of allowing new authors with talent to break into the overcrowded world of publishing. Read more about The Underground Press on www.theundergroundpress.co.uk

www.theundergroundpress.co.uk

CHAPTER ONE

As Derek climbed up on to the chair he wondered if there really was a God, but more importantly, if the act he was about to commit would end in everlasting torment. His mother, a staunch Irish Catholic, had raised him to believe that it would, whereas his father, a cowering English atheist, secretly insisted that God was something grown-ups need to believe in if only to avoid insanity. Glancing at the hangman's noose he held in his right hand, Derek finally conceded that he'd come round to his father's way of thinking or had, at the very least, decided that eternal hell-fire couldn't be worse than what he was going through right now.

Derek took the noose and held it affectionately in both hands. It had taken him two hours to make whilst contemplating over half a bottle of whisky if this really was what he wanted to do. In fact he'd been toying with the idea of suicide for a couple of years now, and had even found the time to go to a DIY shop and purchase the best rope money could buy. Perhaps he had failed miserably at life, but this, this one last act, this he'd do right. Funny he thought to himself as he attached the end of the rope to a wooden beam, which conveniently ran through his small bedsit, funny how mysteriously calm he felt. He'd always imagined that a man who'd chosen to top himself would be charged with emotion, heart thumping, tears flowing, hands shaking, breath heaving. Yet all he felt was a strange emptiness inside. Is this how all suicide victims felt or was it just him? Maybe it was the circumstances that had led to him making this decision that now aided his calmness, or maybe it was the fact that he'd been thinking about topping himself for so long. Who could say for sure? Who the hell cared anymore? All he knew was that this wasn't how he saw himself ending his days, not when he found out that he'd won the biggest ever lottery jackpot in Britain's history. No, not at all, his first plan of action had been to escape from the squalid little hovel he had come to call home. Next on his itinerary of happiness had been telling his boss where to shove his demeaning job and retraining in a profession where he would never again feel exploited. Last, and most importantly of all, Derek had intended to use the money to help secure the future of his two children. Better schools for a start and some money set aside to ensure that they would have a financial safety net at the start of their adult lives. A painful and messy divorce had made Derek feel like a complete failure as a father, and although he was wise enough to know that he wouldn't be able to buy their affection with presents, he couldn't help but fantasize about using the money to spoil them with gifts and holidays he'd never been able to afford before. Well that had been the plan but here he was almost two months later about to hang himself in the same dingy bedsit he'd been forced to move into after his separation.

Derek gave the noose a good tug to check that it would take his weight and smiled, this one last thing he would certainly do right.

'Christ, what a waste,' he muttered to himself, 'how's it come to this?'

Of course Derek knew the answer to his own question, and he certainly didn't expect an answer. As he prepared to slip his head through the noose Derek reflected on the last two months of this roller coaster of a ride. A ride that took him from the brink of despair to the heights of heaven and then crashing back down to lows that he thought weren't humanly possible.

He remembered the day it all started as if it were yesterday. It was a Saturday and, like every Saturday, it was the one day he had visiting rights to his son and daughter. Derek had taken the bus to his old house, the house which he'd spent twenty years of his life paying for but which he'd inevitably lost to his wife after their divorce. He got off at the bus stop, which was situated at the end of his old road, and walked a humiliating three minutes towards what had been his home, hoping that he wouldn't bump into any of his old neighbours. Passing a fairly new BMW he was reminded that it hadn't taken long for his ex-wife to move her new lover into what had been their marital home.

Pressing the doorbell with repressed anger Derek hoped that John, the owner of the BMW, wouldn't be the one to open the door. His hopes were dashed as a slim and fairly good-looking thirty-five year old man opened the door. As usual John was friendly, well-presented and clearly not smug about the fact that he was sleeping with the woman Derek had loved with a passion, living in what had been his home, and spending a lot more time with his kids than Derek could ever hope to. John's lack of smugness and his obvious sincerity didn't help in making Derek hate him any less, if anything Derek hated him all the more for it.

'Hi. Here for the two rug-rats, I guess,' said John with a warm smile. Derek didn't reply.

'They should be ready now,' John continued, 'afraid they had a bit of a scrap earlier on and their mother's still cross with them. Jane, Derek's here, are the kids ready yet?'

'No, they bloody well aren't,' his ex-wife replied.

'You'd better come in while she gets them ready,' said John and reluctantly Derek followed him into the front living room. The place had changed a lot since the last time Derek had seen it, new furniture and new décor, making it obvious that this was a prosperous household. No doubt John, a consultant in IT recruitment, was earning a lot more than Derek had ever done. More than enough to support Jane, who had made a career out of being a housewife, even though Derek had supported her through university during her late thirties. If he could pinpoint a time when she seemed to change it was then, during her university days and the recapturing of her youth.

'But I don't want to go, it's boring!' It was Tom, Derek's son. Their relationship had been patchy during the best of times but after the divorce Tom's indifference towards his father had seemed to turn to outright hatred. He'd obviously wanted Derek to overhear, and if Tom's intention had been to stab at the remaining pieces of an already broken heart, then his ploy had been successful. Derek hoped that it was Tom's age – he'd only recently turned thirteen – that was the cause of the problems but he was already beginning to fear the worst, that it would only be a matter of time before he lost the boy's love, to a younger, richer and more hip man.

'Hi dad,' said a sweet angelic voice, causing Derek to snap out of his thoughts.

It was his daughter, Tina, just nine years old but with an emotional intelligence that he had seen in few adults. She looked at him with solace, causing his emotions to stir. This had been his family, the kids, Jane, they had been his life and now they were gone. Every time he saw Tom and Tina he felt a gnawing sadness inside – they were growing up so fast and he saw them so seldom. He feared that soon they would be strangers and seeing the way Jane looked at John, well that just filled him up with bitterness and a feeling of betrayal so strong that it led to outright indignation.

Tina ran up to him and hugged him tightly around the waist, and he kissed the top of her head.

'I've missed you so much,' Derek said, holding back his tears.

'Me too daddy, where are you taking us today?'

'I thought we might go to London zoo, the weather's so nice and you both loved it there when you were younger. Would you like to go?'

She smiled and nodded enthusiastically and instantly Derek felt a reassuring warmth inside.

'Where's Tom?' he asked her.

'In his bedroom, being an arsehole,' she replied. Quickly she looked away when she saw the shock on her father's face. It was the first time Derek had heard her swear.

'Where did you learn such an awful word?'

She looked down at her shoes and shrugged her shoulders.

'I want you to promise me that you won't ever use such language again,' he said tenderly, afraid that by disciplining her he might very well lose her love in the same way he seemed to have lost Tom's.

She nodded her head slowly, 'I'm sorry dad, I won't do it again.'

'That's a good girl, you know I love you very much,' he said, hugging her tightly.

'Erm, I'll just go and check what's going on upstairs,' said John, interrupting the moment.

'Sure, go ahead,' said Derek.

John disappeared and Derek looked at his daughter.

'Have you and Tom been fighting?'

Again she nodded her head slowly, 'He cut my favourite teddy bear's head off with a knife,' she managed to say before bursting into tears.

'There, there, don't cry I'll buy you a new one.'

'I hate him, all he does is play on that stupid Xbox John bought him, and when he sees me playing with my dolls he laughs at me.'

'Don't worry, he's at a strange age now, he'll change. You remember how you used to play together, don't you?'

'But he's so different now and he says he hates you.'

'Tina don't give your father any more problems than he already has,' a harsh female voice almost hissed. Derek looked up and saw Jane, as she seemed almost to glide into the room. For Derek she had always seemed to radiate a certain aura that despite years of marriage he had never quite been able to identify. It wasn't just her beauty or the way her long dark hair flowed in extravagant waves over the contours of her body until it finally rested at the back of her slim elegant waist. It was that cool inner self-confidence she had always seemed to possess, ever since that first day he had met her at secondary school. She had been very special for him, even back then and he had harboured a secret crush on her for most of his school days.

Of course Derek, being a painfully shy boy, had barely been noticed by Jane, even though they shared many of the same lessons. It wasn't until their final year at school together that he was able to attempt anything that resembled a conversation with her and by then it was way too late, she was already dating Martin Jones, the school stud. A chance encounter, in a shopping centre five years later, when Derek was twenty-one, changed his life. Not only did she remember him but she even smiled patiently as he incoherently mumbled some deeply unimpressive sentence about it being nice if they were to exchange numbers and perhaps go for a drink together.

Jane smiled seductively as she walked over to Tina and Derek. She could see the hunger he still had for her in his eyes. She realised that she had always held a power over him. In fact she fully realised that she held a certain power over most men, after all she was a highly attractive woman, but with Derek it had been so much more. As she looked at him she remembered that sweet mysterious shyness that seemed to ooze so enigmatically out of him. He had always been a lot more attractive than he realised, even now with the middle-aged potbelly he had allowed himself to develop and the slightly balding hair. His charisma, she decided, lay in his eyes, they somehow drew you in. If he had any confidence he would have been highly dangerous to the opposite sex, but the very unpretentiousness that initially attracted women to him eventually drove them away once they realised that this was a deeply complicated and closed man. It had been the same for her, after he had lost his job and his career was in ruins he put up barriers and closed himself off from her. He didn't want to share his thoughts or his worries with her and this had made her feel completely isolated. By the time Derek hit the bottle and his drinking started to become a problem she had met John and fallen for him completely. He made her feel young again but more importantly he made her happy, and although she knew that Derek still blamed her for the breakdown of their marriage, she didn't feel the slightest bit guilty, after all she was entitled to her happiness, wasn't she?

Derek tried his best to avert his eyes away from Jane. Looking at her only caused him pain. He had never been able to recover from the fact that she had left him for John. Despite the fact that he had come to realise that he had pushed Jane into John's arms by his drinking and self-pitying behaviour, he couldn't help but feel deep disappointment in the only woman he had ever loved. It had been just one bad moment in his life, the loss of a job and his career, that's all. He knew he could have been stronger and opened up to her, but he hadn't known how and so he'd chosen the company of alcohol as opposed to his wife. Now that he was sober, he realised what a fool he'd been, but it was all too late. Jane had moved on and he knew that he could never go back to her, not after the divorce, not after all the bitter feelings of betrayal he had suffered and the hatred which had tormented his long lonely nights. If it were possible he would have turned back the hands of time and changed the way he had behaved but that wasn't an option and if Derek had learnt one thing from the whole sorry episode it was that self-pity didn't get you anywhere. If anything it only compounded your problems, but God he wished he could take her clothes off and make love to her one last time.

Looking at her drove him crazy, he couldn't believe that she was the last woman he'd been with and that it had been more than three years ago. Three years of celibacy, sometimes he feared that if he ever had the opportunity to make love to a woman again he wouldn't remember how.

Tina, frightened by her mum's scowl, hid behind Derek, causing Jane to smirk.

'I can see that she can still wrap you around her little finger,' Jane said, her eyes glowing. Just like her mother, Derek thought to himself, keeping his feelings well hidden.

'Where's Tom?' he asked.

'Tom doesn't feel like going out today,' she responded flatly, 'perhaps you'd like to go up and see him?'

'I think that's a good idea,' Derek said, and left mother and daughter in the living room. On his way up the staircase he bumped into John, and the two men sucked in their stomachs to avoid getting stuck.

'Good luck,' John whispered into his ear.

Derek didn't know if John was genuinely wishing him luck or if he was being extremely sarcastic. It was impossible to tell with the man, he managed to keep a straight poker face the whole time Derek was ever in his vicinity. Derek sometimes wondered if he ever displayed any emotion in front of Jane and the kids. Perhaps he was impossible to read only when Derek was around. Unsure of John's intentions Derek let the comment go as if it hadn't been heard and carried on until he reached the end of the staircase.

Nervously he approached Tom's room, the door was open and Derek could see that Tom was playing on the games console John had bought him. He was lost in some kind of game that involved driving absurdly fast and shooting at uniformed police officers. Derek knocked on the door but Tom didn't respond, he didn't even take his eyes off the flickering screen.

'Those things can lead to epilepsy,' Derek said, trying to break the ice, but wincing as his joke fell on deaf ears. Cautiously he sat down next to his son, but Tom pretended not to notice.

'Wouldn't you rather go out with your sister and me than stay in playing games?'

For the first time Tom turned and looked at him before shrugging his shoulders and returning his attention to the game.

'We're going to London zoo.' Tom scoffed, 'London Zoo? That's for little kids, why would I want to go there?'

'Maybe to spend a little time with your dad?'

'London Zoo's boring, in fact everything we do is boring. I don't want to go anywhere.'

'Look Tom, I know I haven't always been there for you but I really want to make the most of the time we have left. Soon you'll have your own life and if we're not careful we'll drift apart.'

Suddenly the car Tom was driving crashed into a

police blockade and the driver was gunned down by an army of police marksmen.

'Fuck,' Tom shouted throwing his hand piece on to the ground, 'that was the furthest I got, shit I could have clocked it.'

Ignoring the swearing Derek tried to remain calm. 'Look, I'm sorry about your game but I really think this is more important.'

'Well I don't, you and mum, you screwed things up right, not me, so don't expect me to try to put them straight. When I have time I'll see you but right now I don't feel like going to London fucking Zoo.'

Derek got up, 'That's OK, I understand son, you play your game, I just hope that you find some time to spend with your old man.' He tried to stroke Tom's hair, but the boy pulled away and Derek's discomfort grew.

'Good luck with your game, I hope you clock it,' he said as he left the room. Downstairs in the living room everyone was staring at him, yet the only eyes which showed some compassion were those of his daughter.

'Tom won't be coming with us today, but we'll still have a good time, just me and you,' he said taking his daughter's hand.

'Look after her,' Jane shouted as they left through the front door, 'and remember that she has to be home before six.'

The day passed quickly and Derek enjoyed the company of his daughter so much that he almost forgot that his only other child seemed to hate his guts. They explored the zoo together; particularly interesting for Tina was the reptile house, which fascinated yet disgusted her at the same time. Derek spoilt her with as many ice-creams as she could eat and by the end of the day he had spent most of his meagre budget. Three o'clock approached fast and with a journey requiring two buses and half-an-hour on the tube it was time to take her home, but not before treating her to a McDonald's meal first. Tucking into her Big Mac, Derek could see that she'd enjoyed her day out and he felt relieved that the day hadn't been completely wasted. An old man on the table opposite left a copy of the Sun as he got up and threw his leftover packaging in the garbage bin not far from where Derek was sitting.

'Take it,' the old man said referring to the paper Derek was glancing at.

'Thank you,' replied Derek as he leant over and grabbed the paper.

The first page wasn't devoted to any acts of terrorism, or revolutions in far-flung corners of the world, but to the fact that tonight would be the biggest ever lottery draw in Britain's history. An unprecedented four consecutive rollovers meant that a fortune large enough to captivate a whole nation was waiting to be won. £25 MI££ILON UP FOR GRABS read the headline, Derek shook his head in disbelief.

'What's wrong daddy?' Tina asked, sipping her strawberry milkshake with a concerned look on her face.

'Oh nothing, just that tonight some lucky person will win more money than I could ever dream about and it hurts a little because I've had so many financial problems since losing my job.'

'I'm sorry,' said Tina as she looked thoughtfully

at the remainder of her fries before quickly devouring two and washing them down with some milkshake.

'Daddy?'

'Yes sweetie?'

'Why don't you play the lottery? Mummy and John play every week and I remember that they once won ten pounds.'

Derek couldn't help smiling, but tried his best not to look condescending, as Tina was quickly offended when she felt that someone was behaving in a patronizing manner towards her. 'I think that perhaps your mother and John have spent a lot more than ten pounds playing the lottery. It really isn't a good investment.'

Again Tina looked thoughtfully at her fries and Derek stopped reading the paper, allowing her time to swallow her food and wash it down with more milkshake. He gave her a wink before taking a couple for himself and she smiled her approval.

'But if it's such a bad investment why do mummy and John play?'

'Maybe because they think they'll win the jackpot one day and become rich.'

'But maybe you could win the jackpot and become rich too daddy.'

Derek let out a little laugh, it was such an interesting contrast to see youth and innocence so clearly complemented by intelligence. Tina looked at him carefully as she finished off what remained of the fries.

'I just don't think I could ever be so lucky. You see the chances of winning the lottery are one in fourteen million, that means fourteen million people have to play and that I would be the only one to win. That would make me one of the luckiest people in the world because over eight million people live in London. So look around this restaurant and see how many people there are and remember all the people we saw on the street and at the zoo, don't you think that's a lot?'

Tina nodded an emphatic yes.

'So I would have to be luckier than all of them put together.'

Tina looked at her milkshake but this time didn't take a sip.

'But if you don't play then you can't be lucky, can you?'

Derek smiled, sometimes there was no arguing with the insight of a nine-year-old.

'True but because I haven't had a very lucky life I don't believe I'll be lucky now.'

'But sometimes you can have bad luck and then good; you told me that daddy, maybe now it's time for you to have some good luck.'

'Maybe, I don't think so but maybe. I tell you what if you like we'll play together, you can choose the numbers.'

'Really? Mummy never let's me play, she says I'm too young.'

'Well, it'll be our secret,' Derek said as he searched his coat pockets for a pen. On finding one he ripped a strip off the top of the Sun newspaper and gave the pen and paper to his daughter.

'Now all you have to do is write down six numbers between one and forty-nine.'

Tina held the pen and paper thoughtfully in her hand, the expression on her face was completely blank.

Derek watched her carefully for at least half a minute, 'What's wrong?'

'I don't know what numbers to write.'

'Just close your eyes and don't think about anything else, now I want you to think of a number, what's the first number that comes to you?'

'Nine, because that's my age.'

'That's a good girl, now think of a second number.'

'Twelve, because my birthday is on the twelfth of March.'

'You see you've got the hang of it now, just four more numbers and we're ready to play.'

It didn't take much longer for Tina to come up with the other numbers and when she'd finished Derek took the strip of paper off her and glanced at the numbers. Nine, twelve, twenty, thirty-two, thirty-eight and forty-one. They don't look like jackpot winners, he thought to himself as he popped the strip of paper and pen into his coat pocket.

'Where will we play it daddy?' Tina asked, with excitement he hadn't seen in her for a long time.

'We can find a place to play on the way home,' Derek replied as he stroked his daughter's hair affectionately. 'Now we better hurry because if we're too late they won't let us play.'

'Let's go then,' she said, quickly putting on her jacket. Derek smiled as once again he repressed the urge to laugh. Oh to be that age just once more, that age of innocence and belief, before life has dragged your dreams out of your heart and smashed them into little pieces in front of you, turning you into nothing more than a jaded cynic. He'd have given anything at the moment to have her youth and all the hope that went along with it, but he'd already acknowledged that sadly life had passed him by.

CHAPTER TWO

Playing the lottery with his daughter had been fun. Her eyes sparkled with excitement and Derek felt like Christmas had come early. She held his hand tightly and skipped as they walked out of the tiny sweetshop together.

'So, should I give you the ticket?' Derek asked. Tina thought about this question seriously, so seriously in fact that she caused her little nose to wrinkle with her deep thoughts.

'No, because I'm supposed to be too young to play. You should keep it and say that the money's yours when we win.'

Derek smiled, life had never been so bleak, yet this little girl could bring the brightest rays of sunshine to the darkest of days.

'Remember we only have a one in fourteen million chance of winning.'

'I know daddy, but I've got a really good feeling.'

'So what do you want to do if we win?'

'Well you paid for the ticket but I chose the numbers, so I think it should be half for me and half for you. But I'm so young I wouldn't know what to do with the money, so you can look after it for me until I'm a grown-up.'

'That sounds fair,' Derek said as he stroked her hair. He took his eyes off his daughter's pretty features and looked at the front door of his old house. They'd arrived and sadly it was time to say goodbye.

He rang the doorbell and his daughter wrapped her arms around his waist.

'I love you daddy,' she said, just as her mother opened the door and gently pulled her in. Derek looked at Jane in disgust.

'You're late,' she said staring at him fiercely.

'What's half an hour matter?' Derek asked brusquely as he looked at his watch.

'It matters because when you're late you spoil the plans John and I have made for the evening. Believe it or not our lives don't revolve around you.'

'Look,' Derek said going against his better judgement and arguing with his ex-wife instead of trying to humour her, 'we were having a really good time, she was really enjoying herself and I see her so seldom that I just lost track of time. I didn't mean any harm.'

'You never do,' Jane said as she prepared to launch into an attack on Derek's lack of consideration. However she was distracted by Tina, who had started tugging at her skirt.

'Mummy, I had a really good time. We went to London Zoo.'

'Yes, but that doesn't mean that you can be late. Anyway it doesn't matter, it's too late now. Just make sure you don't do it again,' Jane said staring at Derek.

Derek frowned apologetically, he knew that Jane had the advantage. The judge had favoured her rights as a mother greatly over Derek's rights as a father. If she wanted to she could make it very difficult for him to have access to the kids even at the weekends. So he forced himself to back down, even though it went against his instincts.

'Say goodbye to daddy then.'

'Bye, bye daddy. I love you,' Tina repeated as she was again pulled in by her mother.

'Remember I love you too,' Derek managed to shout out, just before the door slammed in his face. He looked at the empty place where his daughter had stood for a couple of seconds before having enough strength to turn around and walk towards his bus stop.

The rest of Saturday was spent cleaning his dingy bedsit. It had been a couple of months since his last endeavour to clean the place and just like the last time, the empty beer cans and pizza boxes had become intolerable. Derek tried to work out why cleaning this place was such a chore for him, he'd always been a tidy man and taken pride in such things as his appearance and the immaculate condition of the home he lived in. Maybe losing his job, wife, and kids changed him and he no longer gave a toss. Or maybe it was because he thought staying here was just a temporary measure. He remembered the day he had moved in. The place was small, so small in fact that there was hardly enough room for his bed, an armchair, a chair, his wardrobe, a chest of drawers and a TV. There was a small kitchen area but the bath and toilet, which he had to share with his neighbours, was situated down the hallway. Very little had changed since Derek had moved in, and looking around it felt like nothing had changed at all. He had often complained to his landlord about the damp which covered the wall opposite his bed, causing the wallpaper to peel. He also complained about the kitchen tap, which managed to drip no matter how tightly one turned it off and the state of the carpet which had all kinds of disgusting looking stains covering it. One part of the carpet, right smack bang in the middle of the room, was completely eroded, exposing the floorboards. Derek had covered it up using a cheap rug but that was all he had done in terms of improving the place. After six months he had given up complaining to his landlord, who would always say that he would start work on the place the following week. Yet the following week never seemed to arrive. At least the cockroaches were mostly gone. Derek had managed to get rid of them himself by carefully laying down poison in all the appropriate places. From time to time however a new infestation would occur and Derek would have to start the whole process over again. However the infestations seemed to be less and less. Perhaps the cockroaches had conceded to the fact that they were not welcome and moved to one of Derek's less hygienic neighbours.

As long as they weren't around, Derek didn't care. He could get used to the old peeling wallpaper, the damp on one of his walls, the state of the carpet and the lack of space, but he could never get used to the cockroaches. There were days when Derek considered taking care of all the work himself and paying for the repairs out of his own pocket, but that would have meant admitting that this place really was his home. So he preferred to leave it the way it was and carry on believing that it was just a temporary measure. Well it had been a temporary measure for three years now, just like his job in the meat factory.

To think that he was once the head of an accounts department, a job which had taken him years of hard work to reach. Derek had left school with just his O-Levels and joined a local firm of furniture manufacturers as an office junior. And there he'd stayed, slowly working his way up the corporate ladder and studying accountancy in the evenings, supporting his young family and keeping up with the monthly mortgage repayments, all at the same time. He'd been a certified accountant for five years and head of his department for one when suddenly he arrived at the office one morning to find the company had gone into receivership.

A soaring pound had sent exports plunging whilst an embezzling managing director, with an addiction to cocaine and high class hookers, had wiped out the company's reserves. These two external factors helped pull the trigger which brought Derek's world crashing down. He started looking for a job almost immediately, but oddly enough nobody wanted to give an accounts based job to someone who had been the head of accounts at a company which had gone spectacularly bust. Overnight Derek was unemployable and his years of hard work and studying had been for nothing, just because his MD couldn't keep a reign on his dick. Luckily, Jane, who had recently graduated with a first class degree in computer science, was able to keep up the mortgage repayments. Or at least Derek had thought it was lucky, but little did he know that she had met John, whilst searching for a job and had agreed to take his number.

It wasn't long after this that Derek got his job at the meat factory, and fell into a trough of despair. He stopped smiling, stopped playing with the kids, he even stopped taking Tom to see Arsenal play. In hand with this was an increase in his alcohol consumption and a decrease in his activity in bed, not that Jane seemed to mind.

Three months later she announced that she wanted a divorce, he wasn't the man she'd fallen in love with. Of course he wasn't, he'd gone from being an accounts manager to packing meat! They argued for a week before he realised the devastating effect their fighting was having on the children. Reluctantly he agreed to the divorce and moved into the bedsit.

Two months later John moved into what had been Derek's home. The divorce was a bitter one, and Derek, going against the advice of his solicitor, fought all the way for custody of the kids and possession of the house. After nearly two years of bitter fighting Derek finally conceded to the fact that he didn't stand a chance. He had lost and Jane had won, the kids needed a mother more than a father and their mother needed a stable home to help raise them in, and as she was the one meeting the mortgage repayments then the house should logically go to her. The decree absolute had been issued last year, he could remember holding it in his hands and staring at it in disbelief as the tears ran down his cheeks. Up to that point Derek had managed to survive on the misguided belief that his family wasn't going to be torn apart. Having it confirmed by a legal document not only made him realise the reality of the situation but also brought the long denied grieving process over the death of his relationship to the very forefront of his consciousness.

Derek had won the right to see his kids once a week and was ordered to contribute three hundred pounds a month to their upbringing should he want to keep his visiting rights. Three hundred pounds a month was pretty steep considering Derek was earning nine hundred pounds after tax and had to pay a further three hundred pounds in rent for his stinky little hellhole. Doing the maths, it wasn't hard to tell that Derek had been well and truly shafted. Yet more was to come and Derek's resentment towards his ex-wife grew even more after Jane announced that she was cutting her hours to part-time. It didn't take a genius to see how she could afford it; she had Derek paying for the kids and John paying for the privilege of living in her home, and on twenty pounds per hour, she could afford to go part-time.

Even today the injustice of it all made Derek's stomach churn. Of course he didn't mind paying maintenance towards his children, he saw that as his duty, regardless of his own financial circumstances, but subsidising Jane's lavish lifestyle? It was outrageous! She could earn more per hour than he could in four! It was sad but he had come round to accepting his fate, he didn't see what else he could do and he realised that things could be a lot worse. At least he had two wonderful children, both of whom he loved very much, even if only one of them was willing to acknowledge his existence at present. The hardest thing about the divorce had been losing them, seeing them once a week just wasn't enough. They were growing up so fast and soon they would be gone, living their own lives but Derek was determined to always be there for them no matter where they went and in the meantime he would try to make the most of the time they had together. He might have failed miserably as a husband when he had decided to cut himself off from his wife and hit the bottle but that didn't mean he couldn't be the best dad in the world, and that's exactly what he intended to be.

It was seven pm by the time Derek had finished his cleaning and heated up a discounted microwave meal for one. He ate in a rush, for he knew that soon his best mate Terry would be knocking at his door and they'd be on their way to their ritual Saturday night at the pub. Apart from seeing his kids, going for a drink with Terry was all he had to look forward to. They'd been best mates since school and had both been there for each other when their respective marriages broke down. However Terry, who was a plumber, had faired much better, and after his divorce was still able to buy himself a reasonably sized flat.

Also unlike Derek, who in all fairness could only portion part of the blame for his divorce on himself, Terry had only himself to blame. He had consistently cheated and been unfaithful to his wife right from the start of their marriage. Terry was the first to admit that he'd behaved like a right pig, and sometimes Derek suspected that he was even proud of the fact. There was definitely an irony in the fact that Terry who seemed to view women as nothing more than sex objects had them flocking to him whilst Derek couldn't even get a date. Sometimes Derek felt envious of Terry; they'd both been through the same horrendous life crisis a divorce can bring, yet Terry had emerged almost unscathed and lacking any long term damage whilst Derek had almost fallen to pieces. Seeing Terry brought Derek the kind of happiness only a best friend can bring but at the same time reminded him how badly he had faired himself. Nevertheless Derek wouldn't have had it any other way. His love for Terry was so strong that he would never want them to swap places and for Terry to suffer the way he had. Terry had been a rock for Derek these last few years, saving him from near nervous collapse and helping him pull through with his excess alcohol consumption. Now Derek only ever drank when he went to the pub with Terry. Drinking alone had become a very rare activity and Derek only had Terry to thank for that. Their regular get-togethers in the pub were more like a form of counselling for Derek than your normal two blokes-getting-plastered-together pubscene. Sometimes it felt like it was all Derek had to keep him sane.

The intercom rang and Derek pressed on the buzzer so that Terry could let himself into the building. Derek quickly threw the remainder of the microwave meal with its container into the rubbish bin. The one thing he liked about microwave meals was that there wasn't any washing up to do afterwards. There was a knock on the door and Derek opened it so that Terry could enter his room.

'See you've managed to tidy this place up somewhat,' Terry said looking around, as soon as he came through the door. The last time he'd been here the place had looked like a real dump. Sometimes Derek could really let himself and the place where he lived go, and this always worried Terry. The last thing he wanted was his best friend to fall into depression again, or to start drinking. Of course looking around at the peeling wallpaper and old worn out carpet Terry could understand why Derek just couldn't be bothered with the place.

Especially considering the extortionate price he had to pay to live in it.

'Yeah, well it was high time,' Derek said, closing the door behind Terry.

'So how are you?' Terry asked, taking a seat on Derek's one and only armchair.

'I'll be a lot better after I get a pint down me,' Derek said as he put his shoes on.

'Hey you're not going out like that, are you?' Terry said pointing to the old jumper Derek was wearing. 'It needs throwing out,' he added.

Derek looked at his reflection in the small mirror that hung on his wardrobe, the jumper was awful. Terry was right, he couldn't really go out dressed as he was, even if it was just for a quiet drink with his best mate. The jumper was at least ten years old and wearing it made Derek feel like an old man. It definitely needed throwing out, but he just couldn't afford to buy any new clothes.

'I just can't afford to throw my clothes away,' Derek said, 'not right now.'

'What about that shirt I bought you last week for your birthday? Why don't you wear that?'

Looking again at his reflection Derek conceded that Terry was right, but if he wore the shirt Terry had bought him he would feel like he was trying to be someone he wasn't. The shirt, which was dark navy blue with light blue stripes, might have been considered modest when compared to some of the loud shirts Terry would wear, but Derek still couldn't help feeling that it would attract too much attention, and attention was the last thing he wanted.

'Go on, put it on, you never know there might be some ladies there,' Terry said.

Derek decided to yield to Terry's zealously persuasive technique, it was after all a present and wearing it would make his friend feel good. Terry watched in silence as Derek pulled the shirt out of the wardrobe and put it on. The shirt was a perfect fit and made Derek look a lot better than the jumper, which added at least ten years to his appearance.

Terry carefully studied Derek from head to foot, despite the low self-esteem Derek still had a lot of charisma and was a very good looking bloke. He had wonderfully attractive blue eyes, which Terry had often noted women loved gazing into. He was fairly tall, with broad shoulders and a handsome lived-in face, which contrasted well with his eyes when he smiled. True he was slightly balding but he kept his hair short and didn't make himself look ridiculous by growing his hair long and trying to cover up the bald spots like some men did. If anything the short hair helped direct one's eyes to the more attractive features of his face. Perhaps his one physical flaw was that he was slightly overweight, but even this could be fixed by sometime in a gym and when Derek bothered to dress properly and wore his shirt outside his trousers, like he had done today, instead of tucking it in or wearing some baggy jumper, well then his weight problem was hardly noticeable.

Derek's biggest problem, Terry decided, was his lack of confidence. True enough any man's confidence would be in tatters once they'd been through a divorce the way Derek had, lost their job, had their career ruined and ended up broke and living in a hovel, but tonight Terry was determined to bring Derek out of his shell.

'You look great,' Terry said as he got up and inspected Derek, 'the ladies will be all over you.'

'Mate, a fat bastard in a nice shirt is just a fat bastard in a nice shirt. Besides it's the beer not the ladies I'm interested in tonight.'

'Good to see that you're still the Derek I know and love,' Terry smirked, as he looked round the place for any empty beer cans. Although Derek seemed to be over his drinking problem, it was natural for his best friend to be worried about him.

'So you haven't had anything to drink during the week?'

'I might have had a couple but nothing in excess,' Derek told his friend. 'Look you don't have to worry about me anymore, I'm over it, I promise.'

'That's good to know because I still worry about you sometimes.'

'Well you don't have to worry anymore,' Derek said as he put his arm around his best friend and led him out of the bedsit, 'I'm much saner these days, maybe it's the old age.' In the pub Derek decided to check his wallet, there certainly weren't any notes inside the fake leather container, only bits of change he'd collected over the week. Just enough for a pint of cheap donkey piss, Derek thought to himself shaking his head.

'Let me get the first round in,' Terry said on seeing Derek counting his change. Before Derek had a chance to protest Terry ordered two pints of Stella, 'You can get them next week,' said Terry. Derek noted that it must have been coming up to two months since the last time he'd bought Terry a beer.

Terry eyed the barmaid, and then gave Derek a wink as he handed over a ten-pound note. He certainly didn't look like a womaniser, but he'd had a lot more luck with women since his divorce than Derek had had since his.

Derek admired this about his old friend, for Terry getting divorced seemed to have been a rejuvenating experience. He'd bought himself a bachelor pad, a flash car, nice clothes, went to the gym three times a week and dated as many women as he could get his hands on. In fact Terry often said that this was the best time of his life and that he'd never felt happier. He'd freed himself from his wife, who, Derek reflected after years of enduring Terry's infidelity, was the real victim of their marriage.

Some men just weren't meant to marry and Terry was definitely one of those men, it was just unfortunate that it took Terry nineteen years of marriage to realize that fact. Terry had been happy to go on living the lie but Kate, his wife, could no longer go on with all the deceit. When she filed for divorce Terry was visibly shaken for a while but recovered well. Perhaps he had never truly loved her, it would certainly have been an explanation for all of Terry's affairs. At the time it was Kate, and not his best friend, Derek had felt sorry for.

Terry had acted like a complete idiot and lost a very loving and attractive woman. Recently Derek had heard through a mutual friend that she'd remarried but Terry had failed to mention anything. Derek wished her happiness as he remembered the times he saw Terry and Kate together. At birthday parties, barbecues and family get-togethers. They had always seemed like such a happy, loving couple. At least they had a daughter together, she had recently started working as a model and was rumoured to be destined for great things. So all things considered Terry the playboy bachelor and father wasn't doing too badly at all. A successful daughter, nice clothes, a flash car and a horde of attractive women to date.

Of course being a self-employed plumber meant that Terry's disposable income was much greater than Derek's. Not to mention the fact that Terry had no maintenance to pay, his daughter was already an independent adult. Derek meanwhile could just about afford a pair of new shoes, never mind the new suits.

'Cheer up pal, it can't be that bad,' Terry said, placing the beer under Derek's nose and snapping him out of his thoughts.

'Cheers,' said Derek raising his glass.

'That's more like it, listen what are you doing on Wednesday?'

'Wednesday evening?'

'Yeah, Wednesday evening.'

'Nothing, why?'

'Because my latest, Lisa has a friend, and they'd like to go on a double date, and when I mentioned you Lisa said that you'd be ideal for her mate.'

Derek stared deeply into his beer before taking a sip.

'Well?' Terry asked anxiously.

'I'm just not up to it mate,' replied Derek.

'But why not?'

'I just don't feel ready for a relationship.'

'Who said anything about a relationship? All she wants is a date, it's a bit of female company for heaven's sake. You don't have to commit to her, it's just some fun, some conversation, who knows a little sex,' Terry said, emphasizing the end of his sentence with a nudge.

'I'm just not up to it mate,' Derek said after another swig of his beer. Terry drew closer, so that their faces were almost touching and lowered his voice to a whisper.

'Derek, it's been three years since you and Jane separated, three bloody years. You've got to move on, it's just not normal, a man your age needs a woman, you know what I mean?'

Of course Derek knew what he meant, his genitals reminded him on a daily basis that it had been over three years since he'd had sex. He even felt so desperate that he thought about seeing a prostitute, but that was just too sad, even for him. His body cried out for a woman, but he just didn't have the confidence to go out and meet one. Not with the way things were, he needed to be able to tell any woman he met that he had a job he was proud of, and he needed a place he could take her to and not feel ashamed. How could he attract a woman when he felt like he didn't have anything to offer?

'I'm still not ready, please don't rush me. I need to find my feet first, you know get my life back together, find my confidence, get out of the meat factory.' Terry withdrew slightly and contemplated what his friend had just said, after all he didn't want to push him too hard.

'OK, but promise me that once you're out of that crummy job, you'll let me help you find a bird.'

'OK, I promise,' Derek said. Yet Terry was still deeply concerned about his friend's welfare. He'd helped Derek through his divorce, he'd helped him through the worst of his depression and his near collapse into alcoholism, maybe now he could help him back into the real world. But how could he find a gentle way to do it? One which avoided putting pressure on his friend? Perhaps he could use himself as an example? Sure things felt great for him now but he remembered the time during his divorce when he could just about find the strength to force himself out of bed.

'I do know how you feel,' Terry said tactfully.

Derek raised his eyebrows in interest. How could Terry know how he felt? Terry the womaniser? Terry the Hugh Hefner of the plumbing world? How could Terry possibly understand what he was going through? Derek smiled ironically before shaking his head.

'Straight up Derek, there was a time when I just didn't think I could continue anymore,' Terry said sincerely.

'Who, you? You can't be serious! Yeah sure you were cut up at first, but I do remember you throwing a party when your divorce was finalised!'

'But all that was just a show I was putting on. I may have looked unconcerned and carefree in front of other people but when I was alone it was a different story, a very different story. Especially when I would come home to an empty flat after work, no wife, no daughter, nobody to talk to. Nothing but a cold, large bed to keep me company in the night, and before you interrupt me and say I deserved it for being unfaithful to Kate, knowing it's all your own fault only makes you feel worse. So believe me, I'm telling you the truth when I say that things were bad and at the time I thought they'd never get better, but one day I just got up out of bed and realised that I was crucifying myself over a relationship that had lost its passion a long time ago. So what was the point? In the end I forced myself to start going out and meeting new people, if only to get myself out of that flat. I started attending salsa classes and I attended a French language course.

'If I remember correctly, you were attending the salsa classes long before you got divorced,' Derek chuckled. Terry chose to ignore the comment and carried on with his sermon, 'I met some women, I had some fun but most importantly my confidence started to return. That new found lease on life took me out of my depression and probably saved me from doing something stupid like topping myself.

Look, I'm not a psychologist or an expert or something but I do know that beating yourself up about the past is the worse thing you can do. If all you do is think about the past then you can never progress to the future.' Terry looked at Derek thoughtfully and placed a hand on his shoulder while he waited for some kind of response.

'I know what you're trying to say and I agree with you completely but I just don't have the money to take up hobbies and go salsa dancing. You've always had a better financial position because you don't have to pay any maintenance and your job gives you a much higher income than my dead end job.'

'Well, yeah I know it's tough, but it's not impossible and you could retrain as a plumber, it only takes six months. After that you could come and work for me, it would mean that I could expand my business. I could start you on a salary of about twenty thousand pounds a year. How does that sound?'

Derek smiled, Terry really was the best friend a man could ask for, but plumbing? He'd been an accountant, and he was already tired of the physical work involved in packing meat. He needed something that challenged him intellectually, the way accounting had done.

'Thanks mate, that's a very generous offer but I've never been very good with my hands. I just don't think it's for me.' Derek couldn't help but notice the hurt look on his friend's face but didn't know how he could put things right.

'So what you going to do?' Terry asked finally.

'I'm not sure but I'm working on a few ideas,' Derek lied before slowly taking a sip of his drink. 'Don't worry I'm not planning to end my days packing meat,' he said, even managing a smile to hide the panic caused by the thought of his future. Satisfied that there was still hope for his friend, Terry let out a smile before turning his attention to the television. The latest National lottery show was being broadcast by some comedian attempting to revitalize his flagging career after a three year binge of alcohol and drugs.

'Did you hear that? Twenty-five million, bloody hell,' said Terry, shaking his head in disbelief, before pulling a ticket out of his pocket.

The barmaid scoffed as she pulled a drink for one of the regulars.

'And what might you be laughing at?' Terry said with a twinkle in his eye.

'You, you silly sod, you don't actually think you're going to win, do you?'

'Someone's got to win it and I've got as much chance as anyone else.'

'That's the attitude son,' said the man who was being served.

'Come off it Reginald, we both know he's not

going to win,' said the barmaid as she placed the pint in front of Reginald's eager hands.

'Look love, I know you're new here but that doesn't mean you can go round insulting the customers,' Terry said suddenly losing his humour.

'Hey no need to get cross, I'm only joking with you. I tell you what, if you win, I'll let you take me out to dinner.'

On hearing this Derek almost choked on his drink, he'd seen Terry pull before, but this was ridiculous. Derek looked over at Terry, who was beaming like a kid at Christmas. Taking a swig of his beer, Terry looked at the barmaid with his best come to bed eyes. 'You're on,' he said, causing her to giggle like a schoolgirl.

'Well don't get too excited,' she said, 'you've still got to win it first.'

'Here put the volume up,' bellowed Reginald in excitement, 'the draw's about to start.'

CHAPTER THREE

Justin had rightly anticipated that gaining entry to the building would be easy. He now stood outside one of the many rooms that were vulnerable enough for him to plunder. He knocked on the door to make sure that nobody was in. There wasn't a response, so he knocked harder and louder.

Justin was just seventeen, yet this would probably be his eightieth burglary. He'd only started his criminal career about a year ago after becoming friends with Tony, who was one of the most popular kids at school. Until that point in his life Justin had just been one of the school dweebs, sometimes bullied but mostly ignored by everyone else. Justin had seen Tony smash one of the school windows with a rock but refused to tell the head teacher the truth when he himself was accused of being the vandal. A month in detention had been worth it just to have Tony walk by his side in the school yard and thank him for not grassing. Slowly the two became friends and Justin's status in school quickly rose. To add to his street cred, he'd also nicked cars, been joyriding, mugged a few school kids, dealt some dope and set fire to a derelict church. He'd never been caught, well only once, as a passenger in a car Tony had hotwired. Justin was let off with a warning and Tony had to do ten hours community service in an old people's home. Right now Tony was waiting for him outside in a car they'd hotwired, this wasn't one of their planned crimes, not that their crimes had ever been planned – it was just that they were bored and it was Saturday night. Hotwiring a car and committing a burglary had been Justin's idea. Tony went along with it, but only on the condition that he wouldn't have to take part in the burglary because, 'He'd already been nabbed and done time.' Justin had called Tony a tosser to his face, nobody called community service time. Tony called Justin a virgin, which he was, in fact he was the only one of his mates who hadn't done it yet, so Justin shut his mouth. Tony was the only person he'd trusted with his sexual secret and pissing Tony off meant that everyone else could find out.

Justin rued the day he had ever confessed the worries and regrets that went along with being a virgin, but Tony was the closest thing he had to a brother. The two had become so close that Tony virtually lived at Justin's place. They were linked by an incredibly strong bond, the lack of a father. Tony's had been absent on and off for over ten years whilst serving time in various prisons throughout the country. He was currently banged up for his role in a stolen car ring and wouldn't be eligible for parole for at least another two years. Tony's mother had grown tired of his father's uncontrollable behaviour and inevitably tired of the long lonely nights being a convict's wife brought. She remarried a man Tony had grown to hate with a passion. As step-fathers went he wasn't a bad man, but Tony couldn't stand the idea of another man trying to take his father's place. As a result Tony spent most of his time alone in his room, away from the rest of the family.

If Tony's story was sad, perhaps Justin's was even sadder. His mother was just a teenager when she discovered that she was pregnant with him. After the birth she fled to Spain with a rich, older man. It was left to his grandmother to raise him alone. That sense of abandonment haunted Justin, as did his thirst to know who his father was. His grandmother didn't know who the man was who had got her daughter pregnant. All she knew was that Justin's mother arrived on her doorstep one day after an absence of two years, heavily pregnant and deeply traumatised. She never said who the father was or why she hadn't bothered to visit for two years. There hadn't been any contact, not even a birthday card between Justin and his mother since the day she had walked out on him. He wasn't even six months old. Sometimes his grandmother cried, she just couldn't understand why her daughter didn't even want to visit her and why she had abandoned her grandson. It was left to Justin to sooth the old woman's pain.

That lack of a stable family background had brought the two close enough to consider themselves brothers. They were the only family they had and the only ones who understood each others loneliness and bitterness at being abandoned. Justin by his mother, who had fled the nightmares of teenage motherhood, and Tony, who felt abandoned by his father, who had insisted on a life of crime. The bond was unbreakable, even more so for Justin, who until his friendship with Tony had been a social outcast at school. Added to this was the fact that the only father figure Justin had ever come into contact with was Tony's dad, who relished giving them details of his escapades. It was no wonder the two impressionable teenagers were attracted to crime when their only role model in life was an absent criminal. Tony had first been joyriding at the tender age of twelve after learning the intricate details of how to hotwire a car from his dad, who was out of prison at the time. Now it was Tony's turn to pass on all his knowledge to Justin.

Sometimes Tony would allow Justin to come along for the prison visits he would pay his dad. In a way it was like Tony's dad had taken the place of the father Justin had never had. Justin loved being Tony's partner, although Tony seemed to have become more cautious since his run in with the law.

Sure that nobody was home, Justin surveyed the hallway to check that it was clear. Confident that there weren't any witnesses, and using his shoulder as a battering ram, he charged into the door, disintegrating the twenty-year old lock on impact. Justin felt invincible, but then again he didn't stop to consider that a rather strong fart could have blown the door open. Standing six-foot tall and weighing just seventy kilos, with the skinniest arms and legs this side of Ethiopia, Justin could just about kick a telephone box open. Nevertheless, he had managed to gain access to the room and gently closed the door as he entered.

It was precisely for the reason of ease that Justin's preferred targets for burglaries were large properties where a lot of people resided in separate, smaller rooms. The security of such places was almost nonexistent because most of the occupants felt secure in the knowledge that any intruder would first have to gain access through the front door. Nobody ever stopped to consider that all a potential thief had to do was wait by the actual door until one of the residents entered or left the building and hold it open with a friendly smile, therefore avoiding suspicion. In all the times Justin had used this trick, he'd never once been asked by someone who he was or where he was going, and why would anyone be suspicious? So many people came and went, and half of the residents didn't know who their neighbours were anyway.

Justin carefully walked around the room, he felt bitterly disappointed. Of all the places in the building he could have chosen to burgle, he'd picked the dud. This joker didn't even have a DVD player. And what a tip, the wallpaper was peeling and there were holes in the carpet! Justin quietly swore to himself as he started looking through a chest of drawers hoping to find a stash of cash or drugs, but all he found were old socks filled with holes. 'Shit,' he muttered, as he started slinging the drawers across the room, his frantic search for something worth stealing intensifying.

He sat on the bed and collected his thoughts; it was his own fault for choosing to do a place on the first floor. He wondered about going upstairs and picking another room, but that would involve too much time and greatly improve his chances of getting caught. He got up and turned over the mattress hoping to find some cash or even jewellery, but again nothing. Walking around the room, his eyes darted about, he had to make a list and quick. OK, first things first, the TV, it was brand new and he could definitely get at least fifty pounds for it. He took it off the shoddy table it sat on and placed it in the centre of the room. The remote was placed neatly next to what had been the TV's place, so Justin took it and put it inside his pocket. He quickly rummaged through the wardrobe, which only had two drawers, emptying the contents of each on to the floor. Suddenly a gold wedding ring dropped out and rolled across the room. Justin quickly picked it up before it had finished its journey and placed it in his pocket next to the remote. He smiled, it was thick and solid, and it was definitely worth a few quid down the local pawn brokers. It was also small enough to hide from Tony, so he wouldn't have to go halves on it. OK, just one more thing, again his eyes darted around, he saw a couple of photos on the mantel piece, they were of a boy and a girl. Divorced bloke, thought Justin instantly, no wonder he didn't have anything worth nicking. Next to the photos was an empty vase, Justin picked it up and held it in his hands. It was nicely decorated with red and blue flowers round the side and a gold rim around the top. Justin remembered that it was his grandma's birthday next week and he still hadn't bought her a present. She'd appreciate the vase, Justin thought to himself as he remembered the old dear's fondness for flowers.

He placed the vase on top of the TV before grabbing it in both his arms and then allowing the vase to roll onto his chest. Proficiently he opened the bedsit door with one hand and then began his descent down the stairs of the building, he could see the door which was meant to secure the place and smiled, he was home free. However Justin's smile quickly disappeared as the front door opened and a rather large man entered the corridor.

'Shit,' Justin muttered under his breath as panic began to set in. The guy looked up at Justin and smiled before backing back out on to the street. He kindly held the door open for Justin, unwittingly aiding the young thief in his escape.

'Cheers mate,' Justin said as he passed him by.

'No problem,' the guy said with the same friendly smile, before re-entering the building.

Sap, Justin thought to himself as he walked past Derek's neighbour and towards the car Tony was in. Tony spotted him immediately and got out so that he could open the boot for the TV.

'Is that all you got, a fuckin´ telly?'

'Shut up and get in the car before someone hears you,' Justin said testily. Sometimes Tony could be so unprofessional. Angrily Tony rubbed the two wires together starting the car up, checking that no other cars were about he did a wheel-spin just as he pulled out on to the road. 'Be careful, that's how they nabbed you last time,' Justin said turning around and looking out of the back window.

'I don't know what's wrong with you today but you're really para,' Tony said as he did a right at a set of traffic lights and headed off, back towards his estate.

'I'm not being para, just professional, you should try it.'

'Professional, nickin´ one telly, please tell me you got more than that and that stupid vase, what kind of fool tiefs a vase?'

'The vase is for my grandma, it's her birthday.'

Tony let out a deep sigh, they'd be lucky to get fifty pounds for the TV leaving them with only twenty-five each. Mind you the car had an expensive stereo, which when sold would make them at least another twenty-five notes each. It would be enough to go clubbing with, Tony supposed.

'And there wasn't anything else?' Tony asked, again out of desperation.

Justin put his hand in his left pocket and felt the wedding ring, he rolled it around and wondered whether or not he should cut Tony in on the action.

'No, that's it, the chief didn't have nutin´ worth tiefin´, the place was a real dump. But I've got the remote as well and the telly looks new, we should get a bit for it.'

'Yeah maybe, let's take it round Diamond's, I heard he wants to buy a new telly.'

'All right to Diamond's and yank out that car stereo, he's always on the lookout for one of those,' Justin said feeling that he should definitely be the one in charge and not Tony, after all he was the one generating the cash. Tony was just along for the ride because he didn't have the guts to do anything by himself, or at least it seemed the case recently, but Tony still had his uses, mainly attracting girls. He was good at it, or at least much better than Justin, although that wasn't really saying much. The only girl Justin had ever kissed had been introduced to him by Tony. Yeah Tony definitely had a way with girls and if Justin could just figure out what it was, maybe he could learn to replicate it and get some action for himself. Either way it was well worth having Tony around.

Diamond, whose real name was David, liked to be known as Diamond Dave, he lived on the same estate as Tony. Diamond Dave was the estate's fence, anything that was stolen or dodgy, he bought and sold on for a profit. His elder brother, Simon, was in the same game and had introduced

Diamond into the business. However Simon, influenced by Tony's dad, had got a bit over ambitious and started dealing in stolen cars. The two had gone into partnership together, with Tony's dad stealing the cars and then making them look legit and Simon selling them. The operation was closed down when a dissatisfied customer called trading standards because he suspected that his Ford Fiesta had been clocked. Tony's dad, who hadn't even bothered to check the mileage, except to briefly glance at it when he wrote up the fake MOT certificate had unwittingly stolen a clocked car! Trading standards informed the police, who started to observe the pair before raiding their business premises. As Simon was no longer around it was up to Diamond to take care of the business by himself and use the money he made to pay the mortgage his parents had taken out on their council house.

Tony parked outside Diamond's house and spent two minutes yanking out the car radio. Justin went and rang Diamond's front doorbell. A fairly short but stout man, who looked more like he was in his early thirties than twenties opened it, he had a large, round head and almost no neck.

'What you sayin´ G?' Diamond asked Justin. Diamond wasn't particularly fond of speaking street, his family were originally cockney, but sometimes using the new lingo of the street was good for business, especially when he was dealing with youngsters like Justin and Tony. They had been overly influenced by American films and rap and therefore liked using such words as G, short for gangster, a term of endearment.

'Nutin´ much, got a telly and a car stereo for you.'

'Sweet, bring `em in.'

Tony approached them with the car stereo in his hand, 'What you sayin´ G?'

'Nutin´,' replied Diamond.

Justin returned with the TV and they followed Diamond into his living room. His father was sitting on an armchair watching TV with a beer in his hand. The old man briefly looked up at the two boys, glanced at the stolen TV and stereo, nodded his head in greeting and then returned to watching his film. Justin placed the TV on a table and then placed the remote control next to it. Tony placed the stereo on top of the TV.

'How much will you give us for that lot then?' asked Tony as coolly as he could manage, which seemed pretty uncool to Justin.

Diamond Dave scratched his head and took a deep sigh. He then picked up the remote control and examined it with close scrutiny before bending down and pretending to look at the TV. He then briefly prodded the stereo with his finger before scratching his head again and taking another deep sigh.

'I'll give you twenty-five for the lot, the stereo's a bit naff but I like you boys so I'll take it as well.'

'Twenty-five! Be serious G, that's a brand new telly,' Justin said, remembering the immense effort of carrying it out of the flat and down the stairs.

'We always bring you stuff G, don't screw us over,' Tony added, knowing full well that Diamond was always prepared to pay at least twenty pounds more than his original offer.

Again Diamond scratched his head in mock contemplation, and this time he even circled around the TV before looking wearily into the eyes of his young patronage. 'OK I'll tell you what I'll do,' Dave said as a sneaky smile began to form on his face, 'I'll give you thirty for the lot and you can come with me to Jimmy Jakleson's twenty-first birthday party.'

'No way!' Justin almost squealed. Tony looked at Justin and thought about throttling him, he had just blown whatever negotiating powers they had. Giving Justin a dirty look he sucked his teeth and then let his anger subside, he could understand the reason for Justin's enthusiasm. Jimmy was already a legend on the estate for his wild and raunchy parties, all of which were drug fuelled and lasted until the next morning. Only a chosen few were allowed to attend the parties and Tony had first started hearing rumours of Jimmy having a twenty-first party six months ago.

Justin saw the way Tony had looked at him and realized that he'd blown the deal, slightly embarrassed he looked down at his feet before allowing his short attention span to return to the idea of the party. Apart from the drugs and booze Jimmy's parties were well known for the fit babes, if ever there was an opportunity to lose his virginity this was it.

'I take it we have a deal?' beamed Diamond. Justin nodded his head slowly.

'Yeah all right then,' said Tony coolly extending his hand for the obligatory shake.

'Good,' said Diamond as he began counting out the money from a thick wad of notes he produced from his pocket. Much to Justin's annoyance he gave the money to Tony, making Justin appear as nothing more than a mere sidekick. 'Now go on and tart yourselves up a bit as there'll be a few birds there and come and pick me up in half an hour,' commanded Diamond Dave as he led them to the front door. Needless to say the pair didn't waste anytime in driving over to Justin's home with the sole intention of picking out his finest clothes for themselves. Justin had spent that last couple of years dreaming about being invited to one of Jimmy's parties and now it was coming true. Perhaps it was a sign, perhaps it meant that he could do anything, perhaps it even meant that he would soon lose his virginity.

CHAPTER FOUR

Derek sipped his drink and watched the lottery balls bouncing around with mild curiosity. He'd previously played on two separate occasions and of course hadn't won a penny, which was why he'd given up. As far as he was concerned the lottery was nothing but a tax on the poor and he'd already paid more than enough tax to last a lifetime. The idea of handing anymore of his hard earned money over to the government, even if it was only one pound, made him sick, but for the sake of his daughter, he was willing to make an exception. In fact he would probably have done anything for his daughter, because at that moment in time she was the only person who showed him any love and therefore his only link to life itself.

'It was the last ball last week, but it's the first this week, number thirty-two,' said the announcer.

Thirty-two Derek thought to himself as he was snapped out of his thoughts, he had that one. If he got two more he'd win ten pounds.

'Best not to get your hopes up,' Derek muttered under his breath as he took another swig of his beer.

'What's that my old friend?' asked Terry.

'Oh nothing,' said Derek, 'just talking to myself.'

'You should be careful it's the first sign of madness.'

'So I've heard.'

'Which goes back to my argument about getting yourself a woman.'

Derek chose to ignore the rest of Terry's ranting, the subject of women depressed him, he'd never been any good at going out and picking up strangers and a man like Terry just couldn't get it. He knew that Terry wasn't trying to show off about his own prowess but the fact was the subject was wearing pretty thin.

When Derek next looked at the TV he saw that numbers twenty, thirty-eight and forty-one had also come up. His jaw dropped, he had those numbers! For sure he did, he remembered clearly. Speechless he looked on as Terry continued with his monologue, completely unaware of the event unravelling around him. What occurred next took only a matter of seconds but Derek would have it etched into his mind for the rest of his life as his two remaining numbers tumbled out on to the screen in slow motion. Totally flabbergasted he looked on as the presenter was announcing the week's winning numbers in ascending order; nine, twelve, twenty, thirty-two, thirty-eight and forty-one.

Derek polished off his drink in disbelief, what the hell should he do now? Jump up and down like a lunatic and buy everyone in the pub a drink or keep quite and sneak off home, making damn sure that he really had won and wasn't losing his mind? Instinct told him to follow the latter option, besides he just about had enough cash to buy himself a drink no matter what his new found financial status was.

'Well neither of us are millionaires, but life's not that bad,' said Terry as he nodded towards the barmaid, 'let me buy you a drink and we'll have a toast to the infinite beauty of life's possibilities.'

'That's very philosophical of you Terry, that barmaid must have captured your heart, but yes, let's drink and toast the infinite beauty of life's possibilities.'

Terry briefly glanced at Derek with suspicion before directing his attention back at the barmaid.

'But it's true mummy, I swear on my life it's true,' cried Tina as she rolled around the living room floor in a berserk tantrum. Jane, John and Tom looked on in disbelief; this behaviour was completely uncharacteristic of Tina and rather worrying for Jane.

'Tina, stop it,' shouted Jane as she tried to pull her daughter up off the ground.

'NOOOooo!' cried Tina, tears streaming down her face. 'Daddy won, I tell you, daddy won.'

John frowned in silence, this wasn't his daughter, this wasn't his business, yet he felt obliged to do something. He prised Jane's grip off Tina's wrist and almost instantly the crying and squirming decreased dramatically. Jane looked at him in semi-shock, he'd never interfered in such family disputes before. Her eyes looked at him inquisitively, and his flashed back to her full of reassurance. He bent over Tina, whose crying had faded into mild whimpers and sobs. She now lay on her stomach, with her head buried in her arms.

'Tina, how about we phone your dad? Would you like your mum to phone him and ask if he's won the lottery?' John asked tentatively.

Tina briefly looked up, her eyes red and her

cheeks slightly swollen, she nodded her head slowly before returning to her defensive position.

'This is stupid,' said Jane stubbornly.

'What harm can it do?' John replied looking down at Tina.

'All right, all right you win but I tell you something young lady,' Jane said, directing her anger at Tina, 'if this is some story you've made up, well, you're going to be in for the spanking of a lifetime!' Immediately Tina's sobs started again and quickly developed into one long wailing noise. Jane stormed out of the room, towards the corridor, where the telephone was. Tom, loving every minute of this drama ran after her. John sat down next to Tina and stroked her hair, 'Please don't cry, you know that your mummy loves you don't you?'

'She thinks I'm a liar,' Tina blurted out in between sobs, 'and as soon as she speaks to daddy she's going to regret not believing me.'

'I'm sure she will,' John smiled.

'He's not home,' Jane said as soon as she returned to the room. Tom was by her side, he smiled evilly at his younger sister, who was the only one in the room to notice. She was determined by this reaction not to provide him with any more entertainment.

John spoke to Tina, almost in a whisper, 'So your dad's not home now, it's no big deal, we can phone tomorrow morning.'

'You promise?' Tina asked delicately.

'We promise, don't we baby?' John said as he looked up at Jane.

'We'll phone but only if you promise to go to bed now and be a good girl,' Jane said, her arms crossed against her chest.

'I promise,' Tina said as she slowly rose and wiped her cheeks clean.

Jane sighed, as her daughter left the room, part of her wanted it to be true if only to have some peace in the house and to know that Tina hadn't changed, that she was still the same down to earth well mannered girl she had always been. Yet on the other hand the idea of Derek being worth millions of pounds didn't appeal to her. She could imagine him being all smug and rubbing the fact that he was now worth infinitely more than them in her face. Especially in front of John, of whom Derek was so plainly jealous. Perhaps worst of all would be the gossip the neighbours would spread. After all they had seen Derek move out and John move in. If they found out that he had won the lottery they would be laughing at Jane's poor timing. Derek would probably be living in some mansion somewhere and she would be stuck here putting up with all their gossip mongering. Ah he couldn't have won Jane told herself, Tina had just got the wrong end of the stick. Jane shook her head and laughed at her own stupidity. There was no way that Derek had won the lottery. However, still slightly disturbed, she decided that she'd phone him again later just to put her fears to rest.

Justin carried the vase into his home, trying to carefully conceal it from his Grandma, who was in the living room watching the news. He placed the vase carefully outside the room before he and Tony entered.

'Hello boys,' said Justin's grandmother with an enthusiastic smile. She was seventy-five years old, in fairly good health and adored company.

'Hello, how are you?' Tony asked hoping that she would offer him some tea and some of her home-made scones.

'My back's playing up again,' she complained.

'Oh Gran,' Justin said crouching down beside her, 'I told you to go to the bloody doctor's, init?'

'You remember to watch your language you scallywag,' she said clapping Justin delicately around his head. Tony didn't try to suppress his smirk. Grandmother and grandson both looked up at him simultaneously. Embarrassed, Justin thought of a way to change the subject. Searching for ideas he spotted a lottery ticket on the coffee table.

'Any luck?' he asked nodding in its direction.

Justin's grandma frowned, 'Not even one blooming number,' she almost growled, 'and to think only one person has won this week, the full twenty-five million.'

'Oh well, better luck next time,' Tony said, his attention span already being stretched to its limit. They had a party to go to, beer, drugs, and girls. He knew Justin loved his grandmother deeply, and he admired her for raising the dopy git by herself but this scene, out of some kind of wishy-washy made for TV movie was making him nauseous. He kicked Justin swiftly up the arse, not hard, but quickly so that the old lady couldn't see. Justin got the message.

'OK, going up to my room now gran, we're gonna get changed because we're going to a party tonight.'

'A party, hey? Well just remember to be careful and don't drink too much. Maybe you'd like me to bring you boys up some tea and cakes?'

Tony's eyes lit up at the mere mention of cakes.

'No thanks,' Justin replied, 'we're in a rush.'

Tony's heart sank and he silently cursed his best friend for being the dumbest guy on the planet. He followed Justin out of the living room and into Justin's bedroom. Justin put the vase in the corner, next to his hi-fi.

'She'll love this,' Justin beamed with pride.

'Stop prancing about, we've gotta get changed and go, don't forget there'll be some hot girls at this place,' Tony grumbled.

'Oh yeah the girls,' Justin said out aloud. He had a good feeling about tonight, they'd already made some money and been invited to Jimmy's party. Yeah, tonight was definitely his night.

CHAPTER FIVE

The walk to Derek's home was deliberately slow. He wanted to savour every second of what was now to be the remnants of his life of poverty. Ahead lay a whole future of infinite possibilities. He could finally jack in his job at the meat factory! He could move out of that small, cockroach infested hellhole he'd been forced to call home! Twenty-five million, won by just one person, that's what they'd said on TV. Only one person had won and it was him, twenty-five million! It was more money than he'd know what to do with, he'd be able to enjoy the rest of his life, go on four or five holidays a year and still provide his children with a certain future. He remembered his promise to give half to Tina, but that wouldn't be until she was eighteen. Imagine all the interest her half of the money would have accumulated by then! Why he'd even be able to give Tom a large fortune when he turned eighteen as well.

Imagine all the good things he'd be able to do for his children! Private schools, private tutors, holidays, expensive hobbies he thought he'd never be able to afford, Tina had always wanted to go horse riding. What else could he give them? Well they wouldn't have to get into debt if they wanted to attend a university, that was for sure and when they were ready to settle down he'd be able to buy them a house each. He'd be able to give them all the things he'd never had as a child and all the opportunities that had been denied to him as a young adult.

The icing on the cake would be Jane's expression as he'd pull up every week to pick the kids up in his brand new Bentley, hell he could even afford to buy a Bentley and a Rolls. What kind of car would Tom like his old man to drive? Probably a Ferrari, well he'd buy one of those too, heck maybe even a helicopter, and to think he wouldn't have to share a single penny with Jane because she'd already divorced him. Mrs Stonehold from next door would relish the potential gossip this story could unleash. She and Jane had been archenemies for years and an advanced form of urban warfare through the medium of gossip mongering had emerged between them. Think of all the ammunition he would be supplying Mrs Stonehold in her campaign against Jane! Derek couldn't help letting out a small, evil laugh, the irony of it all was so delightfully exquisite.

He took in a deep breath and increased his pace slightly, his body filled with adrenalin and excitement, he hadn't felt this way for a long time. He wasn't even sure if he'd ever felt this way before. The feeling was unique, only surpassed by the way he felt when his children were born, but this what he felt now, how could he describe it? His body tingled all over for a start and when he walked his steps were so light it was as if he were walking on air. He couldn't stop smiling, suddenly everything in the world seemed OK. Of course, this was what it was like to feel happy, but no happiness wasn't a strong enough word, this was euphoria. Derek had conceded to ending his working life in the meat factory, he had resigned himself to a life of poverty and to finishing his days alone in his bedsit. Now everything had changed, only a prisoner on death row who'd been granted a pardon could understand how he felt.

Would the smile on Derek's face ever go away? Probably one day, one day when he'd become accustomed to the mansions, the flash cars, the luxury holidays, and all the free time in the world. When the extraordinary would become just plain ordinary, but that wouldn't be for a long, long, long time. Yes, Derek was pretty confident that the smiles would keep coming for the next few years.

He thought of Terry, who as usual had taken a taxi after their session in the pub. He'd noticed Derek's strange mood and expressed his concern many times, hah if only he knew! He'd wait until the cheque was in the bank and then surprise his friend with the good news. Terry, he'd been like a brother to Derek over the years, especially during the divorce. Yes, he'd see Terry right, a million at least, hell maybe even two, after all he did have twenty-five million to spend. Just a minute, would he have to pay tax? Shit, imagine losing half to the taxman, thieving bastards, it wouldn't surprise Derek if they did want their pound of flesh. Well he had nothing against tax avoidance, and with his fortune he'd make damn sure he'd hire the best lawyers and accountants money could buy. This was the beginning of a new era, one where Derek would no longer be the one shafted but the one doing the shafting. Yes, there definitely was a God and he wasn't the cruel callous bastard Derek had cursed everyday for the last three years. There was justice! It existed! Maybe he'd pop into his local church tomorrow after he'd claimed his winnings.

He'd always been agnostic but winning twenty-five million suddenly made him feel remorse for his lack of spiritual discipline. Of course he'd donate at least one million to charity, imagine all the good he could do with his money. Derek took out his keys and looked at the building where he lived, soon he'd no longer have to see the place, he probably wouldn't even bother moving the few possessions he had, he'd rather just buy everything new than have to spend a second longer than necessary in that hellhole. Just then it occurred to him how much he actually hated the place. Derek felt like a man who'd just come out of prison, the smile on his face broadened as he opened the door to the building's entrance.

Justin had decided to get stoned before even arriving at the party. He had that slim, red look across the eyes all heavy users of cannabis get when they decide to really go for it and blow their brains out. Tonight he was on skunk, and, damn it, was good! The high was mellowing, making him calm, yet it wasn't the kind of 'relaxing' mellow hash would bring because the chemicals in the skunk had activated Justin's imagination, wrongly giving him the impression that he was all wise. Right now he felt like he knew why everything was the way it was in the world, he felt like he had a solution for every problem and that he could go anywhere and do anything. Justin's skunk-slimmed eyes watched Tony rev the engine of the car as he waited for the lights to go green. Diamond Dave puffed nervously on the spliff Justin had just passed on to him. Tony was driving like a maniac, and he was stoned to boot. Dave made a mental note to catch a ride back with someone else, these two jokers were so stupid they were dangerous. The compulsory wheelspin sent the smell of burnt rubber thundering through the sky as Tony sped them towards their destination.

'Almost there boys,' he shouted as he beeped his horn at a group of young women who were obviously out for a night's partying.

'Damn, they're fit,' Justin whimpered as he looked back at Dave.

'They'll probably be at the party,' Dave said as he finished off the remainder of the joint and threw the roach out of the window.

'Shit,' said Justin, 'we should have stopped and offered ´em a lift.'

'I could turn back,' Tony offered, as he abruptly dropped down a gear in anticipation of the illegal u-turn he was about to perform.

'No, fuck it man, there'll be loads of pussy there, and better quality too!' Diamond Dave shot out more from fear of crashing into a lamppost than true conviction.

'OK G, we trust you,' Justin said as he then turned his attention to Tony, 'carry on my man, ´coz we got some serious partyin´ to do.'

They'd been at the party for five minutes and already Dave was thinking about ways of losing the two fools he'd regretfully invited along. He'd appreciated the lift, but damn they were sticking to him like glue and scaring all the babes away. He wanted to get laid for Christ's sake, not baby sit a pair of adolescent delinquents. Thankfully he spotted Jimmy surrounded by a large group of fans.

'Let's go and say hello to the host,' he said, nodding in Jimmy's direction.

Tony followed Dave coolly and Justin followed Tony, although not with quite the same sophistication as his friend was managing to emit. Justin moved with the fact he didn't like crowds of new people foremost in his mind. This coupled with the skunk he'd been smoking had suddenly turned that previous mellow high into freak paranoia. It was as if everyone there was staring at him or talking about him. He walked past two girls, they looked at him and then started laughing. Were they laughing at him? No they couldn't be, could they? They didn't even know him. Small beads of sweat had already started forming on his forehead and he quickly used the back of his hand to wipe them away before being introduced to Jimmy.

'Always good to have some new guests,' Jimmy beamed at the two boys.

'Great party you've got here G,' Tony said, 'Oh, and happy birthday,' he added quickly.

Justin nodded nervously.

'Cheers lads, have you grabbed yourselves some beers?'

'No, not yet,' said Tony.

'Well help yourselves, you'll find the booze in the kitchen.'

'Cheers G, we'll catch up later, just let us know if you need any skunk, we've got plenty,' Tony boasted loudly for everyone in the crowd to hear.

'Will do,' said Jimmy as he took a pull of a massive spliff someone had just passed on to him.

Tony grabbed Justin's arm and led him to the kitchen.

'Shouldn't we stick to Dave?' Justin asked nervously.

'No G, we've gotta be slick, look like we don't need no one, then the babes will be all over us.'

'But we don't know anyone!' Justin complained.

'Just relax G, and trust me, I know what I'm doing. Now get us two beers from the fridge.'

Justin, listening to the reassurances from his friend felt his pulse slacken. He opened the door and looked around the fridge, which was crammed with assorted beers.

'Stella or Fosters?' he shouted, his head still buried in the fridge.

'Stella of course,' a female voice replied. In disbelief Justin lifted his head out of the fridge. Standing right next to Tony were two girls. Two very attractive girls!

Tony turned to his right and slowly eyed the two girls up and down, a mischievous smile forming on his face. The one closest to him was a dark redhead, wearing a tight t-shirt and an even tighter pair of jeans. Justin's eyes followed Tony's across the same body causing an uncomfortable sensation in his boxer shorts. Next the two boys eyed the tall blonde, whose elegant top was just as tight as her friend's, but barely managed to hide a much larger and fuller shaped pair of breasts. Her short skirt revealed a pair of self-tanned, athletic legs and her high heels made her calf muscles look like a pair of diamonds. Beads of sweat forming on his forehead, Justin imagined what she must look like naked and instantly caused the discomfort in his boxers to become almost unbearable.

The two girls, feeling the uncomfortably silent eyes of Tony and Justin, as they were mentally undressed, looked at each other and shrugged. Being attractive they were used to the unwanted attention, and the way boys and even men would stop and stare at them, unable or unwilling to say anything, just lost in some kind of visually stimulated vortex. What these men would be imaging when they had that strange glazed over look in their eyes just didn't bare thinking about. The two girls were privy to the little known fact that walking into a room filled with people is just as nerve racking for a highly attractive confident woman as it is for her more conventional 'does my bum look big in this?' counterpart. Hungry male stares are the disadvantage of being a very attractive woman, and like all attractive women the two girls had learnt to cast aside the discomfort of the hungry eyes until the brains of the males in the room were able to readjust to the new visual stimuli.

Tony discreetly nodded in the direction of the fridge, but Justin completely disorientated by the presence of female company failed to understand what his friend intended. Instead he merely carried on gazing at the two girls, dumbfounded, with a stupid grin on his face. Tony giving up hope pushed him out of the way and handed the two girls a Stella each. They in turn smiled pleasantly at each other and at Tony, but ignored Justin who failed to make that first all important impression.

'We overheard you saying that you've got some skunk,' said the redhead, her lips uttering the word 'skunk', slowly and seductively.

'Th..that's right,' Justin managed to stammer out loudly, 'we've got loads!'

The two girls looked at each other and giggled.

'Yeah we deal,' Tony said thinking that the girls would be impressed.

'You see mens like us have to be entrepreneurial 'coz the rich folks wantta keep us poor. We can get you anything you need, skunk, hash, weed, charlie, you name it we got it,' Justin managed to add without a single nervous stutter.

'Well, we only want a joint,' the blonde said, her smile enhancing her beauty. Although the two girls could understand Justin and Tony's language, they refused to speak street. Not because they were ashamed of where they were from but because they had simply fallen out of the habit. Both had studied for their A levels at a local college and Karen, the redhead would soon be going to university. Tony quickly sensing that the girls weren't impressed by the use of street or the immature bragging of drug dealing decided to drop the street speak and try another tack.

'Hey don't worry, my mate will roll you one, he rolls the finest spliffs you've ever seen,' Tony said looking in Justin's direction.

'Good with his hands then, is he?' Karen retorted.

Justin, suddenly unable to breath, dropped his beer on the floor, soaking the blonde's feet.

'Shit!' she screamed, causing her friend to burst out laughing.

'Oh, fuck, I'm sorry,' Justin begged apologetically, before dropping to his knees and trying to wipe the beer off her shoes with his hands.

'Fuck off you idiot,' the blonde screamed even louder.

The redhead thoroughly amused at what was happening had to brace herself against the kitchen sink because she was laughing so much. Tony couldn't help but join in.

The blonde completely irritated by her friend's reaction, took off her shoes, and pulled Justin up by his ear.

'Let me give you some advice mate, you use a cloth to wipe liquid off something, not your hands.'

'I'm sorry, I just wanted to get to it quickly,' Justin replied, his breath laboured and his cheeks flushed.

'I'm going to the ladies to clean myself up,' the blonde told her friend, who again burst into a fit of laughter.

'You cow!' the blonde spat out to her friend as she left the kitchen.

'Hey I really like your friend's style,' the redhead said when she finally managed to stop herself from laughing.

'You should see him at a nightclub,' Tony said, causing more fits of laughter. Justin, failing to see the funny side of the situation managed a weak smile.

'My name's Tony, and Casanova over here goes by the name of Justin.'

'Pleased to meet you Tony and Casanova, hah, I mean Justin. My name's Karen and miss happiness is Sarah.'

'Is your friend always so welcoming then?' Tony asked looking deeply into Karen's eyes.

'Oh please forgive her, she's been in a terrible mood all evening, she just needs some skunk, like me, then she'll chill out.'

'Well why don't I take you for a drive, this party's pretty lame and I know a beautiful spot that's ideal for a smoke,' Tony said, his confidence growing by the second.

Karen paused to think before answering, 'Well, you are right about the party, I expected better after hearing about Jimmy's parties, but I don't think that Sarah would be up for a drive.'

Tony looked at Karen intensely, trying his best to lure her with his eyes and his smile. 'I was thinking that you could ditch your friend, after all she doesn't seem to be enjoying herself much.'

'I couldn't do that, she'd kill me!'

'Oh come on, you know you want to. Anyway Justin could look after her, couldn't you Justin?'

'Er, um, er, yeah course I could.'

'You see.'

Karen smiled seductively at Tony. It was obvious he had more than just a drive and smoke in mind, and boy he was seriously sexy, letting him get away would be such a waste. Anyway this could be her last London adventure before she went off to university. 'Let me go and talk to her, see if she's OK with the idea.'

'Sure,' Tony smiled. Both he and Justin watched in silence as she walked provocatively out of the room.

'You fucking jammy bastard,' Justin muttered, shaking his head in disbelief.

'Me! What you talking about you ungrateful git? I'm leaving you with the sexy blonde. I tell you she's well up for it.'

'She hates my guts.'

'Hey man, there's only so much I can do, I let you get first dibs on the fittest girl. If you fuck up it's your fault.'

'That's bullshit G, you saw an opportunity with

the redhead and you grabbed it ´coz you know she's well up for it.'

Tony put an arm round his friend's shoulder, 'Well I didn't see you making no moves, so what was I suppose to do? Let them both get away? Anyway I think the blonde likes you, she's just playing hard to get.'

'For real?'

Tony smiled, 'Trust me, I'm your best friend.'

Justin let out a deep sigh.

Karen had bumped into Sarah on the stairs, just as Sarah had been making a rather incandescent return to her friend and the two idiots they'd had the misfortune to meet on this particular night. Needless to say she didn't take the news of Karen's intentions too well.

'I can't believe you! How can you even think about leaving me with that spastic, here, with no one else I know and going off with some bloke you just met?' Sarah fumed.

'Oh come on, what about that bloke you went off with two weeks ago in that night club? You didn't hear me complaining, did you? I just got in a cab and saw myself home, didn't I?'

'But that was different, I didn't know that you were leaving me and going off to university then. I thought you said that you wanted to spend as much time as possible with me before you went to Manchester.'

'Oh babe, I do, and I will. I mean I've still got another month before I leave and you know I'm going to come back and visit you. We see each other nearly everyday, what more do you want?'

Sarah frowned, she knew that Karen was right

and that she was being selfish, but she couldn't help feeling jealous of her friend. Not only because she was leaving the area and all the problems that went along with it, but because Tony was also seriously sexy and she had hoped that she'd be the one to get off with him. Instead she'd just been lumbered with his retarded sidekick.

'Come on, please. He's so damn fit, I don't want to let him get away,' Karen begged, causing Sarah's heart to melt.

'I don't know, I mean look at the state of his friend. Would you want to be lumbered with him all night?'

'I'd do it for you, you know I would, anyway you can dump him after five minutes and look for some other bloke, come on please, I'll owe you.'

'All right,' Sarah smiled finally giving in, 'but you definitely owe me.'

Justin was drinking his beer in silence as he watched Tony expertly finish rolling a joint. His hands started to shake so much when he noticed Karen and Sarah return that he had to put his can of beer on a table. Still far too nervous he hid his hands in his pockets out of fear of causing another accident. He smiled nervously at the two girls, both of whom surprisingly smiled back.

'There you are,' said Tony placing the finished joint behind his right ear, 'the spliff's ready and so am I. What about you?'

'I'm ready too,' Karen said as she took him by the hand and led him out of the kitchen and towards their exit.

'Now you kids behave,' Tony managed to shout back. Justin could hear Karen's giggle fade off into the distance. Suddenly the sheer horror that he'd been left alone with this extremely attractive girl hit him. A small voice inside his head was telling him to run home, in fact he felt like he was going to puke, but damn it, he was supposed to be a gangster and gangsters were supposed to tap bitches. He forced his hands to stop shaking and picked up his beer, draining the remainder of the can in one big gulp.

With lighting speed he fetched two more cans out of the fridge while Sarah observed him in silence. He opened one of the cans and gave it to Sarah, who accepted it cautiously.

'Don't worry, I'm not usually a butter-fingers,' Justin said with a light smile, desperately trying to break the ice. Sarah sensing his nervousness and feeling slightly sorry for the poor sod, managed to ease up a little.

'Sorry for shouting at you earlier. I was just a little wound up that's all.'

Justin smiled enthusiastically, a full two minutes had passed in the company of this gorgeous girl, some kind of record for sure. He placed the beer back on the kitchen table and began rolling a spliff.

'That's great,' Sarah said. She slowly eased up next to him. 'I've been dying for a spliff all night.'

Justin swallowed hard, he enjoyed this close proximity to her but at the same time it made him distinctly nervous. As he ground the skunk into little pieces and sprinkled it along the paper he could feel her stare, it was intense. Were his spliff making skills impressing her? He took a cigarette out of a pack he kept in his pocket and mixed the tobacco with the ground up skunk.

'Wow, you're really good at that,' she said.

'Jus´ practice, that's all,' he said. She drew closer and he could feel her breath on the back of his neck. Lifting the semi-made joint into the air he rubbed the fine tobacco paper up and down before licking the tip and dextrously rolling it into one tightly packed spliff. Justin smiled to himself, he had been afraid that the pressure of Sarah watching him would have caused him to mess up but it hadn't. He was sure that she'd been impressed by his rolling skills. Hands trembling slightly, he gave her the joint, which she took slowly and calmly, her sultry eyes looking into his. She bit off the end before placing it in her mouth. She waited patiently for Justin to light it for her, but afraid that his unsteady hands would again make him look like a fool, he simply gave her the lighter. She took it and smiled before lighting the joint. Justin studied her carefully, as if she were a painting, while she inhaled and then exhaled those first uplifting tokes of the joint. He watched as her chest rose and fell. His stomach churned as she threw her head back, allowing her golden locks to fall down to her shoulders, and when he watched the smoke as it was expelled through her lips, well damn, he almost wanted to cry.

'This is good stuff,' she said as she passed the joint and the lighter back to Justin.

'Thanks,' he said, as he puffed on the spliff, 'if you ever want some just let me know. You could give me your number and . . . erm, well . . . I could bring it round to you.'

'Thanks, you're so sweet,' she smiled at him and his heart almost melted. He was actually winning her round, she was smiling at him! He smiled back at her whilst his mind frantically searched for something impressive to say. Should he tell her how beautiful he thought she was, or should he tell her how his heart skipped a beat every time he looked into her sparkling eyes? NO! He couldn't talk to her like that, could he? She'd just think he was a wanker, but what should he say? How could he let her know what he thought about her? How could he make her interested in him?

Just as he'd thought of exactly the right thing to tell her, the kitchen door opened and Diamond Dave walked in. He looked at Justin briefly before fixing an incredulous stare onto Sarah.

'All right mate,' Dave said, his words slightly slurred from the skunk and alcohol, 'who's this beautiful angel?'

'Sarah,' blushed the girl Justin was just about to make his move on.

'My name's Dave,' he said taking her hand before gently pressing it against his lips, 'although some people call me Diamond.' She giggled foolishly and Justin couldn't believe she was falling for Dave's crap.

'I've heard about you,' she said, looking girlishly into his eyes.

'Oh really?' Dave said, actually managing to pass himself off as a modest fellow.

'Yeah, on my estate you're really famous,' she purred, tilting her head to one side and slowly mouthing the word 'famous' provocatively. Justin felt like vomiting, his blood was boiling and out of anger he kicked an empty beer can, which was lying on the floor, to the other side of the room. Yet he was totally inconspicuous to Dave and Sarah as they gawped mindlessly at each other.

Filled with rage Justin wanted to punch Dave

straight on the nose, but Diamond Dave was twice his size and Justin was no fighter. In silent indignation he watched Dave confidently strut to the fridge and pull out a beer, before leaning across the kitchen counter in a most masculine pose.

'Well why don't you grab your beer and follow me? I'll introduce you to Jimmy if you like.'

'All right,' Sarah beamed, before almost running out of the door. Dave used his cool strut to leave the kitchen, pausing only briefly to wink at Justin as he passed him by. The kitchen door closed and Justin was left alone. He sunk to the floor and placed his head in his hands. He was never going to lose his virginity, what kind of gangster was he if he was still a virgin? His eyes were watery, tears were on their way but he refused to let them come. He relit the spliff, and taking deep pulls he tried to convince himself that he hadn't really liked Sarah anyway. He got off the floor and straightened up before taking a manly swig of his beer. Five minutes had passed since Sarah had left him alone, she wasn't coming back. Justin quietly left the party pausing only briefly as he saw Dave with his tongue down Sarah's throat and his hand firmly on her left breast. He carried on until he reached the front door, before stopping. He briefly toyed with the idea of staying, there were more girls at the party. Perhaps if he mingled a bit he could meet one of them. Maybe he could stick close to Jimmy, he had girls all over him. But his fragile confidence had already been badly shaken, he just wanted to go home. He quietly closed the door, glad that at least he hadn't drawn any attention as he slinked away.

Shit! He only just now remembered that Tony had taken the car. It was a long walk home, but

Justin didn't care. He just didn't care about anything anymore. Two minutes into his journey, it started to rain, not your usual kind of London drizzle, but that cold, strong, hard stuff that really eats into your clothes and drenches your flesh. Finally, Justin allowed himself to cry, the tears gently mixing in with the rain on his face. He wasn't a gangster he was just a loser.

CHAPTER SIX

Derek whistled the tune of 'If I were a rich man,' as he briskly climbed the staircase, which led to his home. Usually it was a hard arduous, crawl that took him to his small, poky room, but not tonight; tonight he was full of energy. Tonight he was reborn, a multi-millionaire and he was about to show the whole world that it and everybody in it had written him off way too early.

The whistling and rejoicing stopped abruptly once Derek noticed that his door was slightly open. He remembered closing it! Suddenly the unthinkable occurred to him, the lottery ticket! What if someone had taken it? Derek's legs felt like jelly as he entered his room. He quickly checked behind the door to make sure nobody was there, and then under the bed, but whoever was responsible for this was gone. Out of the corner of his eye he noticed that the telly was missing and cursed himself for not having any insurance, and then in panic his attention returned to the lottery ticket! He looked at the mantle piece, the vase, it was gone! God no! That's where he'd put the lottery ticket! In his late mother's vase for safe keeping. Who the fuck would have taken that God-awful vase?

Frantically Derek scoured the room looking for the vase, or its remnants praying that the thief had knocked it over, that it had been broken by accident and that the lottery ticket was lying idly somewhere around the room. After thirty minutes the prayers turned into curses and after an hour the curses turned into sobs as Derek finally accepted the truth – the vase and the lottery ticket inside it had been taken. Understandably he broke down, bursting into tears before sitting on the floor beside his bed, gently rocking backwards and forwards. This was a man, in deep anguish. Derek's reprieve had been snatched away, before he'd even had a chance to breathe the fresh air of his dream. The room started to spin, strange colourful blotches blocked his eyesight and suddenly his stomach started to quiver. His breathing became laboured and his hands started to shake uncontrolably.

The ringing of his phone snapped Derek out of near nervous breakdown. Who could it be? It was rare for Derek to receive a phone call, in fact Terry was his only real mate.

'Hello?' he answered nervously, suspicious of who might be on the other end.

'Hello Derek, it's me Jane.' Derek's ex-wife had been unable to contain her curiosity until the next day. Was it possible that Tina had been telling the truth? Had her father really won the lottery? Jane already knew that twenty-five million pounds was up for grabs.

'Jane? Is everything all right?' Derek asked, instantly concerned about the safety of his children.

'Yes everything's fine. We just had a problem with Tina tonight, that's all.'

'A problem with Tina? What kind of problem?' Derek asked, his apprehensiveness growing.

'Oh nothing to worry about, it's just that . . . erm,

well I feel silly even mentioning it, but, ha, she seems to think that you've won the lottery.'

There was a long silence on the other end as Derek absorbed the information. Of course, Tina, she knew what the numbers were and she must have watched the draw on TV. Bloody hell! Things were worse, not only had he just lost twenty-five million pounds, but everybody that mattered in his life would know what an idiot he was!

'Hello, Derek are you still there? Is everything OK?'

'Yeah, I'm still here.'

'Well did you? I mean win the lottery that is?' she asked with a nervous giggle.

'Er, well yeah I did,' Derek said, instantly wishing he could take it back.

'What? Twenty-five million pounds?' Jane's tone was incredulous.

Derek thought about his next answer. He wanted to lie, but his outdated code of ethics prevented him from doing so. Blast it, why couldn't he just lie and cheat like the rest of the scum that populated the planet? Hadn't his foolish attempt to lead a decent life cost him enough? But he couldn't do it, he just couldn't lie, it went against every fibre of his being. Besides Tina would still know the truth, but worse she would know that her father had lied.

'Yes I won the lottery, all twenty-five million pounds,' Derek said regretfully.

'Well congratulations,' Jane said through clenched teeth, a slight knot forming in her stomach.

'Not so fast,' Derek said.

'What do you mean?'

'I've been burgled and the thief's taken the ticket.'

'What?' Jane screamed down the line. This was unbelievable, it couldn't be happening, could it? What were the odds on winning the lottery and then having the ticket stolen from you? Then she remembered it was Derek, with him anything was possible, a slight smile formed on her face. It looked like he wouldn't be able to rub his new-found wealth in her face after all.

'How the hell did that happen?'

'I left the ticket at home and went for a beer with Terry. At the pub I saw the result of the draw and realized that I'd won. When I got home the place had been burgled and someone had taken the ticket.'

'Well have you at least phoned the police?' Jane asked feeling guilty over her initial reaction to discovering that Derek had lost the ticket. After all, she had loved him at one point in her life and this was the last thing he needed. He was a decent man and deserved some kind of break in life.

'No, I haven't had the chance yet. I'd better do that now.'

'Oh, OK then, well I'll let you get on with things. I'm sorry, I hope you find the ticket, bye.'

'Thanks, bye.'

Quickly he dialled nine, nine, nine.

'Which emergency service do you require?' asked a female operator.

'The police, quick,' Derek said with a sense of urgency. Perhaps if they started looking for the thief now they could catch him before he got too far.

'This is the emergency service for the police, how can we help?' asked another female operator.

'I've been burgled and . . .' but before Derek could finish his sentence the operator interrupted him.

'Is the thief still on the premises sir?'

'No but . . .'

'Is your life or anybody else's in danger?'

'No but . . .'

'I'm afraid that your situation doesn't count as an emergency sir, we appreciate how devastating coming home to a burgled house is but the force is desperately over stretched. Now we will send someone to your home but we have to ask you to be patient, it could take up to an hour.'

'But he's taken my lottery ticket!'

'Sorry, did you say your lottery ticket sir?'

'Yes, I won the jackpot and then I went to the pub and when I got home my room had been burgled and the ticket was gone!' Derek shouted down the line, a vein in his neck throbbing from stress and lack of oxygen. There was a moment's silence on the other line.

'Sir I do hope you realize that wasting police time and tying up our emergency line is a criminal offence.'

'Look this isn't a windup, it's the truth. Some bastard's nicked my lottery ticket!'

'Very well sir,' the operator replied in a slow, agitated voice, 'if you give me your name and address I'll make sure that our officers arrive as soon as possible.'

'When will that be?' Derek asked apprehensively.

'Like I said before sir, in about an hour's time; we're desperately undermanned.'

'But by then the thief could claim my prize!'

'Well I suggest you phone the lottery people and tell them that your ticket has been stolen. I'm sure they have contingency plans for such a situation.'

'But you're the police, surely this falls under your jurisdiction?'

'I'm afraid there's nothing else I can do sir; now will you please give me your name and address so that we can begin to investigate this matter!'

Defeated Derek finally gave the woman his name and address, all he could do now was hope that they would arrive in time.

Almost as fast as he put the receiver down, Derek picked the phone up again in order to dial directory enquires. Eventually he managed to get the number of the lottery claims line. For some incomprehensible reason the line was busy and Derek had to wait ten minutes before he could speak to the operator. In the background played some irritatingly out of tune music, designed, he was sure, to make the caller hang-up.

'Hello, national lottery claims line, this is Lisa speaking, how may I help?'

'Yes I've won the lottery, the jackpot.'

'Well congratulations sir, now if I could just take down a few details . . .'

'No wait you don't understand. I won the jackpot but the ticket has been stolen.'

'Oh . . . I see . . . hmmm have you phoned the police?'

'Yes they're on their way now.'

'Well that's great news sir. I'm sure they'll be able to sort everything out for you. What precisely would you like me to do?'

'To block the ticket of course! Make sure nobody else except me can claim the prize.'

'Aha, I'm afraid I can't do that sir.'

'What do you mean you can't do that? I'm telling you that I won the lottery, don't give the money to anyone else who tries to claim it.'

'Yes, well the problem there sir, is that we have thirty thousand people phoning the line and claiming to have won the jackpot and lost the ticket after every draw. Could you imagine what would happen if we took all of them seriously?'

'But . . .'

'If you are the victim of a crime sir, then you should speak to the police. There isn't anything we can do.'

'But you're the lottery.'

'That's right sir, we're the lottery.'

'And there isn't anything you can do?' Derek asked meekly.

'Not unless you wrote your name and address on the back of the ticket in the space provided. Did you write your name on the back of the ticket sir?'

'No.'

'Well not to worry sir, if you did buy the winning ticket then your finger prints will be on the ticket. You weren't wearing gloves when you bought the ticket, were you sir?'

'No I wasn't,' Derek said raising his voice, irritated by the sarcasm.

'So when the police find the ticket they'll be able to prove the ticket's yours using your fingerprints. Is there anything else I can help you with sir?'

'No,' Derek said as he put the phone down. The people at the lottery were completely useless. It looked as though his only hope now lay with the police, and they couldn't even be bothered to treat his case as an emergency. Tears streaming down his face, he sat down on his one and only armchair and waited for the police to arrive.

CHAPTER SEVEN

A week had passed since that dreadful night and Derek still felt sick. He'd started suffering from insomnia, his mind going over his mistakes again and again. Why hadn't he put the ticket in his wallet? Why hadn't he written his name on the back? But no matter how much alcohol he drank, his nights were still spent tossing and turning.

As of yet nobody had claimed the prize of twenty-five million, another cause for thoughts to surge through Derek's mind. Did the thief know that he'd inadvertently taken the winning lottery ticket? After all it was hidden in the vase, maybe the thief had flogged it at some car boot sale, or just come off whatever drugs he'd been on and realized that he'd just broken into someone's home and stolen a worthless vase. Only it wasn't worthless, was it? It contained the winning ticket for the biggest ever lottery jackpot in English history.

Suddenly Derek felt very ill, he left his room and quickly walked to the communal toilet down the corridor, but someone was already inside. Unable to hold it in he leaned against the wall and vomited into the corner. He felt guilty only for a second, after all he'd seen loads of his neighbours do the same, so why shouldn't he? The stress of this whole damn situation was killing him. For the first time in his life he couldn't even face going into work. No situation had caused Derek to take time off work before, including the death of his parents and his divorce, but now he'd taken the week off sick. As he returned to his room he decided to take next week off sick as well, 'fuck `em, fuck `em all,' he said to himself. What was the fucking point anyway? What was the fucking point in any of it? He'd worked and laboured his whole life, he'd paid his taxes and been an honest man, where had it got him? Where was his good karma? Karma he thought to himself and actually burst out laughing. A kind of hard, desperate laugh, only the deeply tormented or totally insane can ever manage. Derek felt his mental health quickly slipping away. He was aware that if something didn't change soon, he'd end up in a nut house, or prison, or dead. That's when he remembered his daughter, today was Saturday, the one day of the week when he had visiting rights to his children. He'd already confirmed that he was visiting to Jane on Friday. Derek wasn't looking forward to seeing Jane and John, just hearing the sarcasm in Jane's voice over the phone had been more than enough. Worse still Tom had deliberately requested not to see him, it looked like he was so ashamed of Derek that even seeing him had become too much for the boy to bare. Derek wasn't entirely sure he could blame his son, after all how the hell do you lose twenty-five million pounds? Usually when Tom refused to see him, Derek would still try to make contact, regardless of his son's request, but today he just didn't have the strength. Perhaps the rift between father and son had become too much; maybe it was just best to leave things the way they were for a while. At least he still had Tina, loyal, loving Tina, she still wanted to see her dad no matter how much of a loser he was. Derek wiped the remnants of vomit off his mouth before leaving his bedsit and heading towards the bus stop.

He was half an hour late when he arrived to pick Tina up, for some reason, today of all days, the bus which took him to his old house had decided that it wouldn't arrive every fifteen minutes as stated on the timetable but instead would arrive after half an hour.

Nervously he knocked on the door, it only took a few seconds for John to answer it. John looked him up and down very slowly and Derek instantly remembered what a mess he looked like. He must have had about twelve hours sleep in the past week and the alcohol abuse was starting to take its toll. His skin was sickly pale, and his eyes were red, some of the blood vessels seemingly on the verge of bursting. His eyelids were extremely droopy, the bags under his eyes felt like they were almost down to his chin and to top it all off he hadn't had the strength to shave. He looked exactly how he felt, like shit.

'I heard about your fortune, and your misfortune,' John said, whilst not doing a very good job of repressing a smile.

Derek didn't respond, hoping that if he didn't rise to the bate John would seek his twisted pleasures elsewhere.

'Is Tina ready?' Derek asked.

'Yes she's been waiting patiently for ages, I guess the bus was late again, mind you with the cost of petrol these days I can hardly blame you for sticking to public transport. I've been thinking of more economical ways to get into work myself.'

'That's interesting John,' Derek said, impressively keeping his cool, 'but I'm afraid I really don't have time to chat, I'm running behind schedule and I'd like to spend as much time as possible with my daughter.'

'Yes of course. Tina your father's here!'

Tina came to the door with her mother, who looked at Derek distastefully, 'You really don't look very well. Perhaps we should let her stay at home this week?' she scowled.

'Don't worry I'm fine, thanks for your concern though,' Derek said as he took Tina's hand and led her away. Jane had tried her best to scold him, but in front of Tina she knew not to overstep the mark, because his daughter for some reason would defend him. And Jane being highly accomplished in manipulation knew that belittling Derek in front of Tina would only strengthen the child's love for him.

'Well make sure you bring her back on time, because tomorrow we're taking the kids to Chessington World of Adventures, to cheer them up.'

Derek simply nodded his head, before looking down at his daughter. She smiled at him and skipped as they walked down the street.

'I was going to take you to the park today but I think it's too cold now, so what would you like to do?' Derek asked.

'The park daddy, the park, please it's not too cold and we could feed the ducks. Please, mummy never takes me to the park.'

Derek let out a loud laugh, he still didn't understand how this nine year old girl could make all his worries vanish in the blink of an eye and pull him out of the most despairing of times.

'To the park it is then, but first we'll go to the shop and buy some bread so that we can feed the ducks.'

'Oh thanks daddy, you're the best,' she said as she gave him a hug. Derek stopped walking and held her tightly. If one thing made his life worth living it was Tina's love.

'So you're not angry with me then, you know for losing the lottery ticket?' he asked nervously.

'But you didn't lose it daddy. Someone stole it from you, at least that's what mummy said, so it can't be your fault, can it?'

'No I guess it can't; I just thought you might be angry with me, the way Tom is.'

'Oh daddy, you're so silly sometimes. I'm not like Tom, and anyway he's always making problems for one simple reason.'

'What's that?'

'He's a boy!'

Derek let out another roar of laughter before kissing Tina on the head, 'You know I love you very much,' he said.

'And I love you,' she replied with that same sincere and heart melting smile she always carried. He wasn't sure who she took after but it certainly wasn't from anyone in his family, and it most certainly wasn't from her mother. He held her hand again and they started to walk towards the shop in order to buy some bread.

At approximately the same time Derek was feeding the ducks with his daughter, the boy responsible for all his misery, Justin, was upstairs in his bedroom lying on top of his bed with one arm stretched underneath it. His hand searched along the floor as he attempted to find something he had hidden. A very special something, the vase he had stolen a week ago, for today was his grandma's birthday. His fingers brushed across its rim and he gently pulled it up, out of its hiding place and inspected it. It was dusty and grimy and needed a good cleaning before he could give it to his grandma. His eyes searched his room for something suitable, they spotted one of his t-shirts lying in the corner, waiting for his grandma to collect it with the other pile of dirty clothes and wash it.

Justin took the t-shirt and proceeded to wipe away all the dirt and muck that was around the vase. He smiled as he remembered last week's burglary. He'd made a fair amount of cash with Tony and secretly sold the wedding ring for five pounds. It felt good getting one over on Tony, especially after he'd gone off with that redhead. Justin frowned as he remembered Sarah, the blonde who had broken his heart.

At least the night hadn't been a complete waste, he'd spent his share of the loot on high quality skunk. Plus he had the vase, and he just knew that his grandma would love it.

Within seconds his white t-shirt had turned a greeny, black colour. A couple of minutes passed before Justin felt that the vase was clean, he held it up and inspected his handy work. His gran would love it for sure. As he examined it more closely he noticed how dirty it was inside. Well that certainly wouldn't do, and so he took the t-shirt and started to clean the inside of the vase pushing the t-shirt way down with his hand but being careful not to get his arm stuck. As he pulled the t-shirt out bits of fluff and all other kinds of dust and filth came out with it. The inside of the vase was like a dustbin. Justin again looked around for something suitable, lying not far from his bed was a copy of yesterday's Daily Sport, filled with its assortment of naked bombshells. Justin liked to read it and look at the pictures whilst fantasizing about the latest girl who he'd developed a crush on. He spread the newspaper out so that it could cover as much space as possible before turning the vase upside down and roughly shaking it so that its entire contents would fall out. Along with all the dirt and crap, a single neatly crisp lottery ticket fell onto the newspaper. Ironically it landed just underneath a headline concerning the lottery, 'TWENTY-FIVE MILLION POUNDS STILL UNCLAMIED!'

Of course Justin had heard about the biggest jackpot in British history still being unclaimed, the country was in a frenzy. But the one lying on his newspaper couldn't be it, could it? He placed the vase on the floor and gently picked up the ticket. Studying it carefully, he looked at the numbers and then the draw it was intended for. Amazingly enough it was intended for last Saturday's draw, Justin's heart picked up speed as a strange sensation overcame his body. He flipped it over, whoever it belonged to hadn't bothered writing their name on the back.

Holding the ticket in his hands Justin scanned the article for the winning numbers, he read them one by one checking them against the numbers on the ticket he had just found. They were the same numbers!

'Jesus!' Justin muttered out aloud, before checking the numbers a further three times.

'Jesus Christ I don't fucking believe it!' Justin shouted at the top of his voice.

'Justin is everything OK?' his grandma asked from downstairs.

'Yes nan, I'll be down soon. Don't worry about me I'm just fine.'

Justin pondered what to do, in his hand he held the winning lottery ticket for twenty-five million pounds. Twenty-five million pounds! He could buy a mansion and a Ferrari, shit he could even buy a Bentley! Maybe he'd get a chauffeur. He could buy a nightclub! He'd be the coolest guy around, think of all the girls that would throw themselves at him. Hey maybe he could even get Sarah, imagine how good he'd look as he got out of his Lexus with her on his arm. Finally he'd be the gangster he'd always wanted to be.

As Justin fantasized it slowly dawned on him that the ticket wasn't really his, it belonged to the person he'd stolen the vase from. Whoever it was would right now be livid, and they sure as hell wouldn't just step aside and allow Justin to claim the money as his. Maybe the police were even waiting for him to make the claim so that they could prove that it was him that had burgled the bedsit. There was only one person who he knew that would be able to tell him what to do, his trusted friend Tony. Justin picked up his mobile and with the click of a button dialled his friend.

Tony recognised Justin's number immediately, he'd only just woken up and was rolling his first joint. A ritual he practised everyday, before breakfast and just after he'd gone to the toilet to take his morning leak. Tony's motto was, 'A spliff a day helps keep the doctor away.' But he smoked a lot more than a spliff a day.

'What you sayin´ G?' Tony asked, leaving the skunk and rolling papers on the cabinet next to his bed.

'I need help,' Justin blurted out in a hurry. Tony sensed the tension in his voice.

'What's up?' he asked with genuine concern for his friend.

'I've got the winning lottery ticket, the ticket for the twenty-five million pounds but it's not mine and I don't know what to do.'

'Wait, peace, where'd you get the ticket from?' Tony asked, excited but half sure his friend was playing a joke. Justin could just about make out what his friend was saying because the connection between their mobiles was poor. In order to improve the connection he instinctively walked over to his bedroom window, which overlooked the street where his house was situated.

'I found it in a vase.'

'A vase?' Tony questioned, hang on wasn't that the same vase he'd nicked from that bedsit? Instantly Tony's concern grew to reminding his friend that he was entitled to half that money. What was half of twenty-five million? Tony tried to do the sums in his head but quickly gave up. It was more money than he could ever have imagined, that was sure.

'Ain't that the same vase we nicked together?' Tony asked, trying to keep any emotion out of his voice but failing miserably.

Shit! Justin had forgotten that Tony knew about the vase! Now he'd want half of the money! Justin tried to think fast, should he lie to his best mate or tell the truth? He was crap in such situations.

'G, brethren you still there?'

'Yeah, it's from the same vase.'

Pound signs flashed in front of Tony's eyes, beautiful Caribbean beaches with models in skimpy bikinis and pina coladas with cocktail umbrellas filled his head. Under no circumstances could Justin claim the prize himself.

'Listen very carefully,' Tony said slowly and with as much authority as he could muster, 'use a cloth to gently wipe the ticket. Do it all over or the other geezer's prints will be on it.'

Justin obeyed his friend as quickly as he could, 'Done it,' he said when he'd finished.

'OK now put the ticket on the floor so that it is flat and push your fingers onto it. For fingerprints to be clear they need a flat surface. Are you doing it?'

'Yeah.'

'Good, cover the front and then the back with your fingerprints.'

'Both sides are done,' Justin said when he'd finished.

'Safe,' Tony said as he took a deep breath. Was there anything else he had to remember? 'Oh,' Tony said, 'look at the back of the ticket and see if anyone's written their name or address on it.'

'No they haven't, I checked before,' Justin replied enthusiastically.

'Sweet that means we can claim the prize together.'

Shit! Justin thought, phoning Tony had been a massive mistake.

'Are you at home?' Tony asked.

'Yeah,' replied Justin as he stood back up and rested his head wearily against the window. Out of the corner of his eye he noticed a police car pull up outside his grandma's home.

'Fuck it's the police,' Justin screamed down the line.

'Shit, leg it, come round my yard now!' Tony shouted, but it was too late Justin had already thrown the mobile down, kicked the vase aside, smashing it, and run to the toilet which was on the opposite side of the house. He climbed through the window, jumping on to the garden extension and then on to the ground. Just as the police knocked on his grandmother's front door Justin had scaled the garden fence and was running down the street in the opposite direction, with all the strength his body contained.

CHAPTER EIGHT

PCs Haines and Woods were both young and relatively new officers. They had about five years experience between them but shared something in common, a love for the force and a need for adventure and risk. PC Haines hoped to one day join the armed response unit of the Met, whilst PC Woods had ambitions of joining CID. They both had a lot of ground to cover before they could climb up the career ladder and for the time being they had to make do with being thrown bones from CID and higher ranking officers. Neither had really wanted to take on Derek's case, not when they'd heard about the raid being carried out on a local drug den. That sounded much more interesting than a boring burglary, yet they consoled themselves with the certainty that they'd found the suspect; fingerprints had been left on some of the victim's furniture. The fingerprints matched those of Justin Farren, a seventeen year old who'd been arrested not long ago for joyriding but let off with a warning. Nevertheless the fingerprint database still held his fingerprints from the time he'd originally been arrested.

Woods the more senior of the two knocked on the front door. They waited patiently as an elderly woman opened the door.

'Oh dear is there trouble officers?' she asked, almost accustomed to visits by the police regarding her wayward grandson.

'Nothing to worry about, just following routine inquires. We were wondering if we could speak to Justin Farren,' replied Woods.

'Yes of course, I'll just call him. Please come in, he's upstairs in his room.'

The two officers waited patiently at the bottom of the stairs whilst the old lady went to fetch her grandson. They could hear her calling his name and slowly moving from room to room. After a couple of minutes Haines felt agitated.

'Something's not right,' he told his partner, 'lets go up and check.'

Woods nodded his agreement and the two officers quickly climbed the stairs. They found the old lady standing outside what must have been, judging by the mess, Justin's room. The old dear was obviously very distressed and her breathing was slightly laboured.

'I don't understand, he was here a couple of minutes ago. He's not in trouble is he?'

'No not at all, there's nothing for you to worry about dear,' Haines said as he put an arm round the old lady in order to comfort her.

Woods bent down next to the broken vase, he'd read that only three items had been taken from Derek Bonner's bedsit. A wedding ring, a colour TV, and a vase, which the victim claimed contained the winning lottery ticket to last Saturday's jackpot. This had caused some laughs down at the station and it was with great reluctance that Woods and Haines had agreed to investigate the case. Woods put on some rubber gloves and placed the broken pieces of the vase into an evidence bag.

'What's that?' asked Haines.

'A vase was one of the items that was stolen,' replied Woods, 'I'm betting that it was this one.'

'Looks like we've found our culprit then,' said Haines.

Running non-stop for almost an hour, Justin eventually collapsed on the bench of an empty bus stop and heaved in deep breaths of air. Crunched up and held tightly in his right hand was the lottery ticket, and he was almost too scared to unclench his fist for fear that it might some how get away. In his eagerness to escape from the cops, Justin had left his mobile, his wallet and his house keys behind. He had no idea what his next move should be, and he had no idea how to claim the prize. Where were the offices and how was he meant to find out with no money and no phone? He thought about Tony, but if he went to his friend for help he would want half the money. He might even turn greedy and beat Justin up and make the claim by himself. No, Tony could go fuck himself, Justin was going to keep the whole lot, and if Tony didn't like it, well he could go screw himself, but who could he turn to for help? Of course Diamond Dave, he'd lend Justin some money, he might even lend him his mobile. Dave was generous like that. Justin took another deep breath as he prepared for the long run to Dave's house. Then he stopped, hell what was he thinking? He didn't have time to go round on foot, he needed some wheels. Across the road he spotted an old Ford Escort, he walked over to it and checked that there was no car alarm. Perfect, he walked over to the small garden of a house opposite the bus stop and picked up one of the large smooth pebbles situated around a flowerbed.

Returning to the car he threw the pebble into the passenger window. He smiled as the impact of the pebble caused the glass to shatter. Calmly he opened the passenger door and lent into the car so that he could unlock the driver's door. Closing the passenger door he quickly walked around to the driver's door before opening it. He quickly brushed the small amount of broken glass off the driver's seat, using the car owner's squeegee, before getting behind the wheel. Hot-wiring the car was a matter of seconds, and now Justin would be at Diamond Dave's house within fifteen minutes.

Like every Saturday night Derek had agreed to meet his old friend Terry for a drink. As usual Terry had called round to his place first and then they had made their way together to Derek's local. After two pints of beer Derek told Terry about his past week, about winning the lottery and then losing the ticket in a burglary. About his ex-wife and her lover laughing at him, about his sleepless nights and about his son no longer being able to look at him. Terry as usual was like a rock, he listened carefully to his friend, nodding his head in deep understanding and dispensing the best advice he could.

Terry was dumbfounded by the fact that the lottery organisers and the police had so far been of little help, but he told his friend to be patient, that the wheels of justice turned slowly, but they did turn. Derek reminded him of his divorce and Terry couldn't think of a reply. After a third beer Derek said that he felt like going home, he was tired and not much company. Terry said that he understood, that Derek shouldn't give up hope and that it wasn't the end of the world. Derek tried his best not to laugh.

At home Derek opened up the remainder of a bottle of whisky and downed a couple of shots before collapsing on his bed and falling into a heavy, restful sleep.

Four hours had passed since Justin had called Tony, and now Tony was out of his mind with worry. Where could Justin be? He tried his mobile various times but it just rang with no answer. Had the police caught him or was he hiding out somewhere? Or had he gone and made the claim himself? Tony had thought about nothing else for the last four hours before deciding that if Justin was indeed on the run then his first port of call would be Diamond Dave.

Tony briskly walked up to Dave's door and knocked loudly and confidently. As Dave opened the door he noticed a look of urgency on Tony's face.

'Tony I thought you might come round, your mate Justin was here about two hours ago. Terrible state he was in, made no sense at all, what's going on?'

'Justin was here? Where'd he go? What did he want?'

'I don't know where he went but he almost dropped down on his hands and knees and begged to borrow twenty notes. Of course I said that it was no problem and that he could pay me back anytime. Then he said something about paying me back double and ran off as soon as I gave it to him. Covered in sweat he was, the whole thing was nuts.'

'Shit!' Tony screamed.

'What's up? What's going on?' Diamond Dave asked again, intrigued by the events he was witnessing.

'Nutin´, you wouldn't believe me anyways,' Tony said before slowly turning away and walking off. Dave simply shrugged his shoulders, closed his front door and returned to watching the day's football highlights.

A loud ringing sound woke Derek up. At first he thought it was his imagination, but slowly and painfully he realized that someone was ringing the bell to his bedsit. In horror he looked at his clock and saw that it was one o'clock in the afternoon. He'd slept over thirteen hours! How could it be that he'd slept so long? He got up and pressed the buzzer that unlocked the main door to his bedsit, although uncertain who it was he had no choice as his intercom hadn't been working for months. Patiently Derek waited for whoever it was to reach his door, there was no need to get dressed because he'd fallen asleep in his clothes. There was a loud knock on the door and Derek opened it quickly. To his surprise he saw Terry standing there holding a box.

'What's that?' asked Derek.

'It's a TV and it's bloody heavy, so let us in,' said Terry.

Derek stepped aside and allowed Terry in, his mind still hazy from sleep and alcohol. He wasn't sure if this was a dream or reality, so he discreetly reached round and pinched his right buttock, yep he was definitely awake. So what was Terry doing standing in his room and holding a brand new telly at one o'clock on Sunday?

'I bought you this as a gift, in order to cheer you up,' Terry said as if reading Derek's mind.

'I'm sorry but I can't accept this,' Derek said wondering how much it must have set his friend back.

'I won't have any arguments,' Terry said as he started to open the box and pull out the TV, 'it's already been paid for and I'll be damned if I'm going to lug it back to the shop. That means it's yours to do whatever you want with, if you don't want it then throw it away.'

'I can't believe you mate, well, what can I say? Thanks, but I never want to see you pull another stunt like this again.'

'Hey, you're never going to get burgled again, now brew us up a cuppa while I set this baby up for you.'

Derek did as his friend requested and made tea for them both whilst Terry went about the business of setting up the new TV.

After the tea was made and the television set up, with all the channels tuned in the pair settled down to enjoy Derek's new present. Derek again thanked Terry for the gift and Terry told Derek to stop being so silly.

'Seriously though mate, don't ever pull a stunt like that again,' Derek said as he tried to sit comfortably on the small chair. Terry had the armchair, which was only right after all he was Derek's guest. Derek felt conscious of how small his home was, could it have been anymore cramped? Usually when he was alone he'd just lie in his bed and watch the telly.

'Like I said before I won't ever have to,' Terry replied.

'So any plans for tonight?' Derek asked, knowing full well that Terry always had plans.

'Oh yeah, I've got a brand new date set for tonight.'

'What's her name?'

'Kate, you'd like her mate, late thirties, divorced but no kids, goes to the gym everyday. Very nice legs.'

'Where'd you meet her?'

'I put in a new boiler for her.'

'Perk of the job hey,' Derek smirked. At least one of them was enjoying his life. Terry's carefree attitude to life was probably the reason why he had fared so well physically. Derek felt his age, especially recently, whilst Terry, who was two years older, looked and acted like a man in his early thirties. If Derek could have changed anything about his personality it would have been to be more like Terry.

Terry joined in with Derek's laughter, it was good to see that his friend's spirits had picked up since last night.

'I'll ask her if she's got a friend for you, if you like,' Terry said.

'No, don't start again, please. Look when I feel good and ready I'll let you know.'

'OK hint taken I'll stop badgering you. Did I tell you that Elaine's going to be on the front cover of Vogue magazine?'

'No you didn't,' Derek replied impressed. Elaine was Terry's daughter and she'd recently started a career as a model.

'Yeah it's true, next month's cover apparently.'

'Wow you must be so proud.'

'Yeah I am but I can't help but worry sometimes.'

'What about?'

'You know, the glamour and fame, what if it goes to her head? Look how screwed up some of these celebrities become.'

'Don't worry, that won't happed to Elaine, she's always had her head screwed on straight, why I remember . . .'

Terry turned to look at his friend as Derek stopped mid-sentence, his attention attracted to the TV by an item on the afternoon news. Terry watched passively as Derek used the TV's remote to increase the volume.

'It seems that the winner of last week's record lottery jackpot has finally come forward,' a pretty young newsreader beamed enthusiastically. In the background was a picture of Justin posing in a tracksuit and baseball cap outside the national lottery headquarters.

'Seventeen year old Justin Farren walked into the lottery's headquarters early last night with the winning ticket. A press conference is scheduled for six o'clock this evening, when lucky Justin will pick up his check for twenty-five million pounds. Yes, that's twenty-five million pounds, and only seventeen years old, now that's a lot of DVDs and video games. We'll return to the story at six o'clock tonight, where we'll broadcast live from the press conference with the latest news about young Justin's remarkable win. And maybe we'll also find out why it took him so long to come forward and claim his prize.'

In shock and completely speechless Derek switched off the TV and then immediately switched it back on again. Terry took the remote control out of his hands and quickly turned down the volume.

Derek looked at Terry, his eyes seemed glazed

over like his soul was no longer in his body. It seemed like Derek had lost the power of speech, the emotional stress he was suffering was easily evident and Terry was deeply concerned for his friend.

'Derek are you OK?'

'No, I don't feel so well,' Derek said as he got up. Terry could see that he was going to throw up and watched helplessly as Derek ran from the room down the corridor. Luckily this time the toilet was empty, and Derek dropped to his hands and knees as he threw up uncontrollably. Terry, unsure what to do, paced around the room nervously. Eventually Derek returned.

'Do you feel better now?' Terry asked apprehensively.

'I'm a long way away from feeling better,' Derek said as he picked up the phone.

'What're you doing?' Terry asked.

'I'm phoning the police, that little bastard's not going to get away with this, I'll make sure of that if it's the last thing I do.'

Out of relief Terry broke into a smile, his friend still had some fight in him, so maybe, just maybe, he'd be all right after all.

CHAPTER NINE

Tony switched off the telly after watching the afternoon news. He wasn't one for current affairs but he knew that his friend was up to something, and Tony had been sure that if Justin had claimed the lottery jackpot that it would have been covered in the news. That rat! They'd done that job together and now Justin was trying to screw him out of his half of the money.

Tony took a deep pull on his joint and plotted his next move. He wasn't about to just stand aside and let Justin swindle him out of his share of the twenty-five million, but what could he do? He couldn't just threaten to beat him up because then Justin would probably just hire bodyguards and completely cut Tony off. No, no matter what, he had to remain Justin's friend, because the closer he was to Justin the closer he'd be to the money. Just like Al Pacino had said in the Godfather, 'Keep your friends close, but your enemies closer.' Tony nodded as he played the scene from his favourite film through the skunk fuelled imagination of his mind.

Yes, that was definitely the way, stay close to Justin and try to get the money off him amicably. After all Justin might come through as a real mate and give Tony his half of the money, but if not, well then with some patience and planning, Tony would find a way to exact his vengeance.

It was almost six o'clock and Derek settled down with a glass of whisky to watch the live broadcast of Justin being presented with a cheque for twenty-five million pounds. Terry had left a few hours ago, no doubt eager to go home and get ready for his date. Derek couldn't blame Terry for not wanting to waste his time sitting in his dingy, little home. If Derek were Terry, he'd be doing exactly the same thing.

Gently sipping his whisky Derek thought about his conversation with the police. It now seemed that they believed his story about the stolen lottery ticket and had tracked down the thief to his house and found Derek's vase. The news and the press release of Justin's picture had confirmed that the man they suspected had burgled Derek's bedsit and the man claiming the lottery jackpot were the same person. Suddenly things were looking up for Derek. Nervously he sipped more whisky, savouring the taste and promising himself that tonight for the first time in over a week, he wouldn't allow himself to get drunk. He turned up the volume on his new TV as the reporter began his broadcast, live, outside the national lottery headquarters.

'Welcome to this most exciting event, the mystery surrounding this young man will finally come to an end tonight as he has agreed to answer questions from the media after the cheque has been presented to him.'

'And what's the atmosphere like there at the lottery HQ?' asked the newsreader back at the studio.

'As you can imagine, everyone here is highly charged and excited, for not only do they want to get a look at the country's biggest ever jackpot winner, but also the youngest ever winner of the national lottery. This is a most unprecedented story and tonight some of the folks here will hope to unravel the mystery as to why this young man took so long in coming forward and claiming his winnings.'

With perfect timing the reporter touched his ear piece, 'Well it seems that the country is now going to get a glimpse of one of its newest multi-millionaires.'

The camera's focus left the reporter and found its way to the centre of a stage. It quickly focused on a young and extremely nervous Justin as he wiped his sweaty hands against the sides of his tracksuit bottoms and repeatedly fidgeted with his baseball cap. He'd thought about keeping his anonymity but had decided against it. What was the point of having all that money if nobody knew? He wanted to show it off, to show the world that it had been wrong about him. He wanted to be famous and show all the people who had laughed at him or ignored him or bullied him how wrong they really were. At long last people would respect him, he'd be a gangster!

Next to Justin, dressed in expensive suits, stood some official looking men. One of them held a large cheque in his hands. Justin's eyes kept glancing down at the cheque and he'd sometimes tilt his head to the side as if he were trying to read all the zeros that had been written on to the large card.

Out of nowhere the national lottery's famous, ex-alcoholic presenter appeared in front of the microphone. Through luck and contacts he had managed to land the job of presenting the lottery, and it had probably saved what was left of his career and life. He stood between Justin and the man holding the cheque. He put his arm around Justin and picked up the mike, the crowd went wild.

'So tell me how it feels to be the luckiest man in the country,' the presenter said.

The camera zoomed in on Justin's face, which was now contorted as he tried to think of a witty answer.

'It feels . . . er . . . great,' he replied, blushing deeply. The crowd went wild, screaming and shouting, girls were blowing kisses at him. A goofy smile filled his face.

'What are you going to spend the money on?'

'Er . . . I'm gonna . . . erm,' the crowd went silent in anticipation, 'I'm gonna party!'

Again the crowd went wild and Justin smiled, so this was what it was like to be famous! He waved his arm up in the air triumphantly, causing even more screams and hysterics.

The TV presenter felt jealousy surge through his veins because of the attention Justin was getting. The crowd seemed to like this kid more than they liked him. He decided that he'd put an end to the competition and rush Justin through to the press conference and get him off the stage as soon as possible.

'Are you ready to receive your money then?' said the presenter in a booming voice, eyes playing to the cheering crowd.

Justin grabbed the mike, 'You're damn right I am,' he shouted causing the crowd to go berserk. The presenter managed to gently wrestle the mike out of Justin's grip before giving it to the man who held the cheque.

'Congratulations, spend the money wisely,' said

the man shaking Justin's hand, 'It's going to be hard letting go of this cheque,' he continued, getting a laugh from the audience.

Finally the money was in his hands. Justin looked at the crowd with the intention of saying something else to rouse it up even more when his jaw dropped as he noticed two uniformed policemen making their way through the crowd and towards him.

PCs Woods and Haines had been told by powers higher up in the Met to wait until after the press conference to arrest Justin. The official line from the Met was that they wanted Justin's arrest to be as discreet as possible. Arresting a national lottery winner, especially one so young would do the public relations department no good at all. Besides they still weren't a hundred percent sure if he was the one who'd committed the burglary and even if it was him, how would they prove that he'd stolen Derek's lottery ticket? No it was one big mess and a potential headache the Met could do without, so discretion was the key, but even policemen, like all humans, stop thinking rationally when the spell of fame casts its magical cloud over mortal eyes. PC Haines had been bitten by the infectious bug of the limelight, he didn't want to wait until after the press conference, he wanted to arrest Justin publicly, in front of millions of viewers. He'd somehow got it into his head that despite disobeying his superiors the publicity would do his career good. Plus there was the chance that he could sell his story to the papers. Maybe the whole affair could open up other avenues, roads he'd never even considered. Suddenly a career in the Met didn't seem all that glamorous. PC Woods on the other hand was just doing what was expected of all good police officers and backing up his partner.

'Shit!' Justin shouted into the microphone.

'I'm sorry, what did you say?' asked the man who'd just given Justin the cheque for twenty-five million pounds.

'It's the cops!' Justin shouted before tucking the huge cheque under his arm and jumping from the stage in the opposite direction of the two police officers. The crowd gasped in shock as the two officers jumped on to the stage in pursuit of Justin, reporters, photographers and cameramen not far behind.

Justin had only made it a few metres before being apprehended by three other uniformed officers, revealing the scale of the operation to arrest him. In front of millions of viewers, live, Justin was arrested for burglary, fraud and deception.

'But it's my money,' he said as he was gently forced into a police van by camera shy officers, only PC Haines doing his utmost to ensure that his face was broadcast live on TV. The camera kept rolling as the van drove off into the distance, before returning to the original reporter.

'Well an amazing turn of events here tonight in what has become the most extraordinary lottery story ever. Stay tuned for updates as this amazing story unravels, but for now back to the studio.'

'Yes!' Derek shouted at the top of his voice, before rolling on the floor in a fit of laughter. Once he'd caught his breath he poured himself another whisky, perhaps he could get a little tipsy today. After all he had something to celebrate.

Sarah looked at Karen, who in turn looked at

Sarah. Both had been dumbfounded to discover that the mystery jackpot winner had been the dweeb from the party. Even more astonishing was his subsequent arrest, live on TV.

'Bloody hell, what do you reckon's going on there?' Karen asked rhetorically.

'I can't believe it, that twat with twenty-five million pounds?' Sarah said in disbelief.

'I bet he won't keep it, the police have arrested him.'

'But we don't know what they've arrested him for. It could be something completely unrelated which means that once he gets out that money will be waiting for him.'

'Blimey, I bet you wish you'd got off with him now,' Karen joked, prodding Sarah with her elbow and snorting with laughter. Sarah remained quiet, the thought had crossed her mind, yeah he was skinny, and gangly, and not very bright, but he'd carried himself with a lot of charisma on that stage. Besides twenty-five million pounds suddenly made him seem so much more attractive. With a bit of work in the gym and some gentle guidance from herself he might not scrub up too bad, but she'd better move fast because girls would be queuing up to get to him and his money.

'You still got his mate's number?'

'Course I have, did you forget how good in bed he was? I wouldn't lose his number.'

'All right, stop bragging about your sex life and give him a ring, see if they want to meet up,' Sarah said remembering how much she'd fancied Tony.

'What about Diamond Dave? You said you'd got off with him, you're not going to dump him for Justin, are you?'

'Diamond Dave was just a one night stand, and he said that he didn't want any commitments.'

'So you're going after Justin just because he won the lottery?'

'Well it's not for his looks, that's for sure,' Sarah laughed.

Karen smiled in disbelief as she nudged her best friend, 'You gold digging, little tart.'

'I may be a tart, but I'll end up with more money than you, miss university,' Sarah replied with a mischievous grin on her face.

CHAPTER TEN

Seeing the interior of a police station and its interview room wasn't a new experience for Justin. In fact he felt quite at home, not afraid or intimidated like most people would be, but this was mostly down to the fact that Justin felt confident that his young age would protect him. He'd seen so many of his friends let off with warnings or community service that he was sure that he was impervious to the law. Sure the Old Bill would try to terrify him with tales of hard time behind bars and the high possibility of a fresh pup like him being buggered all the way to Timbuktu and back. But that's what they told all the kids. It was common knowledge that no one goes down for their first offence, and seeing how Justin was let off with a warning not too long ago, that's exactly what this would be, his first offence. Besides, Tony's dad, who'd been in and out of prison all his life, had told the two boys no matter what, no matter how much evidence they have against you, no matter how many witnesses identify you, and no matter how many years they threaten you with, deny, deny, deny! Just repeat over and over: 'It wasn't me.' Hell if you did it enough times you'd brainwash yourself into believing it. According to Tony's dad this trick had saved him from a stretch at her Majesty's pleasure more times than not, and it was what all the big time villains did.

Detective Inspector Koleth waited outside the

interview room whilst he pored over the file of Derek's burglary. Normally he wouldn't bother with such a minor case of burglary, preferring to hand it to one of the more ambitious PCs, but this case had turned into an exception. First of all there was a lot of media attention involved and what now looked like the perpetration of a large scale fraud against the national lottery and one of its jackpot winners. Koleth closed the file and waited patiently for PC Woods, who'd been asked to join the case because he was a rising star in the Met and had shown eagerness in joining CID. After the fiasco of Justin's arrest, Koleth had been inclined to throw Woods off the case, but the kid was still being backed by the chief superintendent and Koleth had already taken it upon himself to give Woods a damn, good bollocking.

'Sorry I'm late, the chief was giving me and Haines a bollocking for the public arrest of the suspect,' Woods said as he walked up to Koleth from behind, giving the inspector a scare.

'You're damn lucky he hasn't thrown you off the case,' Koleth bellowed, 'now keep your mouth shut and watch and learn how the job's done.'

Feeling somewhat demeaned Woods silently followed Koleth into the interview room. He kept a stern, serious face and used his eyes to burn his image into Justin's memory. If he wasn't able to take part in the interview the least he could do was try to intimidate the suspect into a confession. The two sat opposite Justin and Koleth started the recording of the interview giving the date, time, and names of the interviewing officers.

'You have the right to a solicitor being present

during this interview,' Koleth continued, 'if you don't have one then we can appoint one for you.'

'I don't need a brief,' Justin said with confidence, returning the cold stares to Woods.

'Why not?' asked Koleth.

'Because I'm innocent and this shouldn't take too long. I just want to get out of here and put my cheque into the bank.'

Koleth smiled and shook his head, this cocky, little bastard really thought he could out smart an inspector like himself, who had over fifteen years experience. Koleth took the insult well, he dealt with idiots like Justin everyday, and the kid had already made the mistake of declining legal representation. With no solicitor present Koleth would have total freedom in leading the interview down any avenue he chose.

'Would you like something to drink or eat?' Koleth asked.

'I'd like a cigarette,' said Justin, who as an occasional smoker of normal cigarettes, for some reason felt compelled to smoke now. Perhaps it was all those Hollywood films he'd seen, where the bad guy would always light up and blow smoke into the cop's face. He remembered the film with Sharon Stone and Michael Douglas and for some reason, which he found slightly disturbing due to the circumstances, he couldn't shake the image of her uncrossing her legs.

Koleth pulled out a packet from his breast pocket and offered it to Justin who took a single cigarette out of the packet, placing it between his lips before throwing the packet back across the table. Koleth then lit the cigarette for Justin, all the kids liked it when he did this, it made them feel big, like they were mafia bosses or something he guessed, but nevertheless it sometimes helped in winning them over.

'Well I'm afraid that the evidence against you really doesn't look too good, we found a broken vase in your room which the victim of a burglary had clearly described. There's no way that vase, which I might add is quite distinguishable, got there by coincidence.'

'I found the vase in a telephone box, just down the road from where I live,' Justin shot out, leaning back confidently in his chair and looking at the ceiling while taking a drag form his cigarette.

'Are you saying that you didn't burgle Mr Bonner's place of residence?'

'Yes, I'm saying I didn't burgle Mr Boner's house,' Justin laughed, impressed by his own wit.

'The victim's name is Mr Bonner,' Koleth reiterated.

'Whatever,' said Justin, 'it wasn't me.'

'Then how do you explain the fact that our forensics team found your finger prints at the scene of the crime?'

Shit! Justin had forgotten about fingerprints. He'd been slightly worried when they'd taken his finger prints a couple of hours ago. Damn it, why hadn't he worn gloves? He stubbed out his cigarette in the ashtray.

'You're bluffing,' he said, leaning forward.

'Really?' Koleth said, smiling and shaking his head. He pulled something out of the file he had in front of him and placed it in front of Justin.

'On the left you'll see two sets of fingerprints that were found at the scene of the crime, on the right you'll find your fingerprints which we took earlier tonight. There're a perfect match.'

Justin studied the pictures carefully, they did look the same but then again didn't all fingerprints? Didn't you have to be some kind of expert to be able to distinguish the difference between them?

'Your fingerprints at the scene of the crime, and the vase found in your room. Do yourself a favour son, admit it and maybe the court will go easy on you.'

Justin had thought about it, he'd thought about it long and hard, he knew that possibly they'd be able to prove the burglary but no way could they prove he hadn't bought the ticket. If he played it cool he could still walk away from this with twenty-five million pounds, he could feel the beat of his heart throbbing in his chest, he wanted that money, no he needed that money. He remembered how the crowd had been cheering for him, the buzz he felt from the glamour of being a winner, if he lost that money then he'd go back to just being a wanker. Admit the burglary but deny having stolen the lottery ticket. Maybe, just maybe, if he admitted to the burglary the cops would be so happy that they'd close the case and he could just go home.

'OK, I'm sorry, I did it, I burgled the guy's yard. I'll buy him a new vase and TV. I'm really sorry, I don't know why I did it, but I just want you to know I'm sorry.'

'So now you admit to the burglary?' Koleth asked.

'Yes,' replied Justin.

'Just once more please, for the benefit of the tape,' Koleth said.

'I admit to the burglary,' Justin said.

Koleth smiled, the kid was falling into his trap just the way he'd planned it. Koleth looked back at PC Woods who gently nodded his head. Koleth could see that he was impressed.

'Can I go home now?' Justin asked nervously, suddenly losing his cool, debonair, hard man image.

'Not so fast,' said Koleth repressing the urge to chuckle, 'you see the victim claims that the vase which we found in your room contained the winning lottery ticket to last week's draw, and well it so happens that you had that ticket in your possession and have recently claimed the prize as your own.'

'He's lying!' Justin shouted out in panic. 'That ticket was mine, I bought it, not him!'

'Then how do you explain his claiming that the vase contained the winning ticket before you even claimed the prize? You see we all thought the victim was crazy but now his story seems very plausible, doesn't it?'

'No, no,' Justin screamed desperately, 'maybe he just planned it like that, I don't know but the ticket's mine, I bought it, I claimed the prize and I've already been given the cheque.' Think you fool think, Justin scolded himself as he felt the money slipping away.

'Who do you think the jury will believe son? You with your previous trouble with the law, or the victim, an upstanding member of society who has been working and paying his taxes for the last thirty odd years? We've already got you lying on tape!'

Tears started to roll down Justin's face and he

sobbed uncontrollably. He shouldn't have admitted to the burglary, he should have listened to Terry's dad's advice. Deny everything you idiot!

'Look I admit to the burglary, I made a mistake but you can't take that money off me, I won it fare and square, I swear on my life!'

Koleth had expected the kid to crack by now, perhaps it was time to increase the pressure, to hit him from a different angle.

'Sounds like a pretty big coincidence,' Koleth said, 'but let's forget that, you see there's one real way to prove who bought the winning ticket.'

'What's that?' Justin asked giving away his apprehension.

'Do you remember where you bought the winning lottery ticket?'

Justin was silent as the gravity of the question sank in. Koleth and Woods both looked at Justin in anticipation.

'I asked you if you remember where you bought the ticket,' Koleth said after a while.

'No, I don't,' Justin said, slumping further into the chair in consternation.

'I thought that might be the case,' Koleth grinned proudly, 'but we know where the winning lottery ticket was bought. You see the national lottery's central computer keeps a record of where all the wining tickets are sold. It wasn't too hard for us to phone up and find out where this particular shop was.'

'So what?' interrupted Justin, 'so I forgot where I bought the ticket, what does that have to do with anything?'

'Well you're right, your apparent lack of memory doesn't prove that you didn't buy the lottery ticket but you see the computer not only knows where the ticket was bought but when. So now all we have to do is go along to the newsagent that sold the winning ticket and check their surveillance cameras at the exact time the ticket was bought and we'll have video evidence of who bought the ticket.' Koleth let this information sink in for a while. Deep inside Justin knew he was beaten, there was no way he could come out of this one.

'Admit that you took the ticket and claimed the prize falsely, give back the money to the victim and save me the journey to the newsagent's and I'll drop the charges of fraud and deception.'

Justin thought about this carefully, he considered the deal being offered. He knew that once they saw the tapes he didn't have a chance but that money was all he had, he couldn't go back to living the way he had before. Not after he'd seen what this new life had to offer.

'Well, do you admit it?' Koleth pushed.

'No, I don't, I bought that ticket, the money's mine.'

'Don't be stupid son. Fraud is a serious crime added to burglary you're looking at five years in prison, first offence or not.'

'It's my money,' Justin said, slamming his fists on to the table.

'OK have it your way, I offered you a way out and you threw it back into my face. You're about to feel the full force of the law, interview suspended.'

Justin watched as the officers left the room with the files and the tape. Tears rolled down his face and he wept uncontrollably. The fear of losing the money was much worse than the fear of going to prison. For the first time in his life people had looked at him with respect and admiration, he loved that feeling, it had been given to him in addition to the money and without the money it would be just as quickly taken away.

CHAPTER ELEVEN

It was Sunday and Tony was so stoned that he couldn't even get out of bed. His step-dad was standing outside his door, demanding to enter his bedroom.

'You've been smoking that crap again, haven't you?' he shouted as he banged on the door. Tony had gone to great lengths to hide the smell of the smoke by placing a t-shirt under the gap of his bedroom door and hanging a pair of his pants over the keyhole, yet somehow his mum and step-dad were still able to smell the skunk. It drove him insane, why couldn't he just have a spliff in peace? Didn't he have enough problems already?

'Do you know how much pain you're causing your mum?' his step-dad bellowed.

'Fuck off and leave me alone,' Tony spat back behind the safety of his locked door, 'before I tell my dad to sort you out.'

'Your dad's banged up, so how can he sort me out?'

'He'll be out one day, init? And the first thing he'll do is come and give you a good kicking if I tell him to.'

'You ungrateful bastard, how dare you talk to me like that. I'm the one that's always sorted out your problems, not him. Well go ahead and rot whatever brain cells you've got left, just don't expect me to wipe your arse after you ever again,' shouted

Tony's step-dad before kicking the door and stomping off into another area of the house.

Tony clutched his head, he heard a million little voices all at the same time and they all talked about the same thing, the money. Somewhere, in some unknown police station his idiot friend was just about to lose them twenty-five million pounds. The greedy fuck! If he'd have come to him instead of trying to keep all the loot for himself they could have gone to his dad and asked for his help. By now they'd be living it up. If Justin lost that money, well, then Tony could only be sure of one thing, that he'd make him pay, boy would he make him pay.

Tony's thoughts were interrupted when his mobile started ringing, his hopes of it being Justin were dashed when he saw that the number belonged to Karen. Suddenly worries about lost fortunes flew from his head replaced by images of the mad bonking session he'd had with her in that stolen car. He was instantly rewarded with a stiffy as he remembered the way she had dug her nails into his buttocks as they banged away at each other like maniacs.

'Hello sexy, I thought you'd forgotten about me and gone to your fancy university,' he said trying to sound cool and indifferent.

'How could I forget about you, especially after all the dirty things you did to me?' she said in her most lush, sluttish voice.

'I'd like to do them again,' he said, 'and more.'
'When?'
'Whenever you want,' he promised eagerly.
'How about tonight?' she asked already feeling horny.
'Tonight's good,' he said.

'What time?'

'I'll pick you up at seven.'

'I'll be waiting, just ring my mobile once and I'll come out.'

'No problem.'

'I'm going to give you the time of your life,' she promised, laughing gently.

'I can't wait,' he said.

'Till then,' she said seductively, and the line went dead.

Tony lay back down on his bed and began to imagine what they could possibly do that they hadn't already done last week.

'You forgot to tell him about the four of us meeting up, you stupid tart,' Sarah forcefully told her friend.

'Keep your hair on! I'll do it tonight, when I meet him.'

'You mean after you've shagged him!'

'Yeah, so what? Anyway it looks less suspicious like that. If I'd just asked him about Justin straight away he'd think I only phoned because of the money.'

'All right, just make sure you don't forget, do it tonight,' Sarah said as she bit her bottom lip in nervous anticipation.

'You can't seriously be going after that guy just because of the money?' Karen said in disdain.

'I just want a second look, I can't remember what he looked like, that's all.'

'You saw him again on the telly and you called him a wanker every time we ever talked about that party!'

'Everyone deserves a second chance,' Sarah said adamantly.

Karen bit her lip, what Sarah chose to do with her life was her business. She was proud that she wouldn't go with a man just because he had money. Yet at the same time she didn't want to judge her best friend. Good luck to her, Karen thought to herself, so long as she's happy that's all that counts.

Derek couldn't hold out any longer, he'd been waiting for news from the police all night and morning, with no word. Finally he cracked and phoned Inspector Koleth.

'Koleth,' answered the inspector in a tone reserved only for the seriously important and busy.

'Hello Inspector Koleth, this is Derek Bonner, I just phoned to enquire about how my case was progressing.'

'Ah yeah, I meant to phone you but haven't had the chance. Well he's admitted to the burglary and we're definitely charging him with that but he refuses to admit to taking the lottery ticket.'

'But he did, I swear to God that's my money he's stolen,' Derek said in desperation.

'Yes, I believe you, but knowing something and proving something are two separate things. Now I'm currently making my way to the newsagent's where you bought the winning ticket. Hopefully the shop's security system should show you buying the winning ticket. If it does, well then that means we'll be able to charge him with fraud and deception.'

'But what if the shop doesn't have a video of me buying the ticket?' Derek asked, concerned.

'Well hopefully we'll have your fingerprints to go

on. If you bought the ticket then they'll be all over it. We should have the results back within two hours.'

Koleth paused for thought, usually fingerprints showed up on flat smooth surfaces and depending on the angle the finger had touched the surface it could sometimes be difficult to prove who the print really belonged to. However there wasn't anything to be gained by worrying Mr Bonner at this stage of the investigation.

'But what if he wiped my prints, I mean that is possible, isn't it?' Derek asked.

'Theoretically yes but having just interviewed the suspect I seriously doubt whether he would be smart enough to do that.'

'But just suppose he did and just suppose there was no video evidence?'

'I have to say that you're being very pessimistic here Mr Bonner.'

'Please humour me.'

'Well I'm afraid the CPS would never prosecute such a case due to lack of evidence. We'd only be able to proceed with the charge of burglary.'

'Does that mean he'd keep the money?'

'I'm afraid you'd have to launch a civil case to recover your winnings.'

Derek was silent, his heart sank and the previous night's hopes seemed dashed again.

'Look, try not to worry Mr Bonner, all shops have surveillance cameras these days, it's standard practice, the odds are in your favour. I'll call as soon as I have more information.'

'I see, well thank you, inspector,' Derek said with a heavy heart before hanging up. It seemed to him that the twenty-five million remained just as elusive as ever.

Inspector Koleth parked his car outside the Sunny Days newsagent's. He had intended to drive straight to Sunny Days after his telephone conversation with Mr Bonner but had been side tracked by a new murder case which had been dumped on him. On the way to Sunny Days he had radioed the station and asked for the results of the fingerprint test. The only prints which were found on the ticket were Justin's. If Koleth were to secure a conviction for fraud and deception then he needed video evidence of Derek buying the ticket. Koleth got out of the car and walked towards the shop, apparently it was owned by a Mr I. Inanilmaz. Probably Turkish, the inspector thought to himself as he made his way into the newsagent's.

The shop was fairly small with just enough room for three or four customers and the usual products that one would expect to find in such an establishment. Behind the counter stood a solitary figure, a tall but overweight man of dark, Mediterranean complexion, who Koleth judged to be in his early forties, but seemed to wear the bored and frustrated frown of a much older man.

Koleth held back and waited for him to finish serving the customers, which he did so in a bland and blasé manner. Once the last customer had left Koleth approached the shopkeeper confidently, 'Mr Inanilmaz?' he asked as he flashed his CID badge. The badge caused the raising of an eyebrow in mild interest.

'Yes, that's me,' the man replied.

'Mr Inanilmaz I was hoping you could help me with a case I'm working on.'

'Please call me Ismail,' the shopkeeper said in a cockney accent.

'Ismail are you aware of the fact that last week's twenty-five million pound lottery ticket was bought here in your shop?'

'Yes I am,' Ismail nodded as he thought about all the ways he'd spend twenty-five million pounds. He caught the inspector looking at him and broke off the fantasizing. 'The computer keeps a record of every single ticket sold, sometimes when I'm bored I check.'

'Are you also aware that last night the person claiming to have won the jackpot prize was arrested for burglary, fraud and deception?'

'Yes I saw it on the news,' Ismail smiled, this was starting to get interesting. 'What did he do?'

'He committed a burglary and I have reason to believe that one of the items he stole was the winning lottery ticket.'

'Oh my God!'

'Yes, exactly.'

'What does that mean? Who gets the money?' Ismail asked, now completely gripped by the story.

'Well that's where I need your help. You see if we had video proof of who bought the winning ticket then we could settle the matter fairly. I can see that you have a surveillance camera just in the right spot, all we have to do now is watch your tape of the day and time the ticket was purchased.'

'Oh I see what you're getting at, but I'm afraid I can't help you.'

'What do you mean?' asked Koleth almost losing his temper.

'The thing is I'm trying to cut down on overheads, business hasn't been that good recently, and, . . . well I simply re-record over the same cassette everyday, unless of course there's been an incident, but luckily we haven't had any trouble for a while.'

'Mr Inanilmaz, I'm sorry, Ismail, please don't tell me you've recorded over last Saturday's video.'

Slowly but regretfully Ismail nodded his head, 'I'm afraid so, I'm very sorry.'

Koleth sighed, without that video there wasn't any hard evidence against Justin.

'Well could you at least identify the person who bought the winning ticket?' It wasn't hard evidence but Koleth hoped that it would be enough to convince the CPS to prosecute. Again Ismail shook his head, 'I'm sorry I get so many different customers coming in and out everyday, and especially on Saturdays. There's just no way I'd have been able to remember who bought the ticket.'

'That's OK, thank you for your help anyway,' the inspector said before walking out of the shop in a huff.

'I'm really sorry,' Ismail shouted out after him, but it was already too late.

Koleth sat in his car and contemplated Derek's situation. How could that poor man possibly be feeling right now, knowing that such an injustice had been committed against him? All too many times Koleth had seen criminals get way with the most appalling acts and their victims simply ask, in bewilderment, how it was all possible. Working within the system was frustrating and sometimes its inadequacies made Koleth sick to the stomach, but there was nothing else he could do. He had a backlog of files piling up on his desk, crimes a lot more serious than burglary and fraud, it was time he closed the case and moved on. Angrily he started his car and sped off.

Ismail Inanilmaz had watched in nervous silence as Koleth sat in his car not moving. He let out a sigh of relief when he watched the car and the officer inside it finally leave. He waited a couple of minutes to make sure the officer wouldn't return before turning the open sign for his shop the other way round and locking his door.

To the back of the shop was a small storage space, where Ismail kept most of his stock, but more importantly a collection of recordable video tapes. He counted the tapes before selecting one. It was without a label, but he was sure it was the one he wanted. Quickly he took it to the counter where he kept a TV and video, which he used to keep himself entertained when the shop was quiet. Ismail placed the cassette inside. The date on the screen showed that the tape was last Saturday's. He rewound the tape to around about the time the winning lottery ticket was purchased. He looked out carefully for a lanky, teenage boy, but Justin wasn't there. Instead the only purchasers of lottery tickets around about that time were a few old biddies and one middle aged man with a small girl. Ismail replayed the tape and then checked the computer to see at precisely what time the winning ticket had been bought. Yes it was definitely the man with the girl.

Ismail ejected the tape from the video and placed it just below the till, so that it would remain within his sight for the rest of the day. Sitting down on his small, uncomfortable stool he ignored a potential customer who gently knocked on the glass door of his shop. Instead of reopening the shop and dealing with the customer Ismail thought back to the one Turkish proverb that was handed down to him by his grandfather, 'When two parties fight, it is the third that is assured victory.' Ismail Inanilmaz scratched the week's worth of stubble that lined his neck, for inside his sharp, corner cutting mind a devious plan was beginning to form.

CHAPTER TWELVE

Derek had thoroughly enjoyed telling his manager how sick he still was and that there was no way he'd be able to come to work for the second consecutive week. Of course his manager had displayed his disdain and took it upon himself to remind Derek that his employees were never sick, they either worked or they left the firm. Derek understood that if he didn't return to work soon his temporary contract wouldn't be renewed. He smiled to himself as he remembered the conversation, he really didn't give a toss anymore. How great it felt to no longer care, to no longer be chained and constricted by the belief that a man should do his best to live a proper, productive life. What the hell was proper anyway?

He was just about to make some tea when the phone rang, pure instinct told him that it was inspector Koleth, the hour of reckoning had come.

'Hello,' he said nervously.

'Hello Mr Bonner, it's Koleth here, I've phoned to inform you about the progress of your case.'

'And?' Derek asked somehow aware that the answer wasn't going to be good.

'I'm afraid it's not good news, I'm sorry.'

'What's happened?'

'The only fingerprints we found on the winning lottery ticket belong to the suspect.'

Derek was silent while the information sank in, then he remembered the possibility of video evidence, 'What about the security video from the shop?'

'I'm afraid there's no video evidence of who bought the winning ticket, and the shop keeper says that he wouldn't be able to identify who bought the ticket. It means that we weren't able to charge Justin Farren with fraud or deception just burglary.'

'So what does that mean?'

'It means that you'll have to consult a solicitor and try to sue him for the money yourself.'

'So he's still got the money?'

'Yes I expect he's probably spending it right now.'

Spending it right now? Derek was bewildered. 'What do you mean? He isn't in prison?'

'No after we charged him with burglary we had to release him, it'll be up to the courts to decide his punishment. Of course that's assuming they find him guilty of burglary.'

'You mean he might still get off the burglary charge?' Derek asked, raising his voice considerably.

'I shouldn't think so,' Koleth responded, trying to sound as soothing as possible, 'the evidence against him is pretty strong.'

'Well if it's so bloody strong, why's he out there now, spending my money?'

'I'm sorry Mr Bonner, I tried my best, there's nothing more I can do, my hands are tied.'

'Well it's not good enough!' Derek shouted before slamming down the phone. His hands started shaking just before a vice like pain gripped his chest causing him to drop to his knees. Just as he thought he was about to pass out and die the pain disappeared. He took deep breaths and tried to clear his head. He didn't need to be a medical expert to guess that his blood pressure must have gone off the scales. Derek knew that he had to find a solution to this mess before it took its toll on his physical and mental health.

After his release Justin had kept low for a few days, staying in a five star hotel, which was ironically paid for by some newspapers that wanted to interview him. The twenty-five million pound cheque he'd used to open a new bank account with had already cleared and he'd been given counselling on how to deal with the burden of becoming a millionaire overnight by employees of the lottery. Counselling! He'd laughed his head off. You don't need counselling when you win twenty-five million pounds! What a bunch of jokers!

They'd also offered him financial advice but it was way too boring. Anyway those fools didn't know how to make money, if they did they'd be millionaires themselves, not licking his arse! No Justin had his own ideas on what to do with the money, like the biggest nightclub in London. He had asked them to help him buy a house though, but not any old house. No they had to find one that fitted the following specifications; minimum six bedrooms, at least three bathrooms, a swimming pool and Jacuzzi and of course a gym. Not to mention a garage with enough space for at least three cars and a garden that was large enough for parties of up to a hundred people. Justin didn't know more than ten people, but he still wanted the large parties! Of course the house had to be located in London and preferably within at least eight miles of the estate where his grandma had raised him.

The estate agent who had the pleasure of finding Justin his new home had of course dealt with lots of cases where his clients had a lot more money than sense, and it always amazed him how stupid the rich could be. Justin however took having more money than sense to a new level and the estate agent decided within five minutes of meeting him that this kid could spend a billion pounds within a couple of months and have nothing to show for it. Nevertheless he went about his job of looking for a house which matched Justin's specifications and found Justin exactly what he was looking for in a quiet suburb of north London. A bargain at three and a half million pounds. Justin bought it without even seeing it, the pictures the estate agent had shown him were more than enough to convince him that the mansion would satisfy his every need. It even contained a second garage, which Justin wanted to convert into a mini house for his nan, so that she could live with him. His new found wealth could now be used to pay her back for raising him alone when his teenage mother had abandoned him in order to run away to Spain.

The tabloid press, which featured at least one story about Justin everyday, went wild when word came out about his most recent purchase. Each paper wanted to be granted an exclusive tour of his mansion, but Justin who had now become accustomed to dealing with the press said that he would hold a press conference outside his new house and that they could ask him any questions they wanted to then. Justin loved being in the limelight and recently had started thinking of more ways in which he could attract media attention.

Derek went livid when he heard that Justin had already spent three and a half million pounds on a mansion. He'd made an appointment to see a solicitor but phoned up three times and badgered her into seeing him earlier due to the importance of his case. Finally she agreed to stay behind longer than usual and see him the following day.

Havers and Co were a small high street firm of solicitors consisting of the proprietor Ms Christine Havers, one salaried partner, one legal executive and one secretary. Christine remembered Derek from when she'd handled his divorce, she had tried her best for him but knew full well that under English law he would be the one to come out of the divorce much worse off. He seemed like a decent man, who adored his children and had been a devoted husband, but of course from her extensive experience of divorce cases it seemed that it was the decent men that wives cheated on or claimed they no longer loved whilst the real bastards were the ones who got away with murder.

Her own inability to find a decent man had left her feeling slightly bitter. She had been a very attractive girl and now at the age of thirty nine was still a head turner. She went swimming every morning before opening up her office and this helped her maintain a slim, youthful figure. Men often complemented her and of course all them said they couldn't believe that such an intelligent and beautiful woman wasn't married or at least didn't have a boyfriend. Yet her work meant that the only men she ever came into contact with were snobbish businessmen, criminals, or even worse, lawyers. Having long ago given up hope of ever finding Mr Right she threw herself into her career fulfilling her ambition to start her own firm at the age of thirty-five, quite an accomplishment, considering the cut-throat nature of the business.

Derek was only kept waiting for ten minutes. He used this time to go over the events of the past week and a half, but by the end of it all still didn't know where to start. Seeing Ms Havers after more than a year snapped him out of his thoughts completely. Surely she hadn't been so attractive when she'd been handling his divorce? Mind you he was in such a mess back then that he wouldn't have noticed if a naked page three girl were representing him.

He followed her to her office, admiring the way her legs worked their way into her elegant but powerful business suit. She sat down behind her desk, if Derek's memory was good it was the same one she had before, but her office had recently been redecorated.

'So Mr Bonner, how are you? How are the children?'

'The children are great thank you very much. I'm surprised you remember me, you must see so many divorce cases.'

She smiled a very charming smile but remained silent. Derek felt his cheeks flush slightly from his attraction towards her. 'And how have you been?' he asked trying to take the focus off himself.

'Oh fine, I've had the place redecorated. What do you think?'

'Oh yes I really like it, looks erm . . . marvellous.' Did he say marvellous? Sometimes Derek could really kick himself. Terry would have all the right words to say to this attractive woman, yet here he was floundering like an idiot.

'So what was all the urgency about?' Christine asked wanting to get down to business. It was late and her day had been long and hard.

Derek took a deep breath and started from the beginning, giving all the details he felt were relevant and answering all of Ms Havers questions as accurately as possible. Christine listened carefully, taking notes on her legal pad, she'd come across some interesting cases in her years of practising the law but this one had to be at the top of her list. After half an hour she put down her pad, speechless by the story Derek had just told her.

'Well what do you think?' he asked anxiously, snapping her back into his world. She had a grave look about her and Derek began to fear the worst, that he simply didn't have a leg to stand on. 'Well,' she said finally, 'the situation isn't exactly good, but on the other hand it isn't irretrievable. However I must warn you that you may not get the full sum back or it may even be advisable to settle outside court, but we'll discuss those kinds of possibilities later.'

'So you think I stand a good chance of getting back at least some of the money?' Derek asked hopefully. At that precise moment in time even a tenth of what was rightfully his would have been considered a hell of a lot better than nothing.

'I think that we have a very good case, it's a fact that he burgled your home, and we can call a police officer as a witness who believes your side of the story. We should also pay that newsagent a visit, with a gentle push he might be able to remember more than he let on to the inspector.'

'Then why didn't the police do more?' Derek asked blustered and frustrated.

'Well the detective inspector was probably right when he said the CPS wouldn't prosecute. You see in order to secure a conviction in a criminal court the defendant must be found guilty beyond all reasonable doubt, something that would be very hard to do in this particular situation, however there is no such constraint in a civil court. Therefore if the defendant appears to be guilty in a civil case, the court can and usually does award in favour of the plaintiff.'

'I can see the logic there,' Derek said, trying his best to understand all the legal jargon. 'So what next?' he asked hopeful that Ms Havers would be able to shed more light into the dark and mysterious world of lawsuits.

'Well the very first thing we're going to have to do is send out a letter of claim, asking that he refunds you the full twenty-five million. He has twenty-one days to respond. Probably he'll seek out a solicitor, now any decent member of the Law Society would recommend that he settle out of court. However you just never know and if he isn't prepared to settle with a sum you are happy with, well then we'll be forced to sue. '

'Sounds good to me.'

'Yes, well I must warn you that such legal proceedings can be very expensive . . .'

'But I don't have any money,' Derek interrupted.

'Well I have enough confidence in your case so far, I must add, because I will of course have to check all the facts you've given me. But I do have enough confidence in this case to provide my services on a no win no fee basis.'

'Oh thank you,' Derek said.

'You have to be made aware however that this means that in the long run my fees will be much more expensive than if you were to just pay them the standard way.'

'How much am I looking at?'

'Twenty percent of whatever amount I recover and I'm afraid that's not negotiable.'

Twenty percent! Derek wanted to walk out of the door, but he somehow knew that Ms Havers was being fair. He seriously doubted whether he could find a better deal somewhere else. Rubbing his temples and taking a deep breath Derek agreed to his solicitor's terms.

CHAPTER THIRTEEN

Justin stood at the top of his staircase and peered down at the party that was taking place in his new home. Over a hundred people he guessed, most of whom he didn't know, but more importantly they all knew him. Everywhere he went people congratulated him on his big win, finally he was getting the respect he felt he deserved. His dream of becoming a gangster was almost complete, all he needed now was a beautiful girl on his arm. Next to him Tony had finished rolling a spliff. He offered it to Justin, who placed it between his lips and waited for Tony to light it. Tony resented the way Justin looked at him, like he was expected to light his joint. He felt that he had shown Justin more than enough respect by rolling him the joint and by letting him take the first pull, but no this didn't seem to be enough for Justin. Justin smiled as Tony lit the joint for him with a gold plated Zippo lighter he had given his best friend just a few days ago. Tony had often rolled spliffs for Justin before, and this wasn't the first time Tony had sparked it on his behalf, but Justin couldn't help but notice the shift in power that had occurred in their relationship since cashing in the lottery ticket. Justin had always been Tony's sidekick, Tony had been the one who was cool, who all the girls liked and who everyone wanted to know but all that had changed. All these people they were at the party for him, not for Tony, and Justin could sense that even Tony was aware of the fact. Lately it seemed that he couldn't stop licking Justin's arse, something that Justin was growing to appreciate by the minute.

'So where's your nan then?' Tony asked trying to stimulate a bit of conversation with his best mate.

'My nan? What the fuck you talking about?' Justin said, vexed.

Tony was silent as he tried to work out why Justin was speaking to him the way he was. He was half tempted to grab him and shake him up a bit. Yet he had to remain calm, he remembered his master plan, to stay close to Justin until he could figure a way of getting his share of the money.

'You said that you'd bring her to live with you that's all,' Tony replied, more than a little agitated.

'How can I bring my nan here? It's a fucking bad boy party,' Justin said, looking at Tony as if he were a complete and utter idiot. 'Look down there, Jimmy and Dave are doing coke for Christ's sake, and what about those girls down there dancing with their tits out? They'd give my nan a heart attack.'

'Shit, just thought I'd ask is all.'

Justin looked at Tony carefully before choosing to ignore the sound of rebellion in his voice.

'Thought I'd get the place decorated and all that before I moved her in. I'm gonna build her a special little house out the back so that she doesn't cramp my style, you get me?'

'Yeah I hear you,' Tony said. Tony started to imagine what he could do with a pad like this and all that money. He'd be able to shag any girl he wanted to and man they'd all be so buff. But it was Justin, not Tony who had the money and the pad. The jammy fucker, Tony thought bitterly. He wondered if Justin had lost his virginity yet, but didn't dare ask for fear of causing his friend to burst into a rage. Justin liked to show that he was the man now, he walked around like he was some kind of gangster, like he was the Don and it didn't seem to stop him if Tony were embarrassed publicly. If anything Justin seemed to take every opportunity he could to make Tony look like an idiot. It was all Tony could do to stop himself from punching Justin in the mouth. Boy, how he'd love to bust his lip right now, but he knew he had to remain in Justin's good books at least until he had a concrete way of getting his share of the loot. Let him play the gangster for now, Tony thought to himself, but it won't be for long.

'Look,' Justin said pointing to his front door, which was open. Tony followed his finger until he spotted Karen and Sarah. He smiled demonically as he remembered the crush Justin had had on Sarah. He also remembered his most recent bonking session with Karen and how she'd begged him to reintroduce Justin to Sarah. No doubt Justin's new found wealth and fame had made Sarah reconsider her opinion about him. Looking at her and remembering how damn good she looked Tony couldn't help but feel envious. To think that she would be wasted on Justin, it was almost a sin.

'Oh yeah I buzzed Karen and told 'em to come round. I's been seeing a lot of Karen lately,' Tony said. Justin didn't take his eyes off Sarah who was wearing a red dress that flowed elegantly over every inch of her body.

'Karen says that Sarah's been asking 'bout you.'

'Yeah?' Justin said pulling so hard on the spliff that it caused his eyes to bulge.

'For real, Karen's been banging on about it twenty-four seven. I did good, init?'

'Yeah you did good.'

'Let's go chirps ´em.'

'Wicked,' Justin said passing what little was left of the spliff to Tony and following his friend with external confidence, but no matter how much he tried to play the gangster inside Justin was a nervous wreck. He couldn't ever imagine a girl like Sarah being interested in someone like him, twenty-five million pounds or not.

By the time they reached them, the girls were already doing lines of coke with Jimmy and Diamond Dave. Justin remembered back to that night when he met Sarah and how she'd dumped him when Diamond Dave had turned up on the scene. Feeling like a fool he hung back and let Tony approach the two girls. On seeing Justin, Dave put his right arm around him and gave him a peck on the cheek. Justin, unused to so much affection from anyone, especially a man, used his shoulder to gently push him away, but Dave's strength and weight made it impossible for Justin to physically budge him without drawing attention to the fact that he didn't like the way Dave was holding him. Turning slightly red, he lent backwards so as to avoid the close proximity of Dave's face.

'This is a fucking great party Jus, I love you man. You can throw a fucking party. Look at those girls over there, they're topless man.' The way Dave slurred his words and the way his eyes roamed around in his head indicated to Justin that the guy was completely out of it. 'Here Jus, have a JD and coke,' he said, taking it out of Jimmy's hand and giving it to Justin. Justin nervous and feeling Sarah's eyes on him downed it.

'That's it, I like a man who can hold his drink,' Jimmy said wanting to join in. 'Have a line with us Jus,' Jimmy continued as he swayed slightly and delicately put a line along the back of his hand. Justin observed as Jimmy snorted it up like a hoover.

'Don't you want some Jus?' Dave asked.

'Yeah course I do,' Justin said, 'give us two lines.'

'I told you, didn't I?' Jimmy shouted in the direction of the two girls, 'I told you that Jus was a hard lad, didn't I?'

'That you did,' Sarah smiled, looking at Justin and giving him a cheeky wink. Justin held out his hand and watched intently as Dave gently poured two short lines down the back of his hand. Justin had never done coke before but he figured that he'd give it a try, especially as Sarah was doing it. Of course he could now easily fund the habit if he needed to. With one quick sniff the first line was done, the hit was instant and indescribable but he felt a burning sensation in his nostrils and the coke caused him to cough slightly. Undeterred he snorted up the second line as Jimmy and Dave cheered him on. By now a small crowd had gathered round, including some of the topless girls, one of whom put her arm around Justin and squashed her large breasts against the side of his body.

'Can I have some?' she asked.

'Course you can, all you fine ladies can, just see my brethren Jimmy and Dave,' he said and watched as she jumped up and down in excitement. 'This is the best party, when are you coming to dance with us?' she asked as a friend of hers joined them. Justin looked on with a stupefied expression on his face.

By now Sarah had had enough of the competition and went up to him, grabbing his arm firmly and whispering into his ear, 'Lets ditch this crowd, they're boring.'

Justin's eyes locked into hers and for an instant the party, the crowd, the topless girls, the music, everything disappeared, there was just him and her. Sarah could blow all the other girls away with the bat of an eyelid. He wanted her on his arm, no other girl because no other girl could match her beauty.

'We could go upstairs to my bedroom, if you like,' he said without managing a single nervous stutter. Justin wondered if it was the money that had given him the newfound confidence. Did all the super rich feel like this?

'That's a great idea,' she whispered again into his ear. She was so close to him he could smell her perfume, and God did she smell good. But it wasn't just her perfume, it was her hair. Justin wanted to reach and grab it with his hand, to feel its texture and bring it to his nose and soak in its aroma. Such a move might have been good or it might not have been, but Justin managed to curb his urges and refrained from touching Sarah's hair. He did however take her hand and winked at Tony as he led her away from all the new found friends and would be groupies, and took her upstairs to his bedroom.

Once they were alone and just after he'd closed the door most of his new found confidence vanished and he felt his old cumbersome self. Sarah sat on the bed and crossed her legs sensuously. Justin offered her the beer he held in his hand, smiling she opened it. Desperately he tried to think of something to say as he watched her take a sip out of the can.

'So how you been?' he asked finally.

'Oh not too bad, not as good as you though. This is a really nice place you've got here.'

'Thanks.'

'I saw you on TV, I thought it was really funny when you ran away from the police. The papers went mad!'

'Yeah that was funny, init?'

They both laughed and then smiled at each other silently.

'Why don't you come and sit next to me?' she asked patting a spot right next to her on his king-sized bed. Nervously he made his way towards her, his legs felt like jelly and the journey seemed to take forever, a couple of times he thought he would fall over before he even made it to the bed. Slowly he sat next to her, staring at her with a hunger she could intuitively feel. It turned her on the way he desired her, the way he needed her, why she could probably make him do anything she wanted.

'Did you really steal the ticket?' she asked placing her hand on his knee and causing an uncomfortable stirring in his trousers. He hesitated, she was the first person apart from the press to ask him that question since he'd left the police station. Up until now he had vehemently denied any wrong doing.

'Come on, you can tell me,' she said leaning closer to him, 'I can keep a secret, I promise I won't tell anyone.'

'Yeah I did it,' he admitted not believing he had told her the truth. She was now the second person in the world to know his secret, Tony being the first.

'It's kind of obvious that you did,' she chuckled, 'but look, you got away with it, the money's yours.'

'Yeah, it's mine, all of it,' Justin said reflecting on his luck.

'You know you can tell me anything, I'll never tell anyone something that you don't want people to know.'

'Thanks, you're just so tick,' he said, reaching forward with his mouth. It felt exquisite as his lips touched hers and she allowed his tongue to explore her mouth. Gently her hand moved up his thigh until it rested on his erect cock. She grabbed it and Justin felt like his heart was going to explode. Oh God, this was it. He was about to lose his virginity to the most beautiful woman he had ever seen. With all the courage he could muster he grabbed at her breasts with his right hand and roughly tongued her neck, just the way he'd seen in the movies, she let out a light groan. His dick started throbbing and he knew that soon he'd reach the point of no return, and he prayed to God that he wouldn't. Then all of a sudden she pushed him away and he looked at her helplessly.

'What's wrong?' he asked desperately, his mind unable to understand what had just happened. She bowed her head slightly, looking away from him but at the same time allowing him to see the beauty of her profile, her thick red lips and her small pert nose, the way her hair flowed over her left ear.

'I'm not sure I can do this,' she said, a confused, guilty expression on her face.

'Why not?' he asked, his eyes pleading, his body hungry.

'You must have so many girls come on to you now, I just need to know that I'm special, not like those other girls.'

Other girls? What was she talking about? 'What other girls?' Justin asked.

'You know those cheap tarts downstairs,' she said, screwing her face in disgust.

Justin remembered the topless girls from the party and the one that had come on to him, how could he forget? But Sarah could make him forget everything, even the girls downstairs. He tried to picture their faces and their breasts but the images just faded into black, there was only Sarah.

'I don't want ´em, all I want is you,' he said besieged by passion, by lust, by want and by need.

'I'd be the only one?' she asked, her eyes now looking into his, a picture of perfect innocence.

'Yes, I just want you, only you.'

She lent forward again and gently kissed along his neck until her tongue reached his ear. She flicked it in and out and the feeling was so pleasurable it bordered on the painful. Again her hand returned to his thigh causing his cock to instantly return to its erect position.

'Do you promise?' she asked.

'Yes I promise.'

She got up and stood in front of him, kicking off her shoes and letting her dress fall to the floor. He stared in disbelief as she undid her bra and allowed her large, round breasts to stand in front of him in all their magnificence. Could this really be happening to him? Taking his hands she gently pulled him towards her and he stood up embracing her tightly as their tongues and mouths meshed into one. She allowed his hands to explore her body freely, gasping when he found the right places. Roughly she pulled his top off and flicked his nipples with her tongue. He did the same to her, his hand by now in her panties, exploring the heat that was between a woman's legs for the first time in his life. She unbuckled his belt and in one swift action threw his jeans and boxers to the floor.

His hard, hot cock landed in her palm and she stroked it gently, he started to groan as her tongue explored his right ear.

'Please wait,' he begged but instead she picked up the pace, moving her hand backwards and forwards furiously. It took but seconds for him to reach his inevitable climax, and as he did so she grabbed him and held him tightly, kissing him roughly.

With a defeated look on his face Justin pulled his jeans back up and slumped onto the bed, 'I'm sorry,' he said shaking his head and refusing to look at her.

Confused she sat down next to him. What was wrong? She hadn't expected him to last very long but most boys his age would try again. She remembered one lad who had done it five times with her, now that had been amazing.

'What's wrong?' she asked, stroking his face gently.

'I'm crap, init?' he said, tears in his eyes.

'No, you're not, I really liked it, you were excellent,' she said running her hand along his bare back.

'I've, I've never done it before,' he said bursting into tears. His crying wasn't strong, moreover it seemed to be like the gentle whimpers a dog would make when it knew it had done something wrong.

Nevertheless tears did flow down his cheeks and she couldn't help but feel sorry for the poor boy.

'Shhh, please don't cry. You've got me now and we're gonna do it lots,' she said as she hugged him tightly. The sobs continued for a few seconds before he wiped his eyes and looked at her.

'You think I'm a wanker,' he said, his voice trembling.

'No. I don't. I think you're really sensitive,' she said holding his head in her hands.

'And you know that women really love sensitive men, don't you?' she smiled seductively.

'Really?'

'Really, you're great,' she said as she lent forward again and kissed him. Justin began to relax and enjoyed the way her tongue explored his mouth, she tasted so good. He felt like the luckiest man alive. She moved her tongue out of his mouth and down his neck, then back up to his ears before slowly running it down his torso. She carried on working her way down until she reached the top of his jeans. She undid them and pulled them and the boxers right off, only stopping to take off his trainers.

She kissed his inner thighs and licked his balls before placing his cock in her mouth. As she felt it grow under the skilled commands of her tongue, Sarah became highly aroused by the power she held, for she knew that she had Justin right where she wanted him.

CHAPTER FOURTEEN

Justin awoke the next morning and looked at the amazingly beautiful woman that slept next to him. Last night had by far been the most amazing of his life. He smiled, it felt great no longer being a virgin. Sex was fantastic and Sarah had promised a lot more to come. Justin peeled back the covers and stared at Sarah in all her naked glory. He didn't know what felt better, the rush he had felt of discovering that he had a ticket worth twenty-five million pounds or last night's activities and the woman he had performed them with. He decided then and there that he would choose Sarah over the money any day of the week. He kissed her and she stirred slightly before turning over and returning to her deep slumber.

'My sleeping beauty,' he whispered as he gently stroked her hair. He remembered how much he had wanted her at Jimmy's party and then how much he had wanted her last night. He had wanted her for her beauty, to show the world that he could have a beautiful woman, because all gangsters need a tick bitch by their side, but after last night he felt so much more. She had taken his virginity, she had been patient with him and shown him everything he should do. He knew that he could trust her, he had even told her about stealing the ticket. Justin was glad that he had thrown the party now, if not he might never have had a second chance with Sarah. He wondered how the party had gone in his absence. It was doubtful if anyone would have noticed he was gone, not with all the drugs and booze that had been flowing about the place. He just hoped that his friends hadn't trashed his new home. Eager to find out he slipped quietly out of bed, careful not to wake Sarah, he quickly put his clothes on.

As Justin emerged out of his bedroom and walked down his long corridor the first thing he noticed were empty beer cans, spliff ends, fag ends, ash, traces of coke, and used condoms, all contributing their part in helping decorate his newly laid down and highly expensive carpet. Peering through the open doors of a couple of the other bedrooms he noticed groups of naked people all bunched up in a very deep sleep. What the fuck had happened here last night? He'd be damned if he'd throw another party, not if that was the way these animals would treat his house!

Justin heard the flush of a toilet come from the en-suite bathroom that belonged to the bedroom he was standing outside of. Stunned he watched Diamond Dave stumble out naked. 'Great fucking party,' Dave said as he approached Justin. 'But the girls hid my clothes, don't suppose you've seen `em?'

'No, sorry mate,' Justin said incredulously.

'Not to worry I'll wake `em up. I hid their clothes pretty well, so if they want `em back they'll have to let the Diamond have his first.'

Justin watched as Dave went over to a mass of bodies and started to wake its female members up. Wondering what had happened to his friend Tony, Justin followed the carnage of beer cans and condoms down the stairs, careful of where he trod.

He'd have to look for a cleaning service in the yellow pages he told himself.

Downstairs lying on the floor and over the furniture were more bodies although most had their clothes on. Those that were naked were just normal boy/girl couples who'd made an attempt at covering themselves up and slept under coats or blankets. Justin guessed that those who were into the hardcore stuff had gone upstairs leaving the more timid downstairs to do whatever they fancied. There was still no sign of Tony however, so Justin carried on until he reached the kitchen.

The smell of bacon and sausages hit him hard as he spotted Karen frying up some breakfast and Tony standing behind her, his arms around her waist as he nibbled on her neck.

'What you sayin´ G,' Tony said when he looked round and saw Justin standing in the doorway. 'We're both starving so we thought we'd help ourselves, all right init?' Tony continued as he left Karen and approached his friend.

'There's plenty to go round,' Karen said briefly looking up at Justin, 'would you like some too?'

'Yeah safe,' Justin said as he put the kettle on and looked at Tony, who took the hint and started searching the cupboards for some cups and teabags.

'Blood that Sarah's well buff, bet you shagged her, init?' Tony asked. Justin remained silent.

'Watch what you're saying, that's my mate you're talking about,' Karen shouted, giving Tony a vexed look.

'Yeah, yeah,' Tony said, 'so what's she like, I bet she's right dirty, init?' Tony said in a lower tone but still audible to Karen.

Justin grabbed Tony by the neck with all his strength, 'Don't you ever talk about my missus like that again,' he snarled into Tony's face, before pushing him with all his strength in an attempt to throw Tony onto the floor. Not quite strong enough, the effect Justin's attack had was to cause Tony to stumble against the cupboards.

Justin stormed out of the kitchen angrily. Tony perplexed by what had just happened simply shrugged his shoulders in Karen's direction before running after his mate.

'What I do?' Tony asked, confused.

'Sarah's with me now so you've got to show her respects, ´coz if she don't get no respects it means I ain't got no respects,' Justin said, pointing his finger towards his chest in an overly dramatic fashion.

'Shit, I didn't know G. I just thought she was a quick ting. Didn't know she was your missus.'

'Well she is my missus,' Justin said, grumpily switching on the large telly that was in the living room.

'Let me apologise then G, I won't ever disrespec´ your missus like that again.'

'Good, don't forget my tea,' Justin said as he started to flick through the channels. Tony left the room before he was overcome by the urge to deck Justin. He didn't know how much longer he could take Justin's outrageous behaviour. The fool was acting like some kind of king, living off half of his money. Now he'd gone and fallen in love with the first girl that came along. His missus indeed! She hadn't even noticed the joker before he had his twenty-five million, and talking about disrespect, how could he disrespect him in front of Karen like that?

Justin carried on flicking through the channels until he saw something he recognised, a street and a building, it was the placed he'd burgled.

'Tony!' he shouted as he turned up the volume.

'Now what?' Tony shouted, as he ran back into the room.

'Look,' Justin pointed at the TV, and instantly Tony recognised the road and the building.

'Shit,' Tony said as the newsreader announced that Derek Bonner, whose bedsit had been burgled by Justin Farren, would be suing the teenager for theft of his winning lottery ticket. The newsreader then disappeared from the screen as recorded footage of Derek pushing his way past a barrage of photographers and into his building was shown. Derek refused to answer all the reporters and journalists questions. In order to build even more tension and intrigue into the story the news programme then showed Derek and his solicitor standing outside her office. Derek remained silent as she read out a statement on his behalf.

'Due to legal reasons we cannot go into detail,' she said, 'but I am able to say on behalf of my client that a letter of claim has been issued against a Justin Farren for the sum of twenty-five million pounds. We expect the letter to reach him any day now and he has the mandatory twenty-one days to reply before we seek legal action.'

'Fuck! What am I going to do?' Justin said clutching his friend by the shoulders. The panic which filled Justin's face transmitted itself to Tony. Gripped by fear he searched the living room for some fags. On seeing a packet he lit one.

'OK the first thing we've got to do is calm down,' Tony said, inhaling deeply. Justin whose nerves were shot to hell by now grabbed the cigarette from him and started smoking, taking deep pulls as if the cigarette were a joint. Tony took another one from the pack and lit up again.

Diamond Dave, who by now had found his clothes, and accompanied by Jimmy, came down the stairs to find out what all the shouting was about. Others who had also partied hard last night but had been awoken by the noise also came to see why the house was suddenly filled with pandemonium. Soon a small crowd gathered round Justin and Tony. Sarah, who had simply used a duvet to cover her nakedness, had also come to investigate. When she saw the state Justin was in she placed her arm around him.

'What's wrong?' she asked.

'I'm being sued for twenty-five million pounds!' he said.

'What? Who by?' asked Dave.

'By the bloke he tiefed the ticket off,' said Tony.

'I didn't tief no fucking ticket!' Justin shouted, at the top of his voice, turning red in the face.

'I mean this bloke says that he tiefed the ticket,' Tony said, as he looked around the crowd of about thirty odd people.

'Everyone just calm down,' said Karen, as she took centre stage. 'You haven't even received the letter of claim yet or spoken to a solicitor, he might not even have a good case.'

'What's she on?' Justin asked, unable to absorb the information and frustrated by the fact that no one seemed to be offering a fast and painless way out of this mess.

'Listen to her,' said Sarah, 'she's off to university soon, to study law.'

'The first thing you have to do is find a good solicitor,' Karen advised confidently, now that her expertise had been confirmed to the crowd. 'Does anyone know a good solicitor?' she asked. There was silence in the room as hazy heads tried to activate their much abused brain cells.

'Hey, I know,' Diamond Dave shot out immediately, 'what about that guy who defended your brother,' he said looking at Jimmy.

'But my brother got sent down, it'll be ages before they let him out of jail.'

'Yeah but your brother was guilty, Justin here's innocent,' Dave said putting his arm around Justin and pinching his cheek. Justin turned red, he was really starting to get fed up with the way Dave kept putting his arm around him or pinching his cheek or both.

'Anyway you'll need a good criminal brief Jus, 'coz you've got that burglary case coming up soon, maybe if you see this geezer about both your problems, you'll get some kind of discount, they do that you know,' Dave finished off. Justin looked confused, what with all the money and celebrating he'd completely forgotten about the approaching trial regarding the burglary he'd confessed to.

'What you reckon?' he asked Sarah, his newest confidant.

'Is this guy good?' she asked looking directly at Jimmy.

'Like I said he didn't get my brother off, but I can remember he got my cousin off a GBH charge, even though my cousin broke the guy's nose. So yeah I guess he must be.'

'You got his number?' Sarah asked.

'Yeah, somewhere at home, so you want him then?'

'We'll go and see him, see if we like him or not. Yeah that's what we'll do babe,' she said prising Justin away from Dave and back into her clutch, 'we'll go and see him and if we don't like the look of him we'll look for some other lawyer, what do you think?'

'That's a wicked idea,' Justin said kissing her in front of the crowd.

'Don't worry babe, I'm here to take care of you now,' she whispered, taking Justin by the hand back in the direction of the bedroom and away from the crowd.

CHAPTER FIFTEEN

Ismail Inanilmaz had called his wife to help him run the shop while he went into the cramped office, which doubled up as his store room, in order to put the finishing touches to his plan. He'd even given the operation a code name, one which he thought was particularly apt for the situation. Operation Freedom wasn't just about scoring some big bucks, it also meant a complete change in his life, a completely new life, for Ismail Inanilmaz was about to score big and then disappear forever.

Ismail had been unhappy for quite sometime, in fact when he reflected on his life it was all he could do to stop himself from crying. An only child, his mother had died when he was young, leaving the arduous duty of raising Ismail to his father, a rather strict, unaffectionate man, whose sole preoccupation in life was the accumulation of money. Almost inevitably Ismail was constantly reminded of how much his upbringing would cost; food, clothes, and books. 'Why do you want books son? You don't need to study. I've provided you with a living right here, this shop.' Ismail shuddered as he remembered his late father's words. It seemed that his whole life had been spent in this damned shop, for he'd been forced to help out after school and at weekends. Yet his father's penny pinching ways earned the family a fortune, for as soon as Ismail turned sixteen his father went on to acquire an off-licence and a few years later a small kebab shop to add to the family's growing empire.

At the age of seventeen, after failing his retakes, Ismail was told that he was to be given the shop. However there was a condition attached to the old man's offer, Ismail would have to marry the daughter of his best friend. An offer the sexually naive and repressed Ismail jumped at. Only to regret later on when he saw what his future wife looked like in person. Ismail recalled how the two had sat in silence unable to look each other in the eye while their fathers discussed the wedding preparations during their first meeting. He had wanted to run out of the house and call the whole thing off. However afraid of his domineering father, Ismail simply obeyed and at the age of nineteen he not only had a shop, a wife and a daughter but was also able to afford a small house for his young family. He reasoned that things could have turned out a lot worse, sure he worked hard and didn't do all the things other kids his age would do, but where would *they* be in five years time? Besides Ismail had a fat inheritance coming his way and all he had to do was stay on the right side of the old man. At the age of twenty-one Ismail's hopes of hitting it big came crashing down when his father died, and Ismail learnt to his horror that the penny pinching miser had left virtually nothing behind.

Having sold the kebab shop and the off-licence for a considerable profit at the age of fifty the old man had decided to go into early retirement. Which was fair enough, Ismail thought at the time, after all he had worked and saved his whole life and done the best he could of raising Ismail by himself, so why shouldn't he put his feet up at the end of his life, right? Unfortunately Ismail was oblivious to the fact that his father, after years of scrimping and saving, had developed a penchant for blowing vast sums of money on the roulette wheel of his local underground casino. In his will Ismail, the sole heir, had been left the sum of ten thousand pounds.

Ismail recovered from the shock well, telling his wife that they still had the shop. The two worked hard and over the years had paid off the mortgage on their small house and managed to raise two daughters, both of whom had done well. His eldest daughter was a solicitor and the other would soon qualify as a doctor. They loved him and he adored them and was immensely proud that they were now able to lead full and independent lives. However, now at the age of forty-two, Ismail had nothing to look forward to but long hours in a shop he had grown to despise, the English winter, and early nights in bed reading a book whilst lying next to a woman for whom he felt great affection but found deeply unattractive.

Yet the beauty of Operation Freedom was that everyone would end up with a fairly decent result. The plan was fiendishly brilliant and completely foolproof. Ismail would send a copy of the video showing Derek buying the winning lottery ticket to Justin's home, the address of which had been fairly easy to find thanks to all the publicity that surrounded the teenager. A note explaining that Ismail wanted the sum of a million pounds would be attached. Next Ismail would take the money and go and live the remainder of his life in a place that was cheap, hot, exotic, but most importantly of all, filled with lots and lots of beautiful women. Brazil!

It had been his life long dream to go there and learn how to samba and surf. He smiled as he thought of those lovely beaches and beautiful, tanned bodies. Sure the first half of his life had been hell but whatever he had left he'd be able to enjoy.

After he'd taken the money and made sure that it was safely out of the country he'd leave his wife and daughters a "Dear John" letter, telling them how much he loved them but that they'd never see him again. Sure they'd be upset and they'd cry but they'd get over it eventually, especially his wife, who he suspected was just as fed up of him as he was of her. He consoled his conscience with the fact that the whole family would be provided for because he'd leave his wife the shop and the house. Yes, it was a win-win situation Ismail convinced himself, and that kid, well he had stolen all that money, so a million pounds would be a small punishment. Why he was even dishing out a bit of justice! Yes, it was indeed the perfect plan, Ismail thought to himself, as he took pen to paper and contemplated about how to start the letter that would explain to Justin that he had just one week to cough up the dough before the original tape of Derek purchasing the ticket would be sent to the police.

'Ismail! Ismail!' It was his wife shouting for him to come to the front of the shop. God all mighty! What did that wretched woman want now?

Ismail got up in a huff, threw the pen onto his desk and marched towards the front of the shop, where his wife was still calling his name.

'All right, all right, shut up, I'm coming for God's sake,' he shouted in Turkish. On reaching the counter he flinched when he saw Derek Bonner standing there with a woman he'd never seen before. Ismail recognised Derek from the video tape he'd watched over and over again, and of course, from the TV and news reports. This was something Ismail hadn't expected at all, for up until this time Derek had been some abstract figure, someone whose existence he'd hardly even been aware of. All that changed now that he was standing here, in person, right in front of him, in his shop.

'They want to talk to you,' his wife said, a trace of concern on her face.

'Go out back and leave me with them,' Ismail commanded in Turkish. She obeyed instantly and without question.

'How can I help you?' Ismail asked, briefly glancing at Derek but letting his eyes rest on the woman, whom he found particularly attractive.

'My name's Christine Havers, I'm a solicitor,' she said handing him a business card, 'and this is my client Derek Bonner.' Derek nodded at Ismail, who tried to smile back pleasantly. Ismail reckoned that Derek was roughly the same age as himself but he seemed even more ragged and jaded. Mind you having your lottery winnings ripped off was bound to have a negative influence on your appearance Ismail reflected.

'You may have seen us on television,' Christine said.

'Yes I have,' Ismail nodded, 'I know about the lottery ticket and everything, I had a policeman here a couple of weeks ago. He asked if I had a video tape of the person who bought the winning lottery ticket.'

'And what was your reply?' Christine inquired.

'I'm afraid I don't have such a tape,' Ismail said as a pang of guilt hit his stomach.

'But you do remember me, don't you?' Derek asked hopefully.

Ismail studied the man's face carefully as he thought about the answer, of course he recognised Derek and damn it he wanted to help the man, not help rip him off, but if Ismail told the truth, Operation Freedom would be completely destroyed.

'No, as I told the officer, I'm afraid I don't I'm sorry. I wish I could help.'

'But you have to, I came in here with my daughter, a little girl, you even asked what her name was,' Derek said, desperately raising his voice an octave or two above what could be considered conversational speech. Ismail looked at him, his eyes paralysed by the pain he saw in the man.

'Are you quite sure?' Christine asked as she put a reassuring hand on Derek's shoulder, calming him down instantly. Ismail nodded his head slowly, unable to look either in the eye.

'If you took part in the trial we would be able to offer financial compensation for your time,' she quickly added.

Ismail considered the proposition for a second before slowly shaking his head, 'I'm sorry I wish I could help but like I told the policeman I just don't remember who bought the ticket.'

Christine nodded her head, hiding her disappointment with great dignity, 'Please keep the card and contact me if you think of anything, absolutely anything that could be of help.'

Ismail watched the pair as they left the shop, his stare no longer on Christine, the attractive woman, but on Derek, the middle-aged, beaten up man. He started to curse himself in Turkish using the exact same words his father would use when scolding him for handing too much change to a customer. Ismail thought that he had come up with a plan that left everyone better off, but he hadn't stopped to consider Derek. For a week now he had been feeling like a genius, a man who was about to dispense justice and compensate himself at the same time, yet all he was really doing was sinking to Justin Farren's level. He held Christine's business card in his hand, thinking carefully about Operation Freedom. Letting out a deep sigh, he called for his wife to return to work. There had to be an answer to all this, some way in which he could balance the injustice which had been committed against Derek as well as carry out the plan that would change his life.

CHAPTER SIXTEEN

Peter J. Cutner peered at the motley crew that sat on the opposite side of his desk. In the ten years he'd been running his practice he'd represented all kinds of criminals, ranging from the deeply sinister and dangerous to the immensely stupid. It took him a second to ascertain into which category Justin and his friend Tony fell. Of course he'd read about the country's youngest ever lottery winner in the papers and like everyone else in Britain he was transfixed by the story.

His eyes bore into Sarah as she bewitched him with her beauty during her explanation of what had happened. She was definitely the brains of the operation, he thought to himself as he focused on those soft, seductive lips. She reminded him of all those sexy, ambitious law students he had met during his younger days. The way beauty and brains melted into one highly sultry embodiment of allure and charm. Yet she had even more, oh yes, so much more, an aura that expelled raw power not just sexual but intellectual and a confidence that defied her age; one that was usually reserved for just the extremely wealthy or talented. He found his eyes wondering downwards, towards her breasts and repeatedly reminded himself that she was just a kid, barely out of school. Yet her confidence and manner portrayed a woman of immense wisdom and worldly knowledge, and of course she was ambitious, her eyes and unassuming demur told him that. Justin was just a way out for her, a one-way meal ticket, the way the law had been a way out of his own working class background. Yes money, civilisation's great equaliser, in no other reality, in no other way, through no conventional means open to normal men could a man like Justin ever hope for a woman like Sarah to give him a second glance. Yet here he was, sitting next to her, proud and arrogant, her hand firmly placed on his thigh as she fought his corner, and judging by the way Justin looked at her when she spoke, she had him wrapped around her little finger. In her hands he was as pliable as plasticine in a kid's playgroup, but did she have the guile to take him all the way?

As a young law student Peter had had dreams of hitting the big time himself, of being a high flying partner in one of the city firms but found upon graduating that the upper-end of the market was tied up. You either had to be a real genius or a member of the old boy's network. Peter who'd had to borrow and steal his way through university and the college of law definitely didn't have any high ranking connections and although he was smart, hardworking and sometimes damn right cunning, he was no legal genius either. The immense competition had confined his role to one of the high street solicitor.

Of course he couldn't complain too ardently, after all he had escaped his working class background, and was able to drive a fairly nice car whilst at the same time paying his mortgage. However he'd grown tired and weary of his clients and had for some years prayed for the one big payoff that could lead to his early retirement. That one old, east-end villain who had been caught importing twenty-million pounds worth of heroin, or that one, fat, old, millionaire businessman, who had fallen for his mistress and was in the midst of a messy divorce battle. He'd never ever thought or hoped that it could come in the form of Justin.

He quickly glanced over the letter Sarah had given him, asking for Justin to appear in court on the charge of burglary, before looking at the letter of claim which had been sent to Justin from Derek's solicitor. A slight shiver crawled its way down Peter's spine as he read the name Christine Havers. He'd crossed swords with her on three previous occasions, all divorces and all outcomes that favoured her clients more than his. She was tough and knew the law like the back of her hand, but she was now in a realm where he felt more comfortable. Part of him couldn't wait to tangle with her again, because like most ambitious solicitors he had his pride and that bloodlust for battle.

'Well,' he said placing the papers neatly on his desk and looking at the three kids with equal measure, 'seeing as your trial for burglary is set for next week it would make sense if we deal with this before moving on to what is possibly the more important legal problem you've brought to me, which, of course, is the claim against you for twenty-five million pounds.'

The three remained silent as they listened to Peter dispense his knowledge as if he were some kind of religious guru. He in turn tried to keep his sentences as brief and free of legal jargon as possible.

'Now you confessed at the police station, and your fingerprints were found all over the victim's place of residence. So it would appear that we have no choice but to put in a plea of guilty, which taking your age and the fact that it's your first offence into consideration might not be such a bad idea. If we also add that there were some mitigating circumstances such as your elderly grandmother not being able to pay her rent on time, well then I think that I might be able to get you off with community service or a fine.'

'That's good news!' Sarah said, leaning over and kissing Justin on the cheek.

'What about the lawsuit?' Tony said, eager to get down to business.

'Well this of course will be a lot more complicated, first lets look at the things you have going against you. You'll have a criminal record and a criminal conviction for burgling this man's property. He is a respectable member of society, you have a reputation as a hoodlum. It's your word against his.'

'Shit,' Justin mumbled as he slowly slumped into his chair.

'However there is also reason not to be too worried by the lawsuit,' Peter continued, 'you see the wheels of justice turn very slowly and we could tie this case up in litigation for many years, all the while you'll be able to spend and enjoy that excessive amount of money, while he on the other hand will be stuck in some cramped up little bedsit. Therefore it's in his interest to settle out of court for a sum of money which could change his life. A couple of million would be pocket change for you but dangled in front of his nose at the right time and in the right way, well who wouldn't take it?'

'So what you're saying is that Justin would be

able to buy him off and keep the rest of the money for himself?' Sarah asked.

'Exactly,' Peter beamed, immensely proud of his cut-throat approach to the law.

'But he tiefed the man's ticket!' Tony exclaimed in disbelief.

Peter rolled his eyes up towards the ceiling, while Justin shot Tony the filthiest look he could manage.

'Shut up you idiot,' Sarah spat out, before thumping him in the shoulder.

'It's very important that you listen to me carefully,' Peter mouthed slowly, 'under no circumstances whatsoever do any of you repeat the fact, privately or publicly that Justin took that ticket. Do I make myself clear?'

The three nodded, and Sarah slapped Tony across the head before calling him an idiot for the second time.

'Now to hasten this strategy I have an idea which should shake the opposition into thinking carefully about how time is against them.'

'What's that?' Justin asked.

'You donate a million pounds to charity, a charity that is dear to the public for example, Save the Children. This will have a two fold effect, it will worry Mr Bonner that you might spend so much that even if he wins the lawsuit there won't be any money left and more importantly it will make you look like a good guy in the eyes of the public.'

'That's smart,' Sarah said in admiration, her eyes and smile uncomfortably distracting Peter from the business at hand. Justin started calculating, although he was just as terrible at maths as he was with any other subject, counting money was something he was quickly becoming apt at. So far he'd spent three and a half million on his house, thirty thousand on furnishings and decorating, a further half a million on a Ferrari, a BMW and a Porsche, seven hundred thousand on various kinds of insurance, but mostly covering the cars and a whacking hundred thousand on gifts to friends, with a further twenty thousand on alcohol, drugs and clothes. That had left him with twenty million and one hundred and fifty thousand pounds. However if he settled with Derek for two million and gave another million to charity, well that would leave him just a paltry eighteen million or so to play with. Of course that was before he paid Peter Cutner for his legal services and bought Sarah an antique diamond ring he heard was being auctioned at Sotheby's, London's most prestigious auction house.

'A million pounds is too much,' Justin said, much to the surprise of everyone in the room.

'What're you talking about?' Sarah asked in disbelief.

'I've only got about twenty-one million pounds left,' Justin said, 'if I give that Bonner guy two million and then another million to charity, that'll leave me with just eighteen large.'

'Shit G what you been doin´?' Tony asked in disbelief. Justin simply shrugged his shoulders.

'OK then, donate three hundred thousand, and issue a statement that you plan to donate a lot more in the future once you've had time to find causes which you feel are worthy. This will have exactly the same effect and cost a lot less,' Peter said in deep contemplation.

'Sweet, I'll do it,' Justin said. His two friends

nodded at Peter in deep appreciation of his wisdom.

'And find yourself a decent financial advisor, because at the rate you seem to be spending money you won't even have enough to pay my fees,' Peter said with a smile. They looked back at him in silence, the irony sadly going above their heads.

'Relax, that was a joke,' he said, managing to get a smile out of Sarah.

'So what next?' Justin asked.

'I'll write up a letter informing Mr Bonner that we deny that he has any claim over the money, however due to the fact the we would like to avoid a very public court battle we might be willing to consider a reasonable out of court settlement. Of course I'll wait nineteen days before sending it out. The longer we make them wait the more powerful our position becomes. In the meantime I'll start preparing your defence on the burglary charge. We'll need to meet again tomorrow so that I can go over a few things.'

'Wicked,' Justin said, seemingly a lot more relaxed and optimistic than he had been when he first walked into Peter Cutner's office. After the three left Peter slowly whirled around in his swivel chair as he thought about Justin, the seventeen year old thief and all that money. There had to be a way for him to get more out of this than his standard hourly rate, all he had to do was find it.

CHAPTER SEVENTEEN

Sarah, like most girls her age, had a love of shopping and could easily spend a whole day choosing what various items of clothing looked best on her. Of course she liked to do this with her best friend Karen, but Karen had deserted her for a new life at Manchester University, where she had begun her law degree. University had also been an option for Sarah, she had left school with two As and a B for her A Levels but she had decided that the conventional route just wasn't for her. Surely there was a better way to live than working or studying. She just couldn't see the point of moving out of home, living in poverty in some unknown area of the country and getting herself in debt just for the privilege of having a career. Karen had said that she was lazy and that someone as smart as her had to study, but Karen didn't know what she was talking about. Like everyone else Sarah had come into contact with, she had tunnel vision and wasn't able to see the world for what it was, one big scam. Life was so short, and for Mr or Mrs Average the most meaningful parts were wasted running around in circles trying to earn a living. No, it definitely wasn't for her. Sarah's only ambition as a child had been to travel and to see the world, there were so many beautiful places out there and all she had ever seen were the concrete blocks which surrounded her. She could remember as a child finding a postcard that had been sent to them by some rich relative who was holidaying in the Bahamas. The picture was of the beach with one solitary palm tree. The sand was pure white, and the sea, which was as clear as a crystal, seemed to sparkle under the gaze of the sun. On finding it in the letterbox Sarah had taken the postcard and shown her mum.

'Yes that's nice, isn't it honey?' said her mum as she glanced at it briefly while changing her younger brother's nappy.

'I want to go too mummy,' Sarah replied.

'Well I'm afraid we can't sugar.'

'Why not?'

'Because only rich people can go to places like that.'

'How can I become rich mummy?'

'Ha, usually when you're born poor you die poor honey. Let's see mummy's poor and my parents were poor and their parents were poor and probably my great grandparents were poor too, but I never met them so I can't be sure.'

'There must be a way mummy.'

Sarah's mum finished putting on her baby brother's nappy and looked at her.

'There is one way.'

'What is it mummy? Please.'

'OK listen to me carefully because I'll only tell you once.'

Sarah nodded her head emphatically.

'When you grow up you have to marry a rich man, not any of the men from around here. They'll just waste your time and break your heart like they did mummy's. So what are you going to do when you grow up?'

'Marry a rich man.'

'That's a good girl.'

'And after I marry the rich man I can go to this place with the white sand?'

'After you marry your rich man you can go anywhere you want honey.'

Perhaps that's where it had all started, the dream of escaping from the inner-city and running away to some far-off land, of finding a rich man that could provide for her, so that she'd never have to work again, so that she'd never have to be like her mother. It seemed like everyone wanted to escape from London, Karen had found her way, now all Sarah had to do was find hers.

Karen's absence sank Sarah's heart, particularly on days like this, where a girl needed her best friend's advice. But Karen's absence had been replaced by the arrival of a new friend, a gold master card, kindly given to her by Justin and with a credit limit of ten thousand pounds! Of course Justin was the guarantor and so it was only with a slight twinge of guilt that she hit Oxford Street determined to wave goodbye to her boredom with a decent day's shopping. What had followed was an orgy of mass spending on goods at extortionately high prices. She'd purchased everything from Gucci shoes to Armani bags and of course had to hire a taxi driver for the day in order to help her carry all her goodies.

On returning home and unpacking all her shopping she started worrying about all the money that she and Justin were spending. Luckily she had persuaded him to seek out the help of a financial advisor just like their solicitor Peter J. Cutner had suggested. She wondered what the J. stood for as she admired the way her new Gucci shoes matched the slick Versace dress she wore. The full length mirror in their bedroom had been her idea but Justin liked it because he could look in it when they had sex. There was another mirror on the ceiling, positioned above the bed. She rolled her eyes in disgust, as she remembered the last time she had to put up with him touching her. She had hoped that with a little practice and training his skills as a lover would have improved, but if anything they'd actually deteriorated. Now that solicitor, he was probably good in bed, as well as being smart and extremely handsome. He was probably wealthy too, although nowhere near as wealthy as Justin. She sighed, her mother had once said that, 'You can't have everything,' and for the first time Sarah understood what she really meant.

Thinking about her mother made Sarah sad, mostly because her mother, who was also a very attractive woman, had lived such a hard life. Three kids from three different men, all of whom were wasters. Sarah had promised herself not to follow in her mother's footsteps. If anything her mother had encouraged her to use her natural attributes and make men work for her. Why should she work if she didn't have to? So far she hadn't done badly at all. Just eighteen years old and living with a multi-millionaire! It was easy to control the younger and more inexperienced Justin and if she played her cards right she might come up with a way of separating him for all that cash. Now wouldn't that be a result? After all, he hardly deserved it, did he? Wouldn't there be a certain irony if Justin lost his fortune to an even more accomplished thief? Sarah smiled as she let her dress fall to the floor and stood in front of the mirror naked, but still in her Gucci shoes. There was a certain sexiness attached to that word, 'thief', she whispered it out of her mouth and felt a tingle run down her spine.

Christine knew exactly why Derek was waiting outside her office to see her. On the front cover of every tabloid paper was the latest news that Justin had donated three hundred thousand pounds to Save the Children. More worrying was his promise of future donations.

Christine also knew that keeping Derek waiting outside wouldn't help in calming him down and so she buzzed her secretary and told her to let him in. In a rage Derek slammed the morning newspaper down on her desk, 'Have you seen this?' he said, his cheeks flushed with rage.

'He can't just go around spending my money like that!'

'Well I'm afraid he can. Of course I'll be applying to the courts requesting that his assets are frozen until after the trial, but until we get some kind of reply in regard to our letter of claim there simply isn't anything else I can do.'

Derek sat down on the chair in front of Christine's desk, his head slumped in his hands. It was a position she had seen Derek adopt fairly often over the time they'd spent together.

'Look, you're just going to have to be patient and trust me, I know what I'm doing.'

'Do you? I wonder sometimes, I mean I hardly came out of my divorce well, did I?'

'Mr Bonner, if you think that I'm not professionally capable of representing you then I suggest you find another solicitor, you know where the door is!'

'Look I'm sorry, I take back what I said, it's just . . .'

'I know, I understand, you're going through a difficult time, but like I said, you're going to have to learn to be patient.'

'It's just that, well I also found out that I lost my job today.'

'Oh God, I'm sorry.'

Derek put up his hands as if her were trying to stop an on coming vehicle, pity was the last thing he wanted.

'It's my fault really, I kept phoning in sick. I just couldn't handle going into work anymore.'

Christine took sometime to reflect, she remembered that he had been an accountant but had lost his job and been forced to take on something menial. Had he been doing the same job all this time?

'What are you going to do?' Christine asked with sincere concern.

'Apply for benefits I guess,' Derek said, unable to look into her eyes.

'Don't worry we all go through bad patches, you're not the first client I've seen go through hell and I'm sure you won't be the last,' Christine said, as she smiled reassuringly at Derek. Derek made an effort and smiled back, she was a great lady but didn't really know what she was talking about. She didn't seem to understand that his bad patch had already lasted over three years.

Tony sat back on Justin's luxury armchair watching the same action film for the third time that week. Justin's large screen TV was great for such films but even better when accompanied by a spliff from a large pile of skunk that Justin had also bought and kept in his living room.

Justin had generously given Tony one of the bedrooms upstairs and now Tony had become a permanent fixture of the house. Tony reasoned that Justin's generosity was because he felt guilty about not splitting the lottery cash with him. Last week Tony had gently broached the subject, but Justin had fobbed him off by saying that they shouldn't divide it up yet. That if he gave half his money to Tony then it would make them look like partners, enforcing Derek's claim against him.

Tony pulled heavily on the spliff, using the fumes to calm his nerves. That Justin had become a right slippery bastard. He knew full well that he had no intention of giving him any money. Did Justin really think he could trick him with that bullshit story about it being too early to divide the money? Justin and the money, the money and Justin, the two whirled around his mind constantly day and night. There had to be a way to get the money. He knew that Justin loved him like a brother, that despite being a greedy bastard he didn't want to lose his friendship. The two had become so close that there wasn't a single day of the year where they didn't see each other or talk to each other on the phone. They'd done jobs together! They were partners in crime, but most importantly Tony had been there for Justin when he had really needed a friend, when no one else had even wanted to know him.

Still the shift in power in their relationship concerned Tony. He didn't want to end up being Justin's 'yes' boy, but at the same time if he pushed him too much for his half of the money Justin might just tell him to fuck off, leaving Tony completely out of the picture and in a worse place than when this whole thing had first started.

Watching the film for the third time bored Tony and so he got up and went to turn on the hi-fi. Like the TV and the DVD player it was the most expensive one on the market. Tony chose one of Justin's rap CDs and turned up the volume until it was loud enough to cause the doors to vibrate.

When Tony turned back round to return to his seat he was surprised to find Sarah standing in the doorway, observing him in silence. He smiled at her in acknowledgment and watched as she walked towards the hi-fi and turned the volume down to a less deafening level.

'Where's Justin?' she asked.

'Don't know,' Tony said, shrugging his shoulders and putting out what was left of the spliff in the ashtray.

'I'm bored,' Sarah said, sitting on the large couch near the hi-fi. Tony joined her, looking into her eyes for any hostility as he did so. Her smile welcomed him.

'Fancy a spliff?' Tony asked.

'No, I'm bored of spliffs, and of coke, and of drink, and of shopping, and of everything.'

Tony didn't respond, but looked at Sarah in silence as he studied the way her legs were now curled up under her buttocks.

'I miss Karen,' he said finally, causing Sarah to look back at him with interest.

'Yeah me too,' she said, shifting slightly closer to him and placing a hand on his shoulder, 'but don't worry you'll find someone else.'

He looked straight into her eyes, did she fancy him as much as he fancied her?

'You for real?' he asked sheepishly.

'Yes, you're very handsome.'

'She'd have to be tick, like you,' he said, as he tried to allure her with his darkly penetrating eyes. His directness caused her to blush but she looked back at the eyes with a primal hunger Tony had learnt to recognise in girls. Slowly but surely he leant forward until his lips touched hers. The kiss started off slowly and gently but quickly grew into one filled with passion and lust. After a while they broke off for air and Tony held her head gently in his hands. No words were spoken because nothing needed to be said, they understood each other completely. They were about to kiss again when they heard the front door slam shut. Quickly Tony jumped onto the armchair and Sarah refolded her long, elegant legs to her side.

'What you doing?' Justin asked, looking at them both.

'Just had a spliff,' Tony said, nodding his head in the direction of the ashtray.

'My day's been shit,' Justin said, as he sat next to Sarah and confidently put his arm around her.

'Why? Where were you?' she asked.

'I was at that financial advisor you kept banging on about and then at my solicitor's,' Justin said, shaking his head in disgust.

'And?' Sarah asked growing impatient.

'The financial advisor told me that I've got to stop spending so much money, that at the rate I'm going my money will be gone within five years.'

'Shit,' said Tony, 'what you gonna do?'

'He goes that what I've got to do is decide how

much I want to spend every year, he reckons it shouldn't be more than a hundred and fifty thousand pounds. Then I have to put that in some kind of current account, while he invests the rest for me in stocks and bonds and funds and all other kinds of shit.'

'So what's the problem?' asked Sarah.

'I goes to him that I want to open up a nightclub somewhere and he just shook his head and looked at me like I'm some kind of idiot. "The last thing you should do Mr Farren is start a business venture; you just don't have the experience," Chief,' Justin said as he sucked his teeth.

Tony bit his lip and repressed a smile, looking over at Sarah he could see that she was doing the same. It seemed that the financial advisor had worked out pretty quickly what a plonker Justin was.

'Oh don't worry baby, I know it's your dream to have a nightclub, but maybe you should listen to the man, after all he is a professional,' Sarah said as she stroked Justin's hair reassuringly.

'Anyways, if you listen to this geezer, he'll increase your moneys, in no time you'll be worth fifty mill G then you can open up a nightclub and if doesn't work just walk away,' Tony said, with a nod and a smile.

'You see that's what we'll do baby, wait a bit and let the money grow. A good business man knows when to be patient,' Sarah said giving Justin a naughty wink. He smiled and relaxed a bit.

'Anyways, I've got other problems.'

'Why ? What else happened baby?' Sarah asked, the beauty of her face crumpled by a frown of worry.

'After all that I went to the solicitor's, he reckons that I should get off with a fine, but was worried ´coz the press, and in particular the Daily Mail was, portraying me in a negative light. They were saying that the three hundred grand might not be mine to give away, that I'm up on a charge of burglary, that I'm being sued for fraud, that criminals in this country were allowed to get away with too much and that I should be made an example of. I asked if it meant that I could get sent down and he said it could. Then he said that I shouldn't worry because if I received a custodial sentence he'd be able to ask for a mistrial claiming that I wasn't able to receive a fair trial because of all the negative statements about me in the press and media.'

'G that means you wouldn't even ´ave to pay the fine, you'd totally get away with it,' Tony said.

'I could still end up doing time.'

'Oh don't worry baby you won't go to prison,' Sarah said, clutching him and cradling his head near her bosom. 'And even if you did, I'd still be here waiting for you.'

'Would you?' Justin asked, looking up at her.

'I'd wait for you my whole life if I had to.'

Tony adverted his eyes, this scene was starting to make him feel sick. Angry and frustrated he started rolling another spliff. Justin reached up with his lips and kissed Sarah who responded enthusiastically. 'Let's go upstairs,' he whispered into her ear, but still loud enough for Tony to hear. She smiled and nodded her head slightly, allowing him to lead her by the hand. As he passed Tony, with Sarah in tow Justin winked at his best friend, who couldn't stop himself from looking up at the couple. Sarah shrugged her shoulders as if to apologize to Tony before rolling her eyes up to the sky, indicating that she didn't really want to go. Tony watched on helplessly as the girl he'd been kissing passionately not long ago was led up the stairs to his best friend's bedroom.

CHAPTER EIGHTEEN

Derek's anticipation grew everyday as the deadline for Justin's solicitor to respond to the letter of claim drew closer. He'd decided that he would settle without a trial for half of the twenty-five million. With no job and his rent already in arrears he was in desperate need of some cash. Signing on had pained him, but he had no choice and after all he was entitled to those benefits, he had worked and paid his taxes all his life. It was about time the state gave him something back, although he hadn't realised how pitiful the money he received would be.

Of course he hoped that Ms Havers, who now insisted that he call her Christine, was capable of negotiating such a substantial sum from that thief. If not, well he might have to consider what his next move would be, but for now he put all thoughts of the lawsuit out of his mind as he approached his former home. For today was Saturday and as usual it was the one day of the week he had visiting rights to see his kids. It had been sometime since his son, Tom, had seen him but at least his daughter, Tina, was interested in seeing her dad. He rang the front doorbell and expected to see John answer the door, as this had been the routine they had fallen into every Saturday. So it was with some understandable apprehension that he greeted his ex-wife when she opened the door.

'You're not seeing her,' Jane sneered at Derek through the half open door.

'What? Why not? What's going on here?' he asked, concerned and angry at the same time.

'You haven't paid this month's maintenance,' she said, before making an attempt to close the door. He stopped her with his foot.

'But I must have forgotten,' he said, 'you know, what with all that's been going on and all, please let me see her, I'll get on to it straight away.' His eyes pleaded for that one ounce of humanity he truly believed she had in her soul.

'No, I'm sorry, but if you don't carry out your duty as a father financially you're not entitled to see them.'

'This isn't fair Jane, I've always paid before.'

'Exactly, so there's no reason you shouldn't pay now, is there? When I get the money I'll let you have the access to them that was agreed in the divorce,' she said before forcefully pushing him out of the front door and almost down the front step. Derek regained his balance just in time to see the front door slam in his face. Pitifully he looked around for any sign of his children and noticed Tina looking at him through the living room window. She'd witnessed the whole ugly scene and had a look of jagged sorrow about her. She put her hand against the window, Derek did the same and they smiled at each other before she was torn away by her mother and the curtain quickly drawn.

Slowly Derek left the front garden and began the forlorn walk back to his bus stop. How could he have forgotten to pay the maintenance for the kids? Of course he knew the answer was simply because he'd been so distracted by the happenings of the recent two months. What worried him more was that being unemployed would mean that he would no longer have the money to pay for the maintenance. If he didn't get his hands on some cash soon he'd be on his way to losing Tina as well. He tried not to cry as he waited for his bus.

Justin had listened in disbelief as he was handed his sentence, a fine of one thousand pounds. He threw his fist into the air and shouted out a big, 'Yes!' before looking around the courtroom and remembering where he was. On seeing the stern look his solicitor was giving him, Justin looked down at his shoes, pretending deep anguish at the situation he found himself in, and an even deeper regret at the actions which had led to him being in the courtroom. He had to bite his tongue as hard as he could in order to repress the laughter that was building inside and dying to get out.

Karen had settled in to university life well, and had even managed to make a few friends. Out of all these new friends the one she felt closest to was Beth. Beth lived in the room next to Karen's and although they were both on different courses it seemed natural that they hung around together.

'Giles is really good looking, but he's such a twat,' Beth said as the two girls assessed the various men who had been presented to them during the Fresher's Ball.

'Tell me about it, at least you don't have him on your course. I have to see him everyday. All he talks about is his father the famous QC. I mean who does he think he's going to impress . . .'

'What's wrong?' asked Beth.

'I think that's my mobile ringing,' Karen sad as she dashed out of the room. Opening the door to her bedroom, she jumped on her bed and quickly grabbed the phone.

'Hello.'

'Hello, Karen, it's me Sarah.'

'Sarah, how are you? I've missed you so much.'

'That's why you've been phoning everyday, isn't it? You cow.'

'Oh, don't be like that, I've just been really busy settling in.'

'How is it up there?'

'It's really great, the people are friendly, although there are lots of wankers, and I've got absolutely no work to do for my course yet, so all we're doing is partying.'

'Wow, that sounds really great.'

'It is. What about you? How are things with Justin?'

'They're OK. I'm living with him in his mansion now.'

'Really? How big is it?'

'It's massive, you'll have to come down and visit.'

'I will do, as soon as I can. So everything's OK?'

'Yeah, the only problem we have is that Justin is in court today on account of that burglary charge.'

'Oh, I'm sorry.'

Sarah laughed, 'Don't be, he'll probably get let off with community service.'

'Well it is his first offence, isn't it?'

'Yeah, that's right.'

'Should be all right then.'

'So what else is new?' Sarah asked.

'Nothing really. I'm glad you phoned, it's so nice to hear your voice.'

'When will you come down and visit?'

'Maybe in a couple of weeks, just for the weekend.'

There was an uncomfortable silence as Sarah thought about what to say.

'You remember Tony, don't you?'

'Oh yeah, of course.'

'He's living with us as well.'

'Is he? How is he?'

'He's all right too. Asks about you sometimes, do you want me to say hi?'

'No, don't bother. There're loads of fit blokes up here.'

'So you're not into him anymore?'

'No, not at all. Why?'

'No reason, just asking. Listen I've got to go, Justin's trial should be over soon. Give us a call and come down soon.'

'I will do. Miss you loads.'

'Miss you too.'

Sarah felt relief as soon as she'd ended the call. She had felt guilty over kissing Tony, but if Karen was no longer into him then everything was OK.

Terry had known that going to the trial with Derek was a mistake, but he just didn't see any alternative. Afraid of the damage Derek could inflict on himself and unable to persuade him to stay away, Terry felt obliged to be by his friend's side when that smarmy bastard was sentenced.

Terry had listened in silence as Derek had let loose about justice finally being done. He had repeated the fact that he hoped they locked up the little toerag and threw away the key. Secretly Terry had feared the worse, that Justin was going to be let off with a slap on the wrists, but not even he had thought that he'd be let off so lightly. A thousand pound fine? For God's sake it was an insult, no wonder the country was being overrun with young hoodlums.

Outside the court Terry urged his friend to leave, but Derek was having none of it.

'I want to tell that little shit exactly what I think of him,' Derek spat out, as he pushed his way through the swarm of reporters and journalists all of whom were tussling with each other for access to Justin. Knocking a few to the ground, Derek finally made it to the front, where in shock horror he saw Justin posing for the cameras, as his solicitor read out some bullshit statement about how his client regretted his past actions, how poverty had led him to crime and how fair the British justice system was in allowing a young man a second chance.

'That's bullshit!' Derek screamed. Suddenly all eyes were on him, TV cameras pointed in his direction, paparazzi photographers lined up their lenses on his face. Justin instantly recognised who the angry man charging towards him was and ran behind his solicitor for protection.

'Now just hold on a second,' Peter said, as Derek came closer, 'you're being recorded and if you touch my client I'll have you up on assault charges.'

'Touch your client, I'm going to kill him,' Derek roared, as he made a lunge at the solicitor who was actually guarding the boy. Luckily Terry managed to grab hold of Derek before his hands could clasp around the solicitor's throat.

'Get off me!' Derek screamed, as a couple of journalists helped Terry hold him back from his quarry.

'As you can see, my client is a peaceful member of society and despite being sworn at and physically threatened hasn't retaliated in anyway,' Peter said, placing his hand around Justin's mouth just as he emerged from behind the solicitor's back on realisation that Derek had been neutralised. Justin took the hint and remained quiet as Derek tried to break through the army of men that were now preventing him from getting through to Justin.

'It's my fucking money!' he screamed. 'Do you hear me? I want my fucking money back!'

'Come on mate this isn't the time or the place, you're just making things worse for yourself,' Terry said, still holding on to Derek with all his strength. When he felt Derek relax he let go of his grip and walked his friend away from the crowd and the court.

Justin shook his head as the TV cameras focused in on his face, one that looked genuinely sad and worried.

'You see that man's really crazy. I don't know if he really believes he won the lottery, or if it's just some scam in order to get money out of me, but I tell you it won't work.'

Peter impressed with his client's on the spot ingenuity, reinforced Justin's position by saying that he now felt afraid for his client's safety, and would be applying to the courts for an injunction. The journalists went wild and fired questions at the pair like a machine gun shoots out bullets, but Peter, who was almost as talented a showman as he was a solicitor, decided that they should end the show on that positive footing, and with merriment raised his hand to the cameras and said, 'I'm sorry but my client won't be answering any more questions.' It was a sentence and a moment he had waited for throughout his career, and he reflected on it with great satisfaction as the two got into the chauffeur driven Mercedes that was awaiting them.

Ismail Inanilmaz watched the whole fiasco outside the courthouse from the comfort of his shop. The distance however didn't stop the gut-wrenching feeling of guilt.

'Do you think he did it?' asked an old woman.

'I don't know,' Ismail said, not really wanting to be reminded of the situation.

'I reckon he did it,' she said, 'he looks like a nasty piece of work that boy, I just hope that poor man gets back his money.'

'Yeah me too, if, of course, the money really is his,' Ismail said, forcing a smile. Being pleasant to customers was the part of his job he'd come to loath the most, worse even than the early morning starts. Why couldn't they just keep their mouths shut, buy whatever it was they wanted and fuck off?

'Oh well all the best dear,' she said, as she slowly plodded along to the exit.

'You too, and watch out it's slippery and wet outside,' Ismail said pleasantly.

'I will do, bye bye then.'

'Yeah fuck off you old bat,' Ismail whispered under his breath as the door closed. He held his head in his hands. What was happening to him? He never used to be so full of hate, he even remembered the time long ago when he had actually enjoyed talking to the customers. Quite simply he'd spent too long in this place, it was starting to eat him up. The shop had been his prison for as long as he could remember, his whole life had been wasted waking up at the crack of dawn, stacking shelves and serving customers. He had to escape before he went mad, and if that meant Derek got the shaft, well then let it be. If he hadn't been so stupid he wouldn't have lost the lottery ticket in the first place, Ismail justified to himself. He'd try to think of another way of getting his million out of Justin and setting things right for Derek at the same time, but if he hadn't thought of anything by the end of the week, well then Derek could go whistle. There was just one person Ismail had to take care of and that was himself.

CHAPTER NINETEEN

Justin rewound the part of the tape where the camera focuses on his very innocent face and he says, 'You see that man's crazy. I don't know if he really believes he won the lottery, or if it's just some scam in order to get money out of me, but I tell you it won't work.'

The room burst into hysterics for the third time. 'That's great Jus,' said Diamond Dave, 'play it for us just one more time.' Justin did as his guest requested and watched in quiet satisfaction at how the audience he had gathered for his party watched the screen, mesmerised by their host's presence. Again they all laughed. 'You're a free man,' Jimmy said.

'That's right, I tief twenty-five mill from the man's yard and they make me pay back a thousand,' Justin boasted proudly, a joint in one hand and a whisky and coke in the other. Of course his guests laughed on cue, Justin had become quite the performer.

In disgust Sarah left the room, sometimes she just couldn't stand the sight of that idiot and his band of arse lickers. Their solicitor had warned the fool never to admit to stealing the ticket to anyone, but here he was showing off and boasting about it in front of people he didn't even know that well. She walked into their bedroom and sat on the king-size bed. They were only here because of the money, she despised them for it. Hollow, shallow people who could be bought at the drop of a hat, but then again wasn't that her? How could she judge them? She was the one who shared his bed, a labour she was fast becoming bored of.

'I saw you leave the party. Are you all right?'

She looked up, it was Tony standing in the doorway. Remembering that first, all important kiss they had, Sarah couldn't help but smile at him.

'I'm all right I suppose, but can you hear that idiot bragging to everyone about how he stole the man's ticket? And after the solicitor told him to keep his mouth shut? Just what the fuck's he playing at?'

'He thinks he's invincible,' Tony said, entering the room and sitting beside her on the bed. She noticed how recently he'd been trying to drop the street language around her. If his intention had been to impress her it was working. She could sense that Tony was a lot more intelligent than he made out.

'It's such a shame it wasn't you who took that ticket,' she said, placing her hand on his knee. He simply shrugged, not knowing what to say. They stared at each other as the sexual tension in the air bubbled. Finally Tony lent forward and they embraced passionately, the kiss strong and hard, like they both needed it more than just wanted it.

'Lock the door,' Sarah said, as they broke for air.

Tony obeyed, only hesitating slightly once the door was securely closed, 'But what if Justin looks for you?'

'Don't worry about Justin,' Sarah smiled, as she stood up and let her dress fall to the floor, 'he'll be far to busy bragging about how great he is to even notice we're gone.'

Christine had braced herself for the meeting with Derek, she didn't have good news and was afraid of how he would react. He seemed to be on a hair-trigger recently, and she worried about what the poor man might do next, especially after his idiotic outburst in front of the TV cameras after Justin's trial.

Of course Christine understood why he had done it, she could only begin to guess at how much he'd suffered these last few years, but that was just an excuse and the law courts could be a most unforgiving place.

Derek sank into the chair, his head in his hands and stared at the floor. Minutes elapsed while the two sat in silence. As ever Christine was pressed for time, but concern for her client kept her eyes off the clock that hung above the door to her office.

'Aren't you going to say something?' she asked, the frown lines on her forehead deepening.

'What should I say?' Derek asked as he looked up at her, desperately holding back the tears, 'I'm stuffed, aren't I?'

'You're not stuffed, we've just been given a couple of bad blows, that's all. The fight is far from over.'

'I messed up, my friend Terry, he warned me to stay away from the trial, but I just wouldn't listen.'

'Look, don't beat yourself up over it. You made a mistake it's not the end of the world, just make sure you don't break any of the rules in the court order.'

Derek nodded his head slowly, right now he hated himself more than ever. How could he be so stupid? Why didn't he ever learn? Because of his stupid behaviour after Justin's trial that son of a bitch solicitor, Cutner, had successfully applied for an injunction banning Derek from having any contact with the thief that had stolen his money!

'Can he use this against me?' Derek asked, already fearing the worse.

Christine took sometime to consider her answer, the law wasn't as clear cut as most would imagine it to be, and sometimes there simply weren't any right or wrong answers. 'Quite possibly if we went to trial, then yes his solicitor could use the fact that you threatened his client with physical violence against you. However the damage this would inflict on the actual case is minimal, after all the case isn't about you. Also one could argue quite reasonably that anyone who'd had twenty-five million pounds stolen from them would also want to throttle the perpetrator,' she smiled at Derek when she said this, and managed to draw a laugh out of him. Christine had seen the footage of his actions and whilst disappointed with the damage it could cause to their case admired Derek for his passion.

'So all isn't lost then?' Derek asked.

'Far from it, but please no more public outbursts like that, things are, lets say fragile enough as they stand.'

Derek nodded.

'Which brings me onto my next point, yesterday I got a reply for our letter of claim . . .'

'And?' Derek asked, full of hope yet also in trepidation.

'Please bear in mind that I was expecting them to play hardball with us . . .'

'They don't want to settle?'

'Now I didn't say that, please remember that we're still sparring right now, the actual fight hasn't begun.'

'What did they say?' Derek asked growing impatient.

'They deny your claim to the money, but in order to avoid a public trial are willing to settle for the amount of ten thousand pounds.'

'Ten thousand pounds!' Derek shouted out incredulously. 'Is this some idea of a sick joke? He steals my money and then offers me ten poxy grand?'

Christine waited for Derek to calm down before she started to address his concerns.

'Yes, ten poxy grand,' Christine said, again smiling. Derek looked at her unable to understand the humour in the situation. 'It's quite common for this kind of negotiating to take months, with the defendant, of course, wanting to settle for the least amount possible. He's just throwing the first stone, testing the waters, hoping that with the advantage of time on his side, that we'll be ground down and forced to settle for an amount that is considerably less than we would expect to see.'

'So what're we going to do?'

'I say lets fight back, lets really show this guy we're ready to fight and at the same time put the fear of God into him. Of course the final decision is yours but I want to write back saying that you feel completely insulted by his offer of ten thousand pounds and that you now want to proceed and sue him for the full amount.'

'But doesn't that mean I could end up with nothing? I mean if we lost the case then he'd walk away with the whole lot.'

'Quite possibly, but would you be able to sleep at night knowing that he bought you off for a few thousand pounds? As the case builds against them, they'll come back to us with another offer, one I'm sure you'll find more reasonable. Why, as soon as the date for trial approaches, he might counter with another offer, or he might write back as soon as he receives our letter saying that we'll see him in court.'

Derek contemplated her words, she was right, he wanted at least a couple of million out of that thief, any less than that and Derek would be tormented for the rest of his life by the fact that he'd beaten the odds and won the lottery only to have it snatched away from him. True he was desperate for cash and couldn't even afford to pay the maintenance required to see his kids, but he needed enough money to last him the rest of his life and also enough to prove to himself that he wasn't a doormat.

'Do it,' Derek said, sucking in a big gulp of air.

CHAPTER TWENTY

Sarah lay on her back, staring up at the ceiling while Justin prodded away coming ever closer to his eventual climax. Occasionally Sarah let out a sigh or groan, if only to speed up the process but most importantly to stop him asking all those stupid questions afterwards about his performance? 'How was it?' 'Did you enjoy it?' and of course her favourite, 'Was I good?' What did he expect her to say? She could hardly turn round and tell him the truth, 'No, Justin you weren't good, in fact you were pretty crap, I've received more sexual pleasure from sitting on top of a washing machine.'

Sarah noted that he seemed to be taking longer today, a full three minutes had elapsed and his pace hadn't slowed at all, nor was he making the usual pathetic noises of holding his breath or that stupid face he'd screw when he'd go over last Sunday's football scores or whatever it was he did to make himself last those two extra vital minutes. Damn he must have smoked a spliff, she thought to herself as she spontaneously let out another moan. If Justin had smoked a spliff it meant that he would carry on for ten minutes. She looked up at him and noticed the screwed up face, if he was counting the football scores and had smoked a spliff that meant twelve minutes, Justin's record. She looked up at him again, yep he was definitely going for the record.

She successfully repressed the urge to burst out laughing, why were men so pitiful? Then she remembered Tony. God, he was so damn good, just like Karen had said, but it wasn't just the way he looked, or that smooth face he possessed, or those big sparkling eyes or the slim but masculine figure, packed with just the right amount of muscle. Nor was it the trim waist and the almost obligatory six-pack, or that big, juicy prick of his. No it was the way he looked at you, as he peeled away those clothes, a hungry, needful look, a look that said 'I want you, therefore I have you.' It was the way he held you, like when you were with him, you were one, but most importantly it was the way he skimmed his fingers along your body with electrifying accuracy, building your excitement until you couldn't bare it any longer and you shouted, 'fuck me, fuck me now! Please fuck me!'

Oh God, had she actually said that out aloud? Justin speeded up his pace, shouting, 'Yeah that's it I'm gonna fuck you, I gonna fuck you good, I'm . . .'

His face contorted and he let out a loud sigh before collapsing on top of her, she bit the inside of her mouth until she tasted her own blood in order to stop her laughter and held him tightly, so close to her body that he couldn't see her face.

Why couldn't it be Tony who had the money instead of Justin? If Tony had the money he would take her to the Bahamas and anywhere else she wanted to go. Justin's only ambition was to stay in London and play the gangster. He was so unimaginative. It was great being a lady of leisure but putting up with Justin was a real chore, much harder than she had originally imagined. If Tony could just get his fair share of the money then everything would be OK. She could still be a lady of leisure but without Justin. It would be nice to be Tony's kept woman. Lady of leisure, kept woman, Sarah smiled. Society looked down on such women, but she knew the truth, whoever insulted such a woman was just jealous because she could do what they never could or dared to do. The only problem facing her now was how to have Tony and the money, and get shot of Justin. It was a conundrum she thought about more and more.

'That was great,' Justin said, finally recapturing his strength and rolling off her. 'Did you like it?'

'Oh yes, very much,' Sarah said, looking into his eyes, 'you were great.'

Derek had phoned Jane two days ago and said that he would bring along two hundred pounds in cash so that he could see his two children. She had said that he was still a hundred short but because of the circumstances she would allow him to visit them this Saturday. Secretly Jane hadn't agreed to allow Derek to visit out of the goodness of her heart, she was hedging her bets in case Derek ever got his money back. John had suggested that she might be entitled to more maintenance for the kids if Derek were a multi-millionaire.

As Derek approached the house he remembered that he had another reason to feel indebted to his friend Terry, who had lent him the two hundred pounds. He didn't know how he'd pay his best friend back for all his kindness but he had to find a way.

Ringing the doorbell Derek somehow knew that it was John who would answer.

'Ah she's all ready for you today, been waiting for two hours to see her daddy,' he said, before leaning forward toward Derek, his face ever so contrite. 'Do you have the money?'

Derek looked at him in astonishment and disgust. John shrugged his shoulders, 'Jane asked me, you know how it is.'

Derek took the wad of cash and thrust it into John's hand, 'I want to see my son too,' he said. John looked at him sheepishly.

'I'm not sure that's such a good idea,' he said.

'Why not?'

'Well you know, with his outburst last time and all, I don't think he's changed his mind about seeing you.'

'Look he's my son and I have a right to see him.'

'OK, have it your way,' John said, stepping aside and allowing Derek into the house.

Derek walked into the living room, where he found Tina putting on her coat. Jane was sitting on the couch drinking some tea.

'What's he doing here?' she asked John, her face almost giving away the fact that she was ready to give him a public scolding.

'He wants to see Tom,' John said.

Jane looked at Derek, her eyes narrowing, 'He's upstairs in his bedroom, make sure you knock before you enter,' she said with a frown that troubled Derek deeply. It was as if Jane was anxious about Derek seeing Tom. Perplexed he climbed the familiar stairs of his old house until he reached the top and with ease found Tom's room. The door was closed and so Derek swallowed hard before nervously knocking on it.

'Come in,' said the much deeper voice of his son. For an instant Derek almost didn't recognise it, but then he understood completely, Tom's voice was breaking. Embittered by how much time he'd lost with his son, Derek slowly opened the door. Tom, who was lying on his bed watching a DVD, looked surprised to see him and stopped the film before sitting up on his bed. He stared at his father hard but didn't say anything.

'Hi,' said Derek nervously before awaiting some kind of response from his son. Tom briefly glanced at him with contempt before looking away in the opposite direction. Slowly and full of hesitation Derek crept into the room before sitting on Tom's bed.

'You've gotten bigger,' he said.

'What do you want?' asked his son coldly.

'The same as every father in the world, the chance to spend some time with his son. I miss you.'

'Well you should have thought about all that before, it's too late now.'

'Look son, what happened between me and your mum, well it doesn't have anything to do with you.'

Tom shook his head, 'You don't understand shit.'

Silently Derek despaired, was there no getting through to this kid?

'Then help me understand son,' his voice was soft, almost a whisper.

'Understand what? That because of you I'm the school joke. Kids make fun of me because I'm the son of the man who won the lottery but lost all the money. They make fun of me.'

Derek breathed in heavily, he couldn't believe what he was hearing. He had thought that things couldn't get any worse, that belief was now blown away in an instant. He tried to think of something to say, but couldn't.

'I'm sorry son.'

'Sorry! Is that it?'

'Tom, please believe me, things will get better.'

'No they won't, how can they? You lost the money and everyone knows it.'

Derek reached up to put his hand on Tom's shoulder but Tom pulled away.

'Don't touch me, I hate you and I never want to see you again.'

'You can't mean that.'

'Just go away!' Tom shouted.

Derek got up and made to leave the room, stopping briefly in the doorway, as he tried to think of something to tell his son. He wanted to say something that would make everything better, or that at the very least would dampen his son's hatred but looking at the revulsion in Tom's eyes he finally acknowledged the fact that he had lost his son. Regretfully he walked out of Tom's room and back down the stairs to the living room, where Tina was waiting for him.

Jane, John and Tina were watching the TV, sitting on the couch together they looked like the perfect family. How Derek envied John. He reflected on the times when it was him who had sat watching the TV with his wife and children. He had taken those times for granted back then. He remembered the times when he would return home tired from work and Tom would annoy him by wanting to play football in the garden, or when Jane would insist on talking when all he wanted to do was switch his brain off and watch telly, or when Tina would want help with her homework. How he wished he could have those times back now.

'I suppose he told you about the trouble he's having at school,' Jane said. Unable to speak Derek simply nodded.

'I think I'll make myself a cup of tea,' said John, as he retreated to the kitchen.

'Well I've spoken to his teachers and they've promised to keep an eye on him but I wouldn't hold my breath, you know how cruel kids can be.'

'Yeah, I remember,' Derek said, having been a victim of bullying himself.

'I've also had a word with Tina's teachers,' Jane said, putting a protective arm around her daughter.

'Tina?'

'Yes, she's been picked on as well.'

Derek looked at his daughter as he was overcome by a deep sadness. When Tom had first started going to school he had been worried that maybe his son would be bullied. After all most boys experience it at some point in their school lives, but Tina? He hadn't ever expected her to have to suffer like that.

Jane looked at Derek, she didn't enjoy seeing him hurt like this but was glad that he knew that his children were suffering. She had been dealing with the problem by herself for over two weeks and felt drained by the whole situation. She had to deal with Tom's moods and Tina's crying almost everyday after school. 'You better get on if you want to spend sometime with her, just remember to bring her back for six,' she said wanting to have some time for herself.

Derek nodded and let out a brief smile, his wife's newfound civility soothing some of his pain.

Justin and Tony were playing their daily game of pool, as usual Tony was winning easily. Fed up,

Justin sucked his teeth as he threw his cue on to the table.

'This game is foolish, I wanna do something else ya know.'

'What you wanna do G?'

'I don't know, but roll me a spliff while I think.'

They went into the living room and Justin put on his favourite rap CD while Tony rolled the joint. Tony tried not to laugh as Justin pathetically limped from left foot to right foot, his head erratically bobbing up and down, as he tried to emulate his favourite gangster rapper. Suddenly he stopped, prompting Tony to turn round and see what he was staring at. In the large doorframe stood Sarah and her friend Karen. Tony dropped the half finished joint on the table as they walked in.

'Hey Karen, what's up?' Justin said as he embraced her.

'I came down from university to visit my parents and Sarah for the weekend. She said that I should check your place out.'

'Well what do you think?' Justin asked.

'It's great, you've done well.'

'That I have. You remember my brethren Tony, init?'

Tony got up and hugged her.

'What you sayin´ girl? I missed you.'

Sarah went red. He wasn't hitting on Karen was he? Surely he wouldn't try to shag her, not after what they'd done together.

'I missed you too,' Karen said.

'Hey I got an idea, why don't we go upstairs and leave these two love birds to catch up?' Justin said, taking Sarah by the hand.

'No, I don't think so, I mean Karen's only here

for the weekend and then she'll be back at university. I want to spend as much time as possible with her.'

'Don't worry,' Karen said as she smiled at Tony, 'they'll be plenty of time.'

'Yeah you two can go, I'll take care of her,' Tony said with a cheeky wink as he put his arm around Karen.

'But . . .' Sarah said as she tried to think of something.

'No more buts,' Justin said as he pulled her by the hand out of the living room. When she turned to look back Tony and Karen were already kissing.

Again Derek was flat broke and didn't have enough money to take Tina anywhere that most children would want to go, so he opted for the cheapest place he could think of, the local library. Tina as ever didn't complain but derived her pleasure from her father's company. She was full of questions and energy but Derek could somehow feel that she wasn't herself. There was a quiet sadness about her. On the way back to her home he thought it best to try and approach the subject.

'Tina, you seem sad, is there something you'd like to tell me?' he asked as he gently placed his hand on her shoulder. She looked up at him in deep consideration and they both stopped walking.

'I'm OK daddy,' she said bravely, her eyes welling up.

Derek bent down and gently held her arms.

'You know if you have a problem, I want to know because I want to help you.'

'But you can't help me daddy,' she said looking away from him.

'Why not? How do you know if you won't tell me?'

'Because mummy's already tried and she just made everything worse.'

'Is it the other children at school, do they make fun out of you because I lost all that money?'

The tears started to stream out of her eyes and she burst into sobs as she embraced him holding on as tightly as she could.

'They make fun of you,' she sobbed, 'they say that you're a loser and that I'm a loser too, and sometimes, sometimes . . .'

'What baby, tell me what else they do.'

'They hit me daddy and they pull my hair,' her sobbing grew louder as she hugged him tightly.

'Don't cry, things will get better I promise,' he said as he held her close to him and fought back his own tears. Derek's soul filled with despair as his daughter cried her eyes out, each tear which dropped onto the cold pavement was like a pellet penetrating his heart. Once the sobs had subsided he wiped away the tear stains from her cheeks and promised her that everything would get better and that he'd get back the money. He didn't believe any of those words himself, but couldn't think of anything else to say. He hated himself for putting his children in this situation but he hated himself even more for lying to his daughter. The last layer of his dignity had finally been shredded away and it was a completely broken man that walked Tina up to the front door of her house and rang the door bell.

When Jane opened the door Tina went to give her dad one last hug, before again bursting into tears. Jane angrily commanded her daughter to go inside before the neighbours saw them.

'Why's she crying?' Jane hissed, the stress of the last few weeks causing her to snap at the person she saw as the cause. It was bad enough she had to nurse her kids and listen to them crying when they came home from school, but she'd be damned if she'd listen to Tina crying after Derek's visits.

'I asked her about the bullying at school, I guess it was a bad idea.'

'You guessed right, I told you that I was dealing with things, the last thing I needed was you sticking your nose in and making things worse.'

'I'm sorry.'

'You always are, but you just can't stop screwing up, can you? Why don't you just sod off and die?' she spat out venomously, before slamming the door in Derek's face.

Derek started the walk back to his bus stop, but halfway down the street was overcome with emotion, and it wasn't long before he broke out into sobs just like his daughter had. The only difference was that there wasn't anyone to comfort Derek, instead he simply carried on walking down the street, his tears leaving a light trail on the pavement.

Sarah sat at the large dining table eating her breakfast alone while Justin slept. Karen had spent most of Saturday afternoon and all of Saturday night in Tony's bedroom. Sarah had felt repulsed as she'd listened to them having sex. That bastard, how could he? She dropped the spoon into her cornflakes bowl when she noticed that Karen had entered the room. She was fully dressed.

'I'm going to have to go,' Karen said.

'Where's Tony?' Sarah asked, trying her best to sound indifferent.

'He's still sleeping. I think I wore him out,' she said with a cheeky wink.

'You were supposed to be here visiting me, not Tony.'

'Hey don't be like that, we spent some time together too. Anyway I'll be back in a couple of weeks.'

'So are you and Tony on again?'

'No, it's just a bit of fun. I can't commit, not when I'm up in Manchester.'

'Don't you have anyone up there?'

'No, I haven't found anyone fit enough yet.' Karen bent down and gave Sarah a kiss on the cheek, before hugging her tightly. 'I've got to go and say goodbye to my mum and dad. Like I said you're always welcome to come up and visit.'

Sarah smiled, 'Thanks.'

'I'll see myself out.'

'Take care, I miss you.'

'I miss you too.'

Sarah watched as Karen left the room, after she'd heard the front door close she got up and threw the cornflakes into the bin. They'd gone all soggy and she hated them like that. In that instant she was sure of just one thing-Tony was a dead man.

CHAPTER TWENTY-ONE

Justin sat on the park bench just like he had been instructed to, he was nervous and scared and looked around the deserted park for any sign of human activity. There was none, it was still too early.

'Did you watch the tape?' asked a voice from behind. Startled, Justin turned round and looked at the man who spoke. He was of a dark, Mediterranean complexion but that meant little to Justin.

'Yeah I watched the tape,' he said, doing a good job of hiding his fear and not stuttering. 'You must be the newsagent,' Justin deduced.

'Who I am isn't important. What's important is that you're prepared to meet my demands,' said Ismail Inanilmaz taking a seat next to Justin on the damp park bench. The early morning air was cold and crisp, exactly the kind of English weather Ismail had grown to loath.

'Are you prepared to meet my demands?'

'I don't have much choice, but how will I know that you've handed me the original tape?'

'You won't, but you have my word.'

'That's not good enough.'

'You have two options, pay me the million pounds and get the tape or don't and watch it along with the rest of the country as it is played repeatedly on the evening news. But you'd better hurry up you've only got four days left.'

'OK I told you I'll do it, but just know this, if you fuck with me the rest of the money goes on your head.'

Ismail gave Justin a contemptuous smile before grabbing him by the collar, 'Don't threaten me boy, I know exactly what you are, a jumped up little thief, not some big time gangster, now you give me the money and then you get the original tape, do I make myself understood?'

Justin nodded his head silently, he didn't want to mess with this guy, he was way too big and strong, and besides Justin knew that he simply wasn't a fighter.

'Good,' said Ismail releasing him and then pushing a folded piece of paper into his hand. 'That's the bank account where I want the funds transferred to. Once the money has cleared we'll meet and I'll give you the tape.'

Ismail stood up, 'And remember if you tell anyone about this I'll expose the truth about your lottery win. Have a nice day, and remember four days.'

Justin held the piece of paper containing the bank details in his hands as he watched the tall figure of Ismail Inanilmaz walk off into the distance. Almost instinctively he could tell that his blackmailer was telling the truth, one wrong move and he'd send the tape to the police, but Justin didn't know how to deal with the situation alone. He had to turn to the only people he could trust, Tony and Sarah.

Sarah held onto Tony tightly as he reached the end of his climax. He'd already satisfied her immensely, giving her two orgasms and making her glad that she'd taken the decision to sneak into his bedroom when she had noticed that Justin had left the house unusually early.

Her original intention had been to tell Tony what a scumbag she thought he was when he'd started sleeping with Karen again.

'How could you? She's my best mate!'

'And what do you think Justin is for me? I was Justin's friend before he had the money, you're just using him.'

'That doesn't mean you can sleep with me and Karen.'

'Why not? You can sleep with me and Justin,' Tony said as he got out of his bed and approached her. His argument, along with his six-pack, seemed to soothe some of her anger away. He did seem to have a point, how could she be angry? He was no worse than her.

He placed his hands on her hips.

'Tony don't, it's wrong. I feel like I'm betraying Karen.'

'Karen isn't into me seriously. She's just wants some fun. Come on Sarah, can't you see that we're the same?'

Slowly he kissed her lips, she didn't try to resist. Slipping out of her nightie as Tony caressed her was easy. Karen had said that she wasn't interested in anything serious and she knew that Justin would be gone a while because he had taken the Ferrari, which he used for trips that lasted more than an hour. For jobs that took half an hour to an hour Justin would take the Porsche, and for anything under thirty minutes it was the BMW.

Afterwards she lay in silence on Tony's chest,

looking up at his eyes and running her hand across his toned torso.

'What's wrong?' he asked.

She smiled, 'Why do you think that something's wrong?'

'Because you're looking at me strange.'

'Oh, I was just thinking, you know, if only it could be me and you living in this place.'

'I've been thinking a lot about us lately too,' he said, gently pushing her off his chest and reaching up for a cigarette.

'Yeah what you been thinking about?' she asked, wrapping her legs around his waist and cuddling him from behind as he sat on the bed, thoughtfully smoking his cigarette.

Tony turned around and looked into her eyes, 'I've been thinking about us running away together, somewhere far away from here.'

She let out a dismissive laugh, 'And how would we survive?'

'I could get a job.'

She laughed even more, 'You a job? What can you do apart from steal cars?'

He didn't attempt an answer, instead Tony just turned away, still puffing on his cigarette. Sarah unable to see that she had hurt Tony's feelings, cuddled him even tighter, kissing him gently on the cheek.

'You're very sweet, that's so romantic, but think about it seriously. What kind of life would we have, even if you could get a job? I mean I want to do more than just get by, I've been getting by all my life. I'm tired of counting pennies and looking at the price tag on things because really I know I can't afford them.'

'So basically you care more about the money than me,' Tony said, pulling away from her and standing up in order to put his trousers on.

'Oh don't get me wrong baby, it's not that I want the money more than you, it's just . . .'

'Just what?'

'Just that I want you and the money, I want both.'

'Well it looks like you've got to make a choice, because like you said, I won't ever have enough money to take care of you the way you want.'

'I don't see why not,' Sarah said looking at him thoughtfully.

'What do you mean?' Tony asked puzzled.

'Well you did the job with him so you're entitled to half of it anyway.'

'No,' Tony said shaking his head, 'I already tried that, he wants to keep it all.'

'But you're his mate, he's got to sort you out!'

'Well he doesn't see it that way,' Tony said bitterly.

Sarah lent forward and taking Tony by the belt pulled him back towards the bed, until he collapsed in it beside her. 'Maybe if we put our heads together we can come up with some way of getting him to part with his cash.'

'Do you have any ideas?' Tony asked.

'No,' she said as she smiled seductively, 'but I'm working on it.' Sarah's eyes lit up, she liked Tony but there was no way she'd be taking him along with her once she'd got the money, not after he'd had the audacity to sleep with her best friend. There was a twinge of guilt as she remembered Karen. Her friend wouldn't have liked being used by Tony like that. She had to tell Karen what Tony had done so that he wouldn't ever be able to be in a position to do it again.

Derek sat on the chair in his bedsit and looked up at the wooden beam, where he intended to attach the hangman's noose. His ex-wife had told him to sod off and die, and quite frankly, feeling the way he did, he thought of it as the best advice anyone had ever given him. His kids were being bullied at school because of his stupid mistakes, his son, Tom, couldn't even look him in the eye and the way things were going Tina was bound to follow suit before long. He was broke and now in debt to his best friend, the whole nation thought he was a joke and right now he felt like the loneliest person in the world.

Suicide had been something Derek had considered before, in fact during his divorce he had felt suicidal. Perhaps it was two years ago that he felt at his lowest, when after sending out his CV to hundreds of companies and employment agencies he finally conceded that he would end his career working in an abattoir. That had been more than enough reason for Derek to consider suicide. He had thought of all the different ways to go, like setting himself on fire, but that was too dramatic (and painful), or jumping under a train, but what about the poor bloke that had to clear up his remains?

Derek found the idea of hanging himself attractive because it wasn't painful or at least he didn't think it was, after all it was pretty quick and efficient, but more importantly it would be left to his landlord to clear up the whole mess afterwards and Derek couldn't think of anyone more deserving of the job than the man who managed the shit hole he lived in.

So two years ago Derek had bought the rope but then changed his mind when his son, who was still speaking to him at the time, told him how much he loved him and missed him and needed him. That had caused Derek to change his mind about topping himself in an instant, but he'd kept the rope. Why had he kept the rope? It was a question he asked himself repeatedly as he attached it to the wooden beam. Maybe it was fate, but Derek didn't believe in fate, he hadn't for a long time. He reasoned that subconsciously he had always known he was a waste of space, and it was only a matter of time before he would again consider taking his life.

He gave the noose a good tug, making sure it was securely attached, before deciding that now was the moment for him to go through with it. Now that he was drunk enough and not scared, but strangely calm and accepting of the end that was awaiting him. He glanced at the phone and made sure it was off the hook. Good, there wouldn't be any interruptions. As he held the noose in his hands, his mind flashed back to the last two months and all the traumatic events that had led up to this moment. They passed before his eyes in a flash, and Derek clenched his teeth in anger. As the tears rolled down his face, he was more determined than ever to go through with this.

The buzzer of his intercom system went off. Somebody wanted him to open the door to the building and let them in. Quite possibly somebody who wanted to see Derek. It sounded again. Who could it be? The press? His solicitor? Terry? As he considered these options it sounded again, this time whoever it was didn't take their finger off the button and let it ring for half a minute. They were obviously either very impatient or in a rush to speak to Derek.

Derek considered what to do, everything was ready for his suicide and the end of his pain. If it was some Jehovah's Witness then he would be even more bitter as he departed this world than he had been before. The likelihood that it was someone who he knew was remote, and anyway the buzzing had stopped now. Derek waited as sweat dripped from his forehead and landed on the cheap carpet below. He looked at the clock which sat on his mantelpiece, a minute had elapsed and the buzzing had stopped. Whoever it was had gone, so it couldn't have been that important anyway. Slowly Derek placed his head into the noose and tightened it around his neck, he closed his eyes, this was it, he was going to go through with it.

CHAPTER TWENTY-TWO

'Derek are you home?' echoed a female voice through Derek's door.

Derek opened his eyes, it was his solicitor Christine.

'I received some news just an hour ago which has led to an interesting development in your case.'

Derek pulled his head out of the noose and considered what he should do. He could hardly kill himself now, not without knowing what this new development was, but how could he let Christine into his home? She'd see that he was just about to commit suicide.

'Just a minute, I'm not decent,' he shouted.

'OK.'

Derek put a lot of effort into untying the noose from the wooden beam, but it took considerable time and energy because he had tied it with the intention of it remaining there indefinitely. However in the end he managed to undo the big, strong knots and threw the noose under his bed.

'Hello, are you OK?' Christine asked starting to grow impatient.

'Almost with you,' Derek shouted as he remembered the empty whisky bottle and placed it beside the noose, under his bed.

Finally he opened the door, 'Please come in,' he gestured to Christine, who looked at him suspiciously.

'How did you get in?' he asked.

'I was buzzing you for ages, but you didn't respond so I buzzed one of your neighbours and they let me in.'

Derek ran his hand nervously through his hair, 'I was fast asleep and I'm a really heavy sleeper. You get to be, living in a place like this, you know with so many neighbours.'

'I see,' Christine said, still not convinced, 'I tried calling but the phone was engaged all the time.'

'Oh thanks for reminding me,' Derek said as he walked over to his phone, 'like I said I wanted to sleep and so I took the handset off, so no one could wake me.' Derek placed the handset back onto the phone.

'Would you like some tea or coffee?' he asked.

'No, I'm fine thanks,' she said taking a seat.

'So what's the big news then?' Derek asked, also making himself comfortable.

'You probably remember the newsagent, Mr Ismail Inanilmaz?'

'Yes, I do.'

'Well he phoned me today and said that he had the tape but that if we want him to hand it over, we should somehow compensate him.'

'How?' asked Derek already fearing that this good news wasn't quite as good as he had hoped it would be.

'He'd like the sum of a million pounds to be paid directly into some offshore account.'

'A million pounds! How does he expect me to pay that?'

Christine smiled, 'That's the good news, he says that he's willing to wait until you've recovered your lottery winnings.'

'So he's going to hand over the tape just like

that? After I get the money, what's to stop me from keeping all of it and not rewarding him?'

'Well nothing, speaking as your legal representative , you wouldn't have to give him a penny.'

'Then I don't think I will give him a penny, after all he should have handed the tape to me from the beginning.'

'If you feel you shouldn't, don't, but what all this means is that we can go ahead with the lawsuit and that we have a very good chance of winning now.'

'Well that's great, I just don't know what to say,' Derek said getting up and pacing the room. Christine noticed the smile that had formed on his face, it was the first time she had seen him smile. He looked good when he smiled.

'He simply said that we should wait a few days for him to get the tape to us.'

'Why?' Derek asked, concerned.

'I don't know but the ball is in his court, for now we have to play his game. Don't worry I have a good feeling about this.'

Derek didn't look totally convinced, and Christine understood why. Mr Inanilmaz was playing some sort of game. What that game was she couldn't even begin to guess, but the fact of the matter was that the tape did actually exist. The tape meant victory for them, so there was still a lot to be happy about.

'Let me take you out for dinner in order to celebrate,' Christine said, breaking Derek's thoughts. He looked at her in bewilderment and she could tell that the request for dinner was more astonishing news than the discovery that the tape of him buying the winning lottery ticket actually existed.

'I don't know what to say, I mean, well, I would like to . . .'

'So grab your coat then,' Christine said getting up, 'we do have something to celebrate and I'm starving.' Derek smiled, thoughts of suicide forgotten as he led the attractive Christine out of his home.

Peter Cutner held the small piece of paper containing the bank account number in his hands. He studied it carefully and then looked up at the three young, concerned faces that sat opposite him. Justin stared at Cutner's eyes before turning his attention to Sarah, it had been her idea to come and see him. Justin reached out his hand and she took the hint, allowing him to place it in hers. When Cutner started talking Justin squeezed her hand, he was nervous and sweaty.

'This isn't a bank account for a British bank, it's definitely offshore.'

'Where?' asked Tony, excited by anything that was linked to crime.

'I'm not sure, I've never seen one like this before,' Cutner said as he pondered the possibilities, 'one thing I am sure of though, is this, blackmailers are never satisfied. You pay him once and he'll comeback again and again.'

'What can I do? If I go to the police he'll tell everyone I tiefed the ticket,' Justin said making no effort in hiding his anguish.

Peter pondered the question, the three watched on in silence until he was ready to speak again.

'As far as I can see you have two alternatives, I would recommend the first one I'm about to suggest.'

'Hit me,' Justin said intrigued but apprehensive at the same time.

'What I'm about to recommend is highly illegal and completely unethical and you mustn't repeat to anyone that I have furnished you with such information.'

The ever sharp and focused eyes of Peter Cutner looked at the three faces carefully. Sarah wondered if he was aware of the way his eyes caused her emotions to stir.

'Go on,' said Sarah, moved by those eyes and aroused by that commanding voice.

'Tell us,' said Tony, now totally captivated.

'You see the problem we have is that Justin Farren is worth millions of pounds, however Justin Farren might lose all that money because of the various external pressures that are placed on him. So if we were to set up a new identity for Mr Farren lets say, John Doe, and then transfer that money into John Doe's name, well who cares what happens to Mr Farren?'

'I don't get it! Why would I give my money to this John Doe?'

'He's talking about money laundering!' Tony shouted, looking at the solicitor in admiration.

Peter smiled, it was a sinister, crooked smile but one that summed up the very nature of the man who sat in front of them.

'Indeed I am talking about money laundering, you see Justin I'll get you a new passport in a completely different name, you'll then open up an account under this new name. Then, using a few shell companies, you wash the money until it's nice and clean and ready to be transferred into the bank account of your new identity, and preferably somewhere far from here like the Caymans or the Bahamas.'

'But I don't want to go to the Bahamas,' Justin whined.

'What? Why not? I would love to live somewhere tropical,' Sarah said, astonished by Justin's lack of daring and adventure.

'It would be possible for you to stay here, but how would you enjoy the money without drawing attention to yourself?' Peter said.

Justin let out a sigh, 'You said there was a second alternative.'

'It's still illegal and also has its risks but you could follow a similar pattern of washing the money through shell companies but eventually transfer it to a real person, someone you trust like your friend Tony or your girlfriend Sarah. It would mean you could stay in England but then you'd be dependent on this person whenever you wanted access to the money.'

'No way,' Justin snorted, his laugh deeply sardonic.

'What's so fucking funny?' Sarah said pushing his hand away and giving him a look that could freeze water.

'Nutin´,' Justin said quietly.

'You don't trust me blood?' Tony said expressing his disappointment.

'I trust you both, for real but I ain't puttin´ my money in someone else's name.'

'Well why not?' Sarah asked, her eyes still boring into his skull.

'Yeah, why not G?' Tony said, hoping that the opportunity had now arisen for him to seize the cash.

'I don't like it and that's it,' Justin said, crossing his arms across his chest.

'Well it looks like the only alternative you have is to comply with this man's demands and hope for the best,' Peter said eager to end the petty bickering.

'So that's what I'll do,' Justin said getting up, keen to leave.

'It is your money, and your choice. Just remember that if you change your mind, or if he comes to you for more money, I'm here to help.'

'I will,' Justin said.

'But also remember that I need at least a week's notice to organise such an operation, it's very complicated and needs lots of planning.'

Justin simply nodded as he walked out of the door, Tony wasn't far behind, leaving Peter the opportunity to escort Sarah to the door. She smiled at him as she was about to leave.

'Bye,' he said as he pressed a small bit of card into her hand. She opened her mouth in shock, but Peter cut her off, 'phone me,' he whispered as delicately as he could.

She smiled and nodded, 'Bye and thank you for all your help,' she said before finally turning her body away from him and walking out of his office. He let out a sigh and leaned against the doorframe as he watched her leave.

CHAPTER TWENTY-THREE

Karen looked out of the window of her parents' house as she waited nervously for Sarah. She'd returned to London on her bi-monthly visit. She'd spoken to Sarah, who'd sounded extremely nervous, on the phone. Something was going on and she didn't have a clue what it was. Sarah was obviously in some kind of trouble, but what could it be?

A Porsche 911 slowly drew up outside her house. It was obviously Sarah.

'Sarah's here, I'll be back later,' Karen shouted as she ran out of the house, slamming the front door shut before her parents could even respond. She could see Sarah sitting in the driver's seat, she was wearing a thick pair of sunglasses. If their purpose had been to completely hide her eyes then they were performing their job well.

'Justin lets you drive his cars then?' Karen couldn't help but ask as she got in.

Sarah smiled, 'He only lets me drive the BM, but I saw the keys to this and thought what the hell. He probably won't even notice.'

Karen quickly put on her seat belt as Sarah unleashed some of the car's power.

'So what did you want to talk to me about? It sounded serious on the phone.'

'I wanted to talk to you about Tony,' Sarah said keeping her eyes fixed straight ahead on the road.

'Go on, what is it?'

'He's been sleeping with both of us.'

Karen was silent. Sarah turned and looked at her but there wasn't a response.

'Well aren't you going to say anything?'

'You mean you've been sleeping with him behind my back, don't you?' Karen said, her voice shaky.

'It's not like that. I'd asked you if you were still interested and you'd said no. Then when you came round the other weekend you were all over him. He'd already started sleeping with me by then. I wanted to say something, but Justin was there and I could hardly say something in front of Justin. I just wanted to tell you this weekend so that he couldn't use you like that again.'

'Or because you want him to yourself.'

'You don't really think that. I only slept with him after you'd said you were no longer interested.'

'What does that matter? You went with a bloke I'd been with. It's disgusting.'

'So what if you'd already been with him? Who cares?'

'Maybe that's why there's something wrong with you.'

Karen couldn't help but notice Sarah's top lip quiver slightly in anger. Her last comment had obviously touched a nerve.

'What do you mean?' Sarah asked testily.

'You're using Justin for his money. You wouldn't even look at him for any other reason and you don't even see that it's wrong.'

'That's because it isn't.'

'It's just a sophisticated form of prostitution.'

'Now you're calling me a prostitute?'

'I'm sorry but that's what you are.'

Sarah hit the breaks and both girls were flung

forwards until their seat belts constricted their chests as the car came to a halt.

'Get out of my car,' Sarah hissed.

'It's not even your car,' Karen responded.

'Just get out!'

'Truth hurts, doesn't it?' Karen said as she unbuckled her seat belt. 'You're using Justin for his money and Tony for his sex. You didn't even stop to consider me.'

'You'd said that you weren't interested!' Sarah shouted.

'You should have asked me before you started sleeping with him!' Karen got out of the car, 'Well you're welcome to him, you're both as bad as each other,' she said as she slammed the door.

Sarah rammed the car into first gear and sped off as quickly as she could. As Karen watched her disappear in a cloud of smoke she couldn't help but wonder if perhaps she'd been too tough on her friend. After all Tony really didn't mean that much to her.

Ismail waited in the shop as patiently as he could. He'd phoned his wife over an hour ago requesting that she came and looked after the shop while he 'popped out' in order to take care of some business. The shop was exceptionally quiet today, even though it was lunch time, a bad indication. A year ago Ismail would have been extremely worried, now he didn't care if he ever saw another customer again. In fact he welcomed the idea. The door opened as his wife came in, drenched from the downpour outside.

'Where the hell have you been woman?' Ismail bellowed.

His long suffering wife ignored the shouting and instead took off her coat before taking her place behind the counter. Ismail silently walked towards the door, his mind preoccupied.

'Your coat,' his wife shouted.

Looking at her contemptuously he went to the back and put on his raincoat.

'Where are you going?' she asked.

'I've got business to attend to,' he said before storming out.

His wife shook her head, what on earth was her stupid husband up to now? Probably another affair. She smiled, if he was seeing another woman she wouldn't have to put up with his advances for a while. The rest would do her good.

Ismail sat on the park bench where he had met Justin a couple of days ago. He was meant to be meeting a tabloid reporter who had sounded very interested in buying the tape off him.

Days of intensive thinking had finally crystallised into a foolproof plan. Ismail was going to get the million off Justin, give him a copy of the tape and then turn around and sell the original to this journalist. Just days ago he had planned on sending the original to Derek's solicitor. It would have been an all round solution for everyone. Derek would have had the evidence he needed and most importantly of all Ismail would have had his million pounds and a guilt free conscience.

He had even phoned Ms Christine Havers informing her that he would hand the tape over on the condition that they promised to pay him a million after they had recovered their money. That meant that Ismail would get a million from both parties but the previous night he was awoken by a frightful dream where Derek had told him to fuck off, because he wouldn't be giving him a penny.

The superstitious Ismail took this as a bad sign, but more importantly it got him thinking, after all why would Derek hand the money over once he had what he wanted? Angry that he hadn't thought about this and distrustful of Derek and Christine, Ismail thought of another solution. To sell the tape to the papers. He'd once read that a simple prostitute, who had slept with a cabinet minister was paid a hundred thousand pounds for telling her story. So how much would they pay for the tape? It was hard evidence in a legal dispute that had gripped the country. More importantly Ismail would get the money, whatever it was upfront, and equally as important, once the tape was aired on TV everyone would know that Derek was telling the truth. Ismail smiled, he was so bloody cunning it hurt.

A rather ragged man with wild, grey hair sat on the bench next to Ismail. Naturally Ismail presumed that he was a tramp.

'I'm sorry, but I'm going to have to ask you to leave, I'm meeting a friend here,' he said in a rather aggressive tone. The tramp searched through his pockets until he found something. He extended his hand towards Ismail, who spotted the business card it clasped. He took it, the man next to him was the reporter whom he was meant to be meeting.

'I'm sorry, but . . .' Ismail said trying to think of a way to apologise.

The reporter put up his hand, 'Don't worry about it, I've just come from a two day stake out.'

'Anything interesting?'

'You can read about it on page five of tomorrow's paper.'

Ismail didn't respond, he wanted to find out how much he could get for the tape, excited and nervous at the same time he tried to look cool. He'd entered new territory, first blackmail and now selling evidence of a crime to a reporter.

'I can see that you want to get down to business,' the reporter said, 'don't worry I can tell, I've done this more times than you've had hot dinners.'

'You've obviously tried my wife's cooking,' Ismail smiled.

The reporter's face remained unemotional, 'How much do you want?'

'I was hoping for lets say a million.'

The reporter burst into laughter, 'A million! You've seen way too many films.'

Ismail felt more than slightly annoyed that the reporter found him so amusing, 'You know there are other papers that would be interested in buying the tape.'

The laughing stopped immediately, 'OK let's cut to the chase, the most our paper's paid for anything related to a story is two hundred and fifty thousand pounds, now considering the public interest in this story I reckon we can pay you that much, but I'll have to clear things with the editor first.'

Ismail nodded, two hundred and fifty thousand was more than enough for his humble needs, and added to the million he was going to extract from Justin, he would have a very comfortable life in Brazil. Yes, a very comfortable life, 'Two hundred and fifty thousand is OK.'

'Of course we'll have to watch the tape first, before we pay out.'

'Not a problem.'

'So when can you get it to us?'

Ismail considered the question, Justin had two more days to cough up. It would take a further five days for the money to clear once it reached Ismail's bank account.

'Give me six days, I'll contact you after then.'

'OK,' the reporter said extending his hand, 'I should have the clearance about the money from my editor by then as well.'

'You better,' Ismail said shaking the reporter's hand, 'remember if you try to play around, the tape goes to one of your rivals.'

'Hey you've got my word.'

'Good,' Ismail said before walking off. In two days he'd have a million pounds to his name, in under a week a further two hundred and fifty thousand. It was time to buy his one way ticket to Brazil.

CHAPTER TWENTY-FOUR

Derek sat nervously in the restaurant as he waited for Christine. This would be their second date. He remembered back to when she'd casually asked him out. At first he had thought that she'd just taken pity on him, but they'd gotten on so well that he felt compelled to ask her out on a second date and couldn't believe it when she had agreed.

He spotted her enter the restaurant and noticed a couple of heads turn as she approached the table where he sat. He got up and extended his hand which she shook gently before kissing him on the cheek. Derek blushed, a response Christine found to be sweet and subtly charming.

'Hope I didn't keep you waiting long,' Christine said taking her seat.

'No, I just got here,' Derek lied. He'd been waiting fifteen minutes.

'That's good, I tried to get away from the office as soon as possible, but sometimes it's almost impossible.'

'You look beautiful,' Derek said. Now it was Christine's turn to blush.

'Thank you,' she beamed, radiating an energy Derek found highly seductive.

The waiter brought them their menus and they ordered their drinks, before sitting in silence and studying the different options available for dinner.

'What are you having?' Christine asked.

'I'm not sure,' Derek mumbled, studying the prices very carefully.

'Well order whatever you want, it's my treat,' Christine said.

'No, I can't allow you to pay. You paid for us last time.'

'So what? Things are going well for me and I want to splash out a bit.'

'But . . .'

'But what? Do you have something against women paying for dinner?' Christine smiled.

'No,' Derek smiled back, 'but you have to promise that I'll pay next time.'

'OK, I promise.'

Well unless she was playing the long game, she sure couldn't be after his money, Derek thought to himself before returning his attention to the menu.

Sarah jumped up and down and rode Peter J. Cutner with all the strength she had. He in turn grabbed her waist and clenched his buttocks, thrusting upwards. This girl was amazing he thought to himself, no wonder she was able to twist an inexperienced kid like Justin around her little finger.

Her groans grew louder indicating to Peter that he no longer had to hold back. It was time for them to ride on the waves of ecstasy together. They'd already been at it for two hours, God damn it.

She slumped down on top of him, her energy gone. Her eyes gazed at him in blissful content.

'You're great,' she whispered into his ear, brushing her hand through his hair affectionately. He rolled her off his chest and they lay side by side looking into each other's eyes.

'You remind me of what it was like to be young,' he said.

'You are young,' she said screwing her face up.

'I'm a lot older than you.'

'You're the best man I've ever had. God, Justin's completely useless in bed.'

Peter smiled arrogantly at the comparison, like all men, a positive evaluation of his sexual prowess helped to reinforce his masculinity.

'If only I could have you and Justin's money.'

'But you can, if you could just convince him to go through with my plan of hiding the cash away in a false name, well then I could get to the account and take it from him.'

Sarah quickly sat up, she wanted to learn more.

'How could you do that?'

'If you know what his password is, and we know the name under which he keeps all his money, well then it's child's play.'

Sarah shook her head, 'Justin would never trust me with the password.'

'But Justin's probably the type of person who writes down his passwords. The one to the Cayman account will no doubt be a ten-digit number. You could find it and give it to me.'

'I suppose I could, it wouldn't be too difficult, but he didn't like your idea.'

'You could make him change his mind. I bet you can be quite convincing when you want to be,' Peter said, taking her face into his hand.

She smiled, 'I'll try my best.'

'That's a good girl, then we'll take the money and run away together, maybe to the Cayman Islands.'

'Oh yes, I hate England, the Cayman Islands

sounds wonderful,' she said jumping on top of Peter and running her nails down his hairy chest. He let out a sigh, half filled with pleasure, half with pain, this girl was mind-blowing he told himself. She started to kiss him passionately, the idea of ripping Justin off and running away to the Cayman Islands with Peter had turned her on immensely.

Derek felt ecstatic when Christine had asked if he didn't mind walking her home. Although it had been her suggestion Derek had been planning on asking her once they had left the restaurant. After two dates he felt confident enough around her to do that; but the fact that she had asked first and appeared to be the one in control was perfectly fine by him.

'So you work in this area, live in this area, and also eat in this area?' Derek asked, although it was more of a statement than a question.

'Yes, it's only fifteen minutes to my house from the office.'

'And you often eat in that restaurant?'

Christine laughed, 'Am I that transparent?'

'No, it's just that the waiter seemed to know you fairly well.'

'I'm afraid I don't have much time for cooking, not with being a busy career woman and all, so most days after I finish work I go there for my evening meal.'

'Is that why you're not married then? Too busy with your career?'

Christine looked at Derek and seemed to get lost in her thoughts.

'I'm sorry if my question was too personal.'

'No, it's not, I was just thinking about the answer,

that's all. I guess it's just that I never met the right man.'

'Well you're still young and very attractive, you have time.'

Christine looked at Derek, 'Maybe I don't need anymore time, maybe the right man has already come into my life.'

'Oh,' said Derek slightly disappointed, he had hoped that she was interested in him romantically. He looked at her, his face puzzled, he wanted to ask who the mystery man was. When she smiled at him and laughed he realised that she was talking about him. But she couldn't be, could she? How could a woman like Christine possibly be interested in a loser like him?

'What about you Derek? You're a lot more attractive than you realise, why didn't you remarry?'

'I guess I was heart broken for a long while, and then, well I found it too difficult to trust anyone else.'

Christine took his hand into hers, 'I hope that you're ready to start trusting again.'

Derek smiled, 'I think I am.'

They continued in silence until they reached Christine's house.

'Well this is it,' she said.

Derek looked at her wistfully, he wanted to say something to let her know how he felt about her. More than that he wanted to hold her, to kiss her, more than he had wanted to hold any other woman in his whole life. She looked at him in anticipation, hoping that he would have the courage to make the first move.

'Thank you for a wonderful time,' he said, moving slightly closer.

She smiled, and despite years of celibacy he instinctively knew that now was the time to make his move, daringly he pressed his lips on to hers. The embrace was short, but passionate. They looked at each other with yearning, it had been a very long time for both. Suddenly they remembered what it felt to be young, and inexperienced and hungry for that other person.

'Would you think badly of me if I asked you in for a coffee?' Christine said as she gently bit her lip, nervously but ever so seductively.

'I certainly wouldn't,' Derek said before following her up the steps which led to her front door. A big smile formed on his face, he couldn't help feeling like maybe things were starting to go his way.

As Peter left his office and strolled down to his favourite restaurant for lunch he couldn't help shake off the feeling that he was being followed. Stopping every now and again and turning round he had hoped on catching his spy, but no luck. Puzzled, he tried a different tack and went for a walk around the block. However as he turned the corner he stopped and waited instead of carrying on. He knew that his spy would soon reveal himself.

Tony gasped as he saw Peter waiting for him as he briskly turned the corner. Before he could say anything the teenager was grabbed by the shoulders and flung against the brick wall where Peter held him roughly.

'What are you doing following me?' Cutner asked, afraid that the teenager knew that he was sleeping with Sarah.

'Nutin´,' said Tony trying to break Peter's grip.

'Don't take me for a fool boy. You've been following me, what do you know about me?'

'I don't nutin´ about you Mr Cutner, honest.'

'Then why are you following me?'

'I was hoping to talk to you alone, I want to learn more about money laundering.'

Peter punched Tony in the stomach, 'Not so loud you idiot, have you forgotten my job?'

'I'm sorry Mr Cutner, you asked is all.'

Cutner drew closer to Tony and whispered in his ear, 'Money laundering is a very complicated process and a buffoon like you will never be able to learn how to do it.'

'Please Mr Cutner, you could teach me.'

Again Peter punched Tony in the stomach.

'Don't be so stupid.'

'OK, what about the fake passports? You could introduce me to the person you get them off.'

'And why would I do that?'

'´Coz you're my friend's brief.'

Cunter paused to consider. The last thing he needed was this idiot following him around. What if he had seen him with Sarah? He needed to be sure that Tony would stop following him. Perhaps if he introduced him to the passport man it would be enough to get Tony off his back. Besides the passport man would be pleased that Peter had introduced him to a new client. But would he be happy with a client like Tony? A spotty faced little buffoon? Tony's idiocy could land anybody who came into contact with him in jail. It wouldn't be good to anger someone as well connected as the passport man. Peter contemplated what to do.

'What do you want fake passports for?' Cutner asked finally, after staring fiercely into Tony's eyes.

Tony shrugged his shoulders, 'Maybe one day I'll need one to get out of the country. Or maybe I can sell ´em to people I know. I don't wanna stay small time forever Mr Cutner. I gotta start earning soon.'

Peter thought some more. He'd been a good client of the passport man's for a few years now. More than likely if Tony screwed things up it would be just him that would be chopped into little pieces and thrown into the Thames. No real skin off Peter's nose.

'OK, if I introduce you to the man who sells fake passports will you stop following me around?' Peter asked eager to get rid of the teenager.

'Yeah for sure.'

Peter punched him in the stomach again. Tony bent over with pain.

'If I ever catch you following me again I'll break your legs, do you understand me?'

'Yeah, I understand Mr Cutner. Just introduce me to that guy you know and I won't ever do it again. I promise.'

'Just remember that if you ever follow me again you're a dead man.'

'I swear . . .' Tony started to whimper.

'And know this, if you cross this man I'm about to introduce you to, your whole family could end up in the Thames.'

Tony nodded his head in understanding. Peter punched him once more in the guts just for good measure and because he enjoyed inflicting pain. Tony doubled over as he tried to get his wind back.

Cutner grabbed hold of Tony's ear and dragged him across the street.

'Where're you takin´ me?' Tony whimpered.

'To the man who can supply you with passports,' Cutner replied.

CHAPTER TWENTY-FIVE

Sarah lay on her back and held Tony closely as he pumped away. They were in Justin's bed, he had left them alone in the house so that he could meet his blackmailer. Justin had paid the man his asking price of a million pounds and now all that remained was to pick up the tape.

Although she hated Tony's guts and blamed him for her bust up with Karen, it didn't stop the sex with him being great. In some perverse way it even made it better. Anyway she'd get her revenge on Tony when her and Peter would run away together with all of Justin's money. She couldn't help but let out a little laugh as she imagined the look on Tony's and Justin's faces as they both realised they'd been duped. Tony, caught in the throws of passion didn't even notice the laugh, instead he bit into her neck, just the way she liked it, roughly but leaving no marks. She dug her nails into his buttocks forcing him to pump harder. God, he was good, but Peter was better. Still it was a tough call, and she would definitely miss her sessions with Tony, but having Peter meant having her man and the money. She'd decided that she would be faithful once they'd run away together to the Cayman Islands, but in the mean time shagging Tony really wouldn't hurt, after all if she stopped sleeping with him, it would only cause him to become suspicious and endanger her plans with Peter.

Tony let out a loud grunt as he climaxed, the sensation of his pulsating penis causing her to orgasm. She clawed at his back as she was overcome by waves of pleasure, the thought of shagging another man in Justin's bed making her extra horny. Finally Tony flopped down beside her and stared into her eyes lovingly. Something she had never experienced from him, had he fallen for her too, the way Justin had?

She kissed his chest, it wasn't covered in hair the way Peter's was, but it was strong and masculine in its own right.

'You're so God damn sexy,' he said.

'I like it when you fuck me,' she teased, holding his cock in her hand and gently massaging it. She knew that once was never enough for Tony, the man was an animal.

'I'm gonna figure a way to get my share of the money, then we'll be long gone, we'll go somewhere hot.'

'Sure we will,' she said as she gently started kissing his stomach, working her way down, until she reached his inner thighs.

'God I'm gonna make you the happiest woman in the world,' Tony murmured as he began to yield to the pleasures of Sarah's tongue.

Derek slowly opened his eyes and then immediately closed them afraid that he would find himself alone in his squalid home and realise that last night had only been a dream. Realise that he hadn't spent all night making passionate love to the most beautiful and intelligent woman he had ever met.

After several minutes of lying in the bed, in near paralysis he was overcome by curiosity and sat up in the bed he was in and looked around. He definitely wasn't in his home but in a rather eloquent bedroom that had been thoughtfully decorated. Light blue walls contrasted with a large gold framed mirror opposite the bed, the windows were large, allowing the sun to fill the room with light when the curtains were drawn back. Small painted pictures of the countryside hung around the room in various places, a large silver candle holder stood in the far corner of the room, next to the wardrobe. He smiled, last night really had happened, but the king-size bed he lay in was empty. Where was Christine? He got up and put his clothes on before noticing the note which lay next to the bed.

The note said that she hoped that last night wasn't just a one off, that he made her happy, and that she was sorry that she left without saying goodbye, but she had to go to work. She finished off by saying that he could make himself breakfast, but only on the condition that he washed up after himself. Derek allowed himself to flop back on to the bed and read the note again. She hoped that last night wasn't a one off! He couldn't believe his luck.

Tony had started his daily routine of watching daytime TV when Justin burst into the living room.

'Where's Sarah?' he asked.

'I think she's having a shower,' Tony said, knowing full well exactly where she was after their sordid session together. He repressed the urge to smile, the guilt over sleeping with Justin's girlfriend ended about the same time Sarah had first taken her bra off.

Justin put the tape he held in his hand into the video and pressed play on the remote control.

'Is that the tape then?' Tony asked.

'What do you think?' Justin said curtly.

They both watched in silence as the image of Ismail Inanilmaz filled the screen.

'What the fuck?' Justin whispered in nervous confusion.

Tony watched on in silent intrigue, as a heinous smile formed across the face of the man on the screen. He started to speak, 'Dear Mr Farren as you are aware we made a deal, you would pay me a million pounds and I would provide you with the original tape of Mr Bonner purchasing the winning lottery ticket which you then stole from his home. I would like to thank you for keeping your end of the bargain and transferring the money to the account as I had instructed. The money is now safely out of the country and as you watch this I am boarding a plane which will enable me to join it. I would also like to take this opportunity to apologise for not being able to keep my end of the deal. You see I was recently overcome by guilt, "How could I stand back and allow this poor, innocent man to be robbed blind?" I asked myself. Well the answer was simple, I couldn't, so this morning, just before our meeting I sold the tape to the press. I now intend to enjoy the money they've given me along with your million for the rest of my life. Again I would like to thank you for this opportunity. I hope there aren't any hard feelings between us; I'm just doing what I think is right and making myself rich at the same time.'

The screen then went blank.

'Looks like you've been screwed G,' Tony said to his expressionless friend.

Derek had treated himself to a full English breakfast, bacon, eggs, sausages, toast and tea. He'd washed up and as had now become routine was wondering what to do with the rest of his day. Having come from a background of hard work Derek found being unemployed extremely difficult. It was the boredom rather than the lack of money that really affected him. The days seemed to stretch on forlornly, mingling into the nights until the two became indistinguishable. Sometimes at night he found himself full of energy, unable to sleep and then during the day he would feel exhausted, unwilling and unable to do anything. Last night was different though, spending it with Christine had led to the most peaceful night's sleep Derek could remember.

The phone rang, he wondered whether he should pick it up. The thought that it could be Christine was overwhelming. Finally he gave in and rushed over to the hallway.

'Hello,' he said nervously.

'Morning sexy,' said Christine.

'I knew it would be you.'

'How are you?'

'Missing you terribly, I was hoping to see you this morning.'

'Well why don't you come over to my office? I've got some good news for you.'

'Really? What is it?'

'That would spoil the surprise, see you soon,' she said before hanging up.

Derek made sure that all the windows and doors were securely closed before leaving. As he left Christine's house he wondered what the surprise could be.

CHAPTER TWENTY-SIX

Peter J. Cutner looked at the three youngsters sitting opposite him. He'd read the morning paper and knew straight away that they would be in to see him. He tried his best to keep his gaze off Sarah, afraid that he could make Justin suspicious. He needed the boy to have complete and utter faith in him.

'I did tell you that you should never deal with a blackmailer,' Peter said.

'I know!' Justin cried, 'But what we gonna do now?'

Peter looked at him, this idiot certainly didn't deserve to have all that money.

'Well forget about the million you paid Mr Inanilmaz, that's long gone and you have bigger problems now. With that evidence there's no way we can win the case, and I bet Mr Bonner's solicitor is preparing an injunction right now. If we don't move the money soon, it'll be gone forever.'

Justin nodded his head slowly, there was a defeated look about him. 'OK, do whatever you have to, just protect my money.'

Peter smiled, the fortune was almost in his grasp.

Derek read the paper Christine had handed him. She observed the smile that grew on his face and the expression which formed conveying his excitement. Inside the paper were stills taken from the tape Ismail had sold. They were of Derek buying the winning lottery ticket. The paper stated that it would be sending the original tape to Derek's solicitor this very morning.

When he finished he looked up at Christine who held a tape in her hand.

'Is that it?' he asked.

'Sure is, a journalist dropped it off about half an hour ago,' she smiled.

Derek let out a sigh of relief, 'So I'm going to get my money back now?'

'You sure are, I'm in the process of getting an injunction served so that Mr Farren can't move any assets around. I'll also apply to the court to bring the case to trial sooner.'

'Thank you, I don't know how I'll ever repay you.'

Christine smiled, 'Well my fees don't come cheap.'

'Oh yeah,' Derek laughed, 'sorry, I forgot about those.'

'I hope you didn't think that I'd let you off just because you were sleeping with me.'

'No, of course not,' Derek laughed before looking at her and taking in her beauty.

'God, you're amazing. When can I see you again?'

Christine looked through her diary, flipping through the pages and looking at Derek in mock thought.

'Hmm let me see, what about tonight?' she smiled.

'Tonight sounds great.'

'Oh I almost forgot, the journalist who delivered the tape said that his paper would like to interview you for your side of the story. They said they were willing to pay, gave me this card.'

'I thought that I couldn't give interviews to the press for legal reasons?'

'That was before, now that the story's been blown wide open there's no reason why you shouldn't cash in too. Plus it'll help tide you over until the lottery money comes through.'

She leaned over and passed him the business card the journalist had given her. They held hands momentarily, gazing into each others eyes. Derek instantly decided that she was by far the most special woman he had ever met.

Jane looked out of the window and waited for John in anticipation. It was already eight o'clock and he usually came home at about six-thirty. She knew exactly where he'd gone because it had been her idea. She smiled as his car finally pulled up outside the house and she watched as he went around to the boot and pulled out a large box.

She opened the door and let him in, 'So you got it then?' she asked once they were in the living room.

'Well you did insist that I bought it.'

'Baby you've been going on about that DVD player for as long as I can remember. Now that Derek looks set to get some money why shouldn't we splash out?' Jane said as she stroked her hand down the side of John's face.

John smiled back, 'Are you sure that we can get some money out of him? I mean you're already divorced.'

Jane sat down on the couch and lit up a cigarette, she observed John as he unpacked the DVD player.

'I spoke to my solicitor today,' she said, 'apparently I should be entitled to more maintenance.'

'Excellent,' said John reading the instructions to the DVD player. 'It seems that you were right.'

'Exactly, so you can relax. I told you I know what I'm doing. That's why I've booked us a luxury holiday to the British Virgin Islands.'

John stopped playing with the DVD player and sat next to Jane on the couch. 'Are you sure that's a good idea? I mean we haven't got any money yet, what if something happens? What if he doesn't win the case?'

'Relax,' said Jane as she took a long drag of her cigarette, 'I've got a good feeling about this. Besides we could do with a break. I'll leave the kids with my mum.'

John took the cigarette out of Jane's mouth and stubbed it out in the ashtray. 'That's a great idea,' he said before leaning forward and kissing her passionately.

Tom who had been sitting on the staircase and listening in on their conversation slowly stood up and made his way to his room. He closed and locked his door, he intended on staying there, alone, for the rest of the evening. The conversation he had just heard disgusted him to the pit of his stomach. His mum and John were behaving like nothing more than leeches. Spending money they didn't even have and expecting a nice cut out of his dad. Any money his dad paid should be spent on him and Tina not luxury holidays for his mum and John, that was the whole point of maintenance after all, wasn't it? How could he have been so stupid? Treating his dad like shit when it was obvious that John and his mum only saw him and his sister as meal tickets? All this time he'd been convinced that it was his dad's fault that his parents had got divorced, now he could see that his dad wasn't the villain he'd thought he was. If only there was a way of making things up to his dad.

CHAPTER TWENTY-SEVEN

Peter J. Cutner had gone through the complexity of laundering Justin's money, but nobody in the room except Peter could understand a damn word he was saying.

'I just don't get it,' said Tony shaking his head.

Peter who had already explained the procedure three times to them was starting to lose the little patience he had left.

'Look,' he said turning to Justin and ignoring Tony, 'it doesn't really matter whether or not you understand the ins and outs of the process, all that matters is that the money is hidden safely and that no one except you can get to it.'

'All right,' Justin said.

'But . . .' Tony started desperate to learn more about this high quality crime.

'Shut up and stop hassling the man,' Sarah interjected. Tony did as he was told.

'Now we've already funnelled the money through a series of shell companies . . .'

'They're those companies that aren't real, right?' Tony asked enthusiastically. Everyone in the room shot him a look that could kill and Tony finally gave in and sat back down in his chair, away from the rest who were huddled over Peter's desk.

'So, as I was saying I've funnelled what's left of the money, some nineteen million pounds, through a series of shell companies. The money now belongs to The Oxford Trading Company, which is based in the Caymans and whose sole director is Collin Matthews.' Peter handed Justin a passport. Justin opened it up at the front page, inside was a picture of him but in the name of Collin Matthews.

'Bloody hell, look,' Justin said showing the passport to Sarah.

'How did you get that?' Justin asked, obviously impressed.

'I have my ways,' Peter said with a smile.

'You did all this in just two days,' Sarah said, looking at him in admiration.

'Well Justin hasn't been the first client of mine interested in moving such a large amount of money out of the country. To be completely honest with you, I suspected that Justin might need this kind of service and so set things moving before you all came to me with the news that Justin had been conned. Of course solicitors aren't meant to perform such functions for their clients but as in most cases theory and practicality are two completely different things.'

'So how do I get the money?' Justin asked, bored by the minor details of how his money was being laundered.

'You simply walk into the Cayman Island International Bank, present them with the passport I've given you, the bank account number and of course the password. You'll then be able to transfer the money to any country in the world, just remember that if you bring it back to England you could end up losing it, just as you will your house which we obviously won't be able to sell in time.'

'I still don't get it,' Tony said, again getting up out of his chair.

'What? What the fuck is it that you don't get?' Peter shouted, finally losing his patience with the boy.

Tony paced around the room, his finger in the air just like some kind of university professor. 'You said you funnelled the money through three different companies until it finally ended up in the bank account of The Oxford Trading Company, of which Collin Matthews is the sole director.'

'Yes,' said Peter crossing his arms across his chest and leaning against his desk in anticipation of the point this financial genius was going to make.

'But you've left a trail for the FEDS to follow, all they have to do is see which company has bought the fake sugar or whatever you've written on those invoices from which company until they finally reach The Oxford Trading Company!'

'First of all, you imbecile, the FEDS only work in the States, they wouldn't be interested in a case like Justin's. Second of all, I haven't left a trail because Justin already closed his original bank account and transferred all the money into a Bahamian company called Rex Incorporated of which a James Ryan is sole director, of course James Ryan just like Collin Matthews doesn't really exist. Rex incorporated bought nineteen million pounds worth of non-existent micro chips from a company based in Guernsey which in turn bought nineteen million pounds worth of non-existent sugar from a company in Bermuda and so on until the money reached the bank account of The Oxford Trading Company. There is no link between Justin and the Oxford Trading Company and any law enforcement agency trying to follow this trail would come up against uncooperative bankers who are paid for their silence. Do you get it yet?'

'But . . .'

'Shut the fuck up Tony,' Justin shouted, pushing his friend back into the chair, 'I've got a fucking headache. All I want to know is that my money is safe.'

'Justin, trust me your money is safe, like I said earlier all you have to do is present the bank in the Cayman Islands with that passport and provide them with the password and the money's yours to do with as you wish.'

'So I have to go over to the Cayman Islands then?'

'No you could fax them a copy of that passport and do the rest over the telephone, but why would you want to do that?'

'No reason, I was just asking,' Justin said rubbing his temples.

Peter himself felt a migraine coming on, he'd never seen a couple of idiots quite like Justin and Tony before. He took in a deep breath hoping it would calm him down. 'Good, well that's it, keep the passport in a safe place and whatever you do don't forget the password the bank manager asked you.' Peter thought back to the time when they opened the account right here in his office, he had thought that perhaps Justin in his naivety would inadvertently divulge the password to that last all important account, but the kid was so paranoid that he had asked Peter to leave the room. Peter could see that he didn't trust anyone, not even his two closest friends, so it shouldn't have been a surprise that he didn't trust a total stranger, even though he was his solicitor. Peter sighed, he had done all he could, so it was back to plan B, he just hoped that Sarah could pull it off.

It was evening and Derek had cooked Christine a meal. Most days of the week were spent at her home now. When he thought about it he was surprised by how quickly things had developed and he even toyed with the idea of proposing to her. Yet the lack of confidence over his financial situation stopped him from going through with it. What kind of life could he provide her? No job, no car, no real home, sure she was loaded but he didn't want to live off her handouts, and sure he'd picked up seventy-five thousand pounds from his interviews with the press but how long would that kind of money last, especially when one stopped to consider his lack of income and all the maintenance he still had to pay Jane?

Christine seemed as though she was in a good mood, more so than usual. He studied her closely as they washed up.

'You've had that big smile on your face ever since you got home, what's going on?' he asked dubiously.

She laughed, 'I guess I can't keep any secrets from you. I wanted to tell you a bit later on but I just can't keep it in any longer.'

'What is it?'

'Tomorrow the injunction against Justin will be served, he won't be able to sell any of his assets or even touch his money. More importantly due to the new evidence in our possession the judge has agreed to bring the trial forward, we go to war in two weeks.'

'That's great,' Derek said, wrapping his arms around Christine and kissing her.

'We're halfway there,' she said gazing into his eyes, but he didn't hear her words, he was lost by the beauty and happiness that now surrounded him.

He wanted to tell her how he felt, how his heart couldn't maintain a constant beat when he thought about her. He wanted to tell her that he had fallen for her, but how could he? It was so early, if he told her the truth she'd run a mile.

As Christine gazed into Derek's blue eyes she wondered what secret thoughts they shielded. Did he feel the same way about her as she felt about him? She wanted her feelings to be reciprocated so desperately that it felt pathetic. She wanted to utter those magic words 'I love you' but how could she? It was way too soon. He was divorced for heaven's sake, if she told him how she felt he'd run a mile. Besides she suspected that she had another bombshell for the poor man. One she feared could end their relationship. It had caused her great concern and the timing couldn't have been worse, not when she stopped to consider how well things had gone so far. But before she told him she had to be absolutely certain.

Justin and Tony were in the games room playing pool and smoking joints, an activity which often kept them occupied for hours. Carefully Sarah searched the bedroom that she shared with Justin. She knew that he had a hiding place somewhere because he would sometimes miraculously produce great wads of cash without ever having to go to a bank. Yet if Justin was anything he was an adept thief and such people knew how to hide things well. His distrust of everyone had made the discovery of his password seem impossible. However Sarah did know one thing, his hiding place was somewhere in this room, it had to be because this is where he'd disappear to just before producing those magical wads of cash.

She looked under the bed, behind the fake Van Gogh paintings, behind the cupboards and closets and under the carpet. Nothing. She was at a loss as to where it could be. In desperation she lay on the bed and stared at her reflection on the large mirror which hung on the ceiling. She remembered how much Justin liked to look at it when they had sex. Sarah in turn liked to look at it when she had sex with Tony. Now out of boredom and frustration she studied it carefully for the first time. She noticed how it wasn't really one large mirror but more over four rectangular mirrors which were screwed into the ceiling. Except they weren't really screwed into the ceiling, they were held there by a series of metallic clips making it easy to remove them.

Sarah stood up on the bed and tried to get a closer look but the ceiling was still too high. She remembered that Justin kept a stepladder in the corridor so that he could have easy access to the loft. She left the room in order to fetch the stepladder, which she brought in as quietly as she could. Sweat now started to line her back, she knew that Justin would be playing pool for hours but there was always that small chance that he might decide to come upstairs.

Nervously she placed the ladder next to the bed and climbed its steps, gently and with all her strength she slid one of the mirrors out of its holding. Nothing, just the ceiling lay behind the area she had uncovered.

'Shit,' she whispered as she gently placed it back into its place. Undeterred she tried the next one, she was now perspiring heavily and beads of sweat dropped off her forehead and on to the ground below. She smiled as she unveiled the safe that was hidden behind this particular mirror and silently commended Justin for his brains. To think that it had been up there all this time, staring right at her, everyday! She tugged at the safe door but inevitably it wouldn't open. She replaced the mirror and wiped the sweat off her forehead before quickly returning the stepladder to its place.

Once her heartbeat had returned to normal she locked herself in the bathroom and used her mobile to phone Peter.

'Peter I've found his safe,' she whispered.

'Good girl,' Peter said, delighted.

'But I don't know the combination for it.'

'Don't worry about that, I'll be able to open it.'

'You can open safes?'

Peter laughed, 'There are lot of things I can do, as you're starting to learn.'

'But how will you get to it?'

Peter was silent as he thought about this, patiently but nervously Sarah listened to his breathing, mindful of any noise that came from outside of the bathroom door.

'OK this is what I want you to do, persuade his friend Tony to take him on a boys' night out somewhere, maybe to a strip club. Make him do it as soon as possible, when you know the exact night they'll be out, phone me back and I'll book us a flight to the Caymans. Do you have your passport?'

'I do.'

'So you understand what you have to do?'

'Yes I do, Peter, I think I love you.'

'I love you too, and soon we'll be together with all that money. We're nearly there baby, I promise.'

Sarah breathed in deeply, 'OK, I'd better get back, bye my love.'

'Be careful,' Peter said before hanging up. Sarah looked at the mobile she held in her hand. Had she actually said the words 'I love you?' She'd always told herself that love was for saps, for women like her mum who didn't know how powerful their femininity was. Yet here she was falling for Peter, but God, what a man, brains, looks, courage and soon they'd have all that money. Yes she would finally get what she wanted, she'd get her man and the money.

CHAPTER TWENTY-EIGHT

Karen ignored the ringing of her mobile as Sarah's name flashed up on the screen. It was the third time she'd phoned in the past hour but Karen chose to ignore her. She had better things to do then talk to that selfish cow. Although Karen had forgiven Sarah for sleeping with Tony, pride still prevented her from talking to her. She wanted her to suffer for a while. Yet she felt uncomfortably guilty as she remembered calling her friend a prostitute. Best friends weren't meant to make judgement calls about each other's morality.

The ringing stopped, allowing Karen's attention to return to writing her essay. She was just about to put down a new sentence when she was interrupted by the familiar sound of an incoming text message. Karen read the message:

> Really sorry. Don't want
> to fight. Leaving country.
> Never coming back. Call
> me. Sarah.

What the hell was Sarah doing now? Karen knew her friend well, if she weren't careful she'd end up getting herself into serious trouble. Letting out a slight sigh, Karen dialled Sarah's number.

'Hello, Karen?' replied Sarah's nervous voice.

'I want you to tell me everything that's been going on.'

Derek smiled as he handed Jane a thousand pounds in cash.

'That should make us square for a while,' he said taking a seat next to Tina on the couch. 'Are you ready? I thought we'd go to Planet Hollywood today, you always wanted to go, didn't you?'

'Oh thanks daddy,' Tina said as she ran to the hallway in order to put her coat on.

'Where did you get this?' Jane asked as she examined the money.

'I've been paid a bit for my interviews with the press.'

'Yes, it seems you're quite the celebrity,' said John, 'how's the case going?'

'Things are looking up,' Derek beamed.

'Well that's good,' Jane said, making a poor attempt at hiding her envy.

'Which reminds me,' Derek said as he searched through his pockets before pulling out a small scrap of paper. 'I'm now able to afford one of those mobile phones you were always nagging me to buy when we were married. Here's the number.'

Jane snapped it out of his hand, giving him a contemptuous look for reminding her about their marriage, 'Well you certainly are moving up in the world,' she said sardonically.

Derek ignored the remark and took great delight as he remembered the old adage that the best revenge is to do better than your enemies.

'I thought I'd try Tom again,' Derek said.

'You don't give up easily that's for sure,' John said, trying to ease the tension in the room. 'As ever you'll find him in his room listening to music. It's all he seems to do these days.'

Jane shot John a berating glance, turning his cheeks slightly red with embarrassment.

'Is something wrong with Tom?' Derek asked, concerned for his son's welfare.

'No, he's just at that funny age that's all,' Jane said quickly, 'go up and see if you can get any sense out of him.'

Again Derek climbed the familiar steps up to Tom's bedroom passing Tina in the hallway and promising her that they would be leaving soon.

To Derek's surprise Tom's room was already open and his son was standing in the doorway as if waiting for him.

'Hello son,' Derek said with a smile of optimism.

Tom nodded in acknowledgment of his dad's presence. He wanted to say hello, to hold his dad and say that he was sorry for the way he had acted, that he missed him and loved him, but he couldn't, he just couldn't. He was too afraid to show his feelings.

'I'm taking Tina to Planet Hollywood today,' Derek said, 'you remember how much you used to hassle me about taking you, don't you?'

Tom broke into a smile, it was the first time Derek could recall seeing his son smile in years, the sight took him aback. 'Would you like to come with us?' he asked.

Tom walked over to his desk and played with the edge of one of his copy books, he looked out of his bedroom window deep in thought. 'Maybe next time, I've already made plans for today,' Tom said.

'Oh.' Derek wanted to ask what those plans might be but thought better of it. 'Well OK, what about next week, would you like to go anywhere in particular?'

Tom thought for a bit, 'I'd like to see that new Batman film if that's OK.'

'Well I can't take Tina to see it, she's too young but if your mother agrees we could go in the evening, just you and me.'

Tom nodded and broke into another smile, 'OK.'

'Well see you next week,' Derek said as he made to leave the room.

'Dad,' Derek stopped and turned back round to face his son, 'congratulations, I read about you in the papers.'

'I still haven't got the money back yet son.'

'I know but at least everyone knows that it was you who won the lottery, and the papers make you out to be a hero.'

'Well you don't want to believe everything you read,' Derek said modestly.

'See you next week,' Tom said.

As Derek walked down the staircase and towards Tina he felt euphoric, for the first time in ages he felt like the relationship with his son was salvageable.

Tony sat down in the corner and watched as the stripper slowly peeled off what little clothing she had for Justin's pleasure. Justin's hand reached up for the third time in an attempt to grab her but she moved out of reach teasingly. Club rules stated that there was no contact allowed between the strippers and their clients.

Tony wondered where all Justin's cash came from, his money was supposed to be out of the country and access to it wasn't exactly easy. He guessed he must have stashed a fair bit at home, but where? More importantly why had Sarah insisted that he take Justin on a boys' night out tonight? She had been adamant, almost begging him to do her this favour. He knew that she was up to something, she'd said that she had a plan to get to the money and that they could run away together but when he pressed her for more details she clammed up saying that he had to trust her, that soon all would be revealed. Trusting Sarah wasn't an easy thing to do, especially when he'd seen the way she used Justin, but what alternative did he have? He wanted her and more importantly he wanted the money, and if anyone could find a way of getting to the money it was Sarah.

Sarah waited by the window looking out for Peter, he was fifteen minutes late. Finally she saw his BMW pull into the driveway and rushed down the stairs to let him in.

'Where have you been? I was worried.'

'Sorry,' Peter apologised, 'but I had some difficulty getting hold of this,' he said pulling out a small packet of Semtex and some fuses.

'Is that a bomb?'

'Sort of. Now where's the safe?'

'Are you sure you know what you're doing?'

'Just trust me OK.'

'Where did you get it from?' Sarah asked as she led him towards the safe.

'I spend most of my life working with hardened criminals, getting hold of a bit of Semtex is hardly difficult.'

Sarah pointed at the safe which hung above the bed, she'd already taken the mirror down.

'Not as stupid as he looks, old Justin,' Peter said

as he filled the cracks of the safe with the Semtex. Sarah bit her lips nervously. She watched on as Peter added the fuse and then lit it.

'Come on, lets go,' he said taking her by the hand and running out of the room and into the corridor. He grabbed her and bent over her as they crouched on the ground.

'Put your fingers in your ears,' he instructed. She obeyed, afraid that they'd both wind up being blown to smithereens.

There was a loud bang which caused the whole house to shake and most of the windows to shatter. Sarah couldn't help but scream and Peter held her closely.

'Don't worry it's over now,' he said as he got up, 'but we better be quick, no doubt the neighbours will be phoning the police right now.'

She followed him into the bedroom and coughed as she breathed in all the dust the explosion had thrown into the air. On the bed lay the safe door along with a large wad of cash and the passport Peter had given Justin.

Peter picked up the cash and stuck it into his coat pocket, there must have been over ten thousand pounds there, all in fifty pound notes. Next he picked up the passport and flipped through its pages, at the back, near Justin's picture was a small scrap of paper, on it, written in black ink was the account number and the address and phone number of the bank in the Cayman Islands. Below was the following ten-digit pass code, 9-12-20-32-38-4. They were all winning numbers from the lottery ticket Justin had stolen, except for the four which Peter presumed came from the number forty-one. Obviously he couldn't fit the original numbers into ten-digits but nevertheless the fact that Justin had to keep this pass code written down reinforced Peter's opinion of him as a complete and utter idiot.

'Not the most original pass code,' Peter smiled showing Sarah the scrap of paper, before placing it again in his coat pocket along with the passport.

'But how will you get the money? That's Justin's picture on the passport,' Sarah asked.

Peter smiled before pulling out a passport from his back pocket. He flipped to the back and showed Sarah his photo; below was thc name Collin Matthews.

'You made two?'

'That's right,' Peter beamed, 'now lets go we've only got an hour to make it to the airport.'

Sarah kissed him passionately and then threw a small envelope on to the bed.

'What's that?' Peter asked.

'I thought I owed Justin a decent goodbye,' she said.

Peter shrugged, he grabbed her hand and they ran out of the house together before getting into his BMW and driving off.

Christine lay on Derek's chest, it was late but she didn't have work tomorrow and so could afford to stay up past twelve. She sighed, but it was a sigh of pleasure, they'd made love every night this week and she couldn't remember the last time she'd been so happy.

'You know right now I feel like the luckiest man alive,' Derek said breaking the blissful silence.

'Is that because you'll soon be a multi-millionaire?'

'No, it's because I'm in love with a gorgeous woman and my son has finally stopped hating my guts.'

She looked at him and wondered if she could finally unburden the secret she felt she had been carrying for an eternity. She took a deep breath, it was now or never.

'Derek I have something to tell you.'

'What is it?' asked Derek, slightly concerned by the way her voiced quivered when she spoke.

Christine bit her bottom lip, she was nervous yet excited at the same time. She sat up in the bed. Derek sensed the nervousness which surrounded her, it caused him concern for he'd never seen her like this before.

'Whatever it is, I'll understand,' Derek said taking her hand into his.

'I'm pregnant,' she said.

The words hit Derek like a sledge hammer. Did she say pregnant? He was sure that was what he had heard.

'I . . . I'm sorry, what did you say?' he muttered in disbelief.

'I'm pregnant.'

Him a father, at his age!

'But I'm too old,' he said.

'The last thing you are is old.'

He grabbed her and held her tightly, the shock subsiding into joy.

'I'm going to be a dad again!'

'Yes you are,' she laughed, glad that he was so happy.

Then he looked at her, a thought crossing his mind. 'How did it happen? I mean I always assumed you were on the pill.'

She looked away, the question staining the moment. 'You're the first man I've been with for a couple of years now. I stopped taking the pill about a year ago. I mean what was the point? I wasn't with anyone, then when we got together, well things happened so fast I didn't even think about it. I'm sorry.'

'Sorry? Why are you sorry?'

'I know you've already got two kids, you're divorced, you've been through all this before. I guess a kid is the last thing you want right now. Look I want you to know that if you want out I'll understand.'

'Out? Are you crazy? You've made me the happiest man in the world. I've got a chance to do everything again and this time I want to do things right.'

He kissed her passionately and they rolled around in the bed like a pair of teenagers both lost in the happiness a new life can bring a loving couple.

Justin and Tony were both drunk but that hadn't stopped them arguing about who would drive the Ferrari home. As usual Justin won the argument, after all it was his car. Spinning the car into his driveway he narrowly avoided crashing into a marked police car.

'What do you think you're playing at?' an officer shouted as Justin stumbled out of his car.

'What the fuck's going on here?' he replied, looking around him and noticing the swarm of police officers.

'Have you been drinking?' the officer asked.

'No, and I asked you what the fuck's going on, this is my house, I'm Justin Farren.'

'Are you indeed, well then Mr Farren I'm placing you under arrest for fraud and money laundering,' the officer said as he grabbed the drunk and swaggering Justin by the arm and shoved him against the Ferrari before cuffing his hands behind his back. Justin tried to resist, but barely able to stand he simply mumbled something incomprehensible to the officer. Tony slowly backed away, afraid that for some reason he might be arrested as well.

'You have the right to remain silent, but anything . . .'

'All right, I know, I've heard it before,' Justin managed to spit out venomously.

'You fucking pigs make me sick.'

The officer shoved Justin into the back of his car, the sudden, violent movements causing Justin to vomit. He made no attempt to keep the contents of the night's drinking session in his stomach and instead, to his great pleasure, puked his guts out over the police car's seats, even managing to spray a little over the driver's seat. When the vomiting had stopped he propped himself up against the back seats only to find the officer holding up a breathalyser.

'Would you mind blowing into this?' the officer asked, a sardonic smile set across the breadth of his face. Justin let out a sigh.

CHAPTER TWENTY-NINE

Sarah looked out of the window, this was the first time she had ever flown, in fact apart from a school daytrip to France, this was the first time she had ever been out of England. She gripped Peter's arm as the plane started its descent. She could see the tiny island of Grand Cayman, from the air it looked like nothing more than a small rock, surrounded by clear sapphire water, which glistened from the sun's rays. It was breathtakingly beautiful and for Sarah there was no turning back now.

As the plane landed on the small air-strip she closed her eyes, holding tightly on to the golden cross that dangled from her neck.

'I didn't take you for a religious girl,' Peter said when the plane stopped moving and she finally opened her eyes. She just shrugged her shoulders and smiled. Peter looked at her in admiration, she had the right quality of feminine beauty and girlish naivety. No wonder men fell in love with her at the drop of a hat.

The first thing that struck her when she walked out of the small plane was the heat followed by the tropical muggy air. She breathed it in and smiled, it was so clean. Peter led her towards immigration control and she held his hand tightly. Would the authorities in England already be looking for them? Would the immigration officer notice that Peter was travelling with a fake passport under a false name? He had reassured her repeatedly that nobody would come looking for them and even if they did they would both have left the Caymans to some other tropical location. Would that be what the rest of her life would be like? Running from one beautiful island to another? It excited her, Peter excited her, he had given her so much and the adventure had only just begun.

Peter gently pushed her forward towards the immigration officer, a dark skinned, elderly gentleman, who had a look of calmness and peace on him that only a life in the Caribbean could bring. He studied her passport photo carefully looking up and comparing it to her face. She started to feel nervous and scared, her pulse beginning to race but as the officer smiled she immediately started to relax. He was only admiring her beauty.

'Are you a model?' he asked in the soft yet confident accent of the Caribbean. She shook her head and smiled shyly. He let out a gentle chuckle.

'Well I hope you enjoy your stay in paradise,' he said. And that was it, she was through immigration. Home free, she turned round to see how Peter faired and hugged him as he was let through almost immediately.

'I love you,' she said without any inhibition and Peter smiled.

'Come on, we've still got to get through customs and then we'll take a taxi to our hotel,' he said. She held him tightly by the waist as they made their way towards customs, she didn't ever want to let him go.

Derek switched on the TV, it was Sunday morning and he was lying in bed with Christine. He was going to be a father again and the beautiful woman who lay in bed next to him was going to be the mother. How lucky was that? He wanted to tell her how he felt about her, how much he loved her but he couldn't, not now. She'd just assume it was because of the pregnancy.

Christine cuddled up to him, 'I don't think you're going to find anything interesting to watch on Sunday morning.'

'I know but old habits die hard I guess,' Derek said giving Christine a peck on the cheek.

'Wait, what's that?' Christine said, pointing towards the TV.

Derek looked at the screen in disbelief as a reporter stood outside Justin's mansion. Behind him Derek could see that the police had cordoned off the area, he turned up the volume so that he could hear every word the reporter said. Christine gripped his arm as she too listened anxiously to what the reporter had to say.

'Neighbours of Justin Farren, the country's youngest ever lottery winner, who is embroiled in an ongoing legal dispute over the validity of his win, say that last night they heard a loud explosion and that later the police arrested Mr Farren on these premises.'

The reporter moved slightly so that the camera could focus on the fairly elderly gentleman who stood next to him. 'Mr Fortt, you live next door to Mr Farren, don't you?'

'Yes, that's right I live in the property just next to Mr Farren's on the left,' he said pointing towards his mansion. The camera focused in on the mansion, which was almost as grand as Justin's before returning its attention back to the reporter and Mr Fortt.

'Please tell us in your own words what you saw and heard last night,' the reporter said.

Mr Fortt looked directly into the camera, 'Well I was at home watching TV with my wife when we heard what can only be described as a large explosion. So loud in fact that there's still a ringing sound in my wife's right ear. She's being visited by a doctor right now.'

The reporter nodded, indicating to Mr Fortt that he would like him to move on.

'Well, then I looked out of my window and saw lots of smoke, so I phoned for the fire brigade. They must have in turn phoned the police because before they left the place was swarming with police officers and police cars, even a helicopter was heard in the sky, for a while anyway . . .'

Mr Fortt again noticed that the reporter was nodding his head, this time rather more anxiously.

'Yes, so,' he continued pausing for a moment while he remembered where he was in his story. 'Oh, yes then Mr Farren arrived, by then the whole neighbourhood had gathered around outside his property, well when he saw the police he started hurling all kinds of abuse at them. It was quite obvious that he was drunk, well then he was arrested and shoved into the back of the car where he threw up.'

The reporter nodded again, 'And tell us Mr Fortt, what kind of neighbour is Mr Farren?'

'Terrible, terrible I say. All kinds of loud music and parties and young hooligans gathering outside his place, he once even told my wife to F off,' Mr Fortt said, looking away from the camera in embarrassment.

'Well thank you for your help,' the reporter said.

Mr Fortt nodded his head in acknowledgment of the camera just before its full attention was diverted back on to the reporter.

'So there you have it, yet another twist in the extraordinary tale of Justin Farren. The police refuse to comment at this point on Justin's involvement with the explosion at his home but have confirmed that he has been arrested on charges of fraud, money laundering, driving while under the influence of alcohol and damage to police property. As always we'll bring you the latest developments as they occur but for now over to the studio and back to you John.'

'Bloody hell,' said Derek.

'Quite,' agreed Christine, 'I wonder what he's done now.'

'How will this affect my case against him?'

Christine shrugged, 'I really don't know, I mean they could have arrested him on the charge of fraud relating to your case. After all they have enough evidence now from the tape to prove that he stole your ticket and claimed the prize as his own, but the money laundering? What's all that about? You don't think he committed some other crime as well, do you?'

'I wouldn't put it past the slimy snake. He obviously doesn't have any morals.'

'Well, whatever's happened, I hope they throw the book at him,' Christine said looking lovingly into Derek's eyes. Just as he was about to tell her how much he loved her his new mobile phone started ringing. Eagerly he grabbed it off the bedside table, expecting Terry he was unpleasantly surprised to hear Jane's voice.

'Hello Derek it's Jane here; I tried you at home but you weren't there, where are you?'

'Oh I stayed at a friend's last night.'

Jane was silent, he hadn't found a girlfriend had he? Jane wondered what she would look like, how old she would be.

'You mean Terry's place?'

Derek laughed, 'No, not at Terry's.'

He was definitely at a woman's place, a touch of jealously crept into the pit of Jane's stomach, she had never thought about Derek ending up with another woman. True she no longer loved him, no longer found him attractive but recently there had been a spring in his step, a quiet confidence which reminded her of the Derek she used to know, before life had ground him down.

Christine prodded him gently, she wanted to know who it was. Derek covered the mobile with his hand, 'It's the ex,' he whispered.

Christine tried to look like she wasn't jealous, but she was.

'Did you watch the news this morning?' Jane asked.

'Yes,' said Derek wondering why Jane was so concerned about his life all of a sudden.

'What will happen to your case?'

'My solicitor says she doesn't know how it will affect us,' he said staring into Christine's eyes. She smiled at him.

'Oh,' said Jane, 'I see, well the reason I'm phoning is that Tom wanted to talk to you about seeing Batman today because next weekend he'll be away on a camping trip with some friends from school.'

'OK.'

There was a moment's silence as Jane passed the phone to Tom.

'Hello dad, I forgot that next Saturday I'm going camping, so I was wondering if maybe you'd like to see the film tonight.'

Derek had already made plans to spend the evening with Christine, however re-establishing his relationship with Tom was vital, he just hoped that Christine would understand.

'Um, yeah sure, what time should I pick you up?'

'I checked the times at the cinema, it's playing at a quarter past five and seven thirty, so whichever one's best for you.'

'Great I'll pick you up at five then.'

'OK, thanks dad, see you at five.'

'Bye.'

Christine looked at Derek in curiosity.

'That was my son Tom, remember that I told you he finally started talking to me, well he wants to see the new Batman film tonight.'

'Oh Derek that's fantastic news, I'm really glad for you.'

'I thought you might be upset because of our plans.'

'Please don't be so silly, your kids are an important part of your life, and I want you to know that I consider them an important part of mine as well. Besides they'll soon have a little half-brother or half-sister to add to their number.'

Her words struck Derek, in his excitement he'd forgotten about Tom and Tina. Running his hand along Christine's back Derek wondered how they would react to the news.

CHAPTER THIRTY

Justin looked at Inspector Koleth in pure and utter contempt, 'Why have you arrested me?' he shouted, banging his fist on the table.

'Calm yourself down boy, I don't want to have to call in the officers in order to restrain you.'

'But you've got no right. I haven't done nutin´ wrong.'

'Haven't you? There's no use lying Justin, we have the tape now, remember? The one of Mr Bonner buying the ticket for the prize you fraudulently claimed, but more importantly we also have evidence that you tried to hide the money. That's called money laundering and it's a very serious crime indeed.'

'I wanna see my solicitor,' Justin said.

'You mean Peter Cutner?' Koleth scoffed.

'Yeah.'

'Well maybe you'd like to see your girlfriend too?'

'What do you mean?'

Koleth looked at Justin and smiled before shaking his head in mock pity, 'Oh dear, oh dear, it seems the conman has been conned.'

Justin looked at the detective inspector, confused and bewildered.

'Don't worry son,' Koleth said handing Justin a handwritten letter, 'maybe this will shed some light on the matter.'

Justin eyed the inspector suspiciously before taking the letter and reading it.

Dear Justin,
By the time you start reading this Peter and I shall be on our way to collect the money you deposited in that off-shore bank account. I wish I could say that I was sorry I'm leaving you like this, but I'm not. Peter has everything I ever wanted in a man, looks, intelligence, courage, a sense of adventure, plus he's really great in bed. In fact when I think about it he's your exact opposite. The times I spent with you pathetically clawing at my body were among the worst moments in my life. Thank God that you could never last very long. However out of the goodness of my heart I would like to offer you the following advice should a woman ever take interest in you again: 1. Make sure you brush your teeth on a regular basis and when you smoke a joint always use mouthwash afterwards, especially if you want to kiss someone. 2. When a woman talks to you, listen to her, it's not that difficult and I mean really listen, don't just nod and keep your eyes fixed to the TV set. 3. When having sex or making love think about the things she would like, things like foreplay, oral sex, cuddling and caressing believe it or not just sticking your penis in won't automatically pleasure her. 4. Now this is the most important of all, treat her like a human being and not a plaything, take her opinions seriously and show her that you trust her. Make her feel that she's more than just a

piece of meat, there for the pleasure of your skinny, little willy.

Well that's about it really, good luck, I hope you have a nice life, I know I will.

Sarah

P.S. Peter has sent the details of the money laundering scam and copies of all the forms you filled in to the police, it should reach them sometime on Monday. I tried to persuade him not to but he said it was his civic duty.

'Bastards!' Justin screamed, jumping out of his chair in a fit of rage and throwing his side of the table up into the air towards Inspector Koleth. The duty officer instantly left his post from the side of the wall and tackled Justin, wrapping his arms around his back.

'Get off me, you fucking pigs! I hate you! I hate all of you!'

'Throw him into the cells to cool off,' Koleth instructed the uniformed officer.

'You're fucking scum, scum you hear?' Justin shouted as he was manhandled out of the room. 'I want a brief, you hear me? I want a fucking lawyer.' Those were the last words Koleth could hear as Justin was dragged to the station's holding cell.

Derek's time with Tom had started off awkwardly, from the time he picked him up to the time it took to take him to the cinema, Derek noticed a distance between the two. It had been so long since he had spent any time with his son the truth was that he no longer knew him. However they both made attempts to fill in the gaps of silence and things dramatically improved once they reached the cinema and had more things to talk about, like where to sit and whether to buy popcorn or tortillas. After the film they talked about how good it was and compared it to the other Batman films. Derek felt confident enough to take Tom to the local McDonald's, where they both ordered Big Mac meals.

'So how's school?' Derek asked now assured that he could approach the more risqué topics of conversation with his son.

'Good, I'm not being bullied anymore if that's what you mean.'

'I'm just worried about you that's all. I don't want you to go through anymore than you already have. I do know that the last few years have been rough on you.'

Tom smiled, he was glad he'd made the decision to reach out to his dad. They'd had a good time together and he could see that his dad really did love him.

'Maybe we can do the same again next week? I mean there are loads of films in the cinema now.'

Derek raised his eyebrows delighted with the way things were progressing with his son.

'Maybe you'd like us to go and see Arsenal play one day, just like we used to?'

'I'd like that dad,' Tom said.

Derek found it difficult to believe how quickly they'd managed to repair their relationship. Perhaps it was a good time to tell Tom about his relationship with Christine, perhaps even about the pregnancy.

'Tom, I have a secret I'd like to tell you.'

Tom looked up slightly confused.

'What is it?'

Derek braced himself, Tom was so unpredictable he just didn't know how he'd react. He looked at his son, who was clearly waiting for what the news could be.

'I've got a girlfriend,' Derek said.

'Is that all? Why the big secret?' Tom asked, obviously bemused.

'There's more,' Derek continued, Tom looked at his father carefully, his eyes giving away the fact that his mind was already trying to figure out what was about to come next.

'Christine, she's the woman I'm seeing, well she's pregnant. You're going to have a little brother or sister.'

Tom looked away in disgust, he obviously wasn't pleased by what he had just heard.

'Well aren't you going to say something?' Derek asked anxiously.

'What do you want me to say? Congratulations? Enjoy your new family?'

'Tom, please don't be like that, I'm still going to love you and Tina the same, like I always have.'

'No you won't, I have friends at school, the dads always forget about the first family.'

'Come on Tom, that can't be true of all the dads.'

'I want to go home, now.'

'Tom, please . . .'

'I said I want to go home!' Tom's raised voice caused a few stares from customers tucking into their Big Macs and cheeseburgers. Derek gave in, the last thing he wanted was a scene.

'OK Tom, let's go home.'

Inspector Koleth entered the interview room for the second time, it seemed that Justin Farren was maturing as a criminal for he had insisted that a solicitor be present during his interview. The solicitor who had been appointed to Justin was a Mr Christopher Welkin, a man Koleth hated with a passion, but then again the inspector had a deep dislike for all members of the legal profession.

He sat down across the table and stared hard at Justin and his solicitor. He came with no cigarettes, or coffee or food, this time he would try a different tact, this time he would be the hard nosed cop who wanted to throw the book at the thieving scumbag and that was exactly what he intended to do.

'You should have taken the money and run,' Koleth said looking at Justin sternly, 'but then again your kind never knows when to call it a day, never knows when they've pushed their luck too far.'

'I would like to object to the harsh tone and manner you are adopting with my client,' Welkin interjected.

Koleth shot the man a look that could kill, 'Your client is going down for a very long time and there's nothing you can do to save him.'

'I'll be the judge of that,' Welkin shot back, matching the inspector's stare.

'Oh no you won't, he'll be tried and judged under a court of law. You're finished Justin, do you hear that? We've got the tape of Mr Bonner buying the lottery ticket, that's five years for fraud, and now we've got evidence of your money laundering scam, that's a maximum penalty of ten years. Fifteen years kid, that's what you're looking at, so you better start thinking about how you can make things real easy on yourself.'

Justin looked at Welkin for help, he was scared,

that much was obvious but his solicitor showed no emotion, the man was like a robot, 'What evidence of money laundering do you mean?' Welkin asked.

Koleth produced a sheet of paper and handed it to the solicitor. It was the letter Sarah had left him. Justin looked on anxiously as Welkin read it, occasionally shaking his head. It was bad, worse than Justin had originally thought, he could feel it. When he finished reading Welkin passed the letter back to Koleth and looked away, his gaze landing upon the table.

'I'd like to spend some time alone with my client.'

'I thought you might,' Koleth said making a show of tucking the letter into his jacket pocket before leaving the room.

CHAPTER THIRTY-ONE

Tony basked in the limelight of the attention he was receiving. He couldn't believe he was actually sitting in a TV studio, make-up being delicately applied to his face by gorgeous babes and about to be interviewed by a world famous TV journalist. He was going to be on the news! He was going to be famous! Justin had had his fifteen minutes of fame, now it was his turn. For the first time in his life he'd decided to wear a suit, and he'd also decided to try and drop the street language, just as he had done with Sarah. He was going to be on TV!

'Are you ready?' the journalist, an attractive brunette in her early thirties asked.

'Yes,' Tony replied confidently. She nodded towards the camera man, 'Rolling,' he shouted.

The journalist looked straight into the camera, 'As most of the nation is wondering exactly what is happening with Justin Farren, the lottery winner who just can't stay out of the headlines, we can bring you this exclusive interview with his best friend Tony Davis. Tony how long have you known Justin?'

'For years. Since we were kids.' Tony looked into the camera as he reflected that really he'd only been friends with Justin for just over a year.

'Now I understand that you've spoken to his solicitor, is that right?'

'Yes the police still won't let me see him, but I

found out who his solicitor was and met him at the police station.'

'So tell me, what exactly has he been charged with?'

'They've arrested him for fraud, money laundering and drink driving.'

'And what does Justin say to these charges?'

'I'm sorry I don't understand.'

'Will he plead innocent or guilty?'

'I don't know, I didn't talk about that with his solicitor.'

'Tell us Tony, do you think Justin is guilty of these charges?'

'I really don't know. There seems to be so much evidence against him, it's possible I suppose,' Tony said, slightly tilting his head for the sake of the cameras. He wanted to show the world that he was basically a good friend, somebody who would stand by Justin, no matter what.

'Now I understand that there have been some developments that only you and Justin's solicitor know about, would you like to share those with us?'

Tony perked up, this was the bit where he could blow them away, this was the bit when he got to deliver the front page news to the whole country, that Justin himself had been robbed of the money.

'Well?' asked the journalist aware of the time constraints.

Tony looked directly at the cameras, his words were slow and precise, 'Justin's money has been stolen by his first solicitor and his girlfriend. They've taken it and run away together.'

'Really? And do you know where they've gone?'

'No, but we believe they may be in the Cayman Islands.'

'Amazing, I take it that the two have eloped together.'

Tony turned slightly red, 'Sorry I don't understand.'

'Justin's solicitor and his girlfriend were having an affair behind Justin's back?'

'Yes that's right.'

'And they've stolen his money and run away together?'

'Yes that's right, something like nineteen million pounds.'

'And are the police looking for them?'

'Sorry, I don't know about that.'

'Tony thanks for your help and for keeping the public informed on what has become the most sensational lottery story in the country's history.'

'My pleasure.'

'Well as ever we'll keep you posted as events unfold . . .'

Derek used the remote to switch the TV off, he couldn't believe what he'd just heard. He walked over to the phone and used it to call Christine, she was still at the office working late. What did it matter if they could prove that Justin had stolen the money when the idiot had gone and lost it all himself?

Sarah stood on the balcony and looked at the view of the sea. Peter had been gone for almost three hours. Since they had arrived Peter had been busy trying to find them more fake passports so that they could assume new identities, transfer the money out of the Collin Matthews account and move on to the next place. She felt safe with him by her side, she knew that nobody would ever be able to find them, Peter was just too smart.

Sipping her Martini she watched as couples walked hand in hand along the clear, sandy beach, not a care in the world. Paradise on earth, she was a whole world away from the bleak working-class area she had grown up in. It felt like a dream, just six months ago she didn't even have two pennies to rub together, no real future, no prospects and no clue what to do with her life and now here she was in one of the most exclusive places in the world. She wanted to stay here but knew that the final decision rested with Peter. He was the one who knew what to do, he was the one in charge.

She heard the door to the room close and came in from the balcony. Peter was standing there, wearing a light, white shirt and matching trousers. He looked so good, the sun had already begun to tan his skin giving him a healthy, vibrant glow.

'How did it go?' she asked sitting on the bed.

'We're almost sorted, tomorrow I'll be able to pick up our new identities and move the money out of the Collin Matthews account.'

'So when do I get my share?'

Peter looked hurt, 'What? You think I'm going to rip you off?'

'No, I was just asking that's all.'

Peter went and joined her by the bed.

'Look right now it's best if we don't separate it, it makes it easier to move about.'

'I see,' Sarah said, slightly disturbed by the fact that right now she had no control over the money or indeed her life.

'Look,' he said gently caressing her face with his

hand, 'you've got to trust me, I'm only doing what's right for us.'

'I know and I do.'

'That's good because we're on the front cover of every single paper on the island.'

'What?' Sarah's voice was panicky and her breathing started to sound laboured.

'Don't panic, nobody on the island really cares, but we still have to be careful, I mean the press from the UK might come here looking for an exclusive story or even the police might be hunting us. So it's imperative that we get off the island as soon as possible and make sure that we leave no trail behind.'

'What are we going to do?'

'Well the first thing we're going to do is cut your hair and dye it brown, that way you'll be harder to recognise. And always keep your sunglasses on when you're outside.'

'What about you?'

'There isn't much I can do really, just wear a hat and keep my sunglasses on. That's why it's so important we leave as soon as possible.'

'When are we going?'

'The day after tomorrow.'

Derek sat in Christine's office, when she'd heard the panic in his voice she'd called him over immediately. She looked calm as he told her about Tony's live interview. It was a shock, a big shock and the last thing they needed right now but she tried to calm Derek down, to reassure him that everything would be all right.

'Don't forget the injunction against the remainder of his assets is now in force, that means that his house and collection of cars is safe.'

'Safe for now.'

'Safe until we win the trial. You've still got over three million pounds coming your way Derek, maybe it's time you started thinking more positively.'

'That's easy for you to say, you weren't robbed of twenty-five million pounds. Can you possibly begin to imagine how it must feel?'

'No I can't, and I'm sure it must be hard but I'm confident that we'll recover what's left. It's still a lot of money,' she said reaching across the desk and placing her hand on top of Derek's, 'besides if your ticket hadn't been stolen we wouldn't ever have got together.'

Derek smiled, 'I never thought about it like that.'

'Do you feel better?'

'Yes I do, I trust you, I know you'll get back what's left but is there any chance that we can get back the nineteen million his solicitor took?'

'First the police have to catch him, and, well, traipsing around the Bahamas or the Cayman Islands isn't really the Met's cup of tea, stuff like that is often left to the kind of law enforcement agencies that track international criminals and I don't think they'll be too interested in a case like yours to pursue Mr Cutner tenaciously. I'm afraid that unless he slips up that money is gone, and from what I remember, Mr Cutner is one very shrewd customer. I'm sorry Derek.'

'That's OK, it's not your fault and like you said if it weren't for this whole mess we wouldn't ever have met.'

Christine squeezed his hand and Derek tried his

best to look happy, but the truth was that although he loved Christine deeply he couldn't help but shake off the feeling of being cheated. Just as he thought the money was in sight it was again taken out of his grasp and with a new child on the way and no job he would need every penny he could get his hands on.

It was Justin's last day at the police station, tomorrow he would have his preliminary hearing at the crown court. If he didn't make bail, well then he'd be transferred to a real prison, where he'd be kept on remand. Justin was afraid, very afraid. He wasn't a fighter, he knew that inside he'd be bullied just like he had been at school, until he'd met Tony. He remembered Tony's dad once telling them that the first few weeks were the hardest because that's when everyone tried to push you around. If you couldn't physically prove yourself, then you were dead. Justin's hands started to shake at the thought of what could happen to him if he were sent to prison. He'd never ever thought that he'd end up in prison. He'd only ever stolen a few cars, burgled a couple of homes, nothing serious. He was just seventeen, he'd only ever imagined his worse punishment being a few hours community service in an old people's home, listening to old biddies complain about their corns. Koleth had said that he could go down for fifteen years. Fifteen years! He'd always thought that his young age would save him from the law but he'd obviously crossed the line from being a kid out for some kicks to being a real criminal, and it now looked like he would be judged like one. Fraud and money laundry, years behind bars, perhaps the best years of his life, spent trying to defend himself against criminals that were harder, bigger, stronger and a lot nastier than he could ever be.

'I don't wanna go inside,' he said looking at Welkin with pleading eyes.

'You won't, I'm sure. Look the crimes you've committed are what we call white collar crimes, usually the courts are easier on white collar criminals. Also there's your age to be taken into consideration, I've never heard of anyone your age being charged with money laundering, let alone convicted for it.'

'But what if they don't give me bail?'

'That's what I'm saying, I'm sure they will.'

'But can you promise?'

Welkin played with his pen, 'No, of course I can't, but if, now that's a big if, if you don't get let out on bail then you'll be kept on remand in a young offenders' institution.'

'You mean Felton?' Justin asked, the panic already creeping into his voice.

'Well that's where most young offenders are sent, but don't worry, that's the worse case scenario and anyway you'll be with boys your age.'

'Some of 'em will be twenty.'

'Yes some, but I'm sure you'll do fine. Look I know lots of people who've been in prison, it really isn't so bad.'

'I can't do time,' Justin said tears rolling down his cheeks. If only he hadn't done what he had, now he was going to get beaten up and buggered. He'd heard stories of what happened to kids in young offenders' institutes, he'd never meant to let things go this far.

Welkin grabbed Justin by the collar, 'Look you're

going to have to toughen up otherwise you won't last five minutes inside.'

Justin started sobbing uncontrollably, Welkin shook him some more. 'Be a man Justin, do you hear me? Be a man. If you have to do the time, then you'll do the time.'

'I don't wanna,' Justin sobbed, green snot running out of his nose.

'Then start listening to me and help me prepare you for tomorrow,' Welkin said handing Justin a tissue. He watched in silence as the sobs died down and Justin wiped the snot and tears off his face. Welkin, an unemotional man, found that he actually felt sorry for the poor kid. Who wouldn't have claimed that lottery ticket as their own? He knew, given the same circumstances that he certainly would have, and now this kid had the prospect of years behind bars. As a criminal lawyer, Welkin had spent a lot of time with all types of criminals, and he'd quickly learnt to tell the men who could handle time and those that would be ripped to shreds inside. It wasn't just about size and physical strength, or the nature of the crime one committed, but more about the mental toughness the criminal possessed. Looking at Justin he saw a boy who was about to be thrown to the wolves.

Justin had finally calmed down and so Welkin took the opportunity to produce some forms which he wanted to fill in.

'What are those?' Justin asked.

'These are legal aid forms, you see you don't have any money, and all your assets have been frozen, so what we have to do is declare you bankrupt so that the state can pay my fees. We'll also need legal aid when it comes to the civil trial.'

Justin had forgotten about the impending civil trial against Derek.

'You mean I can still win that?'

Welkin grinned, despite ten years experience the law's lack of fluidity always caused him some amusement.

'Possibly, or we might be able to cause so much work and hassle that the other side would be willing to settle. Stick with me and you might very well still be a millionaire.'

The words were of little comfort to Justin, who in his terror would have gladly given all his millions in exchange for his freedom.

CHAPTER THIRTY-TWO

The first thing Sarah heard when she awoke was the clear Cayman Sea, only a few yards from her hotel room. Gently she opened her eyes, the sun's rays already filling the room. She'd expected to find Peter lying next to her but he wasn't there. Sitting up in the bed she felt an unnerving emptiness in the room.

'Peter,' she called out, but there was no answer. That's when she noticed the envelope sitting on what would have been his pillow. Her name was written on it, she opened the envelope and saw a large pile of cash. A few thousand pounds at least, suddenly Sarah became very nervous indeed. Carefully she unfolded the letter which was contained inside and started to read.

Dear Sarah,
I remember your fondness of letters, so I thought it only appropriate that we part company in this way. You see for a time I toyed with the idea of taking you along with me, but then I realised that this was never about you, only about the money. Please don't get me wrong, I had a great time and think that you're great, but you didn't really think that we'd really ride off into the sunset together, did you? I'm too young and so are you. In fact you're way too young, but deep down you already knew that, didn't you? In the envelope I've left you three

thousand pounds, perhaps a gentleman would have left you more, but I guess by now you've understood that the last thing I am is a gentleman.
Best wishes
Peter

Sarah read the letter twice before the tears started streaming down her face. Then she read it a third time and that's when the sobs started to hit her. It wasn't just the fact that he'd left her high and dry but also the cruel and callous way in which he'd done it and after everything they'd been through together.

She curled up into a ball, grabbing hold of the pillow where Peter's head used to rest. She held it close to her as she cried in her anguish, she'd loved him and trusted him. In fact he was the first man she'd ever let get really close to her and now he was gone and she was left to fend for herself. What would she do? She couldn't go back to England and she couldn't stay here in the Caymans. She had to go somewhere else, but where? Where would she be safe? And how would she survive? Three thousand pounds wouldn't last long, not in the Caribbean.

As the crying subsided she sat up in the bed and dried her eyes. She'd never felt alone before or afraid, and now the two feelings swept over her body like a storm at sea, it caused her to shiver slightly. Spotting the still half-full bottle of Martini on the other side of the room, she got up and walked over to it. Picking up the bottle she filled her glass; she didn't know how she was going to get out of this mess but the first thing she was going to do was get drunk.

In England the winter had returned and gripped the nation in its cold and icy hand. The retail trade blamed the unusually harsh weather for the drop in sales as the streets were almost deserted in the run up to Christmas. It was dark and drizzly as Derek walked into the pub where he was to meet Terry. Due to one crisis after another Derek had been unable to go for his weekly drink with his friend for some time.

As Derek had expected Terry was already sitting at his usual table, quietly sipping his Guinness. There was another pint at the table, Derek presumed for himself.

'Hello mate, I took the liberty of buying you a pint before you even got here.'

'Thanks,' said Derek, 'I need it.'

'So what's been going on in your life? I thought you'd forgotten about me.'

Derek smiled, 'I don't know where to begin. I guess the main news is that I'm going to be a father again.'

'What? Bloody hell! Is it wanted? I mean I didn't even know you were seeing someone.'

Derek smiled, 'It's definitely wanted by both of us.'

Terry took a big gulp of his drink, this was big news. 'Who is she?' he asked.

'My solicitor,' Derek laughed.

'When do I get to meet her?'

'Soon, I've still got a lot on my plate.'

'Bloody hell, this is a shock, congratulations

mate, I'm really happy for you,' Terry said raising his pint of Guinness into the air.

'Cheers,' said Derek as their pint glasses chinked together. 'Oh before I forget this is for you,' he said producing an envelope and passing it to Terry under the table. 'It's the money you lent me, thank you.'

'There was no rush to give it back you know,' Terry said tucking the envelope into his trouser pocket.

'I know, but things are a bit better on the financial front, I've picked up a few bob for selling my story to the papers.'

'Oh yeah? How much?' Terry asked, his eyebrows raised in interest.

'Seventy-five grand.'

'Wow, you haven't done too bad at all.'

'Depends how you look at it, don't forget I'm down twenty-five million pounds,' Derek said shaking his head incredulously. He still had problems coming to terms with the fact and wondered if he ever would be able to accept it. How does one recover after losing so much money?

'Try not to think about it mate, you'll drive yourself crazy. Anyway seventy-five grand is still better than a poke in the eye.'

'True but you can't help but think about it, especially when you have a little one on the way.'

Terry nodded slowly before taking a slow sip of Guinness, 'Yeah, it must be hard,' he finally agreed.

'Tom still hates my guts, maybe worse than ever.'

'Why's that?' Terry asked. So Derek explained the whole nasty mess of how his son had finally started speaking to him again. About the trip to the cinema, and about breaking the news of Christine's pregnancy to Tom. Barely able to contain his tears Derek carried on the story about Tom's public outburst and his refusal to speak to Derek all the way home. Terry sat and listened in silence, buying Derek more beer. Afterwards he didn't really know what to say, so he bought Derek another round. Merrier, the two joked about a bit and reminisced about old times and Terry told Derek about his latest conquests. Derek listened intently and then told Terry how meeting Christine had given him a new lease on life. Derek bought more drinks and they talked some more. He confessed that he was madly in love with Christine and soon intended on proposing to her. Terry said that he had to buy more drinks seeing as they had more to celebrate. Afterwards Derek insisted on buying another round, he had never been happier and he wanted to share his happiness with his best friend.

Peter J. Cutner slowly walked into the Cayman bank with a confidence that defied description. He liked the layout of the building, the large open spaces prevented the clientele from feeling like trapped farm yard animals. The service was so fast that queues were almost non-existent. It was all such a deep contrast to the UK banking system he had become accustomed to. The décor, although obviously expensive was very modest, no thick extravagant leather chairs like one would expect. Peter approached one of the tables marked 'withdrawals.' He deliberately chose the counter with the most attractive assistant.

'Hello Sir, my name's Delilah, how may I help?' she smiled revealing a perfect set of teeth. Her eyes were emerald green and contrasted wonderfully with her dark skin. God, the women here were beautiful, it was a shame he had to leave so soon, but the next stop was the Bahamas and he imagined that the women there would be equally as attractive.

Peter smiled back at her allowing his penetrating eyes to gaze into hers. 'Yes I'd like to transfer eighteen million pounds from my account into another.'

He had decided to leave a million in the Collin Matthews account just in case he ever needed a ready and waiting account again. From now on his new persona was to be George Cameron, a retired commodities trader.

'Could I have your passport and account number?' Delilah asked eloquently.

Peter passed her the Collin Matthews passport, and a slip of paper on which he had already written down the account number. With no effort the name and account number was typed into the computer in a nanosecond.

'And can I have the first, third, fourth, eight and tenth digits of your ten-digit pass code?'

'Sure, nine, two, two, three and four.'

'Oh,' Delilah said with a stunned expression as her eyes widened. 'Oh,' she repeated as she looked at Peter in what appeared to be disbelief.

'Is something the matter?' Peter asked, a dreaded sense of concern filling his stomach.

'I'm sorry sir could you just repeat those numbers back to me again?'

'Yes of course,' Peter said as he rolled his eyes towards the sky, 'nine, two, two, three and four.'

Delilah carried on staring at the screen. She

picked up his Collin Matthews passport before looking at him carefully.

'I'm sorry sir, please excuse me,' she said as she left her position and walked over to an office. Through the large office windows, Cutner could see the solitary figure of a man sitting behind a desk. The manager, Peter thought to himself. What the hell was going on here? Had he somehow been busted? Peter's gaze stayed transfixed on Delilah as she returned to her desk accompanied by the manager.

'Hello my name's James, I'm the manager here,' said the man as he shook Cutner's hand. He picked up Cutner's fake passport and studied it carefully.

'Is there a problem here?' Peter asked, deeply concerned.

'Yes I'm afraid there is,' said the manager, 'please if you follow me through to the office. Delilah, bring the file for Mr Matthews' account to my office please.'

Delilah gave Cutner a sympathetic smile before disappearing. Peter followed James into his office. Whatever was amiss here had very little to do with any kind of police investigation, of that Peter was entirely sure.

James sat behind the comfort of his desk and gestured for Peter to take a seat.

'Are you going to tell me what's going on here?'

'I'm afraid it appears that you've been the victim of a fraud.'

'Me, the victim of a fraud? Whatever do you mean?' Peter scoffed.

'Yesterday a young lady came into the bank claming to be your sister. She had all the necessary documentation, along with your death certificate and a copy of your last will and testament.'

'What the fuck's going on here? I don't have a fucking sister!' Peter shouted.

'Well I assumed as much, which is why I said that it appears that you've been the victim of a fraud.'

At precisely that moment Delilah knocked on the office door and entered with the file James had requested. Completely avoiding any eye contact with Peter, she handed the file to James before making a hasty exit. James went through the slim file until he found what he wanted. He pulled out two photocopies, one was the last will and testament for Collin Matthews leaving all his worldly goods, including the nineteen million pounds contained in his Cayman bank account to his sister Sarah Matthews. Sarah? Could it be that her hand was in this? Suddenly the cool, sophisticated demeanour of Peter Cutner started to crack. It appeared that he wasn't as slick and intelligent as he'd first imagined. His hands started shaking as he checked the bank account number written in the will. It matched. Next he looked at the photocopied death certificate, it contained everything he'd expect to find in a genuine death certificate. Apparently Collin Matthews had died in a car accident. Peter began to sweat with rage, the cold blast from the bank's air conditioning doing little to cool him down.

'You must know the account of where she transferred my money to!' Peter exclaimed.

'Yes we do.'

'Well then transfer it back to me.'

James shook his head, 'When your sister . . .'

'She's not my fucking sister!'

'I'm sorry, when the lady who perpetrated this crime against you transferred all your money out of your account and into hers she automatically became one of our clients. As you are well aware laws in the Cayman Islands prevent bankers from divulging information about their clients' accounts to absolutely anybody, including the authorities. However, there are certain exceptions and your case seems to fall into one of them. We can contact the Cayman police, who can launch an investigation into what has happened, however as the origin of the fraud seems to stem from the United Kingdom at some stage the authorities there will have to be brought in. Is that something you'd like to happen Mr Matthews?'

Checkmate, there was no way Peter could risk involving the British authorities after he'd laundered nineteen million pounds. He'd have to sort this out himself, he wasn't sure how this had happened to him but so far all clues pointed to Sarah.

'No thanks, I'll deal with this myself,' Peter said as he left the office slamming the door. James watched as Peter stormed out of the bank. Cayman bankers had a term for money which came from dubious sources. It was called funny money and sometimes the tales behind the money could be very funny indeed.

Two hours later Derek stumbled out of the pub, Terry had a taxi waiting for him outside. He asked Derek if he wanted a lift, Derek explained that Christine's house was in the opposite direction, he'd be all right with the bus. Derek waved goodbye to Terry and watched as the taxi drove off. A slight chill hit Derek, making him shiver, damn it was cold. The alcohol hadn't helped, the street was spinning. He blamed it on the lack of sleep he'd been getting but as he started to cross the street he admitted to himself that getting sloshed with Terry hadn't been a good idea. Yet he knew that the real reason for getting drunk was a way of escaping from his problems with Tom. Afraid that he'd revert back to his old drinking habits an image of Tom came to him; it was when he was younger and Derek had taught him how to ride a bike. He remembered the day he'd taken the little stabilisers off Tom's bike and how he rode it just like the big boys. After he had ridden round the block and emerged from round the corner he clung to Derek and asked if he was proud of him. 'Yes of course I'm proud of you son, I always will be.' At the time, when Derek had said those words, he had thought that Tom's love would be forever. He could never have imagined that things would have turned out the way they had and that now his only son couldn't even bare to look him in the face. The unfamiliar noise of a car horn beeping furiously snapped Derek out of his drunken daydream.

Derek barely had enough time to open his mouth in shock as the Ford Sierra ploughed into him. He felt no pain, or fear, just a questioning of what was happening as the car and the sky instantly mingled into one. Then he was on the ground, lying on his back and looking up, he couldn't move, but he could see people gather around him, their mouths were moving but he couldn't hear any sounds. Then everything went black.

Sarah looked at the yachts as she tried to walk as steadily as she could. Half an hour ago she'd stumbled out of the hotel and walked along the beach. She used a hat and sunglasses to disguise her appearance. Her hair had already been dyed and she was a brunette. She had quite liked the new look but now it just reminded her of Peter. Again her eyes started to well up and she cursed the day she ever met Mr Cutner. Suddenly she was on the floor clutching her ankle. She'd bumped into something, something hard enough to knock her down.

'Are you OK?' a deep voice asked.

Sarah looked up and saw a tall, dark man standing in front of her. So it hadn't been a something, she'd bumped into rather a someone. A rather handsome someone.

'I think I've twisted my ankle,' she said.

He bent down and put his hand around it.

'Ouch,' she said looking at him. He smiled gently.

'It looks good to me, but maybe we should put some ice on it just in case.'

'Great, where am I supposed to get ice in the Cayman Islands?'

'I've got some on my yacht.'

'Oh,' said Sarah noticing the gold Rolex on his wrist at precisely the same time as he said 'yacht.'

'Here take my hand,' he said quickly pulling her up with his strength.

Strong, handsome and rich, things were improving by the second Sarah thought to herself.

'Can you walk?' he asked offering his arm for her to lean against.

'Is it far?' she asked.

'No, that's it over there,' he said proudly pointing to the biggest and most extravagant yacht she'd ever seen.

'I think I'll make it,' she said.

'Because I can carry you there if you like.'

'I don't know, I'm heavier than I look,' Sarah said pushing her sunglasses down slightly and peering at him.

'And I'm a lot stronger than I look,' he replied, his smile revealing a perfect set of white teeth.

'OK then, if you don't mind, it's not everyday a handsome man offers to carry me to his yacht.'

And so in an instant she was cradled in his arms, her back able to feel the bulge of his hard biceps. You don't know what's about to hit you, Sarah thought to herself, letting out a little giggle.

CHAPTER THIRTY-THREE

Peter had searched for Sarah everywhere he could imagine she could possibly be on the tiny island, but she was nowhere to be seen. The only good news was that she hadn't yet checked out of their hotel room, and her passport was still there, which meant that she had to return at some point. Peter had staked out her room for the whole night but she hadn't returned, what the hell was going on? Whatever was going on, Cutner knew one thing, sooner or later Sarah would return to the hotel, and when she did, she'd better have some answers.

Derek could hear crying and what came as muffled voices, but he couldn't quite make out what they were saying. He tried to open his eyes but they wouldn't budge and a sharp pain hit the right side of his back before it shot its way up his spine and into the base of his skull causing him to grunt in pain.

He felt a hand on his head and finally he managed to open his eyes, it was Christine, she was standing over him, she'd been crying heavily, that much he could see.

'Derek can you talk?' she asked.

Things started to get blurry, 'I love you,' he managed to say in nothing more than a whisper. Then everything went black again.

'Doctor, doctor, someone help please,' Christine screamed, her voice filled with panic.

Almost immediately doctors and nurses filled the room, pushing Christine aside. She stood alone as they checked Derek over.

'Not to worry,' one of the doctors said as he walked over to Christine, the rush over.

'You mean he's OK?' Christine asked as she dried her eyes.

'He's still stable,' the doctor said.

'But he woke up, he spoke to me and then, and then he was gone again.'

'Well that's a good sign, if he's woken up and spoken to you then the chances of any brain damage are much lower. He's been very badly hurt, it's normal in such cases for the patient to be in and out of consciousness.'

'But he'll make a full recovery?'

'He's stable. We won't know how badly hurt he is until we've had the results for all the tests back, but there isn't any internal bleeding, and it looks like all he's managed to pick up are some broken bones. So yes, at this stage we're optimistic, he's a very lucky man.'

'Thank you doctor.'

Christine sat back down next to him and held his hand. The doctors and nurses were already gone, and so they were alone again. An emptiness slowly overwhelmed Christine, she'd waited all her life to meet a man like Derek and the thought that now, when things were going so well for them, that she might lose him and have to raise their child alone, well that thought was almost unbearable.

Sarah gently opened her eyes, she'd hoped that she'd find her hero lying next to her in the luxury bed of the yacht she'd stayed in last night. Instead she found a single rose in his place. She picked it up and pressed it to her nose and smiled. It was the most romantic gesture she'd ever received.

His name was Alex, and he was as mysterious as he was handsome. He spoke English fluently yet he definitely wasn't British, but he didn't have any kind of accent to give his origins away. The fact that he was so dark gave him that suave Mediterranean appearance. She reckoned he was Italian or, at the very least, had Italian blood. He definitely had the cockiness, trying to sleep with her almost as soon as he'd learnt her name. She held out, even though she wanted him so badly, after all if she gave out on the first night he might think she was some kind of tart.

Sarah decided to look for him out on the deck, and quickly put on her light, summer dress. He wasn't there either, but out on the table was a pot of coffee and some cereal. She touched the coffee pot, it was still warm. There was a note beside it.

Angel,
I've just gone into town to get a few supplies, probably back before you wake up, but just in case help yourself to breakfast. And please don't leave before I arrive!
Alex

Angel had been the nickname he'd given her last night. At first she thought it sounded corny and slushy, but now she quite liked it. She poured some cereal and milk into the bowl he'd left for her. It wasn't quite the five-star breakfast she'd become accustomed to recently but she didn't mind at all.

By the time she was finishing off her coffee Alex arrived with a bag full of groceries.

'I was afraid you'd take off the minute my back was turned,' he said putting the bag down bedside the table and sitting opposite her.

'Not my style,' she said with a flirtatious smile, 'you've been really nice, I couldn't go without saying goodbye.'

Alex smiled back but didn't reply.

'What's wrong?' she asked.

'What do you mean?'

'You're looking at me strange.'

Alex reached into the grocery bag and pulled out a folded up newspaper before gently laying it on the table. Sarah held her breath, he knew, he'd seen her picture in the paper. Shit, this couldn't be happening, not now.

'I thought you looked familiar when I saw you last night, your hair is quite different, but it's you, isn't it?'

Sarah got up, 'I don't know what you're talking about,' she said and made to leave. He grabbed her by the arm, not hard, but firmly enough to make his strength felt.

'I'm not going to rat on you, if that's what you think.'

'What do you want?' she asked, forcefully pulling her arm out of his grip.

'I don't want anything, look I know what you're going through, I know what it's like to be on the run.'

'What do you mean?' she asked, her eyes exploring his face as if seeking out the truth.

'I know about your past, so I guess it's only fair I tell you about mine.'

Slowly the pieces started to come together for Sarah, the yacht, the Rolex, the almost silent demeanour of this man, 'You're a criminal, aren't you?'

Alex didn't respond instantly to Sarah's accusation. He wanted her to know the truth about who he was, about where he'd come from. He'd been alone for so long and finally he'd found a companion, someone who shared his experience, yet he was afraid that the truth would scare her away. Almost reluctantly he decided that the truth was all he could offer her. Half his life had been a lie, it was time for the lies to end.

'I was, and pretty big time, but not anymore. Please take a seat, let me explain.'

Eyeing him suspiciously, Sarah carried out his request.

'I was born in Palermo, Sicily, my mother died giving birth to me and when I was ten years old my father died in a car accident. My uncle, who also happened to be my Godfather, decided that the best thing for me would be to go and live with a wealthy relative in the States. That relative was my father's second cousin, but Sicilian families are very close. The cousin, Johnny, he looked after me well; you know I was like one of his kids. When I grew up, Johnny said that I should work for him and I did so without question. Johnny worked for Florida's biggest mob boss and was in charge of the family's cocaine business. Unknown to me he liked to skim a little off the top of each deal, and when Johnny's boss found out he ordered a hit on Johnny, his wife, his two sons and me. The DEA arrested me and one of Johnny's sons just two days before the guy who was meant to carry out his contract on us got the chance. The rest of the family wasn't so lucky.

The DEA offered us a deal, new identities and enough cash to get out of the States but only if we ratted on our bosses. The alternative was years behind bars, and so we took the only option open to us. That was eight years ago and I've been hiding here ever since, always looking over my shoulder, afraid that one day someone would come to collect the contract out on my head.'

Alex looked away from Sarah, out on to the harbour and all the other luxury yachts stationed there. Her gaze followed his and she wondered how many other yacht owners here had similar stories to tell.

'You're the first person I've told that too. I guess after all this time I feel kind of lonely, when I saw that paper today and your picture, I felt like, well maybe we had something in common, something that could bind us together.'

Sarah nodded her head in sympathy, 'I think I understand what you mean, I'm sorry I had no idea.'

'Hey it's OK, it's not your fault, sometimes people just kind of fall into something, things happen and no matter how hard we try we've got no control over them.'

'Yeah I guess so,' Sarah said looking down at the wooden deck.

'Is that what happened with you? Or is it true, what the papers say?'

'Yeah it's true, I didn't fall into it like you did, I planned to rob him.'

'I see,' Alex said. She could see that he was disappointed. 'Why?' he asked.

She almost laughed, it was a question she didn't really know the answer to, or maybe she did know the answer only she was too afraid to ask it of herself, for fear of what she might find out; for fear of knowing what kind of person she was. Her eyes started to well up but she refused to allow herself to cry. She wanted, no, she needed to answer Alex's question with dignity.

'I guess it was just greed, I didn't really know what I wanted from my life. All I knew was that I was just sick of being poor, of thinking about where the next penny would come from, afraid of ending up like my mum. When I found Justin, it was like a way out, so I grabbed it even though I knew I could never love him.'

'And your boyfriend, the lawyer, where's he?'

'Gone, along with the money,' Sarah said as she finally burst into tears.

Alex immediately got up out of his seat and crouched down beside her.

'Don't cry please, I didn't mean to upset you.'

'You don't understand, I did some really awful stuff,' she sobbed, 'the way I behaved, I'm so ashamed. I deserve everything that's happened to me.'

'Hey don't be so hard on yourself, maybe you did some stuff that was bad, but we all make mistakes and we all deserve a second chance. Look at me.'

'Do you really think so?'

'Yeah, I do. Listen I'm setting sail for Jamaica tonight. Do you want to come with me? It's no longer safe for you here.'

Sarah was quiet as she considered her options. She didn't really know this man, yet he had confessed his darkest secret to her.

'Hey I'm not asking you just because I want to sleep with you, I'd really like the company,' he said.

'Is that true?' she asked looking down into his eyes.

'Yes it's true,' he said gently using his hand to wipe away her tears, 'so what do you say?'

'Yes,' she nodded, managing a smile.

Justin sat in the van and tried not to look at its other passengers. In fact everybody tried their best to ignore everyone else. He couldn't believe that he hadn't been granted bail. Welkin had assured him that today he'd be going home. Instead, his worst fears were coming true. He'd be kept behind bars until the trial. That bastard Cutner had really stuck it to him. Based on the evidence he had sent to the police regarding the money laundering scam the judge had said that anyone able to organise such sophisticated criminal activity should be regarded as highly dangerous and likely to abscond. Also to be considered was his previous run-ins with the law and his conviction for burglary. It was in the nation's interest to keep him incarcerated until it was clear that he wasn't a danger to the public. Justin was petrified, it was all he could do to stop himself from breaking down and crying. Fear of looking weak in front of his contemporaries was driving him now. If Justin knew one thing he knew that looking weak when you were banged up, even in a young offenders' institute meant only one thing, annihilation.

Out of the corner of his eye he tried to study the three other boys, they were all bigger than him and they all looked a hell of a lot meaner.

'What the fuck you looking at?' the big one in

the middle shouted at Justin, his eyes bulging in rage. Justin knew that now was the time to step up, to show that he couldn't be intimidated or bullied to show all present that he was just as hard as the rest of them. But for some reason he just couldn't do it, deep down he knew he just couldn't beat the boy opposite him, not in a straight fight anyway and so Justin simply looked away.

'Pussy,' the boy spat out, his eyes boring into Justin and not leaving him alone for the remainder of the journey.

Eventually the van stopped, and Justin's heart raced as he heard the driver's door open and close. They'd arrived. The back of the van suddenly opened up, filling it with light.

'Come on, out you come,' a guard said.

Slowly all the boys left the van and were made to line up against a wall, just in front of the entrance. They were out numbered by five guards, all of whom would have looked like convicts themselves were it not for the fact that they were wearing sparklingly clean uniforms. The guards were big and muscular and made all the boys there, even the big one who'd taunted Justin, feel small and insignificant. The smallest of them was just a couple of inches shorter than Justin, but he had a thick neck that was probably necessary to prop up the boulder he had for a head. He walked slowly up and down, inspecting them.

'Well what a bunch of sweethearts we have here,' he said. 'Now I'm only going to say this once, so you better listen good. We don't take any shit off anyone in here, you step out of line and you'll pay for it. My name is Mr Johnson and you shall address me as Mr Johnson or Sir, or preferably both and you shall pay me and all the other guards here the due respect we deserve. Do I make myself clear?'

He approached Justin and stood in front of him, his face so close that Justin could smell his breath. 'I said do I make myself clear?' he shouted, spit from his mouth landing on Justin's face.

'Yes,' Justin replied.

'Yes what?'

'Yes Sir, Mr Johnson.'

The other boy, who had taunted Justin earlier, let out a sneer but quickly lost it when the guard's attention turned to him.

'You have something to say?' Johnson said standing in equally close proximity to the boy as he had Justin.

'No Sir,' the boy replied.

Johnson took out his truncheon and waved it in the air, 'It's funny how there's always one volunteer,' he said before ramming the truncheon into the boy's solar plexus. The boy buckled over on to his knees, his face saved from hitting the ground by Johnson's hand.

'You watch your step boy,' he said holding the boy's face in his hands, 'I'll be keeping my eye on you. On all of you, so remember that when you're all cold and lonely at night, and you cry out for your mummies, you'd better behave, because it won't be mummy who comes,' he said letting go of the boy and allowing him to slump on to the floor, 'it'll be me,' Johnson said, looking at all the boys with a sadistic smile on his face. Speech over and point made, Johnson turned to the other guards.

'Let's get these virgins inside, they've got a lot of settling in to do.'

Sarah rushed into her hotel room with Alex by her side, throwing her clothes into her suitcase as fast as possible.

'Hey you don't have to rush,' Alex said taking a seat on her bed and flicking through the TV channels.

'I want to get out of this place as fast as possible, it gives me the creeps,' she said as she looked around the hotel room. She opened her hotel room safe, her passport was still inside but the money Peter had left her was missing. A chill ran down her spine. Who had taken the money?

'Something wrong?' Alex asked.

Sarah considered telling him about the missing money but intuitively she knew that he would go to the hotel reception and cause a scene. She just wanted to get off the island and go somewhere she could feel safe as soon as possible. Sod Cutner's money she thought, whoever had taken it was welcome to it.

'Nothing's wrong,' Sarah said placing her passport in her handbag, 'just thinking about which clothes I should take.'

Peter watched from a bench by the hotel gardens as Sarah emerged with a man who was carrying her suitcase. He was big and muscular and looked like he could rip Peter's head off if he wanted to. He'd obviously played a part in helping Sarah to steal his money. Peter fumed, this was starting to get complicated. He'd probably need a gun to deal with the likes of Sarah's new boyfriend. He watched as they hailed a taxi. Getting up and rushing over to his hired car he followed them as closely as he could, careful to blend into the background of the traffic.

CHAPTER THIRTY-FOUR

The coast of Jamaica came into view and Alex quietly killed the engines.

'Why have you stopped?' Sarah asked walking towards Alex.

'I always stop for a few hours far away from the coastline for some privacy. It's beautiful, isn't it?' he said walking up onto the deck and surveying the surroundings. There wasn't another yacht in sight, just the clear, sapphire water of the Caribbean Sea and far off in the distance, barely visible to the eye was the coast of Jamaica.

'It's like right now, at this moment, this place is our home. This part of the world belongs to us, because we're the only ones here and we can do whatever we want.'

'You're very philosophical,' Sarah said, wrapping her arms around his waist and pecking him on the side of his neck. Last night in the middle of the sea, she'd finally given herself to him. They'd slept together in the same bed for four consecutive nights and she'd done her best to resist his advances but last night she couldn't stand it any longer. She had wanted him from the moment she'd laid her eyes on him and she knew that he had wanted her just as desperately.

'If it wasn't for the beauty of the Caribbean I'd have lost my sanity long ago. For so long this place has been my jail.'

She turned him around and looked into his eyes

completely unaware that she made his stomach flip with every sensuous gaze she gave him. She kissed him, gently, not passionately, making the kiss all the more erotic.

'There are worse jails,' she smiled seductively.

'Have you ever swum naked in the sea?' he asked.

'No, never,' she smiled.

'You don't know what you've been missing, do you want to try?'

'Why not?'

She watched him strip and admired the hard, tanned body he possessed. He dived in completely nude.

'Come in, the waters great,' he shouted. He looked up and watched her as she undid her bikini top and let it drop to the floor. Instinctively she turned around in order to make sure that they were alone before removing her G-string. There wasn't a soul in sight and so with complete freedom she followed his lead and dived in completely naked. The cooling water hit her, and flowed with abandonment over every millimetre of her body. He was right, it was a completely liberating experience.

He watched her swim, fulfilled by the sight of her enjoyment. She swam towards him and they embraced each other in the deep sea.

'It feels like a dream,' she said gazing into his eyes.

'Well this dream's yours as long as you want it,' he said.

'What if I never want to leave?'

'Then this is what the rest of your life will be like. Nobody will ever find you here, I'll take care of you for as long as you want, I promise.'

She couldn't help but kiss those soft lips of his,

she knew she didn't deserve this piece of luck. Sarah remembered her childhood dream of finding a man that could take her to a place like this, of walking on the white sandy beaches she had seen in that post card from the Bahamas. She knew that she didn't deserve to spend the rest of her life living in a place as beautiful as this with a man as great as Alex, but that's why she'd never screw things up. She promised herself that she'd never let him go, she'd found her place now, she was home.

Justin lay in his bed and enjoyed the quiet and the solitude for as long as it would last. His cellmate was in the prison chapel, praying. Justin looked at the bible his cellmate read constantly, it lay on the small table they were forced to share beside the bucket they used as a toilet in the night. Justin's cellmate was called Paul, he was twenty-years old and had spent a year in custody for stabbing his brother in-law with a screwdriver. Next month he would turn twenty-one and be transferred to an adult prison.

Paul said that he wasn't scared, he knew that Jesus would protect him. Paul had found Jesus inside, he said that you needed Jesus in a place like this. Paul talked about Jesus all the time. It had started to drive Justin insane but it also made him curious, for Paul's belief gave him a calmness few other inmates possessed and a strength Justin had never seen the likes of before. He knew that if he were in Paul's place and about to be transferred to an adult prison, well it wasn't an easy thing to admit but he knew he'd be crying himself to sleep every night. He sat up careful not to hit his head on the bed above and took the bible into his hands. Slowly he started to flick through it, stopping at random pages and reading the odd passage here and there.

'You can borrow it if you like,' a voice said. Justin looked up, it was Paul. 'I've read it so many times I know it off by heart.'

'How can you be so sure?' Justin asked.

'Sure of what?' Paul asked, confused.

'Sure that he exists.'

'There'll come a time Justin, when you'll need him and you'll pray for his protection and then he'll be there for you. That's when you'll know he exists. That's what happened to me anyway.'

'But you said you found him in ´ere.'

'In here's where you need him the most Justin, and pretty soon you'll be needing him more than most.'

'What you mean?'

'You're the new boy Justin, the others will come for you soon. In fact I'm surprised they haven't already.'

'Paul, you gotta protect me.'

Paul shook his head, 'In here it's each man for himself, I can't protect you. The only person who can protect you is yourself, with God's good grace of course.'

Justin tightened his grip on the bible, Paul was one of the oldest lads in the place. If he wouldn't protect Justin then no one would.

The bell indicating lunchtime sounded. It was time for the inmates to make their way to the canteen.

'Come on,' Paul said, 'it's not the best food in the world but it'll help keep your strength up.'

Justin followed him as everyone made their way to the canteen. As he was almost outside the entrance to the canteen Justin felt three big figures converge behind him, he looked at Paul and could see that he also felt their presence. Neither of them dared turn around, instinctively they knew it meant a fight.

'New boy,' a voice behind Justin said. Justin turned round, the guy who had called him was short and fat, but he had a nasty scar that ran along his face. His two other friends were much bigger but it was obvious that Scar-face was the leader.

'Yeah you,' he said, 'I want your lunch, you hear me? Me and my brethren gotta eat and a skinny little fuck like you don't need a whole portion.' On cue Scar-face's two companions laughed at their leader's witty joke.

Justin looked at Paul for help. Paul slowly shook his head, he'd told Justin before that the others would try and size him up. They'd try him first, see if he was a soft touch before they really started to go to work on him.

'Whatever you do, don't give into them,' Paul had said.

Justin stopped walking and turned round. He had planned on telling them to fuck off but when they closed in on him he suddenly lost his nerve.

'What you stopping for fool?' said Scar-face's big friend. His eyes bore into Justin like he wanted to kill him.

'My man thinks he's got something to show us,' said the third one who was slightly taller than Justin but twice as wide, his breadth made up of pure muscle.

'Look I don't want no trouble,' Justin said.

'Well you got trouble, fool,' Scar-face said as he slapped him across the face.

Justin backed off slightly, the slap stung but he knew that worse would follow soon if he didn't think of something fast.

'Come on, why don't you leave him alone?' Paul said.

'What's it got to do with you preacher boy? Back off before we send you back to church.'

Scar-face's two friends walked into Paul, the really big one giving him a shove. Together they cut him off from access to Justin. It was Justin and Scar-face, alone now and toe to toe. Justin's heart started to race, he wanted to run away but his legs felt like jelly.

'Are you going to give me my food?' Scar-face said staring at him, his face showing the anger caused by Justin's insolence.

Justin knew he couldn't give in, if he did they'd make him their bitch and gang rape him on a regular basis. At least that's what Paul had said happened to the newcomers who buckled under pressure.

'No,' Justin said, his voice almost quivering.

Scar-face punched him in the gut and Justin keeled over on to the floor. The next thing he felt was Scar-face's foot connect with his testicles and that's when Justin screamed out in agony. Scar-face and his friends laughed, a small crowd gathered round now to enjoy the show.

'Break it up,' a booming voice shouted and suddenly everyone froze. The prison guards were coming to break it up.

'What's going on here?' one of them asked Justin as he got up off the floor.

'Nutin´,' he replied.

'Then what you doing on the floor? Fell did you?' the guard said eyeing Scar-face.

'Yes Sir, I fell,' Justin said.

'Go on get out of here the lot of you, before I send you to your cells with no food.'

The crowd started to fan out, the show was over and the guards returned to their posts.

'This isn't over bitch,' Scar-face told Justin as he barged past him, his two companions following suit. Paul looked at him, 'Don't worry, you did good,' he said, before walking off with everyone else for his lunch.

Justin watched Paul walk off, what did he mean, he'd done good?

Elmore had spent the last ten years of his life living on his yacht and sailing around the Caribbean, Grand Cayman was one of his favourite islands but more through its rich history rather than the merit of its outstanding beauty. Grand Cayman is where Blackbeard the pirate is said to have buried his treasure. His ten years of travel had brought Elmore into contact with all kinds of weird and wonderful people, yet none of them had such a serious demeanour about them as the man who now stood in front of his yacht.

'Can I help you?' Elmore asked as he walked towards the man.

'I hope so,' replied Peter. 'A friend of mine was staying here but his yacht has disappeared, I'm worried about him.'

Elmore scratched his beard, 'You mean Alex?'

Peter smiled, 'Yes Alex, big strong guy, isn't he?'

'Oh yes, that's Alex, built like a tank.'

'Well do you know where he's gone?'

'I heard his new girlfriend mention that they were setting sail for Jamaica. If I remember correctly Alex has a house there.'

'A girlfriend hey, the sly dog, he didn't mention anything to me. Nor did I know about the house in Jamaica.'

'I've seen Alex around these islands for the last five years, he's always been a bit of a dark horse. Keeps to himself.'

'Yes, I know, I've known Alex for quite sometime. Still I need to speak to him urgently, I don't suppose you know where this house of his is?'

''Fraid not, but you could try Ed,' Elmore said pointing towards a bar named Ed's, 'they're quite the drinking buddies.'

'Thanks, I appreciate your help.'

'Not a problem, say hello to Alex when you see him.'

'Will do,' Peter said as he walked off in the direction of Ed's.

Christine held Derek's hand. The doctors said that he should be waking up any day now. Apart from a few broken bones, which at times he would probably find painful, he should be OK, or at least that's what they said. Christine was an optimist, well that's how she preferred to think of herself but she couldn't help listen to those little black thoughts that would creep into her head.

'Oh Derek when are you going to wake up? I need you more than you'll ever know.'

Derek opened his eyes, 'I love you,' he said. She looked at him and started crying. She'd waited so long for him to speak, she'd put her whole life on hold for this man, sacrificing work and sleep and now, finally, he'd woken up.

'Are you in pain?' she asked.

Derek smiled, and his eyes flickered slightly, 'I'm not sure,' he said letting out a small laugh, 'I can't feel anything.'

'That'll be the painkillers, at least they're working. You were hit by a car.'

'Yes I remember. How long have I been unconscious?'

His voice started to fade and for a moment she thought he'd pass out again but then his eyes opened up and they had that familiar sparkle she remembered from the times when he'd gaze lovingly at her.

'You've been out for more than a week,' she said. 'Truth be known, even I'm not sure, the days, they all blurred into one,' she continued before bursting into tears.

'Hey,' he cooed, 'don't cry I'm OK, I've been through worse this year than getting run over.'

She laughed and dried her eyes with some tissues. They held hands and looked into each others eyes.

'Will I be able to walk again?' he asked.

'Oh yes, the doctors expect you to make a full recovery, they say you were very lucky. Both your legs are broken, as are your ribs and you banged your head pretty hard, which led to the concussion, but nothing permanent.'

'Maybe I am lucky. I was lucky enough to find you.'

She smiled, she just wanted to take him home and take care of him.

'Derek I want you to know that I love you very

much,' she said as she clutched his neck tightly. Derek smiled, at long last they were able to admit to themselves that they were in love.

'I can't breathe,' he said finally.

'I'm sorry,' she said as she let go and wiped away her tears again.

'You had everyone so worried about you.'

'Everyone? Aren't you alone?' he asked.

'No, Tom's outside. Everyone's been to visit you, Tina, Terry, even your ex-wife. Both your children wanted to stay here with me, but of course we couldn't allow that but Tom simply refused to leave. He's practically lived here since you arrived.'

'Can I see him?'

'Of course you can. They only let one visitor in the room at a time. I'll go and get him.'

'Thank you,' Derek said holding her hand tightly before letting her go. He waited in anticipation for Tom to enter the room. Why had Tom stayed here so long? The last time they had seen each other Tom had returned to hating his guts. Did he want to see Derek die? Was that what Tom had wanted?

'Dad,' Tom said, standing in the room but at a fair distance from the bed.

'I can't see you all the way over there,' Derek said.

Tom moved much closer, and was now standing right next to Derek, he held his father's hand.

'Are you going to be all right dad?' he asked.

'Yeah I am son.'

'I'm sorry about the things I said to you. I was just jealous.'

'That's OK, I understand. Do you know I love you very much?'

'I love you too dad,' Tom said, the tears of humility finally breaking through. He lent across the bed and rested his head on his dad's chest. Derek held Tom's head, it felt good to have his son's love back, even if it meant getting run over.

'Dad.'

'Yes Tom?'

'I met Christine, I think she's great,' Derek's son said as he stood straight so that he could look at his father properly.

'I'm glad you like her son.'

'And I can't wait to have a little brother or sister.'

'Thank you Tom that means a lot to me.'

It was lights out in the young offenders' institution, time for its guests to turn in for the night, although few would really be asleep at such an early hour. Most, like Justin, simply lay in their beds, lost in thought.

'Why'd you say I did good today?' Justin asked breaking the silence. He heard Paul turn round in the bed above and then his face was in the air hanging just above Justin's bed.

'Because you showed Hannibal that you won't take any shit. You showed everyone that you won't be pushed around.'

'You mean the guy with the scar?'

'Yeah.'

'Why they call him Hannibal?'

'Hannibal's only got one ambition, to be the prison Daddy, but there are other contenders for the job. A few months ago he got into a fight with someone who also wanted the post. Hannibal ripped the guy's ear clean off his head, he's been called Hannibal ever since. I know he looks like a fat fuck, but the man's an animal. Everyone's scared of him and for good reason.'

'What happened to the other guy?'

'He slashed his wrists, I guess he decided being the Daddy wasn't for him after all.'

'And now he's after me. Why?'

'There's no point asking that question, if Hannibal weren't after you then someone else would be. You're the new guy, everyone goes through it, you're just unlucky enough to be the one to have caught Hannibal's eye.'

Justin had to get out of bed and take a leak in the bucket that adorned the corner of his cell. His initial fear over his confrontation earlier today was now turning into terror. What chance did he have against Hannibal and his gang?

'What am I gonna do?' Justin asked getting back into his bed. His voice actually quivered with fear.

'There's only one thing you can do, challenge him publicly to a fight. Then you and him will meet in the laundry room and settle things with your fists. It's just the way things are done around here.'

'But he ripped somebody's ear off. I can't fight him.' Tears were actually rolling down Justin's face but he managed to hold back the sobs. Perhaps Paul wouldn't notice that he was crying, perhaps he could keep hold of some kind of dignity.

'If you don't fight him, then you'll have his whole gang to deal with, that big one, remember him, he's known as Little John, and the other one we call him Dirty Dennis because of the things he likes to do to the others in the showers. And there are more of them, they'll make you their bitch. Is that what you want?'

'No,' the sobs hit Justin and he held his pillow

close to his chest. He just wanted to go home, back to his grandma's house. He just wanted things to be the way they were before he stole that stupid ticket.

'Don't cry Justin. Do as I say, you may get the beating of a life time off Hannibal but it'll be better than the alternative.'

'Then it'll stop after I fight Hannibal?'

'When you've made it clear that you won't let anyone push you about, they'll look for an easier target, it's the law of the jungle in here.'

'But I'm scared.'

'You should be, anyone who had to take on Hannibal would be mad if they weren't.' Paul's hand came into view, it held a little book. Justin took it, it was the Bible he had left lying on the table.

'Do you believe in God Justin?'

'I don't know.'

'Well now's a good time to find out. Do you remember that I told you in here was the right time to find Jesus?'

'Yes,' Justin wept quietly.

'Then read that and make sure you challenge Hannibal to that fight tomorrow, before it's too late. I'll pray for you Justin.'

Justin held the Bible close to his chest as he quietly fought back the tears.

It was 5am and Ed was tired. It had been a busy night and the clients just didn't seem to want to sleep. The girls had left at three leaving just him to serve the remaining customers. Two hours later everyone had gone home except for that lonely English man, who had been sitting by himself in the corner.

'Time to go to bed, bar's closed,' Ed shouted. The man moved slightly, his head was lying on the table, cushioned by his arms. Great thought Ed, he was probably so drunk that he wouldn't even be able to move. Ed would have to carry him out and leave him in front of the bar to sleep it off.

'Don't touch me,' the man said as Ed approached. An uneasiness bore down on Ed as the man's sinister eyes focused on their target. Whoever he was he'd spent the last three hours pretending to be drunk and unconscious. Ed could tell that this man was as sober as the day. 'What do you want?' he asked nervously.

'You're a friend of Alex's, aren't you?'

Alex, he was Ed's friend. He had known that Alex had a past, that he'd been running away from something, whatever it was had obviously caught up with him.

'I'm sorry but I don't know anyone called Alex,' Ed said, determined to protect his friend.

'Perhaps this will help refresh your memory,' the man said, pulling out a gun and pointing it at Ed.

'Look mister, I don't know what this is about but you're making a terrible mistake. I really don't know any Alex.'

There was a loud bang and then Ed was one the floor clutching his leg in agony, blood was pouring out of it at an alarming rate. The man now stood over him and pointed the gun at his chest.

'You don't have to die like this Ed, I just want to know where he lives.'

'Please . . . I . . .'

'Don't be stupid Ed, you need a doctor and fast.'

'OK, OK I'll tell you, God damn it.'

'That's a good boy,' said the man.

Slowly Ed told him everything he wanted to know, he'd planned on phoning Alex as soon as he'd got his leg looked at but little did Ed know that Peter J. Cutner would gun him down in cold blood as soon as he had the information he wanted. As he stepped over Ed's lifeless body and towards the bar Peter reflected that killing a man had been pretty easy. He'd always heard it was hard the first time round, yet shooting Ed had been no more difficult than slapping a mosquito. After pouring the spirits from behind the bar over Ed's body and lighting a match, Peter made a hasty exit. He wanted to stick around and watch the bar burn to the ground but he had things to do. Namely tracking down the couple that had stolen his money before ensuring they met a slow and painful death.

CHAPTER THIRTY-FIVE

Justin knelt in front of his bed, the Bible in his hands and prayed to God for strength and protection. He had followed Paul's advice and publicly challenged Hannibal to a fight. Now the hour of reckoning was drawing close, in less than ten minutes Justin was expected to show up in the prison laundry. If he didn't then he'd be branded a pussy and the remainder of his time in the institution would be hell on earth.

'That's it my friend, pray to God and Jesus, they will protect you. Jesus knows everything you're going through, after all he was crucified on the cross for our sins.'

Justin rose up off his knees and left the Bible on his bed.

'Paul I'm really scared.'

Paul placed a hand on Justin's shoulder. 'I know you are, but do you think David wasn't scared when he went to meet Goliath? This is a test Justin, a test of your faith. Remember that Jesus will be right behind you, and nothing can stand before the power of the Lord.'

Justin nodded, he felt courage enter his body and a strange detachment to the world quickly followed. He wasn't sure if it was Paul's presence there in the cell with him or because he really believed the words his cellmate spoke. The only thing he was sure of was that if it weren't for Paul he'd be a shambling wreck.

'Do you remember everything I told you?'

Justin nodded, 'Yeah use my height advantage, keep my jab up and dance round him.'

Paul smiled, 'Good, just don't let him grab you, never forget that he's got gravity on his side. If you keep away with your jab you can wear him down. When he comes close enough to grab you, back away and keep the jabs flowing into his face.'

Justin took in a deep breath and started praying again.

'Here take this,' Paul said taking off the gold cross he wore around his neck. Justin didn't know how to thank him, the gesture was almost overwhelming.

'When you feel so scared that you want to run away, touch it with your hand and remember that he is with you. Your cause is just, my friend.'

'Thank you,' Justin said putting the cross on around his neck, it felt good. Suddenly he didn't feel so alone.

'It's time for you to go,' Paul said.

'You're not coming,' Justin asked nervously.

'No, I'm going to stay here and pray for you,' Paul said dropping to his knees in front of Justin's bed and taking the Bible into his hands.

Justin simply nodded before he made his way out of the cell. He walked down the metal stairs and down towards the laundry. On his way he couldn't help but notice how quiet the institution was. Some of the other boys smiled and nodded at him, showing him their respect. Others simply looked away. The guards glanced at him phlegmatically as he passed them.

He held the cross tightly and started to pray as his heart raced and every instinct in his body told him to turn and run. Nearing the laundry entrance he spotted Little John and the rest of Hannibal's cronies waiting outside. They blocked his path. He turned to look around, it wasn't too late to run but standing behind him was Johnson. The guard he remembered from the first day held his truncheon in his hand and sneered at Justin and the other boys. He didn't want any of them to forget who the real boss was. Little John and the others stepped aside in order to allow Justin through and then Johnson nodded for him to continue towards his final destination.

With hesitation, and not daring to look at the other boys as he passed them by, Justin carried on. The laundry was dark and it felt cold, a chill shot down his spine. He looked for Hannibal but he couldn't see him. Maybe he'd decided not to turn up. Maybe that was it, maybe it was over, maybe Justin could return to his cell and go to sleep. Then all hope was dashed as a shadow emerged from the darkness.

'I didn't think you'd show up,' Hannibal said walking towards Justin.

Justin simply remained quiet, again reaching up for the cross and saying a little prayer.

'You know why they call me Hannibal, don't you?' he sneered.

'Yeah I do,' Justin nodded.

Hannibal walked closer, until they could see the whites of each others' eyes.

'Look, why don't we call this off? I mean we don't have to do this,' Justin said cautiously extending his hand.

Hannibal laughed before slapping his hand away.

'I don't want to hurt you, but I will if you don't

stop this,' Justin said, almost able to convince himself.

'Oh you're the one who's gonna feel pain bitch, lots of pain,' Hannibal growled as he lunged forward, his arms extended as he aimed to grab Justin by the collar. Justin remembered Paul's advice and quickly extended his left arm forming a jab. It struck Hannibal straight on the nose and caused him to stagger back. Inspired with confidence he let out another one and another one before letting out a flurry of punches. Before he knew it Hannibal was on the floor looking up at Justin towering over him.

'Give it up,' Justin said heaving for breath.

'You're gonna pay for that,' Hannibal said, standing back up and examining the blood which had spilt out from his nose. He rushed forward at Justin ducking below his jab but Justin managed to hit him with an upper-cut, again another flurry of punches and Hannibal was back on the ground. This time Justin decided not to allow him up and fighting to catch his breath rushed forward, his foot aimed at Hannibal's midsection. Somehow Hannibal managed to grab Justin's leg and before he realised it the two of them were on the ground rolling in the dirt, punching, biting and clawing to get the upper hand.

Justin felt Hannibal's hand on his testicles and cried out in pain as his opponent started to crush them. In desperation Justin thrust his thumb into Hannibal's right eye. Suddenly he was free, and again they were rolling around and thrashing at each other. Then Hannibal was on top of him, pinning him down and punching at his face. He looked up trying to fend off the blows and saw the sheer determination and hatred in Hannibal's face. He saw Hannibal's right hand come crashing down as it struck him and felt his head crack back and hit the hard surface of the laundry floor. As he lost consciousness Justin prayed, he prayed for Jesus to save him.

Alex's secluded beach house on the Jamaican coast was amazing. There wasn't a soul in sight for miles around and every morning, before her breakfast, Sarah would go for a swim or a jog. She usually accompanied Alex twice a week into town, in order to help with the shopping but today she felt exceptionally lazy and had decided to stay home and sunbathe on Alex's private beach. She was about to doze off blissfully when she felt a shadow cast its presence over her.

'You're back early,' Sarah said opening her eyes and seeing the tall figure of a man.

'I thought I'd surprise you honey,' said Peter Cutner just as Sarah's sleepy eyes started to register the fact that it wasn't Alex standing in front of her. She screamed as he grabbed her by the hair and dragged her towards the house.

'What do you want?' she cried out in pain.

'What the fuck do you think I want? I want my fucking money!'

Confused Sarah looked up at him, had he gone mad? What was he talking about?

'But you took the money,' she cried, tears emerging from her eyes, caused by the pain of being dragged by the hair across the beach and into the house. Cutner let go of her hair and slapped her across the face, sending her flying on to the sofa.

'You can stop the acting, my dear, the cameras have stopped filming.'

'Please Peter I really don't know what you're talking about.'

'The money, I'm talking about the fucking money,' Peter shouted rolling his hands into fists.

'But I thought you took the money, you wrote that letter and left me.'

'Oh you're a very clever girl Sarah, a very clever girl. I don't quite know how you pulled it off but you see apart from Justin and myself, you are the only other person who knew about the bank details and the name the money was hidden under.'

'There's Tony,' Sarah said, desperately afraid. Cutner burst into a fit of laughter.

'Tony? Tony couldn't organise a piss up in a brewery! No you must have had help but I'm sure it wasn't Tony. Maybe your new boyfriend had a part to play in things.'

Sarah started to cry harder, she'd never seen Peter like this before. Fear gripped her as she realised how well he'd kept his real self hidden.

'Oh yes, I've been observing you both for sometime,' he said as he pulled a pistol out from behind his back, 'and so I thought I'd come prepared in case your new boyfriend thought he could make use of those muscles of his. Has a lot of stamina, has he?'

'You're insane,' Sarah cried.

'I'm more than insane dear, I'm extremely pissed off. But I'll tell you what your mistake was, using your own name as Collin Matthews' sister. I mean surely you have more imagination than that?'

'Please Peter, I don't know what you're talking about.'

The front door opened, it was Alex holding a bag of groceries. He dropped them to the floor as Peter aimed the pistol at him. Sarah, afraid that Peter was about to pull the trigger, barged into him from behind. Quickly recovering his balance, Peter slapped the pistol across Sarah's head, sending her crashing to the floor. Barely hanging onto her consciousness, Sarah clutched her head as the room span. She could just about make out Alex's figure as he launched himself on to Cutner. Sarah sat up, blood dripping down her forehead, she tried to get up, but stumbled as the room continued to spin. The two men were rolling around the floor, she looked on helplessly. Suddenly the unfamiliar sound of a gunshot rang out deafening her ears.

'Alex, Alex!' Sarah cried as she crawled towards the two men.

'Are you all right?' Alex asked as he hugged her and examined her head.

'I think so,' she said as she looked down at the motionless body of Peter Cutner. Blood seemed to be gushing out of his chest, his eyes flickered with the remnants of life. Alex took off his t-shirt and used it to stem the bleeding from Sarah's forehead.

'Is he dead?' she asked nodding towards Peter. Alex looked at him, his blood was all over the floor and his breathing had become laboured and erratic.

'No, he isn't dead, but he will be soon. He's lost too much blood, I guess the bullet must have hit an artery. Who was he?'

'He was the solicitor I ran away with.'

'What the hell's he doing here?'

'He thought I took the money.'

'What?' Alex exclaimed, 'but I thought he'd ripped you off and left you with just a note?'

'He did, but I guess someone must have got to the money before he did.'

Alex looked down at Peter quizzically, confusion filling his face. Cutner could feel his life force rapidly leaving his body, as his eyes opened and closed his gaze fell upon Sarah. So she had been telling the truth, but if she didn't take the money, who did? It was Cutner's last thought as his eyes closed never to open again.

They'd made Derek wait three whole days after waking up before discharging him from the hospital. Just as well because the boredom had started to get to him. Christine said that he had spent a total of thirteen days in hospital. It kind of made him glad that he had been unconscious for ten of them. Now he was back at Christine's house and she was looking after him. The first thing he had done when she returned to work was phone Terry and ask him to buy and then bring round an engagement ring. Christine had accepted Derek's proposal with tears in her eyes. Derek's life now seemed so surreal that he toyed with the idea of writing an autobiography.

Today he planned on surprising Christine by cooking her a meal. It was hard though because he was confined to a wheelchair and his head still throbbed with pain. The doorbell rang and Derek remembered that Terry had mentioned that he might pop round.

'Blimey you look like you've been in a car accident,' Terry joked as Derek let him in.

'Sorry mate, couldn't help myself,' Terry said as he handed Derek a bunch of flowers.

'You always were a comedian,' Derek said as he wheeled himself into the living room.

'What you been up to today?'

'I'm going to surprise Christine by cooking her a meal, so just getting things ready for that really. It's hard to do even the simplest things when you're stuck in a wheelchair.'

'Just make sure you don't strain yourself. Take things easy.'

'I intend to,' Derek said with a smile.

'We were all worried about you, even Tom. Are things better there?'

'Yes much.'

'Nothing like a near death experience to help solidify a father and son relationship,' Terry joked.

'If that's what had to happen to get him to speak to me, then I'd do it all again.'

'Just don't make a habit out of it, there's only so many times a man can get run over.'

'I'm afraid you'll have to make yourself tea if you want it,' Derek said nodding towards the kitchen.

'Would you like some?' Terry asked.

'I thought you'd never ask,' Derek laughed.

'Just don't get used to this royal treatment,' Terry shouted from the adjacent kitchen.

'Who me? Never!'

'Course not, you sly sod, bet you can make tea by yourself just fine.'

'I guess I can but what are friends for?'

'Does Christine look after you when she comes home from work then?' Terry asked as he emerged from the kitchen with two cups of tea. He placed them on the table next to Derek.

'She tries her best, poor girl. But she gets back really late. She fell behind so much when she took time off to spend with me at the hospital.'

'You're lucky to have her mate. She's a keeper. Hey what's she going to do about maternity leave? It sounds like her whole practice falls apart when she takes any time off.'

'She's going to take on a new trainee and give more responsibility to her salaried partner, but she hopes to return to work as soon as possible.'

'Must be hard.'

'Yes it is. You're right though, I'm lucky to have her. Maybe one day you'll find someone and give it all a go again!'

'Me? No way! I'm having way too much fun mate.'

'But doesn't it get boring, one meaningless fling after another?'

'Hmm let me think about that. No!'

Terry emerged with two cups of tea and put them down on the coffee table next to Derek.

'Look I'm glad for you mate,' Terry said, 'really I am. But the whole marriage thing, I tried it and it didn't work. It's not for me.'

'So long as you're happy, that's all that counts.'

'I am. And what about you, are you happy?' Terry asked.

'Happier than I ever remember,' Derek said.

'That's good. And what about the case? Is there any sight of all those elusive millions?'

Derek laughed.

'What's so funny?' Terry asked slightly flustered.

'Can you believe I completely forgot about the money? What with everything that's happened recently, Christine and I haven't even talked about it.'

'But you're not going to give up, are you?'

Derek shrugged his shoulders, 'I guess I'll ask Christine about it when she gets home, but to be honest with you I couldn't give a monkey's about the money right now. I've got everything that I want.'

Welkin sat in the room and waited for Justin to be escorted in. When he first started practising criminal law he had hated visiting his clients in their various prisons. Now he'd grown quite indifferent towards them. He still hated the screws though, they treated everyone as if they were criminals.

The door opened and Justin entered, the guard looked at Welkin with contempt before closing the door. Welkin immediately noticed the bruises covering Justin's face.

'Bloody hell,' he said as Justin sat down, 'are you all right?'

'Yeah fine thanks.'

'I'm trying my best to get you out,' Welkin said opening his briefcase.

Justin smiled, 'Don't worry about it, really I'm fine,' he said, although he was clearly in pain.

'You don't look fine,' Welkin said.

Justin shrugged his shoulders, 'Look the reason I called you is that I want to change a few things.'

'Oh yeah?' Welkin said intrigued, 'Like what?'

'First of all I want to plead guilty.'

'But if you plead guilty it will affect your civil case.'

'That's the other thing I want to talk to you

about. I want to give back all the money or what's left of it to Mr Bonner.'

'What?' Welkin almost shouted incredulously.

'I took that money Mr Welkin, I don't deserve it.'

'Has someone in here got to you? Is that it? Is that why you have all those bruises?'

'No, don't be silly.'

'Then why? We're talking about millions of pounds. I'm telling you it's still possible . . .'

'I'm not interested in the money. It's not mine and it's not right if I were to keep it.'

'But what's made you change your mind?'

'Jesus, Mr Welkin.'

Welkin sat back in his chair. He'd seen prisoners turn crazy before, sometimes they'd slash their wrists or turn into violent animals, sometimes they'd catch religion and turn into bible bashers. He hadn't really expected it to happen to Justin. Welkin felt his slice of Justin's millions slipping through his fingers. Justin's had been the biggest case ever to come his way, he saw Justin as his big break. It could be years or maybe even never, before he got another opportunity like this.

'You mean Jesus has told you to give back the money?' Welkin asked sarcastically.

'Of course not and please don't talk to me as if I were crazy.'

'Then explain it to me. What's this whole thing with Jesus? I never had you down as a Jehovah's Witness.'

Justin let out a deep sigh, he hadn't expected Welkin to understand and nor did he expect him to understand now. 'Three days ago I had a fight with one of the hardest, toughest and craziest people I ever met. I had no choice because if I didn't stand up to him his gang would have made me their bitch. I was scared man, scared like I've never been before in my life, so scared that I wanted to cry out for my grandma to come and take me home, scared enough to be afraid that I'd wet my pants, but a friend, a close friend, he told me about Jesus and about God and it gave me strength. Strength enough to face this guy and stand my ground. I didn't win the fight but I won my respect and that's all I ever wanted. I remember as I faced this monster how I wanted to cry and how I prayed and then I felt his presence, Jesus was there right next to me. He touched me, I swear to you he did and then I knew everything would be all right.'

'All right lets just say Jesus was there for you, lets just say he did touch you. That still doesn't mean you have to give away all that money!'

Justin shook his head in disbelief, 'Can't you see? Are you really so blind?'

'What? See what?' Welkin asked raising his voice in frustration.

'All this happened for a reason, everything that's happened to me has happened for a reason. I did the wrong thing and I must be punished and I must put right what I did wrong. I came here because I was blind, but now Jesus has found me and shown me the light.'

'Look, why don't you think all this over for a few more days. Maybe after you've . . .'

'NO!' Justin shouted slamming his fist on to the table. 'I must put right what I did wrong, NOW!'

Welkin was silent, unable to comprehend what was happening and how he could deter his client from the actions he was about to take.

'I want you to prepare everything, for all my

assets to be transferred to Mr Bonner's name and I want you to send this letter to Mr Bonner's solicitor,' Justin said placing an envelope, addressed to Derek on the table.

'I can't,' Welkin almost whimpered.

'I'm instructing you as my solicitor,' Justin barked, 'if you won't do it then I'll find another one that will. So what's it going to be? Will you carry out my instructions?'

Welkin nodded.

Justin got up and walked towards the door, 'Guard!' he shouted.

The guard opened the door for Justin to leave.

'I'll pray for you Mr Welkin,' Justin said and then left.

Sarah sat on the porch and looked up at the clear Jamaican night as an infinite number of stars shone on a perfect black canvas. She breathed in some of the clean air, holding it in her lungs, savouring its purity before slowly releasing it. It was a stark contrast to the London smog she had grown up in. Alex was somewhere off the Jamaican coast, dumping Peter's body into the sea. She felt sorry that his greed had led to his death and understood that there was a poignant lesson to be learnt. Yet the unanswered question still perplexed her. Who had the money? Who could have known the bank account number and the address of the bank? Peter was right, it couldn't be Tony, it was doubtful if Justin would trust him with such information and even if he had, she just couldn't imagine Tony being able to pull it off. Besides Peter had said that it was a woman who had taken the money. A woman . . . Karen? Sarah remembered back to the time Karen had phoned her, directly after she'd sent her the text telling her that she was leaving the county for good. Karen had insisted on knowing everything to the smallest detail once she had found out Sarah and Peter were running away together. She'd found out about the money laundering scam and the name the money would end up in. Karen had known about the bank account and its number, Sarah would phone her and tell her any new developments as soon as she found out herself. Peter didn't seem to mind revealing the details of how everything would work or the name of the bank, where the money would be hidden. He obviously didn't think that Sarah had posed a threat but he had no idea that Karen was in the equation. She had thought that telling her best friend all the details would provide her with a safety net in case anything went wrong. She couldn't ever have imagined Karen using the information to get to the money first, but it had to be Karen Sarah thought to herself.

CHAPTER THIRTY-SIX

Derek was lying on the couch watching TV when he heard the front door open. Christine was home, Derek checked the time using the TV's Teletext. It was seven o'clock, which meant that Christine was home a whole hour earlier than usual.

She walked into the room with a big smile on her face and stroked Derek's hair before kissing him fully on the lips.

'My, you are in a good mood,' he said looking up at her in mild surprise.

She sat down next to him on the couch, her smile irrepressible.

'I received some really good news today,' she said.

Derek sat up intrigued, 'Oh yeah, are you going to tell me or let the suspense finish me off?'

'I received a letter from Justin Farren's solicitor basically stating that he now admits liability for his actions and would like to transfer the remainder of his assets into your name.'

'What? After all this time he's just giving up?'

Christine nodded, 'Apparently he's already signed all the necessary paper work and now all you have to do is sign that you accept and it's over. I phoned his solicitor and we've arranged a meeting in my office tomorrow morning in order for the documentation to be finalised. It requires your presence.'

'But why? Why after all this time?'

'I don't know,' Christine said shrugging her shoulders, 'but maybe the answer's in here,' she said producing the envelope with Derek's name on it.

'What is it?' Derek asked taking it from her.

'It's a letter from him to you.'

Carefully Derek opened it, half expecting it to explode in his face. He was excited but he was also understandably apprehensive about what it could contain.

He unfolded the single piece of paper and glanced over it briefly. The handwriting was extremely neat, leading Derek to the conclusion that the writer had put a lot of thought and effort into it. Christine also looked at it from her vantage point and the two virtually read it at the same time.

Dear Mr Bonner,

I've thought a great deal about what I'd like to write in this letter, about the kind of things I could say that perhaps might make you think better of me as a man. Yet the more I think the more clearly I see that someone like me would never be able to find the words to express how sincerely they regret their actions. All I can do is offer my apologies and pray that one day you will find it in your heart to forgive me.

Prison has taught me a lot Mr Bonner, but more importantly it has shown me that a real man must at some stage be responsible for his actions, it is with this view that I have instructed my solicitor to transfer the remainder of my assets into your name. Of course what is left is nowhere near the amount of money you won but I think that you should find that once you have sold my house, it is still substantial.

I know that I will never be able to pay you back the full amount, but hope that this gesture will in part go someway to compensate for the emotional and financial pain I have caused you. For now it is the only thing I can think of, although I pray everyday for some new means by which I may redeem myself.

Mr Bonner I believe things happen for a reason, before I came to prison I led a Godless and selfish life. I believe that the actions I took were meant to be so that I could come to this place, where I discovered Jesus, in order to learn what a fickle and meaningless road I had embarked on. I am sorry Mr Bonner and if there is anything more I can do in order to make amends for my inexcusable behaviour you may contact me. I will be now and forever your humblest servant.

In deepest humility
Justin Farren

After reading the letter Derek and Christine both looked at each other in disbelief.

'This has to be a joke,' Derek said screwing up the piece of paper.

'No wait,' Christine said taking it out of his hand, 'you never know when we may need it for documentary evidence.'

'So you think it's a hoax as well then.'

'No I don't, if it were a hoax then we wouldn't be meeting his solicitor tomorrow. I just like to err on the side of caution, that's all.'

'A leopard never changes its spots Christine.'

'He is awfully young, maybe you're being too hard.'

'Too hard, he stole twenty-five million pounds from me!'

'More like twenty-one now,' Christine said, placing her hand on his shoulder in an attempt to sooth his anger.

'I'll believe it when I see it,' Derek said.

'I guess we'll both find out tomorrow.'

Karen lay on the Bahamian beach while she awaited Sarah's call. She'd been waiting for Sarah to contact her for over two weeks. Karen was starting to get worried. Beside her was her UK mobile, it had international roaming, so why hadn't Sarah called? Was she in some kind of trouble? Perhaps she'd been wrong about Cutner, perhaps he hadn't been planning on ripping Sarah off after all. Perhaps the two were now wandering around the Cayman Islands penniless and unable to return to the UK. But surely she'd have enough money to call her best friend and ask for help? Damn it, she'd been sure that Cutner was untrustworthy, the way he'd come up with the scam to rip Justin off, the way he'd conveniently started sleeping with Sarah and the way in which all the money would have ended up in his off-shore bank account. It just didn't seem right, and concerned for her friend's safety, she was determined to get to the money before Cutner. Finding a corrupt printer's willing to forge the death certificate had been easy thanks to Diamond Dave. Also easy had been drawing up a false will and making it look official. She'd spent part of her summer holiday volunteering at a solicitor's and had seen how wills were drawn up.

Putting the name and address of a made up firm on top Collin Mathews' will had hardly been daring because she knew that the Cayman bank would never check. The only real hurdle had been obtaining the fake passport in the name of Sarah Matthews. Surprisingly Diamond Dave had said that Tony was able to get passports and to Karen's surprise he could.

Karen had managed to get to the bank and the money way before Cutner because Sarah had already told her everything she needed to know and the beauty of it all was that there wasn't a damn thing he could do because he had stolen the money from someone else. Slimy git, probably thought he was a real genius. Imagine the look on his face if he ever found out that he'd been outmanoeuvred by an eighteen year old! The phone started ringing, Karen answered it full of anticipation. Yes it was Sarah.

'You've got a lot of explaining to do,' said her friend's voice. Karen smiled, Sarah was fine.

Justin closed the Bible, the bell rang indicating lunch time had come. He knew that by now Derek would have read his letter and that most probably all of his assets would be in Derek's name. He wondered what had happened to Sarah, how her life was in the Caribbean with Peter Cutner. Justin didn't feel bitter at all, he had always known that Sarah was with him because of the money. He could see now that it wasn't the way, and that maybe one day, a long time from now, when he left this place he would find a girl who wanted to be with him just because she liked him, not because he had something he could offer her.

Justin walked down the metal steps, the sight of seeing the other inmates as they walked single file towards the canteen had a deep humility about it. Inside they were all equal, no matter what the reasons were for their incarceration. From his vantage point he could see Hannibal and a small group of his followers. Hannibal looked up at him just as Justin descended the stairs and joined the others on the ground floor of the institution. The two locked eyes, and then Hannibal nodded. It was a nod of reconciliation, the uttering of an unsaid truce. Justin nodded back and momentarily the two walked side by side in silence until his old tormentor passed him by. Justin smiled to himself, it was over, he had stood his ground and gained the respect of his contemporaries. He didn't know how long he would spend in this place, nor did he care anymore. He just wanted to pay his debt to society and to Derek before returning home and starting fresh. He had stolen the money because he had wanted people to respect him. Now penniless and denied his freedom he had won respect here in this place, and realised that true respect isn't won by money or possessions, it is won by the character and moral fibre of a person. Justin knew that no matter what happened from this point onwards he would be fine, he just had to remain true to himself.

Derek still found it hard to believe that he was worth some four million pounds. He had already put all of Justin's cars up for sale. All that remained was to get an estate agent for the mansion. He had wanted to see what kind of place Justin had lived in and now able to move around on crutches had persuaded Terry to drive him there.

'It's an amazing place,' Terry said after they had both taken a tour of it in silent awe.

'Yes,' Derek agreed. Despite having been stripped of all its furnishings and fittings by Tony, who'd even managed to take the kitchen sink before moving back to his mum's house, the mansion was opulent and easily worth the multi-million pound price tag it would command on the open market.

'I guess you could always live here,' Terry said.

'No,' Derek said, a broad smile growing on his face at the thought of the idea.

'You'll sell it then, like everything else?'

'Yes, it would be far too expensive to maintain.'

'What are you going to do with all that money?'

'Well I'll have to give half of it to Tina when she turns eighteen. It was my promise to her.'

'OK but what will you do with the rest?'

Derek shrugged, 'I spoke to Christine about us getting a house together but she doesn't want to move, said that her house was easily big enough for us and the little one. She suggested that I see a financial adviser. Invest in lots of safe products like government bonds, she thinks that I could probably earn about two hundred thousand pounds a year in interest.'

'So you'll be a man of leisure?' Terry said imaging what it would be like to retire at the age of forty odd.

'I'll be the one to bring our kid up while Christine runs her practice, there's even talk of another baby some day in the not too distant future. Then, when they're old enough to go to school, I'll think about retraining.'

'What would you like to do?'

'I'm not too sure, I think I'd like to work with my hands. Maybe plumbing, like you.'

'Well you'll probably be the world's richest plumber,' Terry said with an incredulous smile.

Derek let out a laugh, he couldn't believe it was all finally over. He had enough money to look after his children and a chance to turn his life around, but most importantly of all he had Christine. He had thought that winning the lottery would be like owning some magical wand, and that he'd able to do whatever he wished. Ironically if Justin hadn't stolen the ticket he would probably have ended up as a very rich but very lonely man. It occurred to Derek that he had wasted so many years with self-loathing, unable to believe that a woman could find him attractive. Yet Christine had taken him on when he didn't have a penny to his name, and she still didn't want any of his money.

Christine loved him for being plain old Derek, and really isn't that what any man wants? The unconditional love of that one, special woman? In an instant Derek realised that it was Christine's love that made him lucky, not the millions he would have in the bank. The whole fiasco with Justin had showed him that and maybe one day he would be able to find it in his heart to forgive the boy, simply because if it weren't for Justin he wouldn't have found Christine nor would he be so appreciative of all that he now possessed. Most importantly of all Justin had shown him that the future was far from being the dark, hopeless place he once thought it to be. The future was bright, filled with unknown excitement, and Derek promised himself that he wouldn't squander a single second of it.

The Bahamian beach was just the way Sarah had imagined it to be from her childhood memories, inspired by that postcard she had seen so many years ago. As she walked on the fine sand she looked at Alex on her right, who was sitting by an open bar drinking a cocktail. To her left gently swimming in the sea was Karen. It was still hard getting used to the fact that Karen had taken them all in, and at the beginning Sarah had been resentful that her friend hadn't told her what she was planning. Still, if it weren't for Karen, Peter Cutner would have gotten away with the full nineteen million, a horrendous thought if ever there was one.

Sarah hadn't been sure if her friend was sincere when she had said that she wanted to split the money in half. Their relationship during the end of this adventure had been shaky to say the least. She was just glad that Karen had forgiven her for sleeping with Tony. The money in Sarah's Bahamian account had cleared two days ago and she was worth nine and a half million pounds. It was nice to have so much money, but not as nice as having her friend back or as nice as the man who now sat at the bar and who was so obviously into her.

As Sarah walked into the crystal clear sea Karen stopped swimming and walked towards her. They met each other halfway. Karen smiled, 'I don't think I'll ever get used to the beauty here.'

'Me too,' said Sarah.

'He's a great guy,' she said nodding towards Alex.

'I know, I'm very lucky.'

'Make sure you never lose him.'

'I don't intend to,' Sarah said.

The two were silent as Karen looked off into the distance, the sea seemed never ending.

'I don't know how I can thank you,' Sarah said, a tear in her eye.

'You don't have to, we're friends.'

'But I didn't behave like a friend, did I?'

'You were just doing what you thought was right. I was doing the same thing. Hey if anyone should be sorry it should be me.'

'Why's that?' Sarah asked.

'Because of my actions you and Alex were almost killed by Cutner.'

'Oh yeah that's true,' Sarah laughed.

'Hey you don't have to agree,' Karen said, punching her friend in the shoulder.

Sarah laughed some more, 'But it is true, isn't it?'

'So maybe that makes us even? Friends?'

'Friends,' said Sarah as the two girls hugged each other.

'So what are you going to do with the rest of your life?' Karen asked.

Sarah smiled, 'Live here with Alex, maybe have some kids.'

'Well don't rush,' Karen said.

'Hey I know, there's no rush. But for the first time in my life I'm really happy. I think he's great.'

'That's good. You deserve to be happy,' Karen said.

'What about you? What are you going to do?' Sarah asked.

'Me? Next week I'm going back to England to carry on with my law degree.'

'Your law degree? What for? You've got so much money!' Sarah exclaimed.

Karen smiled, her friend still had so much more to learn.